Also by Sherri Hayes

Hidden Threat
A Christmas Proposal (a Hidden Threat short story)
Slave (Finding Anna, Book 1)
Need (Finding Anna, Book 2)
Behind Closed Doors (Daniels Brothers, Book 1)
Red Zone (Daniels Brothers, Book 2)

D1495476

Sherri Hayes

Truth

Finding Anna Book Three

The Writer's Coffee Shop Publishing House

First published by The Writer's Coffee Shop, 2013

The Writer's Coffee Shop
(Australia)   PO Box 447 Cherrybrook NSW 2126
(USA)   PO Box 2116 Waxahachie TX 75168

Paperback ISBN- 978-1-61213-161-0
E-book ISBN- 978-1-61213-162-7

A CIP catalogue record for this book is available from the US Congress Library.

Cover image by: © Depositphotos.com/ Yuri Arcurs
Cover design by: Jennifer McGuire

www.thewriterscoffeeshop.com/shayes

About the Author

Sherri is the author of five novels: *Hidden Threat, Slave* (*Finding Anna, Book 1*), *Need* (*Finding Anna,* Book 2), *Behind Closed Doors* (A Daniels Brothers Novel), *Red Zone* (A Daniels Brothers Novel), and a short story, "A Christmas Proposal." She lives in central Ohio with her husband and three cats. Her mother fostered her love for books at a young age by reading to her as a child. Stories have been floating around in her head for as long as she can remember; however, she didn't start writing them down until she turned thirty. It has become a creative outlet that allows her to explore a wide range of emotions, while having fun taking her characters through all the twists and turns she can create. When she's not writing, she can usually be found helping her husband in his woodworking shop.

To all my readers, thank you for your continued support.

Acknowledgments

I want to thank my beta. She is there to be a cheerleader when I get bogged down, and gives me that extra push when I need it.

A special thank you to Mack for his advice on several scenes throughout this book. He let me bounce ideas off him, and gave me several suggestions on how to make the BDSM more accurate and believable.

For authors good editors are invaluable, and mine are no different. I have a team of three editors who not only make the story look good, but they care about these characters as much as I do. Thank you so much for all you do.

This book contains conversations, flashbacks, and various other items regarding abuse that may be disturbing to some readers.

Chapter 1

Brianna

"I'm so glad I found you. You have no idea what it took for me to find you, baby girl."

His words echoed in my ears as I stood there staring. He was here. He was really here. I was frozen, unable to move. I needed to get away. Away from him. Away from here.

Red! screamed in my head but refused to come out of my mouth. It was as if I'd suddenly swallowed a mouthful of cotton. I couldn't move. I couldn't speak. Fear took over. My chest tightened, making it harder to breathe.

I stumbled backward, still trying to speak, but nothing would come out. I had to get away. Stephan. I needed Stephan.

As I moved farther into the living room, he followed me. He was like a giant, filling the space. I'd always thought Stephan's place was large, but now it felt very small as John stalked toward me. The panic continued to rise, but I fought it. *Breathe. Remember to breathe. Stephan. Think about Stephan.*

Oxygen tore through my lungs with every intake of air. I was breathing, but it wasn't doing its job. It wasn't calming me. My father had come for me.

Every step I took, he matched and then some. I couldn't get away. He was bigger, stronger. Why? Why was he here? What did he want with me?

Turning my back on him for the first time, I ran toward the phone. I stumbled over the coffee table on my way and righted myself. I knew he was close, but I had to try. I had to try to call Stephan.

My hands trembled as I picked up the phone. I didn't get any further than that. Before my fingers could touch the keys, he snatched the phone out of my hands, tossing it to the floor behind him. He was too close.

I stepped back again, trying to get away. He said something, but I couldn't understand it. His words echoed through my head like the rumble of cars through a tunnel.

He reached out, his fingers grazing my arm as I moved. Again he spoke, and again I couldn't make out his words. I cringed at his touch, taking another step away from him and bumping into the couch. The collision jarred me from my stupor, and I tried again to utter my safeword.

"R-red. Red!"

Instead of stepping back, leaving, he continued to approach me, his brow furrowed in confusion. I wanted him to leave. Why wouldn't he just *leave*?

"Anna, honey. It's okay. It's me, your father."

Shaking my head, I did the only thing I could think to do. I ran toward my bedroom. He was blocking my path to the front door, so my bedroom was my only hope. If I could get inside, shut the door behind me, and lock it—I would be safe.

Unfortunately, a split second after I started running, so did he. I heard his footsteps behind me, gaining. John reached the door almost at the same time I did, and I was trapped. I knew in that moment I wouldn't be able to get away from him. That the happiness I'd experienced with Stephan was over. John was going to take it away from me, and I was powerless to stop it.

John called my name again, and I whipped my head around to stare at him. Something tugged at my neck, and I reached up to feel Stephan's collar. I couldn't give up. I couldn't. He wouldn't want that.

Closing my eyes for a moment, I decided to give it one last try and took off toward my bathroom. It was a feeble attempt at best. He'd already proven he could catch me, but I couldn't give up. Not when there was still a chance.

Once again, he was there almost before I was. His hand lay flat against the door, and I was unable to close it behind me. I ran to the far corner of the room, pressing myself against the wall. He stood there staring at me for a minute before he came closer. Every step he took was measured, as if gauging my reaction.

I wanted to close my eyes, but I didn't. Instead, I tried yelling my safeword again as loud as I could. He didn't listen. He didn't stop his approach.

My cell phone vibrated in my pocket, drawing my attention away from him. I glanced down, taking in a deep breath, hope swelling in my chest. *Stephan?*

Reaching into my pocket, I struggled to remove the phone. It was my last chance.

I finally wrestled it free of my jeans, but as soon as John realized what I had in my hand, he knocked it away. Tears welled up in my eyes as I heard the clatter of my phone hitting the tile floor on the other side of the room. I was on my own. No one was going to save me this time.

I slid to the floor, and huddled into a ball, accepting my fate. I had begun to hope. I'd begun to be happy. Now it was going to end. John would take me away. He would take me away from Stephan, from my life. Would he take me back to Ian, or would it be someone else this time, someone worse? I reached up and touched my collar. *Stephan.*

"Anna? Anna, honey, can you hear me? Do you know who I am? I came to get you. I'm sorry it took so long, but I couldn't find you. I looked everywhere for you, baby. You have no idea how I looked."

Did I know who he was? Of course, I knew. I also knew what he'd done to me. He'd let Ian have me, and he'd left me there. For ten months. He let that man do things to me. Horrible, horrible things. I didn't understand why he'd been looking for me. Was it because he'd learned Ian had sold me to Stephan and he didn't want Stephan to have me? How did he know? Did Ian tell him? Were they friends? The thought sent a shiver down my spine, and I clasped my arms tighter around my legs.

I didn't want to go back to the life I'd had before with Ian. As a slave, I was nothing. Here it was different. Stephan was different. He was nice to me, made me feel things—good things. I wanted to stay with Stephan. I felt warm and safe and happy here. I didn't want to go.

My father lowered himself to the floor and began inching toward me. I repeated my safeword over and over again. He continued to ignore it.

The walls began to close in on me as the panic started to take over once more. I was shaking, and I couldn't get enough air in my lungs. This couldn't be happening. It couldn't.

Stephan

I picked up my cell again, punching the speed dial for what felt like the hundredth time, hoping she'd answer, as I weaved through traffic toward our home. Instead, the sound of my voice on the answering machine greeted me. I tried both the home number and her cell again. She wasn't answering either.

With more force than necessary, I threw the phone against the passenger seat. She wasn't answering, and I knew why.

Tom's haunting words echoed in my ears. *"Mr. Coleman, we have a problem."*

My stomach churned as the conversation replayed in my mind. He'd only been gone for five minutes, leaving one of the security guards to watch over the lobby. When he returned, the guard was out cold on the floor behind the desk with two Taser wires still attached to his chest, the Taser lying discarded on the floor several feet away. After checking the other man was still breathing, Tom had immediately checked the security monitors. He'd been just in time to see a strange man step off the elevator at the top floor and walk toward the door to my condo. Given the current situation, I knew it had to have been Jonathan Reeves, Brianna's father.

Just thinking about it sent a shot of fear through my chest and caused me to press my foot harder on the gas pedal. There were too many unanswered questions when it came to Brianna's father. The one thing that was certain, however, was that she was terrified of him. If he got inside, got to her, I had no idea how she'd react. I'd promised to protect her. To keep her safe. She needed me. I had to get to her.

All other thoughts were pushed to the back of my mind as I weaved through downtown traffic. I'd always been a fairly patient driver until Brianna came into my life. I wouldn't have it any other way, though. Just thinking about her not being there every day when I came home from work brought that pain back to my chest.

I felt a sense of déjà vu when I pulled up in front of my building, jumped out of the car, and ran inside. Jesse, one of the security guards, was sitting behind the desk looking a little paler than normal. He must have been the one Reeves used the Taser on.

As soon as he saw me, he stood. "Tom's upstairs waiting on you, Mr. Coleman."

I nodded, increasing my pace as I hurried across the lobby.

The elevator ride seemed to take forever, but I knew it was quicker than taking the stairs. I was in good shape, but racing to the top floor would be pushing it, even for me.

When the doors opened and I saw Tom standing there, I breathed a small sigh of relief. If he was there, Brianna was still inside.

As soon as he saw me, he was moving. "The door's locked, sir. I checked. As far as I can tell, he's inside, but I haven't been able to hear much from out here."

Tom had been ready to call the police when I'd talked to him on the phone earlier, but I'd stopped him. I understood his thinking, but it was the last thing I wanted. The police would only complicate things at this point. They would barrage Brianna with questions, demanding answers. Her father was in law enforcement. Even if he wasn't local, I had little doubt the police would believe whatever lies he spun. I wouldn't let him take her.

That was the only thing I knew for sure, and the point I drove home to Tom. He was to make sure Jonathan Reeves didn't leave the building with Brianna. I would take care of the rest.

Barely acknowledging Tom's words, I moved to the door to listen. He was right—I couldn't hear anything from out here. Then again, if they were far enough away from the door, I wouldn't. Given my lifestyle, and what I liked, I'd invested in extra insulation to cut down on noise. At the moment, I was cursing that decision.

Using my keys, I opened the door slowly. I had no idea what I'd find once I stepped into the condo. Everything inside me screamed to barge inside, but the last thing I wanted to do was give him the advantage. So even though it nearly killed me, I quietly slipped inside.

To my surprise, the main room was empty. I stepped farther inside, aware that Tom was right behind me. Something had definitely happened. The table beside the couch was turned over, and several things that had been lying on various surfaces were on the floor. The pattern of debris guided my steps.

Halfway to her bedroom, I heard what sounded like muffled sobs and whispering. I picked up my pace. Tom followed me step for step.

The sounds took me to her bathroom, where I got my first glimpse of Brianna huddled against the far wall, knees to her chest, trying desperately to get away from her father. He hovered over her, even though he was on his hands and knees, hand outstretched and attempting to coax her into coming with him. Brianna's only response was to push herself harder against the wall.

Seeing so much fear in her eyes reminded me again of those first few days, and I reacted without thought or care for myself. She was the only thing that was important. I gripped his shoulders and pulled with enough force to throw us both off balance. Concentrating too much on Brianna, he hadn't seen me coming, which worked in my favor. He wasn't passive for long, however. I was barely up on my feet before his arm collided with the back of my knees, sending me sprawling again. The side of my head knocked into the cabinet, but it didn't seem to cause much damage.

As I shook my head to clear it, I saw Tom reach around Reeves's torso, trying to subdue him. Reeves's response was to elbow Tom in the gut before twisting around and landing a solid punch to Tom's jaw. Tom released his hold on Reeves, and the man took full advantage, kicking Tom in the stomach and sending him flying backward into Brianna's room.

Confident he was safe from Tom for the time being, Reeves turned his attention back to me. Noticing I was once again on my feet, he pulled his arm back, ready to strike. I'd take a million hits for Brianna if it meant she was safe, but giving Reeves a free shot wasn't on my to-do list. Shifting my weight, I lunged at his lower body, landing us both on the floor again.

He must have hit his head against the wall, because he was slow getting up. It gave me just enough time to land a solid punch to the side of his face. And then another. Finally, his body sagged, and I released him. He fell back, his head bouncing off the side of the bathtub before he landed limp on the floor. My knuckles were sore, my hands bloody, but none of that mattered.

Tom stood, massaging his jaw. He followed my gaze down to where Reeves lay unconscious on the bathroom floor. Tom walked over in front of Reeves. I'd known Tom for two years. He wasn't a small man, and he was in great shape for his age. By Tom's response, Reeves must have put quite a lot behind that punch.

Twisting around, I crawled across the floor to Brianna. She was wide-eyed and staring at her father. The moment I tried to touch her, she jerked.

"Brianna. Look at me," I demanded. Her eyes snapped to mine. "Good girl." This time when I reached out to caress her face, she didn't flinch. "Are you hurt?"

She shook her head.

"You and I are going to go into my bedroom and get something while Tom stays here and watches your father. Can you walk?"

She nodded. Without another word, I helped her stand.

Once on our feet, Brianna clung to me as if her life depended on it, her fingers digging into my skin. There would probably be marks there later, but it was the least of my worries. I needed to get to my room quickly, but there was no way I was leaving her here in the same room with her father, Tom or no Tom.

Inch by inch, we walked to the door leading to her bedroom. I was careful to keep my body between Brianna and her father. She stayed with me step for step until we reached his head, which was lying about a foot from the opening. She stopped moving, and a shiver ran through her body. A sob ripped from her throat, and she buried her face in my chest. With a firm, hopefully comforting squeeze, I placed a gentle kiss on the top of her head before bending and lifting her into my arms.

It was a little tight getting out of the bathroom carrying her, but I could tell by her immediate response that it was the right decision. I was here for her. I'd promised to protect her, and I would.

When we made it to my bedroom, I carried her over to the bed and set her down. Her arms locked around my shoulders, not wanting to let go. Wrapping my fingers around her wrists, I urged her to release me.

"I need you to let go, Brianna, just for a minute, so I can get something. I need to tie your father up, so he can't hurt you or anyone else, okay?" I said, holding her gaze.

I saw the battle waging inside her—it was written all over her face. She didn't want to loosen her hold on me.

Reluctantly, her grip slackened, and I brought her hands up to my lips and kissed the backs of them. "Good girl. Thank you."

Turning to my left side, I opened the bottom drawer of my nightstand. The cotton ropes I always kept there lay in the back, just as I'd left them more than six months ago. Grabbing two of them, I faced Brianna again. "I need to go back in there. Do you want to stay here or come with me?"

"I want . . . I want to stay with you," she whispered.

One thing I knew for sure—he was not leaving here without giving me some answers. I wanted to know how he could turn his daughter over to a monster like Ian Pierce. Once I found that out, I'd make a decision on what to do with him.

Chapter 2

Brianna

I was scared. More scared than I'd been in weeks. The only thing that made it better was that Stephan was there. He would take care of me. He would keep me safe. I trusted him.

Stephan held tight to my hand as we walked back into my room. I had to consciously put one foot in front of the other, forcing myself to take the next step, and then the next, because all I wanted to do was run the other way.

The closer we came, the heavier my legs felt and the more effort it took to continue moving. I stepped closer to Stephan, wrapping my hand around his upper arm. He glanced down at me, and I held tighter.

"I'm right here, Brianna. You're fine now." His fingers brushed against my cheek, dragging the rope with it. It felt soft yet strange, and the thought of what he was going to do with it sent a shiver up my spine.

We took the final steps through my bedroom and into the bathroom. John was still unconscious but was now propped up against the wall, his head hanging to one side. I stopped, and tugged on Stephan's arm. I didn't want to go any closer. I didn't want him going any closer.

Instead of remaining by my side, as I wanted him to, Stephan placed a soft kiss on my forehead before releasing my hand. "Stand right here, Brianna. Don't move until I tell you."

I tried to do what he said. The desire to run was still there, and I had to force myself to do as he'd instructed. I'd already made one mistake.

Tom stood over John with a menacing look on his face, his arms crossed over his chest. He looked scary. I'd never been frightened of Tom until that moment. I took a step back.

"Brianna."

Stephan's voice brought my attention back to him. He wasn't looking at me, but I knew he must have heard me move. Disappointment mixed with my fear as I realized I'd messed up yet again. I vowed to do better.

He knelt down in front of John, dropping one of the ropes to the floor. With the remaining rope still in his grasp, he looped it around itself until there were two distinct holes. Then, with Tom's help, Stephan brought John's hands behind his body and slipped the two holes he'd made with the rope over John's hands and up to his wrists. With a quick pull, the ropes tightened, effectively creating handcuffs.

Seeing my father bound helped calm my fears a little more. He could no longer reach out and grab me or take me away. Although I knew Stephan would never willingly allow him to remove me, seeing him restrained was comforting.

Stephan picked up a second length of rope and repeated the same process around John's ankles. Once the ropes were secure, Tom helped Stephan move John into the main room. Stephan instructed me to follow them but not get too close. I made sure I stayed back far enough that John would have no hope of reaching me even if his hands weren't tied, but close enough that I could always see Stephan. It was a careful balance, made easier once we were out in the main room.

John didn't move as they carried him, Stephan at his head, Tom at his feet. I watched carefully, looking for any signs that he'd regained conciousness, but there was nothing. They sat him in one of the dining room chairs and tied him to it with the ends of the ropes.

Once Stephan appeared satisfied that John wasn't going anywhere, he walked to where I'd stopped by the end of the couch, and stood in front of me. His arms wrapped around me, hugging me close. I could feel his lips brushing against my hair. For the first time since I'd seen my father standing in the doorway, I felt as if I could breathe.

"Did you want me to stay, sir?" Tom asked.

Stephan turned to face him but didn't release his hold on me. "No. I think we'll be fine for now. Thank you, Tom."

There was a rough edge to Stephan's voice. I looked up into his face and could see the anger boiling beneath the surface, the vein in his neck pulsing vigorously.

Even though I knew he'd be leaving, when Tom moved toward the door, I jumped. Stephan rubbed his hand up and down my side. I closed my eyes and tried to take a deep breath.

If I hadn't opened the door, none of this would be happening. Why had I opened the door?

"Deep breaths, Brianna."

He looked down at me, concern on his face.

He brought his hands up to cup my cheeks, and I instantly missed his arms around me. I wanted to sit in his chair with him, lay my head on his shoulder, and forget everything outside the two of us existed. Closing my eyes, I leaned into his hands, taking what he was willing to give me.

John groaned, grabbing both of our attentions. I cringed back, but Stephan refused to release me.

He tilted my chin up, making me look at him. "Your father and I are going to talk. Do you wish to stay or go into the other room?"

"I want to stay with you," I whispered.

He smiled and brushed his lips against mine in the softest of kisses. "I want you to sit in my chair. You can watch and listen, but if he tries to speak to you, I don't want you to answer. Not yet anyway. Do you understand?"

"Yes, Sir." I nodded.

"Good girl." He rewarded me with another gentle kiss before releasing me.

I did what he'd asked, taking a seat in his chair. It was a good fifteen feet away from where he and John were in the dining room, but I could still see everything. Stephan stood, towering over John as he began to stir. It didn't take him long to realize his hands were tied, and I saw him pull on the ropes sharply to test their strength. I breathed a sigh of relief when I saw the look of frustration cross his face. He wasn't going anywhere.

John lifted his head. He first looked at Stephan, frowned, and then turned his head. I knew he was looking for me, and I burrowed further into the chair, pulling my legs up onto the cushion. Once he located me across the room, his expression changed. It softened for just a moment before going hard again.

"Welcome back," Stephan said, his voice anything but welcoming.

My father tore his gaze away from me and glared at Stephan. "I underestimated you."

Stephan ignored his comment.

"What are you doing here?"

John spit out blood from where Stephan had busted his lip in their fight. I glanced up at Stephan and realized that he'd been injured as well. Moisture pooled in my eyes. He'd been hurt trying to protect me, and I hadn't even noticed. A sob ripped from my throat. I couldn't stop it.

They both heard me. Stephan left my father and walked over to me, kneeling in front of where I was sitting in his chair. He rested his hands on my bare legs.

"What's wrong?" he whispered so that only I could hear.

I reached out, my fingers grazing over his wounds. "You're hurt."

He smiled and kissed my fingers. "I'm fine."

"How'd you do it?" John's voice cut through the room, interrupting. We both turned our heads toward him, my hands falling back into my lap as Stephan stood. I missed his touch instantly.

"I don't believe you're in any position to ask questions," Stephan said, stalking back toward John.

John laughed, but it wasn't a happy sound. "I knew rich boys like you got your kicks in strange ways, but I didn't think you'd be into kidnapping, what with you being such an upstanding citizen and all. I've done my research on you, Mr. Coleman. I wonder what all those rich people who throw their money at you and your foundation would think if they found out you like to take young girls."

Stephan

I laughed. I couldn't help it. The man was unbelievable. He broke into my house, scared Brianna, and then had the nerve to threaten me?

"I think you should choose your words wisely. As for Brianna . . . she isn't your concern anymore. You gave up that right when you sold her."

His eyes went wide. Shock?

He looked at me, then at Brianna.

"Eyes over here." He returned his gaze to mine. "Good. Now. Where were we? Oh yes, you were going to explain to me how a father can justify selling his one and only daughter."

He turned his head again to look at Brianna.

"I said eyes on me," I snapped. I stalked toward him, and was pleased to see that I had his full attention. "You will keep your focus on me, or I will restrain you in a way to force you to. Your choice."

He furrowed his brow in concentration. I had no doubt he was gauging how serious I was. If he decided to push back, he'd find out exactly how serious I could be. I had a posture collar upstairs that would solve his wandering eye problem perfectly. It wasn't something I used often. Actually, I'd gotten it specifically for Tami. She got off on being restrained. The more restrained the better. I may never use it again, but in this situation, it might come in handy.

After a rather lengthy staring contest, Jonathan Reeves slumped back in his seat and said, "I didn't sell her."

I looked at him in disbelief. He was honestly going to try to feed me a story. Did he think I was stupid?

"Let me bring you up to speed about what I *do* know," I said, allowing him to hear my repulsion. "I know that you had a gambling problem. I also know that you borrowed money from Jean Dumas to pay off your debts. Now my question is what exactly did you promised Dumas in return?"

Reeves pressed his lips tightly together, much like his daughter did when she was nervous. It was the only outward sign of his discomfort. Thankfully I'd learned Brianna's tells well, and they were useful tools when dealing with her father.

"Cat got your tongue?" I wanted to beat the man to a bloody pulp for what he did to Brianna. Unfortunately, with Brianna in the room, I had to restrain myself. I didn't think she would react well to such a display of violence.

"You don't understand."

His voice was almost pleading, as if begging for sympathy. That wasn't something he was likely to get from me, not after everything I'd learned from Brianna. Not after seeing her deal with debilitating panic attacks over and over again. There were many people who were responsible, and

Jonathan Reeves was one of them.

"Perhaps you'd care to explain it to me, then."

He stared at me and then jerked, testing the restraints for a second time. His tenacity made me smile. Reeves could test his bindings all he wanted. They would hold. I wasn't a Shibari expert by any means, but I was proficient in the basics. He wouldn't be getting free until I allowed it.

"You could loosen these, you know. They're a little tight."

"The ropes are fine, and I'm waiting."

The man was stubborn, I'd give him that. He continued to assess me, trying to look for a way out of the situation he currently found himself in, a weakness. He wouldn't find one. Jonathan Reeves wasn't leaving here until he started talking.

Another five minutes passed before he finally slumped back in his chair, resigning himself to the situation. I didn't say anything, just waited for him to start speaking. He met my gaze, and I could see the disgust in his eyes. I was sure he saw a similar reflection in mine.

"I messed up," he muttered. I thought the fact that he messed up was a given, but apparently he felt the need to preface whatever he was about to say with that fact.

He paused.

I waited.

"When . . . when I found out Anna's mom, Carrie, was sick—dying—I sank into some sort of depression." He closed his eyes and shook his head. "I should never have gone with Chad, but I did. It was only supposed to be something to take my mind off of things, a distraction." His voice drifted off, and I knew from experience with Brianna that he was falling into a past memory. Like father like daughter, I supposed.

"He took you gambling."

Reeves opened his eyes and met my stare. "Yes." He swallowed. "I couldn't stop."

"I know this part," I said, getting agitated. "What I want to know is at what point did you think it was a good idea to *sell* your daughter?" My voice rose giving way to my irritation.

"I didn't!"

I lifted my eyebrows, showing him my doubt at his declaration.

"I didn't," he insisted.

Again, his eyes pleaded with me to believe him. I didn't. I'd done my research on him, too. The man was a cop, yet there was no missing person's report on Brianna. If he were not to blame for her ten months of hell, why didn't he do everything within his power to find her?

Eventually, when I didn't soften my stance, Reeves continued. "I had no idea what Dumas had planned to do. Until that day, I didn't even know he was aware of Anna."

"You called her. You told her to get into that car."

"Yes." He nodded, seeming stunned that I knew what had transpired that day. "Yes. I called her. He said he wanted her to join us for dinner. That if I didn't call her, he would make sure he met her on his own. I didn't have a choice. Anna didn't know anything about what I'd done. I'd tried to keep her out of it. Tried to keep her safe."

At that point, I walked away from him. I had to. The man was trying to convince himself, and me, that he was a good father who had been coerced into allowing Brianna to fall into the hands of that sadistic bastard.

I walked across the room to Brianna. She was huddled into a ball in my chair. Bending over, I scooped her up into my arms and sat down. She wrapped her arms around my neck and laid her head on my shoulder. I started to calm down, if only a little. Ignoring the man sitting across the room for the time being, I closed my eyes and breathed in the coconut scent of her hair. Jonathan Reeves still had some explaining to do, but at that moment I needed the love and comfort only Brianna could provide. Reeves wasn't going anywhere.

Chapter 3

Stephan
I ran my hands over her back, her hips, and halfway down her legs before trailing back up and starting over again. With every inch of her skin I touched, my anger slowly receded. I took a deep breath and opened my eyes.

The first thing I noticed was Brianna. Her eyes were closed, just as mine had been. All the tension I'd felt in her muscles when I'd picked her up and placed her in my lap was gone. She was completely content, relaxed, sitting in my arms. I brushed my lips gently against her forehead. She sighed. If only we could stay like this.

That wasn't possible, however, and I knew it. I turned my head, resting my cheek on her hair, and glanced over at the man tied to one of my dining room chairs. He was watching us. All the pleading desperation he'd had in his face while he told me his story not ten minutes before was gone. In its place was what looked to be anger and . . . hatred? I had no idea what he was reading into my interaction with his daughter, but I couldn't have cared less. Even if she weren't already a legal adult, he'd lost all say in her life a long time ago.

When he realized I was watching him, the center of his eyebrows angled down, and his chest rose and fell with his exaggerated breathing. I knew he was gearing up to say something, and maybe I should have waylaid it by getting up and walking over to him, but I wasn't quite ready to let Brianna go.

"How dare you!" He spat out the words between clenched teeth.

Brianna jerked at the sound of his voice. She curled her fingers around my shirt, holding it in a death grip. I ran my fingers through her hair, trying to calm her.

"In case you haven't noticed, you're frightening her. If you do, in fact, care for her, even a little, then perhaps you should consider your words and your tone before you speak," I said with a slight edge of irritation.

The man was testing my patience. While I doubted Reeves had any real fatherly love or compassion for Brianna, I was hoping that, at the very least, the act he was trying to portray of the devoted father who'd been searching desperately for his daughter would carry over. It was worth a try.

To my great surprise, he appeared shocked at my words and lowered his gaze to Brianna. I watched his expression morph into what looked like genuine concern. Either he was a good actor, or he was bad at reading people. I had a hard time believing the latter, considering he was a cop. Being able to read a person was part of the job description, wasn't it? Then again, I wasn't all that convinced he was a good cop.

I pulled my attention away from him and focused once again on the woman in my arms. Brianna was still clutching my shirt, but her grip wasn't as tight as it had been. She had her face pressed against my neck. I could feel every exhale and knew her breathing had slowed. I caressed her cheek several times before tilting her chin up so she was looking at me. Her eyes were so full of trust, and it continued to amaze me how far she'd come in such a short amount of time. She was so strong.

"I need to go talk to your father again, Brianna."

She shook her head, her eyes pleading with me.

I cupped her face with my hands. "You'll be fine. I'll be right over there if you need me. He won't hurt you," I whispered.

She didn't want me to leave—that was plain to see on her face—but she nodded and relaxed her fingers. I leaned closer, caressing my lips against her temple and trailing them down to her ear. "Good girl."

Standing up, I sat her back down in my chair. I made sure she was okay before walking back across the room to where Reeves was sitting. His hostility was back, but he appeared to be trying to rein it in for Brianna's sake. I appreciated the effort, but it was too little, too late.

This time when he spoke, it was with less volume and not quite as aggressive. "You've brainwashed her," he accused.

I cocked my head to the side, observing him. Reeves still thought he was running the show. I shook my head and ignored his accusation. What he thought of me was irrelevant.

"Tell me how you know Ian Pierce."

At the sound of his name, Brianna whimpered. I glanced over to check on her. She was once again huddled into a ball, her knees pulled up tight to her chest. I sighed and turned back to Reeves. The sooner we got this over with, the sooner I could give her the comfort she required from me.

"Who is Ian Pierce?"

Jonathan Reeves appeared confused with my current line of questioning. I wondered if he really didn't know, or was playing dumb for some ulterior motive.

"He's a friend of your benefactor, Dumas. You mean to tell me that you have no idea who he is?"

"No," he said, shaking his head. "I've never heard of him. Why would I?

Who is he, and what does he have to do with Anna?"

I leaned back against the table casually. It was still taking effort not to pummel Brianna's father, but he didn't need to know that. If he knew how angry I was, he might be able to use that against me, and I wasn't willing to let that happen.

"For a cop, you have a lot of questions and not very many answers."

"I don't know what you want from me," he spat, getting frustrated. "I've been looking for my daughter for the last year. I don't know who this Ian Pierce is. I've never heard of the man before today. All I want to do is get my daughter and take her home where she belongs." His agitation peaked, and he pulled at the ropes.

I pushed myself away from the table and stalked toward him. He sat up straight, or at least as much as he was able, at my approach. His eyes were wary, no doubt wondering what my reaction would be to his declaration. I leaned down so that my face was directly in front of his. I didn't want there to be a single miscommunication about what I was going to say. "That is *never* going to happen."

He was quiet for several minutes. He seemed to be carefully considering his next words. I walked back over to my previous position against the dining room table and waited.

"You can't keep her here. I won't let you. She's a young girl with her whole life in front of her. I won't let you take that away from her."

I laughed. "You think I'm forcing Brianna to stay here with me?"

That confused look was back, but it was soon replaced with determination. "Of course you are. Look at her. She's absolutely terrified. I don't know how, but you've obviously convinced her to be dependent on you and only you. What did you do to her? What sick game are you playing?"

The more I listened to him, the more I began to believe his assertion that he had no clue about Ian Pierce or Brianna's time with him. I only wished his assumption that Brianna had been with me the last year were correct. I would have loved to have met the girl who didn't second-guess herself at every turn. The girl who didn't have nightmares about being tortured and raped.

I sighed and walked back over to Brianna. Extending my hand, I offered it to her. She glanced up at me, unsure.

"Come."

She slid her small fingers through my hand and unfolded herself from the chair. I wrapped my arm around her waist to steady her. She clung to me.

With my free hand, I touched the side of her face. "I want you to keep your eyes on me at all times, do you understand? No matter what happens, no matter what's said, you are to look at me and only me." She pressed her lips together and nodded. "Good girl."

Slowly, we walked back toward her father. His eyes were intense, watching every move, every step. I held tight to her, one arm firmly around her waist, the other still holding her hand. She did exactly as I asked.

I brought her over to stand near the table where I'd been previously. Once we reached our destination, I pulled her body closer to me. I could feel the tension in her muscles. This was going to be difficult for her, but it couldn't be helped. This would have to be dealt with sooner or later. She locked her gaze with mine. I smiled, letting her know I was pleased.

"Brianna is here because she chooses to be, and she will be here until she chooses not to be. You seem to be under the impression that Brianna's fear is something I cultivated. I assure you, I did not. Her anxiety is a product of what you did to her. You have no idea what the last year has been like for her, and you may never know. In my opinion, you don't deserve to know."

"She's my daughter. Of course I deserve to know."

"If you want to help Brianna, then tell me what you know. *That* is what's best for her right now." I never broke my gaze with Brianna as I spoke to her father, and neither did she with me. Every time Reeves spoke, her fingers dug into my flesh. I held on tight, giving her the lifeline she needed.

"Then what?"

"Then . . ." I paused, turning my focus away from Brianna for the first time. "You leave. You leave and you never come back."

"I won't just leave her. How will I know . . . how will I know she's safe?"

I looked down at Brianna. Her beautiful blue eyes stared back at me, and I felt that all-too-familiar tug in my chest. "If Brianna ever wishes to contact you, I won't stop her, but it will be *her* choice, not yours. If you really care for her as you claim you do, then you will allow her to do this on her terms. I will not let you bully your way back into her life."

His silence told me he didn't like what I'd said, but I meant every word. I firmly believed that Brianna would be much better off without her father in her life, but given everything that had already been taken from her, I wouldn't deny her if it was something she desired. At this point, however, I was confident it was not something Brianna wanted. It might never be. That was a fact he was going to have to accept.

Brianna

I didn't like this. I didn't like being so close to John. He was tied up, and I knew Stephan wouldn't let him hurt me, but I wanted him to go away. I'd listened to everything he'd said. I didn't want to hear any more.

Focusing on Stephan, I tried to block out everything else, but it was impossible. I heard John tell Stephan about the day the car came to pick me up, the day I met . . . Ian. Just thinking his name made my heart pound in my chest. It was almost painful. I held on to the one person who made me feel safe as I tried to remember where I was and that Stephan was here with me. My fingers held tight to his shirt, grabbing for anything that would anchor me to him.

He responded by rubbing his hand up and down my back, trying to soothe me. It helped. Air entered and exited my lungs a little easier with every pass of his hand. I wanted this to be over. I wanted it to be just him and me.

Stephan's chest vibrated as a low sound rumbled in his throat. "And you didn't think to file a missing person's report when she never showed up to dinner?"

John was speaking again. He was saying something about not knowing for sure, hoping he was wrong, and then feeling guilty. Tears pricked my eyes as I realized that his guilt over what he thought might have happened to me had overridden the need for him to file a report. I had no idea if such a report would have saved me from everything I went through, but if no one knew I was missing, that I had been taken, how could I have ever been found? I suddenly felt cold, empty. I shuddered with the knowledge that if Stephan hadn't bought me, I most likely would have been there, or with someone else like Ian, for the rest of my life, however long that may have been.

Stephan pulled away suddenly, catching me off guard. I almost lost my balance, since I'd been leaning into him. He steadied me. "Stay right here, Brianna."

He walked to stand behind John and pulled out his cell phone. By the way he was holding himself, I could tell he was very upset. I wanted him back in front of me, holding me, touching me. He was too far away.

I stayed where I was, as he had instructed, keeping my focus on him and trying to ignore John. I could tell my father was watching me, but I was trying my hardest not to pay any attention to him.

"I could use some assistance. Mr. Reeves is ready to leave," Stephan said to whomever he was speaking.

Stephan pocketed his phone and then knelt down to check the restraints. He didn't untie them, but he did slip his finger inside each of the loops to check them. John twisted in his seat, trying to look at what Stephan was doing, but I didn't think he could see much.

I was so wrapped up in watching Stephan's hands that the knock on the door startled me. Stephan stood and went to get the door. Tom and another man I didn't know were standing on the other side. As they entered the room, I instinctively took a step back, then stopped myself. Stephan ordered me to stay where I was, and I would obey.

Tom and the other man walked directly to John and stood on either side of him. Stephan knelt behind the dining room chair again, this time untying the ropes. As soon as he was free, John massaged his wrists. From where I stood, I could see the red marks where the ropes had bit into his skin.

I'd been in ropes a few times. Ian preferred cuffs and chains, but some of his friends liked to use rope. I knew from experience that pulling against the bindings caused marks and sometimes pain.

It also didn't get you free.

Stephan removed the ropes from John's ankles. He leaned back and stood as soon as John's feet were clear of the rope. Before John could reach down and see the damage, Tom and the other man each took hold of one of his arms, pulling him to his feet. John began to resist.

"I wouldn't do that if I were you. I still owe you for earlier, and I'd love for an excuse to pay you back," said the man I didn't know. There was a devilish smile on his face. John paled slightly.

The two men practically carried John to the door. He looked back at me as they left. There was sadness in his eyes, all the anger from before gone. For a moment, I was reminded of the man from my childhood. The man who'd taken me to the park and pushed me on the swing as high as it would go until I was squealing at the top of my lungs. The man I didn't know anymore.

The door shut, removing John from my view. Stephan crossed the room and pulled me into his embrace. I let out a sigh of relief. He was home. We were alone. I circled my arms around his waist and rested my head against his chest.

"Are you all right?" he asked.

I nodded, letting the warmth and comfort I'd been seeking seep into me.

For the longest time, we stood there, holding each other. I closed my eyes and enjoyed the feel of him, the smell of him. Every now and then his lips would brush against my hair, my temple, and I'd relax a little more. Being in his arms was the one thing that felt right.

I could have stayed there all night, but all too soon, he pulled back. He placed a hand on each side of my face and brushed his lips against mine, giving me the gentlest of kisses. "It's dinnertime. I'm going to order us a pizza. We can watch a movie while we eat."

I nodded. He stepped back, and I felt empty and cold when he walked across the room toward the phone. As much as I hated to admit it to myself, I was disappointed. Pizza meant we would be spending the evening on the couch. All I wanted was to spend the rest of the evening curled up with Stephan in his chair. I didn't care about the movie, and I wasn't all that hungry. I just wanted him.

Chapter 4

Brianna

He had me select a movie from his collection for us to watch. I took my time, but he was patient with me. In the past, I had stayed away from the romantic comedies I'd used to favor. Action movies didn't make me think of all the things I could no longer have. As I ran my fingers over the titles, I realized that might not be the case now. I wasn't sure what one would call my relationship with Stephan, but I knew that I cared for him. I loved seeing him smile, happy. I wanted to do everything in my power to see him look like that as often as possible.

I continued to argue with myself, unsure of what I should select. There was no right or wrong answer, I knew that. He wouldn't get upset with my choice no matter what it was. I just needed to pick one. The problem was, without his touch to calm me, I was beginning to feel numb. What did it matter what movie I picked?

The telephone rang in the background, and I heard Stephan answer it. The pizza was here, and I still hadn't chosen. Pressing my lips together, I closed my eyes, trying to concentrate. I could do this. Looking back at the rows of movies, one I had barely noticed before stood out, almost calling to me. It was a movie I hadn't seen in a long time, one that brought back a lot of memories.

Stephan wrapped his arms around my waist, making me realize I'd been standing there much longer than what I had thought. I leaned into him, letting my eyes drift closed. Feeling began to return, and the numbness started to fade. He hugged me closer, trailing his nose down my hairline to my neck and placing a kiss there. I sighed.

"You seem to be thinking very hard about something. Tell me."

"I was thinking . . . I was thinking about my dad." My words came out not much louder than a whisper, but I knew he'd heard me when his body tensed.

"What about him?"

Even though his tone didn't show any agitation, his body couldn't hide his reaction to the mention of my father. I hated that I'd upset him, but I knew better than to lie.

"I miss . . . I miss the way he used to be. When I would visit him, we would watch movies sometimes. We were always trying to find ones we'd both like."

He didn't respond right away. Instead, he reached out to touch the movies, his fingers grazing over the ones directly in front of us. "You found one you used to watch with your father."

I nodded.

"Which one? Show me."

I lifted my arm toward the bookcase where the movies were lined up in neat rows. When I came to the movie in question, I indicated that it was the one and quickly dropped my arm. Unfortunately, Stephan reached for my arm and guided my hand back to the bookcase. Together, we pulled it off the shelf.

"Is this the one?"

"Yes."

He turned me around to face him and tilted my chin up. "Your father likes baseball."

I nodded.

I couldn't remember how old I'd been the first time John and I watched *A League of Their Own*. The movie hadn't been new, but it had looked interesting enough to both of us that he'd rented it from the local video store. We'd liked it so much that he'd bought a copy of his own. It had become sort of a tradition, and we'd watched it together almost every time I came to visit. I hadn't seen it years. Not since before my mom had died.

He released my chin and stepped around me to put the movie into the player. Once he turned everything on, he reached for my hands and led me over to the couch. To my surprise, he already had everything laid out and ready. The pizza sat on the coffee table along with plates and two glasses of water. I'd been lost in my head again and hadn't been paying attention. He would be so disappointed in me.

We sat down, and I lowered my head, placing my hands in my lap.

"What's wrong, Brianna?" He brushed my hair away from my face so I couldn't hide.

"I wasn't paying attention."

He was quiet. I had no idea how he would react. It wasn't the first time I'd gotten lost in my thoughts. Every time he caught me, he stressed the importance of paying attention to my surroundings. He'd even taken away my books once.

"You think you deserve to be punished?"

"I don't know," I whispered.

Stephan leaned back and pulled me into his arms. I rested my head on his chest and began playing with the buttons on his shirt.

"Thank you for telling me."

When he didn't add anything else, I felt I should say something. "You're welcome."

He chuckled.

I looked up into his face. He stared down at me with amusement.

"You had a very stressful day, sweetheart. Although I do wish you would pay more attention to what is going on around you at all times, I do understand that it's not always going to be possible. Life is not black and white. There have to be exceptions."

"You're not . . . disappointed?"

"With you not paying attention? No. Not at all." As soon as he finished speaking, he kissed me. The kisses began with his lips barely touching my forehead, and slowly, as he worked his way down to my mouth, he increased the pressure. With every kiss, my heart rate accelerated, and I felt that now-familiar heat in my belly. Thoughts of my father and everything that had happened that day faded into the back of my mind.

I slid my hands up his chest, his neck, and into his hair, feeling the silky texture beneath my fingers. He pressed his lips against mine, dipping his tongue inside my mouth. I held tighter, trying to get closer. It seemed I could never get close enough to him anymore.

He grasped the back of my neck, pulling us apart. I frowned. I didn't want to stop.

Stephan laughed.

"Don't look so disappointed, Brianna. We both need to eat." Then he pulled me back against him, harder than before, and placed a solid kiss on my mouth. "And I promise you, there will be more time for this later," he said, rubbing his thumb against my bottom lip.

Reluctantly, I nodded, and we both sat up. He reached for the pizza and placed a piece on each of our plates before handing me mine.

There were several parts of the movie I'd forgotten. Although some scenes did remind me of my father, I found myself getting lost in the story. There were times I laughed and even a few where I cried. At one point, Stephan leaned down to whisper in my ear, "There's no crying in baseball," mimicking what Tom Hanks's character had said earlier in the movie. It made me laugh. By the end, I remembered why I'd always liked it so much. It wasn't really about baseball. It was about friendship.

He put the movie away when it was over, and we both took our plates into the kitchen. Stephan shoved the pizza box into the refrigerator and then walked over to circle his arms around my waist.

"Time to get ready for bed."

I nodded.

He stepped back, and I immediately felt the loss of his heat against me. Without a word, he took my hand, and we walked into his bedroom.

Stephan

After the stressful afternoon Brianna had, I wanted to make the evening as relaxing as possible. We needed to talk about what had happened with her father, but that could wait. She was already stressed out. Making her relive it so soon after wasn't something I wanted to do. While waiting on the pizza to arrive and Brianna to pick out a movie, I'd sent Jamie an e-mail letting her know I'd be in late the following day. I'd also asked her to send a security company over first thing in the morning to install a camera outside my door. What happened earlier would never happen again. I wanted a video panel installed that would be motion-activated from the outside and display anyone standing outside our door. The peephole was obviously not enough.

When checking my phone, I'd noticed a missed call from my lawyer. I listened to the message, but it wasn't anything I hadn't already figured out on my own. Jonathan Reeves had lost his tail. Reeves deserved some credit. He must have realized he was being followed, and once he'd gotten free, he'd worked quickly. I'd need to call Oscar eventually, but tonight was about Brianna and making sure she was okay. Instead, I'd sent him a quick text letting him know I received his message.

There were still a lot of unanswered questions, like how Reeves had gotten into our home. There were no signs of forced entry, so I had to assume she'd let him in on her own. It was obvious, however, that she'd not welcomed his arrival. So how had he gotten through the door without breaking it down?

Once we were inside my bedroom, I brought her to stand at the end of my bed and began to remove her clothing. I didn't stop until she was completely naked. She was beautiful and sexy and absolutely perfect. I cupped the back of her head, twisting her hair around my hand, and pulled her against me.

Feeling her body pressed to mine, seeing the trust in her eyes, was a high I couldn't explain. Her trust meant more to me than any gift I'd ever been given, and I hoped I'd never lose it. She deserved everything in life, and I wanted to be the one to give it to her.

Her nipples hardened as she swayed against me, and my body responded. I had no idea if I'd ever be able to resist her. Sex wasn't what I was setting out to do tonight. I wanted to give her pleasure, yes, but I wasn't worried about me. She was what was important. She was always what was important. Her needs had to come first, and tonight, she needed to forget about everything.

I ran my free hand down her back and cupped her ass. She twitched, and I smiled. Releasing her, I took a step back.

"Lie down on the bed, Brianna."

It took her a few seconds, but she complied.

"Slide closer to the edge," I instructed, showing her where I wanted her.

When she was finally in place, she lay on the edge of the bed with her legs spread, her knees bent, and her hands and feet flat. She was completely open to me.

I knelt between her legs and placed my hands on her inner thighs. She was watching me.

"What number, Brianna?"

"One, Sir."

"Good girl." I smiled.

She was already moist and ready for me. I couldn't wait to dive in and taste her delicious pussy again, but I wanted to address something first. Pubic hair on my partners wasn't something I particularly cared for. It got in the way and was plain inconvenient.

"I want you to talk to Lily about getting this waxed," I said, touching the fuzzy hair between her legs.

She stiffened, and her legs jerked as if she were thinking about closing them.

"Number?"

She didn't answer.

I waited.

"F-five."

"Tell me why."

"It . . . it hurts. And . . ."

"And?"

"I don't . . . I don't want anyone else to touch me. I don't . . . not like that." She shook her head, looking as if she were about to cry.

I rubbed her thighs, trying to comfort her. Had Ian made waxing sexual, too? Was there anything that man hadn't perverted for her?

"Brianna, I want you to talk to Lily about it, because it's something she has done as well. I was thinking she could go with you. She would stay with you the entire time and make sure nothing would happen to you other than getting the hair removed."

"No one would—"

"No. I promise you that."

She took a deep breath and closed her eyes.

"Okay."

I smiled and placed a soft kiss directly on top of her clit.

"Thank you," I whispered, allowing my breath to wash over her sensitive skin.

She shivered, and I knew I once again had her attention on more pleasant things.

"I want you to close your eyes and keep them closed. If you start to get anxious or something doesn't feel right, I want you to tell me. Use your numbers."

She nodded and closed her eyes.

I continued to rub her inner thighs for several minutes, willing her to completely relax. Finally, I heard a sigh escape her lips, and I knew she was ready.

Sherri Hayes

Starting from the outside, I began to probe her lips with my tongue. Even there she was moist, and I wondered what had caused her arousal. I would have to experiment to see what turned her on and what didn't. I knew she'd enjoyed our kiss earlier, but I wouldn't have thought it would have produced this type of response.

With every lick, every sweep of my tongue, more moisture pooled at her opening, until I could no longer resist going straight to the source. The first taste was even sweeter than I'd remembered from the night before. I had no idea why. Then again, it could also be that the memory had nothing on the present. My erection was straining in my pants, begging to get free. I took a deep breath, trying to calm myself, only to get another lungful of her scent. Needless to say, that did nothing to help my situation.

Replacing my tongue at her entrance with my fingers, I moved up to give her clit some attention. I could already feel her legs beginning to tremble. She'd been such a good girl, remaining still for me while I partook of her, that I wasn't going to draw this out any longer. I wanted her to come. I wanted to feel her inner muscles pulsing on my fingers.

I wrapped my lips around her clit and began licking and sucking in alternate motions as two of my fingers moved inside her. Soon her legs were no longer trembling. They were shaking. I could feel the vibrations getting faster, more intense. I adjusted my fingers to rub against the front of her vaginal wall with every pass, and I increased the pressure on her clit.

She no longer had her hands flat against the mattress. The blanket was now bunched between her fists as she held on tight, trying to ground herself. When her muscles began to spasm, I released my mouth from her clit long enough to tell her to come before returning my attention to my mission of making her world explode.

Brianna didn't disappoint. Twenty seconds after I'd given her permission to come, I felt her muscles clamp down hard onto my fingers, and what almost sounded like a wounded cry left her lips. Her back arched up off the bed, thrusting her pussy into my face. I wrapped an arm around her leg, placing a hand over her stomach and holding her in place as she rode out her orgasm.

As she came back down to earth, I removed my fingers from her pussy. My entire hand was soaked.

I stood, waiting between her spread legs for her to open her eyes. When she did, they were glassy and dilated. I smiled and extended my hand, helping her to sit up.

Once her feet were on the floor, I cupped her face in my hands and kissed her, plunging my tongue into her mouth, letting her taste herself. Then I pulled back slightly and, with my still wet hand, brushed some of her moisture over her lips before resuming our kiss. It wasn't quite as good as getting it directly from the source, but it still tasted amazing.

When I ended the kiss, I looked down into her eyes. More than anything, I wanted to tell her how much I loved her, but I was afraid it was too soon.

The one time I'd let it slip, she'd completely missed my declaration. The next time I told her I loved her, I wanted there to be no doubt that she understood what I'd said and what it meant.

"Ready for our shower?"

"Yes, Sir." The darkness that had been clouding her expression since I came home was gone, at least temporarily.

I helped her to stand, and we walked into my bathroom. Although I'd helped her with her problem, I now had one of my own to deal with. Hopefully a shower would calm my body down. If not, it would be a very long and restless night.

Chapter 5

Brianna

Before I opened my eyes, I was aware of him beside me. He had his arm draped over my stomach. It was warm and heavy, so I knew he was asleep.

I turned my head to look at him. He was lying on his stomach, his face toward me, one hand tucked under his pillow. This was only the second time I'd seen him asleep. The first was shortly after I'd come to live with him. I'd snuck into his bedroom—without permission—to give him a blowjob. It hadn't ended how I'd thought it would. Then again, back then I'd known next to nothing about him. I'd thought it would be what he wanted. Instead of being pleased, he'd ordered me out of his room and proceeded to give me a lecture on how to thank him.

That morning seemed like a lifetime ago. A lot had changed since then. Stephan was no longer a stranger to me. He had helped me not be afraid all the time. He'd also opened up an entirely new world to me over the last two days. Before him, my sexual experiences had been of the nightmare variety. Sex wasn't something I enjoyed. It was something I hated. Sex had never been enjoyable for me, and I hadn't expected it to be with Stephan either. At best, I'd hoped it wouldn't hurt like it had before and I'd be able to endure it for him. What I'd discovered, however, was that I liked it. A lot.

As I watched him sleep, I remembered our conversation less than a month ago when he'd told me that in some ways he was like Ian. I still wasn't sure what he'd meant by that because he was nothing like the man who used to own me. Stephan was kind. He never forced me to do anything or hurt me just to hear me scream out in pain.

Were there some things he'd had me do that were uncomfortable? Yes, lots of times. Talking about all the things that had happened to me wasn't comfortable. Neither was sleeping on the floor. But after all that I'd been through, they were minor things. He always explained why he was doing something, letting me know there was a purpose behind the discomfort.

With every day that passed, I became more determined to please him, to be what he needed me to be. Sex had ended up being an extremely pleasurable surprise. He'd given that to me. In return, I was determined to give him what he needed.

Movement drew my attention back to his face. He opened his eyes and smiled.

"Morning, Brianna," he said in a groggy voice.

"Morning, Sir."

He rolled onto his side and pulled me up against him. We were both naked, and I could feel his penis hard against my stomach.

He kissed me. It was soft and slow, with no tongue, but I could tell he was restraining himself. I held on to his arms, allowing him to take whatever it was he wanted.

"Hmm. I think I like waking up like this. I may never let you go back in your own bed."

"Okay." He would get no argument from me, if that was what he wanted.

He sighed and rolled onto his back, turning his head to look at the clock. I followed his gaze. It was already seven thirty. We'd overslept.

Stephan must have felt me tense, because he turned his attention back to me and ran his fingers down my cheek, along my jaw.

"What's wrong, sweetheart?"

"You're going to be late for work."

"It's all right. I let Jamie know yesterday that I wouldn't be in until this afternoon." He leaned in, kissed my forehead, and then sighed. "We do need to get up, though. Someone is coming over to install a video camera outside our door." He paused. "Then you and I need to talk about what happened yesterday."

I felt an unpleasant pull in my chest and a sinking feeling in the pit of my stomach. The last thing I wanted to do was tell Stephan how I'd messed up the day before by opening the door to my father, but I knew I had to. Stephan had told me time and time again that communication was the number one thing he required of me. I'd learned the hard way just how serious he felt about the subject.

He lay there, waiting. My distress must have been clear on my face.

"Don't be anxious, Brianna. Whatever it is, we'll deal with it. Right now, we need to get dressed and get breakfast before the security company arrives."

Before I could respond, he threw off the sheet, revealing what I'd felt pressed against me earlier. He sat up, then stood and walked over to his dresser. Removing a pair of boxers and jeans, he pulled them up over his long legs and then turned to look at me still in the bed.

"Go to your room and get dressed, Brianna. Meet me in the kitchen when you're done."

I scurried to get out of the bed and went to my room. As soon as I walked through the door, all the feelings from the day before hit me again, and I ran back out to the main room. Stephan was just walking out of his bedroom, and I headed straight toward him. He caught me as I flung my arms around his neck.

"Hey, what is it?"

I pressed my face into his neck, plastering my body as close to him as I could get it. "I can't . . ."

There was a long pause where neither one of us spoke. He just held me, rubbing his hands up and down my back.

"Would it help if I go in with you?"

I nodded.

Stephan reached up, untangled my arms from around his neck, and then took both of my hands in his. He looked serious but not angry.

"I'll go into your bedroom with you, but I'm going to remain by the door. You'll be able to see me, but you'll have to go to your closet and retrieve your things by yourself."

What sounded like a whimper left my throat.

"You can do this, Brianna. I'll be right here with you, but you can do this." He rested his palm on the side of my face and stared at me intently.

I closed my eyes and gave myself a pep talk. I could do this. He was right. I could do this.

Opening my eyes, I met his gaze again and nodded.

"Okay." I knew I didn't sound very confident, but it was the best I could do.

Stephan

I stood just inside Brianna's bedroom door while she rushed around the room getting her things. She didn't linger, and I doubted she gave what she grabbed more than a cursory glance before picking it up. Once she had everything she needed in her arms, she came to where I stood. She made no movement to put any of the clothing onto her body.

I waited, but she still didn't move. "Were you planning on running around naked all day?"

She shook her head.

"Then I suggest you put on those things you have in your hands."

Brianna's forehead creased in concentration but she didn't speak. I checked my watch. Seven forty-five. The person from the security firm was due in fifteen minutes.

"Would you rather I leave?"

She looked up at me, her eyes wide, and shook her head again. I understood she didn't want to be in this room anymore, but I was right here, and I was not going to let her run away just because it was easier. No one was going to hurt her. It was all in her mind. I wasn't going to allow Jonathan Reeves the power to make Brianna afraid in her own home.

"Dress." It wasn't a request, and by her immediate response, she knew it.

I stood with my arms crossed over my chest while she finished. After she put on her bra and panties, she moved faster. I wasn't sure if she hurried because she'd gotten over her fear or if it was *due* to her fear. It was another thing we'd have to address after the camera was installed.

As soon as she was finished, I cupped her face, leaned forward, and gave her a kiss. "Good girl. Don't let your fear have so much control over you. You should feel safe inside these walls. Don't allow him and what happened yesterday to change that."

We were walking back into the main room when the phone rang. It was the front desk letting me know a man from the security firm had arrived, and I gave Tom clearance to send the man on up. The sooner this was done, the better.

I had enough time to set the table before I heard a knock on the door.

"Keep working on breakfast. I'll be back to help in a minute," I said, leaving her in the kitchen. She was going to make her homemade waffles. I'd given her the choice, and that was what she'd picked. She'd made them a couple of times before, and each and every time I'd stuffed myself. I would have to be more cautious this time, as we had things to discuss. Today wasn't about relaxing.

The man on the other side of the door was older, about Richard's age, give or take five years. After introducing himself, Danny confirmed with me the information he'd received from my assistant. I explained to him in more detail what I was looking for, and he showed me a couple of different options. In the end, I chose a high-resolution motion-sensitive camera. The picture was clear, and in full color. Neither Brianna nor I would have any trouble seeing who was on the other side of the door.

Danny went to work, and I walked back into the kitchen where Brianna was already plating the waffles. Looking over all the options, and then discussing specifics, had taken longer than I'd planned.

I walked up beside her and placed a kiss on her cheek. She smiled. We each took our plates over to the table and sat down.

Brianna was distracted all during breakfast. She kept glancing at the door where Danny was working and then back down at her plate. She didn't appear panicked, so I was fairly sure her anxiety had nothing to do with Danny himself. As I continued to watch her reactions, I began to think that what she was actually doing was watching to see how much longer it would take him to finish. Brianna was never eager to talk things out. Even after two months, getting information out of her, especially information she didn't think I'd like, was a challenge.

We were almost finished with breakfast when the telephone rang again. Wiping off my mouth with my napkin, I stood and walked over to answer it, leaving Brianna at the table. Aside from Danny, we weren't expecting any visitors to my knowledge. I also knew that if Reeves showed up again, Tom would gladly have him physically removed from the premises.

"Hello."

There was a long pause. If I hadn't heard breathing on the other end of the line, I would have thought no one was there.

"Coleman?"

"Yes. This is Stephan Coleman. Who is this?"

"Why are you home? Where's Anna?" There was no longer a question as to who was on the other end of the phone. The demanding and impolite attitude gave him away.

"Good morning to you, too, Ross."

"Cut the crap, Coleman," he snapped. "John came to see me last night. I know he was there."

Glancing across the room, I saw Brianna had stopped eating and was watching me. I met her gaze and nodded toward her plate. *Eat*, I mouthed. She lowered her head and picked up her fork.

"What did he say?" I asked.

Ross snorted. It wasn't a pleasant sound.

"He said he'd found Anna and that, other than being scared witless, she looked okay. That she wouldn't leave with him, which considering what you told me . . ." Ross paused. "He also said you tied him up and questioned him. He's got some pretty nasty red marks on his wrists."

Reeves's all-out confession to Ross didn't surprise me. I was sure he'd been livid when he left here. Ross was a family friend who lived nearby. Of course he'd go there to vent his frustrations.

"Yes, I did."

Ross was silent for a long moment.

"Is she all right?"

"She's fine."

He snorted again. Could the man hold a conversation without all the theatrics?

"Would you tell me if she wasn't?"

I smiled.

"Maybe."

This time he chuckled.

"Well, at least you're honest."

Considering Ross had been forthcoming with information about Reeves being in town, I decided I would be nice. "Brianna's finishing her breakfast right now, and we have a few things to take care of after that. I'll let her know you called, and if she wishes, she can call you back this afternoon."

"I just want to know she's all right. John was really upset last night. I hope you have something in place to keep him away from her."

"Did he say something to you about returning, trying to take Brianna away again?"

"Not in so many words, no. It's just that I know John. He's not one to give up. I know you think he's responsible for what happened to Anna. I don't know if that's true or not, but it's what Anna believes. He loves her, though. I know he does."

"His love for Brianna is irrelevant."

"How can you say that? He's her father. He's the only family she has left." This conversation was quickly giving me a headache. Besides, Brianna was finished with her breakfast, and Danny was already packing up his tools.

"I'll let Brianna know you called."

He sighed in frustration.

"Okay. Fine. Whatever. Just have her call me." Without another word, he hung up the phone. His lack of manners never ceased to amaze me.

After placing the phone back on the receiver, I walked over to Danny. He stood at my approach and smiled.

"Everything is all set up, Mr. Coleman."

He then proceeded to show me how everything worked. The camera was positioned so that not only could you see directly in front of the door, but it was also at enough of an angle that you could see anyone approaching from the elevator as well. He demonstrated by walking down the hall toward the door, activating the motion sensor.

He'd installed a flat-panel screen into the wall that resembled a small television. The picture was crisp and clear. It was exactly what I'd wanted.

Once I signed the paperwork, I thanked Danny for coming over so promptly and saw him down the hall to the elevator.

He shook my hand again as he left. "Call me if you have any questions or problems, Mr. Coleman."

Walking back into the condo, I noticed Brianna was still sitting at the table. Her plate was empty, her glass drained, and she had her hands folded neatly in her lap. I strolled over to her, and picked up my own plate I'd left on the table when Ross called. I could see her pressing her lips together, broadcasting her nerves.

"Grab your plate. We need to clean up, and then we need to talk."

Brianna's shoulders slumped slightly, and I saw her flex her fingers before she nodded and stood. With the way she was acting, I had a feeling I really wasn't going to like what she had to tell me.

Chapter 6

Brianna

I'd been covertly watching the guy who'd come to install the security camera. He looked like he knew what he was doing, so I didn't think it would take him long. I was right. By the time we finished eating breakfast, he was finished. Once he was gone, there would be no avoiding Stephan and his questions.

My responsibility in what happened weighed me down. I knew I shouldn't have opened the door without checking to see who it was first, but I had anyway. It was stupid and reckless.

Cal's call only delayed the inevitable. Stephan had given me last night. He wouldn't put off our conversation any longer. He wasn't like that.

By the time Stephan returned to the table, I was near tears. I'd done the wrong thing, and I knew there would be consequences. Although I had no idea what those consequences would be, I wasn't as worried about that as much as I was about having to confess to him what I'd done.

We rinsed and loaded our dishes into the machine before walking over to his chair. I trailed behind, dragging my feet. He noticed and snapped his fingers, pointing to the spot beside him. Picking up my pace, I met him beside his chair. He let me stand there for several minutes, looking me up and down as if trying to see something. I started to get nervous.

"Don't fidget."

I stopped moving. Why was I moving? I'd learned how to stand stock-still with Ian. I'd learned the hard way, like I had everything else. Why was it difficult now?

He made me stand beside the chair for several more minutes before he invited me to sit on his lap. I wasn't sure what to do with myself. Usually I would cuddle up to him and lay my head on his shoulder, but that didn't seem right. I was in trouble, and I knew it.

"Tell me what happened yesterday, Brianna, and don't leave anything out."

"I was cleaning your bathroom when I thought I heard the phone ring," I said, looking down at my lap. He wasn't having it and lifted my chin up with his hand, forcing me to look at him. He wasn't going to let me hide.

"That's better. Start again. And this time look at me."

"I . . . I was cleaning your bathroom. I thought I heard the phone. But I had your radio on. I wasn't sure."

"Then what did you do?" he asked when I didn't say anything else.

"I heard a knock . . . on the door."

"You were still in the bathroom?"

"No." I shook my head. "In your bedroom."

He nodded but didn't say anything else. I knew he was waiting for me.

"The knocking got louder, and then I thought about the phone . . . how I'd thought I'd heard it . . . I thought maybe . . . Tom . . . had tried to call me, and when I didn't . . . when I didn't answer, he came up to check on me."

"So you thought it was Tom?"

"Yes," I whispered.

"When did you realize it wasn't?"

I pressed my lips together, not wanting to say that part.

"Brianna."

"When I opened the door."

He placed his hands on either side of my face. I could feel the tension in them. It wasn't the same loving gesture from the night before. He was angry with me, and he had every right to be.

"You opened the door without checking to see who it was first?"

I closed my eyes. I couldn't look at him.

"Open your eyes. Now," Stephan ordered.

I quickly reopened my eyes and met his angry stare.

"Answer the question."

"Yes."

"Yes, what?"

I swallowed.

"Yes, Sir. I answered the door without . . . without checking."

He dropped his hands into his lap and looked at me. For the longest time, he didn't say anything, and I could feel the uncertainty take hold. He'd said many times that he didn't own me, that I wasn't his slave. I believed that now, but what would happen if he didn't want me to be here anymore? Stephan wouldn't sell me, but he could make me leave. Where would I go? What would I do? How would I—

"Calm down, Brianna."

I took several deep breaths, trying to do as he said.

"You know you did wrong, correct?"

"Yes, Sir." I nodded.

"Good. That's a start." He paused. "You do realize I can't just let this go, don't you?"

"Yes, Sir."

"You deliberately put yourself in danger."

I nodded and looked down. This time, he didn't stop me.

"Stand up."

I moved quickly to obey him. Whatever my punishment was, I'd take it. Anything was better than having to leave.

He stood and walked around me to the small side table where he kept his keys. Opening the drawer, he removed something about a half-inch thick and rectangular and then placed it on the floor in front of the door. He straightened back up to his full height and waited. I realized he was waiting for me and moved quickly to stand in front of him.

"Kneel facing the door." He nodded, motioning for me to kneel on what I now realized was a thin cushion.

I didn't hesitate in complying and lowered myself to the floor.

He knelt down and adjusted the position of my legs, spreading them farther apart to where they were not far from the edges of the rectangle. I didn't understand what was going on, but I didn't question him.

"Now rise up onto your knees."

I did as instructed, lifting my butt off my legs so that all my weight was supported by my knees. Once I was in position, he stood and walked around the other side of me.

"Place your arms behind your back and grasp your forearms."

It had been a while since I'd been in this position, but I remembered it well. I fought a moment of panic at the memory. This was Stephan. I was fine. I was safe. He wouldn't hurt me.

He reached into his pocket and removed a coin. When he brought it in front of my face, I realized it was a quarter. I had no idea what he planned on doing with it, but I didn't ask. I was in enough trouble as it was.

Stephan placed the quarter between his thumb and index finger and held it against the door. "Lean forward and press your nose against the quarter, Brianna."

I leaned forward, pressing my nose against the round metal coin. It was warm, probably from being in his pocket. The metallic scent filled my nostrils when I inhaled.

He backed away and walked around me again. His movements were slow and deliberate, each step measured. When he finally came to a stop, I could feel him staring down at me. From the position I was in, I couldn't see his face. I could only imagine the disappointment in his eyes. I hated disappointing him.

"You are to stay in this position until I tell you otherwise. Do not let the quarter drop." He paused. "Maybe next time you will stop and think before you open the door without looking, since you are going to be staring at it for a while."

I closed my eyes and swallowed. I could do this.

Stephan

Once I was sure Brianna was in the correct position, I left her for a few moments to retrieve my laptop from my bedroom. Grabbing a dining room chair, I positioned it where I would have a clear view of her but she wasn't able to see me. So far, she was doing fine, although I hadn't expected her to have trouble yet. Holding that position for a short amount of time was easy. Her legs, however, would eventually start to feel the strain.

I opened my laptop and began checking e-mails. It was hard to tell how long it would take before she reached the point where I would stop her discipline. She'd come very close to being taken from me, and the responsibility for that ultimately lay upon her shoulders. If she'd waited another five minutes, Reeves would have been forced to leave the building while she remained safely inside our home. Opening the door without looking to see who it was first had been a stupid decision, and it was one I was bound and determined to make sure she thought long and hard about before doing again.

Once I finished going through my inbox, I sent an e-mail to Lily. I needed to go into work this afternoon, but I wasn't comfortable leaving Brianna alone. If Lily couldn't come and stay with her, then Brianna would have to come to the office with me. There were no other options.

Two minutes after I pressed send, Lily responded. I hadn't gone into details in my message, just letting her know something had happened the night before and I didn't want Brianna to be by herself. Her response was perfect. She would bring lunch around noon, and she could stay with Brianna until five. With that taken care of, I leaned back in my chair and pulled up a document I'd been working on the previous day. There was little I could do with it at home, but it would help me pass the time.

It was about fifteen minutes later when I noticed some movement from her. Her breathing had changed a little as well. The effort of holding the position was getting to her, as was intended.

Standing, I returned the chair to the dining room and left my laptop on the table. From the way she was acting, I estimated we had another five minutes left before her legs began to tremble with fatigue. I propped myself up against the back of the couch and waited.

As it turned out, I didn't need to watch all that closely. In an almost coordinated fashion, her legs began to shake and a weak whimper escaped her lips. Pushing myself away from the couch, I walked across the room to tower over her.

Brianna glanced up at me, pleading in her eyes. Her lips were pressed so tightly together they were white. I waited for another thirty seconds, unmoving, before I reached down and took hold of the coin.

"You may sit down now, Brianna." A large gush of air left her lungs as she sat back on her heels. I could still see the muscles in her legs flexing, trying to recover from the strain.

As I slipped the coin back into my pants pocket, I noted it was warmer than it had been when I'd placed it into position against the door. Hopefully she wouldn't make me remove it again anytime soon. I was accustomed to using slightly more physical discipline with my submissives, spanking or possibly even gagging them. I didn't think Brianna was ready for that, however. She might never be. Even if I could get her to the point of enjoying types of play that blurred the boundaries of pain and pleasure, I doubted that would ever carry over into discipline. I didn't want Brianna confusing the two.

Looking down at her, I saw a red mark on the tip of her nose from where she'd pressed it up against the coin. It was rather cute, and it took effort for me not to smile.

Brianna wasn't looking at me, though. She had her head tilted down, and I realized she was crying. Squatting down next to her, I brushed the moisture from her cheek.

"Talk to me. Tell me what's wrong."

"I . . . I'm . . . I didn't mean to. I . . ."

I gathered her into my arms and carried her back over to my chair. Laying her head on my shoulder, I let her cry it out while I consoled her the best I could and rubbed the muscles in her legs so they wouldn't cramp up on her.

A submissive was supposed to feel remorse when they received correction for something they'd done wrong, but I hadn't expected it to cause her tears, especially not to the extent where she was having difficulty speaking coherently. As with so much when it came to Brianna, her reactions rarely made sense unless you took into consideration the whole of her life and circumstances. I could safely say my point was driven home. I doubted she would ever open the door again without checking to see who it was first.

It took a long while before her tears subsided, and her breathing returned to normal.

"How are you feeling, Brianna?"

"I didn't mean to do something reckless."

I cupped her face gently with my hands and kissed her forehead, before tilting her head up so I could look into her eyes. "I know you didn't mean to, Brianna, but I can only do so much to try to keep you safe. You have to help me by doing your part. That means not opening the door without knowing who it is. It means paying attention to your surroundings, especially when you're out in public or not with me. I don't want anything to happen to you. I don't know if I could take it."

"I'll do better, Sir."

"Good girl."

I gave her a soft kiss, and she met my lips eagerly. It could have easily gotten out of control, but I broke the connection before it got that far. As much as I would have loved to get lost in her and forget about everything else, there were still a few things we needed to discuss. I laid her head back on my shoulder and hugged her close.

"Your father went to see Ross last night."

She tensed but didn't comment.

"He was upset I wouldn't let you leave with him."

"I don't want to go," she whispered.

"Shh. No one is going to make you go anywhere you don't want to go, Brianna."

She pressed her face into my neck and played with the buttons on my shirt. I'd gone ahead and put on a dress shirt and slacks earlier, but I should have known better. By the time I was ready to leave for work, it would be wrinkled. Brianna loved to play with the front of my dress shirts.

We sat there for several minutes before she finally spoke up. "Why?"

"Why what?" I asked, brushing my lips against her hair.

"Why did he . . . why did he let . . . Ian . . . have me?"

I sighed and held her tighter, knowing this was going to be difficult for her. She must have blocked out most of the conversation I'd had with her father.

"He says he didn't. He claims he doesn't know who Pierce is."

"How?" she asked, holding tighter to my shirt.

There was a part of me that didn't want her to know this. I wanted to shield her from the pain. Logic, however, told me I needed to tell her. This was her life. She'd suffered for her father's mistakes, and she should know the extent of it.

"When your mother got sick, your father started gambling. He got in over his head and had to borrow money from a man named Dumas to pay off his debts. He says he didn't want to involve you, and a part of me buys that, but it doesn't change what happened."

She was quiet for a long time, but I waited. I knew she'd want more, but I wanted to give her a chance to digest the new information I'd provided.

"But . . ."

"But what?"

"The car. What about the car he sent for me?" My shirt was bunched tight in her hands. There would be no saving it.

"Your father says he went to see Dumas that day and that Dumas brought you up in conversation. Dumas said he wanted to meet you. The car was his idea, according to your father. You were supposed to be joining them for dinner." I paused. "When you didn't arrive, Dumas let your father know that his debts had been paid in full."

"Ian," she whispered.

"Yes."

There was a long pause.

"So, John didn't know? He didn't . . . sell me?"

"That's his story."

"You don't believe him?"

"I don't know if I believe him or not. He's an officer of the law, yet at no point in time did he file a missing person's report for you. If he wasn't involved, why didn't he do that? If I suspected my daughter had been taken, I would move heaven and earth to find her."

Chapter 7

Brianna

Stephan held me in his lap until Lily arrived. Even then, he seemed reluctant to let me go. It was only as I noticed his struggle to release me that I realized how much what I'd done must have bothered him. It wasn't just me my bad choice affected, it was him, too.

He answered the door, and I hung back. Lily was dressed in one of her designer suits and had a large plastic bag in her arms. Stephan took the bag from her, and she walked over and hugged me. I hesitated for a brief moment, before hugging her back. In some ways, it felt odd having her comfort me after what I'd done. It was different with Stephan, almost as if we were comforting each other. Lily didn't need comfort. It was all for me, and I didn't feel as if I deserved it.

We walked over to the table where Stephan was laying out the contents of the bag Lily had brought with her. There were sandwiches, chips, and cupcakes with icing towering so high it was almost as tall as the cake part.

I waited until both Stephan and Lily took their seats before I sat down. They both selected a sandwich. I knew I should follow their lead as well, but I held back. I wasn't sure why, exactly, other than the guilt I still felt. Stephan reached over and took my hand. I looked up to meet his gaze.

"Stop worrying about what you can't change. We learn from our mistakes, and we move forward. Do you understand?"

"Yes," I said.

He smiled.

"What kind of sandwich would you like? Lily brought a little bit of everything. I think maybe she bought out the store."

"Very funny, Stephan."

He chuckled and then turned his attention back to me. Although he didn't say anything more, I knew he was waiting on me to pick a sandwich. I reached out with my free hand and took the one closest to me. He tightened his hold on my fingers for a second before releasing them and unwrapping his own sandwich.

Over lunch, Stephan and Lily mostly talked business. There was supposed to be a board meeting on Friday to approve the new chief financial officer. He would be the man taking Karl Walker's place at the foundation. From what they said, he sounded like a nice man. I could only hope he was nothing like Karl and would leave me alone.

Once we were all finished, Stephan stood. I knew he'd be leaving soon, and I didn't want him to go.

"Stop looking so sad," he said, gently cupping my chin. "I'll be home before Lily has to leave."

I nodded, and he leaned down to give me a kiss before strolling across the room and disappearing into his bedroom.

Lily began to clear off the table, and I jumped up to help her. She smiled but didn't say anything. It made me wonder how much she knew, how much Stephan had told her. I didn't care that she knew, exactly, but I didn't want her to be disappointed in me, too.

We'd just finished wiping off the table when Stephan reappeared. He'd changed his clothes and was now wearing a light blue shirt with a pinstriped jacket and tie. As he walked toward me, it felt like something was flip-flopping in my stomach. It wasn't the first time I'd felt it—Stephan had a way of making my body react in ways I was only beginning to understand.

He came to a stop in front of me and pulled me into his arms. "I'll be in a meeting this afternoon, but if you need me, call."

I nodded.

"I want you to talk to Lily today about waxing. I know you're nervous, but I think she can help you with that. She can answer any questions you have."

I pressed my lips together and nodded again. He ran his thumb along my bottom lip until I relaxed my mouth, then cupped my cheek and tilted my head to bring it at exactly the right angle to meet his lips in a kiss.

There was nothing soft or gentle about this kiss. He nipped at my lips with his teeth before plunging his tongue into my mouth and taking. By the time he separated his mouth from mine I was panting and holding on to his arms, fearing I might lose my balance since I was so lightheaded. He was breathing hard, too, but he was smiling down at me.

He pressed one short kiss to my forehead before turning to leave. Then he walked across the room, picked up his briefcase, and opened the door. Seconds later, he was gone, and I was left alone with Lily.

I stood there unmoving for a while, staring after him. He'd said I needed to talk to Lily, and as much as I didn't want to, I would because he asked it of me. I also had to return Cal's call. After weighing my two options, I decided I would try Cal first. Without saying anything to Lily, I went to pick up my cell phone from where it had been charging overnight and dialed Cal's number.

"Anna!" His voice was so loud, I pulled the phone away from my ear for a second.

"Hi."

My voice shook slightly. I wanted to talk to him, but at the same time I didn't. John had been to see him, and I had no idea what he'd told him. Would Cal believe my father or me?

"How are you? Are you all right?"

"Yes. I'm all right."

He released a loud gush of air, and I could hear how relieved he was. If he was happy I was okay, that had to mean he believed me, right? I walked over to the couch and curled up into the corner, pulling my legs under me.

Lily was still in the kitchen, but I could tell she was listening. The thought crossed my mind that maybe she'd tell Stephan and he'd be upset, but I knew better. Stephan told me I could talk to Cal any time I wanted. I locked gazes with her for a second before refocusing on my phone conversation.

"I'm glad you aren't hurt, Anna. I was worried. Did Coleman tell you that your dad came by my place last night?"

"Yes," I whispered.

He paused.

"I'm sorry he scared you. If he was anywhere near as worked up with you as he was when he got here, I know you had to be frightened. He told me what happened. Not every detail, but the basics. He thinks Coleman is the one who took you and that he's brainwashed you."

"He's not like that. Stephan has helped me so much. He wouldn't hurt me."

"I know you believe that, but . . . Anna, I've heard rumors. About Coleman. I don't know if they're true or not, considering the source, but I want you to be careful. If you ever need or want to leave him, you call me and I'll come and get you, all right?"

"What rumors?"

He was silent for a long time. So long that I didn't think he was going to answer.

"Cal?"

He sighed. "Promise me you won't get upset?"

"I'll try," I said, bracing myself for whatever bad thing he was going to tell me.

"About a week after Coleman fired Karl Walker, I ran into him in a local bar. I don't think he recognized me. He was three sheets to the wind by the time I got there. He was talking to whoever would listen, and when I heard him mention Coleman, I moved closer and started paying attention."

I wanted to forget about Karl Walker. He was a vile man, and I was glad Stephan fired him. If he was making trouble for Stephan, however, I knew I needed to find out. I didn't want someone doing something or saying something that would hurt him or his business.

"What did he say?" I asked when Cal didn't continue.

"He said Coleman liked to hurt women." After he said it, he let it hang in the air.

"He wouldn't do that," I said, shaking my head even though he couldn't see me.

"I'm not saying he would or he wouldn't, but Karl mentioned one of Coleman's old girlfriends. He said she'd told him all about Coleman tying her up and beating her. And after what John told me last night about Coleman tying him to a chair . . . I'm wondering if it might be true."

"No." I shook my head back and forth, violently denying his claims.

A hand touched my arm out of nowhere, and I jumped. Lily. She was sitting beside me, her face full of worry.

"Are you all right?" she asked, rubbing her hand up and down my arm.

I took a deep breath and nodded.

She didn't look convinced.

"Who is that? Doesn't sound like Coleman. Who's with you?" Cal's voice cut through the fog clouding my brain.

"Lily."

He paused.

"Lily Adams? The event coordinator?"

"Yes."

"Why is she there? Is something wrong?"

"Lily's a friend. She's staying with me this afternoon while Stephan's at work."

"If you didn't want to be alone, I could have come and stayed with you, Anna. All you had to do was ask."

I pressed my lips together, unsure how to answer. Stephan didn't want me to be alone with Cal. I didn't think it would be good to tell him that, though.

"It's okay. I like Lily."

He sighed again, but this time he sounded frustrated.

"Just be careful. I know you trust Coleman, but I don't know that I do."

"He won't hurt me," I said again, insistent.

He paused, and I wondered if he was going to argue with me.

"What do you want me to do about your dad? He wants to see you, and he wants me to help him. I won't, though, unless you want me to."

It was my turn stay silent. What did I want? I knew I wasn't ready to see him again. Maybe I never would. That's all I knew for sure right now.

"I . . . I don't want to see him."

"Okay." He paused. "I don't know what I'll tell him, but I'll figure out something."

"Thank you, Cal."

"I'd do anything for you, Anna. I hope you know that."

After that, we talked a little about his morning. He told me how he'd gone to a jobsite where there'd been a water main break and he'd had to wear boots up to his waist to walk through the basement. His description of him walking in the bulky rubber made me laugh.

He didn't ask any more about Stephan or John. I got the feeling he knew it would upset me if he did. All too soon he had to go, and we said good-bye. He promised to call me again soon.

When I hung up the phone, Lily was still sitting beside me. The frown was gone, but she still looked concerned. I didn't want her to worry.

"I'm okay."

"Are you sure?"

I nodded.

"All right," she said, hesitant.

The two of us sat for a long time, not saying anything. I knew she was waiting on me. She had to have heard what Stephan had said to me before he left, that he wanted me to talk to her, and she was obviously giving me time.

I hated that I was so nervous. I didn't like being afraid. Ian had always waxed me himself. He'd made sure it was as painful as possible, and it had usually been followed by some kind of sex. I would already be sore from the waxing, and he would always wear a big smile when he'd see me wince or try to get away from him, knowing I was strapped down and not going anywhere.

As I relived the memory, breathing became more difficult. My chest constricted, and I felt trapped all over again.

"Brianna?"

I didn't answer. Lily sounded far away.

"Brianna? Can you hear me?"

I felt her hands on my arms, my face.

Not real. It's not real.

I tried to take a deep breath. Then another, fighting the images I was seeing. *Lily is real. She's here. Now.*

The pressure in my chest eased. My breathing slowed down, and I began to feel calmer. I had no idea how much time had passed before I opened my eyes again and looked at Lily.

"Better?" she asked.

I nodded.

"Do you need me to call Stephan for you?"

I shook my head.

I *did* want him there, but I also knew he was working. As much as I wanted him with me, I knew I was safe. Lily wouldn't hurt me, and it was just her and me. I was fine. I would be fine.

"Do you want to tell me what happened?"

I swallowed.

"I was . . . remembering." Just mentioning it again had my chest tightening, my breath quickening. I grabbed hold of Lily's hand, wishing it were Stephan's.

"What were you remembering?"

"Stephan . . . he wants me to talk to you about . . . about getting waxed."

"I know. I heard him talking to you." She gave me a small smile.

"I was remembering . . . the last time." Closing my eyes, I tried to block out the images that once again threatened to creep into my head.

"Oh," she said.

Lily released my hands and looked out the large windows showcasing the city. It was a beautiful view of downtown Minneapolis. I never got tired of looking at it.

"He used that to hurt you, too." Her voice was flat as she said the words. She didn't ask it as a question. She stated it like it was a fact. I was beginning to realize that it was hard for people to fathom all the ways Ian had devised to torture me. If something could be twisted to cause pain, humiliation, or even discomfort, he found it and used it.

"What's it like?" I asked, trying to steer the conversation away from my time with Ian. If I continued to talk about it, I would go into a panic again, and I didn't want that. Stephan wasn't here, and he was the only person who could make me feel better afterward. Even now, I felt how far away he was, and I wanted him here with me.

"Waxing?" she asked.

"Yes. I never had anything waxed . . . before." I didn't have to elaborate. She knew what I meant.

"Well . . . it does hurt some, but only in certain spots and it's not that bad. Plus, after a few seconds the pain is gone and so is the hair." She smiled.

"They don't . . . do anything . . . else?"

She bunched up her nose. "No. I mean she has to touch you in order to get the hair, but that part doesn't hurt or anything. And it's not sexual at all, if that's what you're asking. She just removes the hair and then it's done."

"She?"

Lily giggled.

"Julie is my esthetician. She's really nice. I think you'll like her. I've been going to her for years, and she's always been great."

"Will you . . . will you go with me?"

"Of course. Besides, I doubt Stephan would let you go alone, especially not your first time, knowing how nervous you are."

I nodded.

"What do you say I make us some popcorn and we watch a movie?"

"Okay."

"Come on," she said, dragging me over to the bookcase where Stephan kept all the movies.

She ran her hand over the titles until she landed on *Pretty Woman*. I couldn't remember ever watching it. Lily was stunned when I told her. She insisted it was a classic and that everyone had to watch it at least once. I didn't argue. I was just happy to do something that didn't require thinking for a while.

When Stephan arrived home that night, he held me in his arms and asked me about my day. I started by telling him about my conversation with Lily. He said he was proud of me for facing my fears. It felt good to be in his arms, like I could take a deep breath again.

Then he'd asked about Cal. "How do you feel about what Ross said?"

"I don't understand," I told him, truly not getting what he was asking me.

"Karl told Ross I like to hurt women. How do you feel about that?"

"You won't hurt me." I trusted Stephan more than any other person. He'd had plenty of opportunities to hurt me, and he hadn't.

He kissed my forehead. "No, love, I won't. You are precious to me."

Time ticked by as we sat together with his arms around me. Everything was peaceful. Everything was right.

We stayed in his chair until it was time for bed, and he guided me into his bedroom. Like the night before, he stripped me of my clothes, touching me in ways that made me feel warm all over. This time, however, after I was naked, he led me into the bathroom. After removing his own clothes, we stepped into the huge marble shower stall that I'd come to love. He washed me and let me wash him. I loved feeling his body under my hands. There were certain places where I'd touch and he would flex in response. I found one of those areas on his stomach, and I touched it over and over just to see his muscles move.

"What do you think you're doing?" He smiled.

I giggled. "It moves."

"You think that's funny do you?" he asked, stepping toward me.

"Yes."

He moved closer still, until our bodies were flush against each other. I could feel his penis, hard and pressing against me. It had also been subject to my exploration. His body was still so new to me, and he seemed to like it when I touched him, so I kept doing it, trying to learn what he liked.

I expected him to stop moving once we were body against body, but he didn't. He gripped my shoulders and continued walking us backward until my back was up against the cool tile wall and my front was pressed against the heat of him.

"I think you are being a very naughty girl, Brianna."

I froze. Was I in trouble? Did I really do something wrong? I felt my anxiety building.

He leaned forward and kissed me with the slightest brush of his mouth, slipping out his tongue to slide gently along the seam of my lips. It was in complete contrast to what he'd just said.

"Sir?"

"You're not in trouble, sweetheart. I'm not talking about that kind of naughty."

I took a deep breath and tried to relax.

"Okay."

"Brianna, I want to tell you something. Are you listening?" he asked as he moved his mouth from my lips and trailed down my jaw to my neck. I tilted my head back instinctively, asking for more. His mouth felt amazing, and it was hard to think straight.

"Yes," I gasped.

"I will never, ever, use sex against you as a punishment. Sex is meant to be fun and pleasurable. I would never do anything to make you feel otherwise, do you understand?"

I nodded.

"I want to hear you say it, Brianna," he said, sinking his teeth with the slightest pressure into the skin just above my collarbone.

"I understand . . . Sir." I gripped the tops of his arms, feeling the need to hold on to something even though I was pressed against the wall barely able to move.

"Good girl. Now I want you to close your eyes and relax. You've had your fun exploring my body, and now I'm going to have fun exploring yours."

A shiver ran up my spine at his words. This time, however, there was no fear. I loved when Stephan touched me.

He knelt in front of me, and I looked down, following his movement. He gazed up at me, waiting. It wasn't until he quirked his eyebrow at me that I realized I was disobeying him. I quickly closed my eyes.

I heard some movement, then nothing for several seconds. The temptation to look was almost overwhelming, but I controlled myself. I would be good.

Stephan didn't make me wait long. He picked up my right leg, and rested my foot on what I assumed was his shoulder. I felt a pressure against the back of my knee, and realized he was kissing me there. First, he only used his lips, and then he added his tongue and then finally his teeth. It was like the skin beneath his mouth came alive and tingled. As he continued, I relaxed back into the wall.

Just when I began to get used to the sensations, he moved. Up, up, up, he kissed, licked, sucked, and nipped me with his teeth, until he came to the junction between my legs. He kissed everywhere but where I ached for him the most, and I whimpered when he abandoned the area altogether and moved to my other leg. Like before, he kissed the back of my knee, using his entire mouth to explore and probe. The pattern repeated itself as he slowly worked his way back up my leg until he was again between my thighs. By then, I was arching toward him, the space between my legs aching, silently begging him for more.

"No." He stopped his kisses entirely, and I wanted to cry.

Thankfully, after some time had passed, he began kissing me again, but instead of continuing between my legs, he moved up to my stomach. I had to press my lips together, attempting to stay quiet when all I wanted was to cry out in frustration. He'd pleasured me with his mouth the night before, so I knew it was greedy of me to want it again, but I did.

My stomach muscles contracted under his mouth as he teased them. There was nothing funny about it, and I wondered if this was his way of teaching me a lesson. Was this anything close to what he'd felt when I'd been playing with his stomach? With every touch, my body temperature seemed to rise. No wonder people loved sex, if this was how it always felt. I wanted to reach out to him, but I didn't dare. He'd told me not to move, and I was trying very hard not to.

He inched his way up my torso and sucked first one breast, and then the other, into his mouth. I moaned when he dragged his teeth over one of them and then bit down not so gently on my nipple. I could feel the moisture between my legs and knew it wasn't the water from the shower. I was wet and ready for him to take me whenever he wanted.

My mouth was open. I couldn't seem to get enough air to fill my lungs anymore. Every breath in seemed to be filled with a mixture of him and me and sex.

Stephan reached for my arms and lifted them one at a time, kissing and nipping his way across their length. I was a mess of feeling by the time he reached my mouth again, my arms held firmly above my head with both of his hands.

He took control of my lips, thrusting his tongue inside and stroking. His hands encircled my wrists, holding tighter. His body was flush against mine, even closer than before if that were possible. I could feel all of him, including his fully erect penis pressing eagerly between my parted legs, teasing my clit as he bumped against it. More. I needed more.

He repositioned my wrists so both of them were being held by only one of his hands. The new position caused me to arch my back, but he didn't seem to care. As my breasts brushed against his chest, he groaned and increased the grip on my wrists. Something told me I should be frightened since he had me pressed against the wall, holding me like this, but I wasn't. This was Stephan, and instead of feeling trapped, I felt safe. I could feel him, smell him, surrounding me.

I jumped a little when he slipped his hand between my legs, but I recovered quickly. He rubbed his fingers back and forth a few times, and I moaned, trying to press against the friction as best I could. Then he pushed his fingers inside me. I couldn't tell how many fingers, but it didn't matter. Everything felt so good. The familiar pressure began to build inside me, driving me toward my climax, but before I could reach the peak, he removed his hands.

Before I could form words to beg him to please not stop touching me, he was back. This time, however, it wasn't his fingers pressing into me. He hitched my leg up around his hip, opening me further to him, and lifted me slightly before his penis glided inside me, stretching me until I felt completely full. Everything felt more for some reason. My whole body was on fire, from where he held my wrists to where we were joined, down to where my leg was wrapped around him.

He released my lips and ravished my neck with his mouth as he began to move inside me. There was no going slow. Every thrust of his hips pressed me hard against the tiles, but it only added to the sensation. The only things holding me in place were his hands. My legs were both off the floor and encircling his waist. With every movement, every kiss, I came closer and closer to the goal I was searching for. Every muscle in my body tensed.

"Come for me!" he shouted against my neck before biting down hard. I felt the sting of his teeth as they dug into my skin, and I screamed. The pressure that had been building between my legs exploded.

Chapter 8

Stephan

On Thursday I ended up working from home since I couldn't bring myself to leave her alone yet and there wasn't anything pressing that needed me to be in the office. Nothing I couldn't delegate anyway. Brianna appeared to be doing fine for the most part, but she always kept me in sight. One time, I came out of the bathroom to find her sitting on the floor just inside my bedroom. She glanced up at me, nervous she'd done something wrong, and I quickly made sure those doubts left her mind completely.

Ross called again, wanting to talk to her. I stayed close, in case she needed me, but she did well. There were a few moments when I noticed her tense, but she closed her eyes and breathed through it. When she opened her eyes and glanced over at me, I stood from where I was working at the dining room table and walked over to where she was curled up on the couch talking to him. She placed the phone in her lap as I approached, and I could hear Ross yelling through the phone.

"Tell him to hold on a minute," I whispered once I was standing in front of her.

She picked up the phone and did as instructed before laying it back down. I could still hear Ross's voice getting progressively louder. He wanted to know what was wrong, if she was all right. I'd heard her tell him I was working from home for the day, so why he thought I wouldn't make sure Brianna's needs were met was slightly irritating. The man needed to understand that she was my responsibility.

Ignoring Ross, I leaned down, and placed my hands on the back of the couch. Brianna's eyes grew wide as I towered over her, but she didn't move. I brushed my lips against her ear and felt a shudder ripple through her.

I smiled and stood. This time when Brianna glanced up at me, there wasn't a look of shock or uncertainty. Her chest rose and fell with increased awareness. She knew the pleasure I could pull from her body, and she craved it. I loved that I was the one able to put that look in her eyes. If I had my way, I would work to see that look from her each and every day of our lives.

She picked the phone back up as I returned to where my laptop sat. I heard her answer him but not his reply. They didn't talk long after that, and she seemed frustrated when she hung up.

I spent most of the afternoon on the phone. First with Jamie, then with Oscar. My lawyer was trying to figure out how to get a restraining order on Reeves without Brianna having to go before a judge. It would be tricky, but he felt, given his connections, he could accomplish it. While it wouldn't guarantee Reeves would keep his distance, it would allow him to be reported for a violation of his restraining order should he ever come to the building again in an attempt to get to her.

We also talked about Ian Pierce. Oscar had finally gotten all the financials on both him and Dumas. He was sending them over to my office so I could go through them. We needed to find something in them that would implicate Pierce. Otherwise, it was just Brianna's word against his. I kept my voice low so Brianna wouldn't be able to overhear, but she seemed to sense something wasn't quite right and kept turning her head to check on me. She'd been hurt, abused, and yet she was worried about me.

Later that night, when we were lying in bed with her head resting on my shoulder, I asked about her phone call. Ross wouldn't let go of his concern that I would hurt her, no matter how much she reassured him. I didn't really care what he thought of me, but I didn't want his opinion to cause problems for Brianna. She shouldn't have to defend me. It was my job to protect her, not the other way around.

The next day, I had to go into the office. I didn't want to leave Brianna, so I decided to bring her with me. It wasn't ideal, but there was a comfortable couch in my office where she could read while I was in my meeting if she wanted. Jamie would also be there if she needed anything.

To my surprise, Brianna was thrilled when I told her she would be going with me. The last time I'd taken her to my office she'd been frightened. Then again, she and I had built a lot of trust since then.

Jamie greeted me when we walked off the elevator, and I formally introduced her to Brianna. My assistant knew about Brianna, of course. At least, she knew that Brianna existed and what had happened with Karl. Jamie, however, was a compassionate person. She loved her job, and I had no doubts about leaving Brianna in her care for the morning. Jamie would make sure Brianna had what she needed.

I led Brianna into my office and showed her around. My desk was at the back of the room along a large bank of windows overlooking the city. I loved being able to see the outside. It was one of the things I loved best about both my home and office.

In front of the desk were two padded chairs, slightly angled to give a more comforting feel. To the left there was a small, more relaxed meeting area made up of a coffee table and four chairs. I rarely used the space other than to have lunch with Lily occasionally. Meetings with clients normally occurred down the hall in the conference room, and the employees and executives who came to meet with me used the two chairs in front of my desk.

On the other side of the room sat a black leather couch. To my knowledge, I was the only person to ever use the couch since I'd been in charge at the foundation. About a year ago, there had been a problem matching up some figures on a grant that had to go out the next day. Karl and one of the other executives had stayed with me trying to sort it out until I'd sent them both home around midnight. That night should have forewarned me about the true nature of Karl Walker, but I'd chalked it up to us all being tired and irritated. Every time we'd rerun the numbers and they wouldn't add up, he'd become increasingly flustered and throw something across the room. It was usually a pen or a balled up piece of paper. Nothing major, but telling. By the time I had been satisfied the calculations were fixed and the grant proposal was ready, it was nearly three in the morning. I'd been exhausted and crashed on the sofa. Jamie had found me the next morning.

Brianna brought with her a small backpack of things to occupy her while I was in my meeting today. I tossed it on the couch before I guided her behind the desk with me. Sitting down in my high-backed chair, I positioned her to stand in front of me with her back against the desk and her legs bracketed between mine. She was wearing a skirt that ended halfway down her thighs, showcasing her legs. It didn't take much for my mind to fixate on how those legs had wrapped around me the previous night, and how great it would feel to have a repeat performance right here in my office. I'd never had sex with a woman at work before, but with Brianna the thought was very appealing. Exhibitionism wasn't normally my thing, but that was what locks were for.

Gripping her hips, I pulled her toward me. The movement happened so fast, she reached out to steady herself, holding tight to my shoulders. I smiled. "My meeting is going to start soon. If you need anything, let Jamie know and she'll get it for you. "

"Okay." I detected a note of sadness in her response.

"Is something wrong, Brianna?" I asked, bringing her even closer to me.

She shook her head. "No, Sir."

I held her face between both of my hands and brought her lips down to mine for a chaste kiss. At the contact, some of the tension eased from her body. She was as reluctant for me to leave as I was to go. I would only be down the hall, however, and I wasn't expecting the meeting to go past lunchtime. We would be able to spend the entire afternoon and evening together.

As I was about to pull her in for another kiss, I heard a familiar voice outside my door, followed by Jamie's frustrated one. "I do believe he's busy, Dr. Cooper—"

The door to my office opened and in walked my uncle.

He stopped, blinked, and then strategically cleared his throat. Given the look on his face, I wasn't sure if I should be upset by his behavior or amused. He moved his gaze back and forth from me to Brianna, even though her back was still toward him. At the sound of his voice, she'd ducked her head. Her breath ruffled my hair, and I could tell she was no longer as relaxed as she'd been before Richard's arrival. That alone made me lean more toward irritated.

"Good morning, Uncle." The greeting wasn't overly pleasant, but it wasn't meant to be. Richard may have tried to make an amends with Brianna, but I was under no misgivings as to his view of our relationship.

He straightened his posture, broadcasting his displeasure in finding Brianna and I in what he was sure to view as a compromising position. It wouldn't matter that we were both fully clothed and doing nothing that wouldn't be perfectly acceptable on a city street. To him, my showing Brianna anything beyond friendship was unacceptable.

"Good morning, Stephan. I didn't realize Brianna would be with you today."

Placing my hands on Brianna's waist, I turned her around and sat her down on my lap so we were both facing Richard. She gravitated to her favorite position and laid her head on my shoulder. I placed a kiss at her temple before turning back to my uncle.

"We have plans today after the board meeting." It was all I was willing to offer him. He needed to get over his aversion to my relationship with Brianna.

"I see," he said without elaborating.

"Was there something you needed before the meeting?"

He'd been staring at Brianna but snapped his eyes to me. "Your aunt was hoping I could convince you to come to dinner this Sunday. She told me to tell you she's making her homemade spaghetti and meatballs."

I chuckled. After my parents' deaths, I'd lost my appetite. No matter what my aunt had put in front of me, I would eat a couple of bites and then stop. It had all tasted bland to me. Then one day she'd pulled me into the kitchen with her, pleading for my help to make homemade spaghetti and meatballs. We'd worked for hours making the sauce and the meatballs, even the bread. That night, I'd sat down and eaten the fruits of my labors, and for the first time in months, I ate everything on my plate.

Diane bribing me with her spaghetti and meatballs was a plea. One I couldn't deny her.

"Let Diane know we'll be there."

"Thank you." He sighed in relief.

I glanced over at the clock on my desk and realized it was almost time for the meeting to start.

"I'll meet you in the conference room. I need to make sure Brianna's settled."

"Of course."

He turned to go but then stopped and looked at Brianna.

"It was good seeing you again, Brianna." Before she could respond, he walked out the door.

Brianna

I was glad when Dr. Cooper left, but I also knew that meant Stephan would be leaving soon, too. When Stephan told me I'd be going to work with him, I'd felt relieved. Even though I knew eventually I'd have to be left alone again, I wasn't ready. Plus, I liked being with him.

"I need to go to my meeting, sweetheart." He patted my leg, letting me know he wanted me to move from his lap.

Stephan stood, reached over to the phone on the desk, and pressed a few buttons. I had no idea what he was doing, so I waited.

"I've forwarded my phone so all my calls will go out to Jamie. She's been instructed not to let anyone into my office while I'm gone, but if you should need anything, press this button here. Jamie will answer." He stood there waiting, and I realized he wanted me to answer him.

"Yes, Sir."

He tilted my chin up with two fingers until I was looking at him.

"I'm hoping this meeting won't last more than a few hours. You can read, listen to music, or take a nap . . . the bathroom is through that door if you need to use it. If you need something that isn't in this room, you call Jamie."

"Okay."

"Good girl. Now give me a kiss so that I have something to think about while I'm sitting in this boring meeting."

Stephan released my chin, and I didn't waste any time wrapping my arms around his neck. He smiled as he bent his head to kiss me.

The kiss didn't last nearly long enough. I wanted more. Then again, I always seemed to want more of Stephan's kisses.

He chuckled as he stepped back. "More later. I promise."

Stephan walked to the door, straightening his jacket and tie. He paused and turned to look at me from head to toe. I was right where I'd been moments before, still enjoying the impression of his mouth on mine. There was something in his stare that made my heart beat faster. He smiled at me, and I smiled back. Then he was gone, leaving me alone.

I looked around his office, not knowing what to do with myself. There were very few signs of him in the space. Most of the furnishings were generic things found in almost any office. There were only two exceptions. On the wall was a picture of him and his uncle at what looked to be a ribbon cutting, and there was a picture of me on his desk.

My picture was something I hadn't expected to see. I was pretty sure Stephan cared about me. He was so nice to me, and he made sure I had what I needed. Did his having a picture of me in his office mean it was more than that? The thought that it could had me smiling so wide my cheeks began to hurt.

I walked over to the couch and picked up the small bag I'd brought with me. At first, I'd been happy I wouldn't have to stay in the condo by myself and that I'd get more time with him. That had lasted for all of thirty seconds before he'd told me it was because he and Lily had to attend a board meeting and he didn't want to leave me alone just yet.

At his instruction, I'd packed a bag with two of the books I'd been reading, my journal, and some magazines Lily had brought me. Picking up the bag, I pulled everything out. For some reason, reading the books I'd been working on didn't appeal to me, so I set them aside. I glanced at my journal, remembering how Stephan had me write down my feelings about what had happened with John. It had been difficult, and I'd needed to stop a few times. Stephan had held me, comforted me, until I could go back to it. I didn't want to think about that right now, however, so I picked up one of the magazines.

The cover of the first one claimed to have all the secrets to snaring the perfect boyfriend, along with makeup tips and the ten hottest guys of summer. I flipped through the pages briefly. The tips on a boyfriend weren't for me. I had no desire to get a boyfriend. I had Stephan, and he could keep me for as long as he wanted. The ten hottest guys were okay. I'd seen some of them on television before. They were all celebrities and cute in their own way. Some of them had a lot of muscles, others not so much. None of them, however, had anything on Stephan. His body was beautiful to me. I loved seeing it, touching it . . .

I leaned my head back and closed my eyes, remembering the previous night. After an all-too-quick shower, he'd taken me back to his bed. He'd held my wrists over my head as his penis filled me. It was as if he'd been surrounding me, protecting me. Like if I fell, he'd be there to catch me.

Thinking about him holding me down, restraining me, I remembered the rope. Stephan had been honest with me. I knew he was what he called a Dominant and that he wanted me to be his submissive. We'd talked a little about what he liked, what he expected of me, but that had been before we'd had sex. Would he want to tie me up? I didn't know how I felt about that, but I also knew I wanted to make him happy.

There was a knock at the door.

I threw the magazine down on the couch, anxious. Who was there?

A second later, my question was answered. The woman Stephan had introduced me to as his assistant, Jamie, peeked her head in the door. When she glanced over at me on the couch, she smiled.

"Sorry to bother you, but I wanted to check and see if you'd like anything to drink. We have water or coffee. Or I can call down to the café and have them deliver something else."

Although Jamie seemed nice, I was nervous. I didn't like new people.

"I'm . . . okay."

She grinned.

"All right. Well, if you change your mind just call me. Mr. Coleman said he showed you how to use the phone?"

"Yes." I nodded.

"I'll leave you to your reading, then," she said, closing the door behind her.

I sat staring at the door for several minutes after she left. Jamie was very pretty. She was taller than me, maybe five foot seven or eight, and she had long blond hair. I knew Stephan worked with Jamie all the time—she was his assistant, after all—but did he feel anything else for her?

The possibility made me feel sick to my stomach. While I knew I had no real claim on Stephan, I didn't want anyone else to have him. He was mine. I knew it wasn't right to feel that way, but I couldn't help it. My gaze drifted over to where the picture of me sat on his desk. That had to mean what I thought it did, didn't it? I was important to him, wasn't I?

By the time Stephan returned, there were tears in my eyes. He noticed immediately, of course, and gathered me into his arms.

"What's wrong?" he asked, tucking my head against his chest.

I instantly felt better. The anxiety that had been plaguing me fell away, and I was left with a warm, tingly feeling.

"Is everything all right?" I jumped a little when I heard Dr. Cooper's voice behind Stephan.

Instead of answering Dr. Cooper, Stephan tilted my face up to look at me, brushing the tears that had fallen off my cheeks. He just stared, and I realized he was waiting for me to answer his question. "I'm okay."

He continued to look at me as if searching for something. I knew I'd have to tell him what had been bothering me, but I didn't want to say anything in front of Dr. Cooper. He already didn't like me much. I didn't want to give him any more reasons to think Stephan shouldn't be with me.

After a long pause, Stephan nodded and then turned to address his uncle. "Everything's fine. Did you need something?"

"I was going to grab lunch before heading back to the office this afternoon, and wanted to know if you two would like to join me."

"Thank you for the offer, but we've already got plans for this afternoon," Stephan said, continuing to rub his hands up and down my back.

The two exchanged a few more words, but I wasn't paying attention to them. All I wanted was for Dr. Cooper to leave already so Stephan and I could be together.

Chapter 9

Stephan

The only thing on my mind was getting Brianna out of my office so we could talk. Even though she said she was okay, I knew something was on her mind. One thing I'd learned about her over the last two months was that emotional worries tended to do more damage to her than physical ones. Whatever this was, she needed to talk about it. Doing so here, however, wasn't a good idea.

My uncle following me out of the meeting and finding me holding a crying Brianna in my office only complicated things further. I was beginning to think Richard had some sort of radar where she and I were concerned. It wasn't helping his opinion of the situation, nor was it helping Brianna's comfort level with him.

As quickly as I could, I gathered Brianna's things back into her bag and got us out of there. Jamie waved good-bye to Brianna as we stepped onto the elevator, and while Brianna responded, she seemed reluctant. It made me wonder if something had happened between the two. Jamie had been my assistant since I'd taken over The Coleman Foundation. She was efficient and reliable. I'd never had a problem with her. However, Brianna's response to her had changed. Something had happened.

"What would you like for lunch, Brianna?"

She looked up at me, her blue eyes wide.

I waited. What we had for lunch wasn't all that important to me. It had to be portable, that was all.

Her lips pressed together hard, and she glanced down. She was thinking. "Cheeseburger?"

In all the time Brianna had been with me, I realized we'd only ever indulged in a simple burger once, when I'd taken her to the zoo. That seemed like a lifetime ago. So much had changed. In college, I'd practically lived on cheeseburgers. They were fast, could be eaten on the run and, as long as you bought it at a decent place, tasted good.

"Cheeseburgers it is," I said, helping her into the car.

We drove to a restaurant near Minnehaha Park. I'd heard they had good burgers. It was time I found out what all the fuss was about.

It was almost noon, and the restaurant was busy. Brianna held tight to my hand as we entered, and I pulled her close to my side. A man greeted us and handed me a menu to look over. They had a whole page of different types of burgers. Everything from a simple cheeseburger with all the usual toppings, to something they called a Garbage Burger with an egg on it.

"They have a lot to choose from, Brianna. What kind of cheeseburger would you like?"

She pointed to the classic cheeseburger at the top of the page. I had no idea if she'd even read the rest, but if that was what she wanted, then that was what she would get. I went for something a little more adventurous, a chipotle burger with jalapenos.

With our orders in, we walked over to the long bench along the wall and waited. Brianna kept looking around at all the people. I knew she was nervous, but she was going to have to get used to being around people to some degree. At least this way I knew she was safe. I had no idea if she'd be ready to go to school in the fall, but I wanted her to try. She needed to have some independence, some schooling she could use out in the world, even if she never used it.

About fifteen minutes later, the man approached us again, this time carrying two bags. Brianna cringed and stepped closer to me. I gave her fingers a squeeze before releasing my hold on her and taking the bags from the restaurant employee. She stayed glued to my side, rigid, until the man walked back behind the host podium.

"Number?" I leaned down to whisper in her ear.

"F-four."

Shifting the bags to one hand, I made her look at me. "Only four?"

She pressed her lips together and nodded.

I pulled her into my arms briefly, and kissed her. "Let's go before our food gets cold."

The ride to the park was quiet. Brianna looked out the window. It was a beautiful day, and there were quite a few people out enjoying it. I knew the park wouldn't be any different.

I made sure to park as close to where we were going as possible. Thankfully, there were parking areas inside the park itself, not just on the perimeter. Brianna was still unpredictable around people, and if we needed to leave quickly, I didn't want to have to walk three blocks to reach the car.

She didn't say anything as I threw my suit jacket in the backseat and then grabbed the food and the blanket I kept in the trunk. I helped her out of the vehicle, balancing the food and the blanket in one arm, and laced our fingers together. It was a gorgeous spring day in Minneapolis, and I wanted to share it with her. I also thought it would be good for her to be around people in what I hoped was a less-threatening environment.

I found a spot not far from the wading pond. We were close to the Mississippi River—I could hear the sound of flowing water in the distance —but it was out of view. If things went well, maybe we'd walk down to where we could see it after we ate.

First things first, however. I gave her hand a squeeze before releasing it and set the food down on the grass near the base of a large maple tree. Looking over the area, it looked level enough, and I spread out the blanket. She stood watching with her hands balled into fists at her side.

After straightening the blanket, I motioned for her to join me. She hurried over to sit down. I smiled and handed her the container with her sandwich.

We sat in silence for a while, eating. Brianna hadn't relaxed. She would take a bite of her sandwich and then glance up, her eyes darting from side to side at all the people around us. The nearest person was over twenty feet away. I didn't understand what had her so nervous unless it was the openness of the environment itself.

I sighed and reached for her, situating her between my legs, her back against my chest. As soon as we made contact, the tension began to release from her muscles. Even though I loved that my touch calmed her, Brianna needed to find strength within herself as well.

"Close your eyes," I whispered in her ear.

It took her only a moment's pause before she complied.

"Good girl," I said, placing a kiss on her shoulder. "Now tell me what you hear."

"People."

I smiled. Such a simple answer, but not what I was looking for. Lily had told me what happened the other day while I was at the office. Although Brianna had managed to find her way back to the present without me, it had taken nearly twenty minutes. Lily had been frightened seeing Brianna like that, completely unaware of her surroundings. I'd taken the time while I was working from home on Thursday to do some research.

"What about the people? What do you hear them doing?"

She was quiet for several very long minutes. I watched as she scrunched up her nose, pressed her lips together, and tilted her head. It was extremely cute, and the urge to kiss her surfaced, but I forced myself to remain still and allow her to follow through on the exercise.

"Kids . . . splashing in water. A woman . . . laughing. Someone running?" She paused.

"Anything else?"

"Dogs barking." She smiled. "They sound happy."

I wrapped her in my arms and held her close, my nose skimming along her neck to her ear. "Very good. And do any of those things sound like they are going to cause you harm?"

"No." Her response was quiet, barely even a sound at all. Of course, that probably had something to do with my mouth on her neck and my hand creeping up her bare thigh. I'd wanted to distract her, and I was pleased to have accomplished my goal.

"Open your eyes, Brianna."

She opened her eyes and blinked against the sunlight.

"Do you see the people now? They are still doing all the things you heard. Just because you can see them doesn't make them any more frightening."

She didn't respond, but I knew she'd heard as she looked around again. I could almost see her mind working through the new concept. Just like with the cane, she had to learn that it wasn't the thing—or in this case, people—that were the danger. It was the who, the person themselves.

"When you feel frightened by a situation, I want you to stop and listen. Concentrate on what is around you, what's happening in the here and now, not the past, and decide if it's truly a danger."

Brianna nodded and sank back against my chest. I tightened my hold on her and kissed the exposed skin on her neck where her hair had fallen to the side.

Although everything felt right for the moment, I knew we needed to talk. I took her hand in mine, rubbing my thumb over her fingers. "Tell me what upset you earlier in my office. Did something happen while I was gone?"

She shook her head. "No."

"Why where you crying?"

"I was . . . I don't know," she whispered.

Turning her around in my arms so I could see her face, I tilted her chin up so I could look in her eyes. "Yes, you do. What was going through that head of yours?"

"Jamie."

"My assistant? What about her?"

Brianna pressed her lips together for a long moment. "She's pretty."

I tilted my head to the side and appraised her. "Yes. Jamie is attractive. What does that . . ."

I paused, and she looked down. Was she really jealous?

For several minutes, I watched her and tried to digest the information she'd just hit me with. Never in a million years would it have crossed my mind that Brianna would be jealous of Jamie, but it did explain the difference in Brianna's reaction to Jamie from when we'd arrived to when we'd left.

Cupping her face with my hand, I massaged her cheek with my thumb. "Brianna, you never have to be jealous when it comes to other women. I promise you that. I . . .." The words died in my throat. She wasn't ready. "I care about you. A lot. I said once that I'd be here until you ordered me away, and I meant it. I'm not going anywhere. Not unless it's what you want."

She looked up, tears in her eyes again. This time, however, I knew they weren't because of distress.

Leaning down, I captured her lips with mine, sucking first her bottom lip, then her top into my mouth. It was a slow kiss, one meant to show her the depth of my feelings. When we finally broke apart, I brushed the remaining moisture from her cheeks and smiled. She smiled back.

For the next hour, we sat on the blanket, ate the rest of our cheeseburgers, and people watched. By the time we walked over to the water, she was much calmer than she'd been when we'd entered the park. Brianna was amazing, and she constantly made me so proud of her I could barely contain it. She was brave beyond what any person should have to be. It made my love for her increase with every passing day. I couldn't imagine my life without her.

She was bracketed by my arms as we stood in front of the railing, looking out at the river. Although I couldn't see her face very well from this angle, I could tell she was smiling. A warmth grew in my chest at seeing her so happy. I felt like I was floating, and I didn't want to come down, ever.

As I rested my chin on top of Brianna's head, completely content, the sound of laughter nearby drew my attention. Some thirty or so feet away was a group of four playing Frisbee—two guys and two girls. They didn't look much older than Brianna, and I wondered if, had it not been for what had happened, that could have been her playing out in the sun on a spring day with her friends, not seeming to have a care in the world beyond catching the Frisbee being tossed their way.

Like a cold slap in the face, my conversation with Oscar replayed in my head. I wasn't willing to let Ian get away with what he did to Brianna. One way or another, he was going to pay for breaking this beautiful woman. The chances of that happening and me not being pulled into the fray were next to impossible. I'd written a large check to him recently for something I couldn't easily explain. Although I had every confidence in my lawyer, there was no telling what would happen, especially once the press got involved. There would be lots of questions and not many answers.

There was also the matter of her father. The man ranked right up there with Ian and Karl in my book. Actually, he was worse. Any man who would sit back and allow his daughter to be taken . . . just the thought had me wanting to punch something.

I tightened my hold on Brianna, letting her warmth seep into me. Taking a deep breath, her scent filled my nostrils, and the tension in my muscles eased.

All three of them needed to be strung up and beaten for what they'd done to her. Ian was no longer a part of her life, and I was working to help her deal with all that he'd done. I hoped that one day she'd be able to completely put that part of her life behind her, although I was sure she'd never be able to entirely forget.

Karl's influence had been less, but his actions certainly hadn't helped how she viewed people in general. Her uncertainty of people and the world around her had only increased.

Her father, however, was different. Nothing I could do would make him any less than what he was. I could try to protect her, keep her away from him, but I had no idea if that would be enough. I had to hope that it would, for her sake.

With that thought, I pulled her back against my chest and placed a kiss on her cheek. "It's time to go."

Brianna

The park was nice once I relaxed. I didn't like being around people. Stephan said I had to get used to it, and I did understand, sort of, but it was still hard. I don't think I could've done it if he hadn't been there.

After the park, he drove us across town to get ice cream. "I'd like one scoop of each of these in a large bowl with two spoons, please."

"You want a scoop of each of these, sir?" The woman behind the counter asked, pointing to the large case in front of her. I didn't blame her for asking, because there were at least thirty different types of ice cream.

"Yes. Is that a problem?"

"No. Not at all. That's just a lot of ice cream for one person, or even two," she said, looking over at me.

"I think we'll manage." Stephan looked down and kissed me. He squeezed my hand and smiled as he turned back to the lady behind the counter.

We waited for several minutes while the woman scooped out the ice cream and placed it in a large bowl. With each scoop, my eyes opened wider. No wonder she'd asked for clarification. By the time she was finished, the bowl, which was the size of a large mixing bowl I sometimes used to cook, was heaped with all different colors of ice cream. I had no idea how Stephan and I were going to eat all of that, but I didn't question him.

After paying for the ice cream, he guided me over to a small table along the wall. He set the bowl down on the table between us and handed me one of the spoons. "Go ahead," he encouraged.

One at a time, I tasted each of the different flavors of ice cream. I liked most of them. There were two, however, I had no desire to try again—coffee and key lime. Both had me scrunching up my nose in distaste as I tried to force the bite I'd taken down my throat.

Stephan chuckled at the faces I made, which eventually caused me to giggle as well. Some people looked at us, and it made me slightly uncomfortable but not enough for me not to enjoy the moment with him. He didn't have to do this for me. He didn't have to do anything for me.

That night, as we sat in his chair after a light dinner, I began to wonder what I could do to thank him for all that he'd done for me. I knew that he would appreciate a simple thank you, and I could do that, too, but I also knew what he ultimately wanted from me—to be his submissive. Although we had talked about it some before, I knew he had to want more than what I was currently giving him. The idea still terrified me, but I would do it for him.

"Sir?"

"Yes, Brianna?" he asked, stroking my hair.

I paused, thinking of the best way to approach this. Then I remembered the ropes. The ropes he'd used to tie John. The ropes he'd gotten from the drawer in his bedroom. The fact that they were there had to mean something, right? Why would he have them if he didn't use them? And why in his bedroom?

He reached out and caressed the side of my face with his fingers, tilting my chin up, making me look at him. I must have taken too long to gather my thoughts. Pressing my lips together, I gathered my courage. "I was wondering . . . I was wondering about the ropes."

"What about them?"

Stephan continued to massage my cheek with his thumb. It was distracting, but I tried to stay focused, to remember what I needed to say and why. "Do you . . . why are they there? In your bedroom?"

With my question, he smiled. "They're there for me to use."

I closed my eyes. They were there for him to use, but how? Why?

Even as the question floated in my head, I already knew the answer. He'd never hidden what he was from me. He'd never tried to be something he wasn't. I'd been tied up before, and I'd watched other people be tied up. Was that something he wanted to do to me?

"Do you have another question for me, Brianna?"

I opened my eyes, but I couldn't bring myself to look at him. "Do you want to use them . . . on me?"

His hand stopped moving, and I tensed. Had I asked the wrong question? "Look at me."

Slowly, I raised my head to look at him. What I saw caused me to release the breath I hadn't realized I'd been holding. There was no tension in his features, no anger, no disappointment. The look in his eyes was one of gentleness. It was a look I'd seen from him many times.

Stephan cupped my face with both of his hands, running his thumbs along my cheeks. "Yes." He paused and cleared his throat. "Yes, I'd like to use them on you. Is that something you'd be willing to try?"

I nodded and started to look down. He stopped the movement by tightening his hold on my face.

"Keep your eyes on me, and I want to hear you say it."

Swallowing, I looked into his eyes. What I saw only confirmed what I already knew. I'd do anything for him. Be anything he needed me to be. "Yes. I'm . . . I'd like to try."

He smiled and kissed me. It was hard at first, and I could feel his excitement growing. I grasped the front of his shirt. No matter what happened, I knew above all else that I trusted him. He wouldn't hurt me. And as long as he was there by my side, I knew I could do whatever he asked of me.

Chapter 10

Brianna

On Sunday morning after our workout, Stephan had me take a shower in his bathroom while he made some calls. After our conversation on Friday night, I'd been waiting for him to pull out the ropes and use them on me, but so far . . . nothing. I tried not to think about it, but I couldn't help my nerves. Would he just take me into his room one day and tie me to his bed? I didn't know.

Pushing the thoughts to the back of my mind, I grabbed the shower gel and began washing my body with the large sponge Stephan had bought for me. As I washed the sweat from our workout from my body, I tried to prepare myself for the day. We were going to his aunt and uncle's house for dinner. Stephan said his uncle had promised to be on his best behavior, but I was still anxious.

Stephan had given me some rules to follow for the day. I wasn't to look down for more than five seconds at a time. I was also to ask both his aunt and uncle one question each. He clarified that it couldn't be the same question for both either. I had no idea what I wanted to ask them, but I hoped I could come up with something. The last and most important rule, he'd said, was that if at any time I was in a situation where I felt threatened or reached a five or higher, I was to squeeze his hand twice.

When I finished my shower, Stephan was in his bedroom waiting on me. He'd removed the shirt, shoes, and socks he'd worn during our workout and stood at the end of his bed in only his shorts. I waited, not moving, watching him, and remembering what he'd felt like the night before, when he'd had me climb on top of him and run my hands up and down his chest while he played with my breasts. I was becoming more comfortable with sex and touching him in different ways. I wasn't scared he was going to get upset anymore.

A smile slowly spread across Stephan's face, and I realized I was staring. I looked down, averting my gaze and feeling self-conscious for some reason.

He laughed.

Before I knew it, he was there in front of me, lifting my chin. "Don't be shy, sweetheart. You can ogle my body all you want. I don't mind."

I didn't respond.

Stephan leaned down and brushed his mouth against mine before using his tongue to trace the outline of my lips. Then, to my great disappointment, he was gone.

I opened my eyes to find him looking down at me, smiling. "I laid the clothes I want you to wear on the bed. I'm going to take my shower. Be ready by the time I get out."

Without another word, he walked into the bathroom, leaving me standing there.

I didn't move until I heard the shower turn on in the other room. It was enough to wake me from whatever trance I was in, and I went to see what clothes he'd picked out for me.

Stephan didn't often choose the clothes I was to wear—he'd only done it twice before—but I didn't mind. Although he did tend to pick skirts instead of the pants I favored, I was learning that skirts and dresses weren't so bad. Not when Stephan was around anyway.

The outfit he'd chosen for me was a lot like the one I'd worn on Friday to his office, except instead of a skirt and top, it was a dress. It was dark green and had a skirt that flared out a little. It was pretty.

Beside the dress was a matching bra and panty set, also a dark green color. I reached out and ran my fingers along the edge of the lace and silk before putting them on. They felt nice and soft against my skin.

The dress was next and then a pair of nude thigh-high stockings with lace around the tops. I was just slipping into the tan heels he'd selected when he strolled out of the bathroom with a towel wrapped around his waist. He stopped and stared, looking me over from head to toe. I felt warm under his gaze, and I instinctively looked down.

His bare feet come into view and then disappeared as he moved behind me. He wrapped his arms around my waist. I jumped a little, and he chuckled, burying his face in my neck. "You look beautiful," he whispered.

"Thank you."

He trailed his hands down my dress and then gathered the hem until he was touching skin. My breathing began to accelerate as I waited to see what he'd do next. When he reached the top of my leg, he stopped.

"What are you thinking, Brianna?"

It took me a moment to register what he'd asked and that he was waiting for me to answer. "I'm wondering . . . what you're going to do."

"Is there something you want me to do?" he asked as he began drawing circles on the inside of my thighs.

I sucked in a ragged breath as he moved higher and higher.

"Tell me what you want." I could feel his breath as it ghosted across my neck, causing me to shiver.

When he reached the edge of my panties, he let his fingers hover there, unmoving. My chest clenched. "I want . . ."

"Yes," he said, kissing his way up my neck and then taking my earlobe between his teeth.

I gasped. "I want . . . you to touch me."

"I am touching you, sweetheart. Is there some place specific you want me to touch you?"

"Yes."

"Tell me."

As my mind tried to think of a way to tell him what I wanted, I froze. Ian, and all the men he'd given me to, flashed through my mind. All the words I'd heard them mumble, yell, and spit at me in disgust repeated over and over. It was as if they were there. It wasn't a memory. It was real.

Hands. I felt hands on my face. Gentle hands. Hands I knew.

"Brianna. Listen to my voice. Remember where you are. What do you hear? What can you feel around you? Tell me."

My throat felt tight as I opened my mouthed and tried to speak. "Hands," I choked out.

"Good girl. Now tell me what else. Concentrate."

"C-cold. I feel . . . cold."

The hands left my face and arms circled around my back and shoulders. Then there was warmth. Warmth and the clean smell of soap I recognized. Stephan.

I reached for him, wrapping my arms around his waist, and holding as tight as I could. He brushed his lips across my forehead. "I feel . . . your arms . . . holding me. Your lips. You."

His chest vibrated beneath my cheek, and he kissed the top of my head. "Good girl. What number?"

Sucking in a deep breath, and burrowing deeper into the comfort of his arms, I took the time to consider my answer. "Three."

He hugged me before loosening his grip and pulling me down to the bed to sit on his lap. It was then I noticed he was no longer wearing his towel. Glancing down, I saw it pooled in a heap on the floor.

"Did you have a flashback?"

"I don't know." Had it been a flashback? It was different than what had happened before, so I wasn't sure.

"Take your time and tell me what happened. Remember, slow, deep breaths. There's no hurry."

I took a deep breath just like he'd said and leaned into his chest. Opening my eyes, I saw the beautiful green fabric of the dress he'd picked out for me. The dress I was to wear to dinner with his family. I sat up quickly. Or I tried to. Stephan held me in place, not letting me go very far.

"Brianna?"

"Dinner. Your . . . your family—"

"They'll wait."

Looking up at him, I saw that he was completely serious.

"Now relax and tell me what happened. Why did you panic?"

Closing my eyes, I tried to will myself to relax. Stephan pulled me back against him, laying my head on his shoulder. It wasn't quite the same as his chair, but it was close. I circled my arms around his waist and sighed. "I could hear them."

"Hear who?"

I swallowed, holding him tighter.

"Shh, sweetheart. You're fine. You're safe. Whose voices did you hear?"

I opened my mouth to answer, but the words wouldn't come. They stuck in my throat, gagging me. I wanted to answer him. I wanted to give him what he asked for, but I couldn't. No matter how hard I tried, I couldn't get it out.

"Calm down," he whispered.

It was then I tasted the salty moisture running down my cheeks and realized I was crying. I tucked my head into the crook of his neck as he ran his fingers through my hair. The constant motion soothed me.

We sat there for a long time not saying anything. The only sounds in the room were the steady rhythm of our breathing and the gentle rustling of his hand as it moved through my hair. Slowly, the tension drained away, and I relaxed.

Stephan

I had no idea what happened. One minute she was aroused and on edge in the best way, and the next she was lost in one of her panic attacks. I had been standing behind her, and maybe that had been the problem, but I'd touched her from behind before and she'd been fine. She had trouble when I attempted to spoon her at night—often waking up scared. Never once, however, had she reacted negatively while she was fully awake and aware of her surroundings.

It took a while for her to calm down, but eventually, she did. We were going to be late to Richard and Diane's, but that was the least of my concerns at the moment. I'd sent my aunt a text. It was the best I could do given the circumstances. I needed to know what had happened and why. Brianna had managed to tell me she'd heard voices. Just getting that much out had been challenging for her.

Her hair was still slightly damp as I ran my fingers through it. I loved touching her hair. It was soft, and the motion seemed to calm her as much as it soothed and relaxed me. We needed to get to the bottom of this, however.

"Do you think you can tell me what happened now?"

Her fingers dug into my back in response.

"Sit up and look at me."

She retracted her fingers one by one and sat up to face me. Her eyes were bloodshot from crying.

Placing my hands on each side of her face, I leaned in and gave her a chaste kiss. "I want you to keep looking at me and tell me what happened. You are right here. With me. You're safe. No one is going to hurt you. Do you understand?"

She nodded. "Yes."

"Good girl." I kissed her again, keeping it short, even though it was always tempting to get carried away.

Making myself pull back from her, I sat and waited. I would wait all day if that was what it took, but I was confident that wouldn't be the case. Brianna had an inner strength I admired and, in some ways, envied. When I'd lost my parents, I'd fallen apart inside. No one had been able to reach me for months. I'd been a walking zombie.

My family and Logan never gave up on me, and eventually, they'd helped me through to the other side. Even then, I'd shut out most people. Daren was the first person I'd told what had happened other than Logan, and the only reason Logan had found out was because he was there right after it happened. Logan had seen firsthand what losing my parents had done to me. It took me years to get over it, to move past the pain and anger.

Losing my parents paled in comparison to what the woman in front of me had lived through, yet she never gave up, never stopped trying. I knew I would never stop loving her.

I brushed some loose strands of hair away from her face. She closed her eyes for a few seconds and then seemed to realize what she'd done and opened them again. Her eyes were wide as she stared, and I could tell her anxiety was increasing again.

"Deep, even breaths, Brianna. Take one word at a time. There's no rush."

She did as I'd instructed, her chest rising and falling steadily with each breath. I tried not to pay attention to how the fabric of her dress brushed against me with every movement, drawing my attention to her breasts. Closing my eyes, I made myself block out my body's natural reaction to her.

When I opened my eyes, she had a determined look on her face and her hands were balled into fists in her lap.

"I could . . . hear . . . them."

She reached toward my chest, but when she touched my bare skin, she pulled back. I realized she was used to holding on to my shirt. Since I wasn't wearing anything, it was throwing her off. I didn't want that, so I lowered my right hand and laced our fingers together. Brianna's fingers clasped my hands tighter than I thought possible.

"The . . . the men. They . . . the words . . . what they'd . . . say . . ."

Brianna was doing well, but I could see the panic rising. I brought her face closer to mine, touching my nose with hers. Gradually, she relaxed again, and I thought about what she'd said and what we'd been doing right before her panic had begun to spiral out of control.

I'd asked where she wanted me to touch her. It had been a simple question with an obvious answer. "You're talking about the men Ian shared you with."

She didn't need to confirm it, but she did with a nod.

For some reason, I felt I needed to clarify something. "When I asked you where you wanted me to touch you, it reminded you of those men?"

Brianna opened her mouth and then shut it. She did this several times, never uttering a word.

"There isn't a wrong answer, love."

"When you . . . asked me . . ."

"Yes," I prompted. She tried to glance down, but I tapped the underside of her chin, and she looked back up at me.

"I didn't know . . . how to answer. What word . . . to use." She took a deep breath. "Then I heard them. All the words, the names, they used to say, to call me. It . . . ." A shudder ripped through her body as she rushed through the last few words.

"Come here." I released her hands and turned her around in my lap so her back was to my chest.

Almost instinctively, she leaned back and rested her head on my shoulder.

I ran my hands down her sides, her legs, until I reached the hem of her skirt. This time, I wasted no time in lifting it, bunching it up around her hips, and revealing her silky dark green panties. Lacking pretense, I spread her legs and cupped my hand over her mound. She glanced up at me and waited.

"What words you use to describe your body aren't as important as the meaning behind them, Brianna. Those men—did the words they used convey the pleasure, the beauty of what they were talking about? I doubt it. The way you've described them, it was more about degrading you than anything else. I never want you to feel that way. Ever. Your body is beautiful to me. Every single part of it. It should be beautiful to you, too."

Removing my hand, I fixed her dress and cradled the back of her head. I leaned down to brush my mouth against hers before deepening the kiss. She parted her lips, responding.

I broke the kiss before it could get out of hand and smiled. "We are going to revisit this later, sweetheart, but for now, we have a dinner to attend."

I patted her leg, and she stood.

"Finish getting ready," I instructed, giving her a light swat on her behind as I walked around her to get to my closet. Brianna stood unmoving for several seconds, much as she had the first time I'd spanked her, as if waiting for something, and then she scurried off to the bathroom to fix her hair.

On our way to Richard and Diane's, I asked if she remembered her rules for the day, and made her repeat them back to me. Brianna needed to get used to interacting with people. Although I didn't fully trust my uncle, I did trust Diane to make Brianna feel welcomed and provide a somewhat safe environment for her. Requiring her to ask questions, something she wouldn't naturally do in a social situation, would hopefully push her out of her comfort zone a little without sending her into another panic attack.

As I pulled up in front of their home, I noticed a familiar car already in the driveway. While I'd hoped it would just be us and my aunt and uncle, I wasn't surprised by their presence. It just added another complication.

I helped Brianna out of the car, closed the door behind her, and gathered her into my arms. "Jimmy and Samantha are here." She tensed. "It's all right. Remember your rules and you'll be fine. Do we need to go over them again?"

"No, Sir. I remember."

"Good girl. Now try to relax. You're safe."

We were two steps from the front door when it opened. I'd expected my aunt, but instead Richard stood ominously in the doorway, his features unreadable.

"You're late."

His tone was tempered, but his eyes were fierce as he stared at me. I sighed and stepped forward to go around him. Even though I knew another lecture was most likely coming, I did my best to act as if he were only irritated about our tardiness.

With my arm tucked around Brianna's waist, I smiled at my uncle. "I sent Diane a message. I do hope we haven't kept everyone waiting too long."

He looked at me again and then turned his attention to Brianna. His features softened. She wasn't paying attention to Richard, though. Instead, her focus appeared to be a picture on the other side of the room. It was a family portrait taken two years before my parents' deaths. I made a mental note to get her a closer look after dinner.

"No. She's just putting everything out on the table now."

"Great!" I said with exaggerated enthusiasm, and began steering Brianna toward the dining room. A half second later, Richard followed. I had a feeling it was going to be another interesting Sunday afternoon.

Chapter 11

Stephan

Jimmy was the first to see us when we walked into the room. Once he'd announced he was going into medicine, Richard had taken him under his wing. Apparently he and his wife were going to be regular guests in my aunt and uncle's home from here on out. Jimmy smiled. "About time you showed up. I'm starved."

This, of course, got the attention of both his wife and my aunt. Diane set down the bowl of salad she had in her hands and walked toward us without preamble. She pulled me in for a hug, squeezing with more force than necessary. "I'm so glad you came," she whispered.

I hugged her back with one arm, refusing to let go of Brianna. "I couldn't turn down your spaghetti and meatballs, could I?"

She stepped back, smacking my shoulder playfully. "If that's all it takes to get you to come see me, I'll serve spaghetti every week."

I laughed.

Brianna had been standing stoically beside me until Diane turned her attention from me to her. Diane wasted no time stepping forward and hugging Brianna as well. Brianna remained stiff for a long moment and then returned my aunt's hug with her free hand.

"It's so good to see you again."

"Thank you," Brianna responded as my aunt stepped back.

Diane smiled. "I hope you're all hungry," she said as she turned her attention to the food once more.

Without further delay, we all took our seats around the table. Diane and Richard were at each end, with Brianna and me on one side, and Jimmy and Samantha on the other. I hadn't missed Samantha's intense scrutiny of Brianna, but she hadn't said anything and Brianna hadn't reacted to it, so I chose to ignore it. At least for the time being.

As I took the first bite of spaghetti, I was transported back to the many times I'd spent helping both my aunt and my mom in the kitchen. My parents had employed a cook who had come in during the week, but on the weekends Mom had insisted we could cook for ourselves, and she'd required that we all help. It was because of her I could cook as well as I did. Not that I was a stellar chef or anything, but I could hold my own, especially with a recipe in front of me.

I hadn't realized my trip down memory lane had drawn the attention of my dinner companions until Brianna touched my arm. I looked over at her and could see the worry on her face. Taking her hand, I laced our fingers together and gave her hand a gentle squeeze. She didn't look convinced.

"Is everything all right, Stephan?" Samantha asked. It was the first time she'd spoken since we'd arrived.

"Yes. I'm fine." Then to get the attention off me, I asked Jimmy how things were going at the hospital.

Throughout the rest of dinner, he regaled us with stories. Everyone appeared to be enthralled and thoroughly distracted by Jimmy's tales—everyone but Brianna. Worry lines creased her forehead, even as she ate.

I leaned over and spoke softly in her ear. "I'm fine, sweetheart. I promise. Relax and enjoy your meal." She nodded, and I could tell she was trying to obey. Lifting her hand, I placed a kiss on her knuckles before releasing my hold and going back to my food. I didn't want her worrying about me. I really was fine.

Diane stood as everyone was finishing. "Brianna, would you like to help me bring in dessert?"

Brianna stared up at me, unsure.

I nodded, letting her know it was all right. She took a deep breath and pushed back her chair. I knew the effort it took for her to do something as simple as go into the kitchen and help my aunt with dessert, but she was doing it, and I was proud of her.

As soon as they were out of earshot, my uncle pounced. "Should I even ask why you were late today?"

I picked up my water and took a drink before addressing him. "If there's something you wish to say, Richard, please say it. As we've already established, I'm an adult and so is Brianna. What we do, or don't do, is none of your business."

"Now, Stephan, I don't think your uncle—"

"Stay out of this, Samantha. I have no interest in your mind games."

"Stephan! I don't appreciate you using that tone with my wife," Jimmy said, all his usual lightheartedness gone.

"Jimmy, I appreciate you defending your wife, but if she is going to stick her nose into someone else's business, then both of you are going to have to learn to deal with the consequences. I won't be one of her psych studies."

"And what about your consequences?" Samantha piped in.

Unfortunately, I was unable to respond. Diane and Brianna walked around the corner with dessert. Even with the tension in the room, I couldn't help but smile when I saw what she was carrying. It seemed my aunt was pulling out all my favorites.

Brianna waited patiently behind her with a stack of plates and a handful of forks, while Diane laid the three-layer chocolate and strawberry swirl cake on the table and began to slice it. One by one, Brianna handed my aunt a plate, which she filled with a piece of cake.

"Thank you, dear," she said to Brianna, taking the last two plates from her.

Brianna resumed her place beside me quickly. Soon we were all eating again. Unfortunately, the tension in the room hadn't dissipated much.

"Dr. Cooper?" Brianna's voice was barely above a whisper, but since they were the first words anyone at the table had heard her speak all day, everyone stopped and waited.

There was an unnatural pause before my uncle answered her. "Yes, Brianna?"

She pressed her lips together for five very long seconds before she spoke. "What made you . . . want to become a doctor?"

No one spoke for the longest time, but I reached out and took her hand in mine, smiling the entire time. I knew she was only following the instructions I'd given her, but she could have picked something simple like asking him his favorite color. It would have only required a one-word answer on his part, and once the response was given, her task would have been completed. By asking something more open ended, she also opened herself up to a more lengthy conversation.

"My father was a doctor. I used to go into the office with him on Saturdays when I was younger. Then in my teenage years, I volunteered at the hospital." He paused, glancing over at me before returning to Brianna. "I admired my father a great deal. He knew every one of his patients by name. He knew their families." There was a long silence before he added, "I wanted to be just like him."

We could have heard a pin drop in the room after that. There wasn't even the sound of forks scraping against plates. Richard's father had died last year, and it was clear that talking about him had brought his grief back to the surface.

"Ted was a good man and a great doctor," Diane said, breaking through the silence.

"Yes," Richard said, clearing his throat. "Yes, he was."

I decided I needed to fill Brianna in on what was going on. I didn't want her to be confused. "Richard's father, Ted, died a little over a year ago. They were close."

She looked up at me, eyes wide. Brianna closed her eyes momentarily, before turning to face my uncle. I knew she was trying to keep herself from crying. "I'm so sorry."

He cleared his throat again and picked up his napkin to wipe his mouth. It was a purely reactionary gesture. "No need to be sorry, Brianna. You didn't know. Besides, talking about our loved ones who've passed on is a way for us to honor their memory. They are only truly gone if we choose to forget them."

The way my uncle glanced over to me as he spoke was not lost on me. I knew exactly what he was implying, but he was wrong. Just because I didn't like to talk about my parents didn't mean I'd forgotten them. Far from it. They were a part of me. A part of me that I didn't share easily. A part of me that I wanted to share with only one person.

Brianna

I was nervous when Stephan's aunt asked for my help in the kitchen, but I didn't know how to get out of it. It turned out not to be as scary as I thought it would be. She was really nice. I even felt comfortable enough to ask her my question.

At first, I thought I'd asked something wrong because she stopped what she was doing and turned to look at me. Then she smiled and continued to place slices of strawberries on top of the chocolate cake. "Stephan didn't come to live with us until he was almost fifteen, you know."

She paused, glancing up at me again.

When I nodded, she continued. "His mother and I were only a year apart, so we were close. But like most families, we didn't see each other all the time. They were busy with their lives, and we were busy with ours."

She finished decorating the cake and then began removing plates and utensils from the drawers and cabinets.

"He was a good kid. Happy. A little spoiled, but most kids who grew up with what he did would be. My sister tried very hard to make sure he appreciated what he had, though."

Diane handed the stack of plates to me, along with enough forks for everyone. She turned around and reached for the cake and the cake server but halted her movement mid-reach.

I was just about to ask if something was wrong when she spoke.

"He was devastated after they died. For the first three months, he barely spoke to anyone. Even after he did start talking again, you could just tell. He wasn't the same." She looked at me and smiled. "He's happy with you. Happier than I've seen him in a long time. Even when he doesn't have a smile on his face, I can see it in the relaxed set of his shoulders, the way he leans into you when you're close."

She paused.

"Thank you."

I didn't respond. I didn't know what to say. Throughout dinner, I'd been trying to think of a question I could ask her. Asking about something that I had no interest in seemed fake somehow, so I'd asked her something I'd truly been curious about. Stephan. I was curious what he'd been like growing up.

Somehow the conversation had turned back to me, and that made me uncomfortable. Diane seemed to sense my anxiety and refocused her attention on the cake. "Are you ready?" she asked, picking up the delicious-looking dessert.

"Yes."

When we walked back into the dining room, I could tell something was wrong. Stephan was sitting way too straight, and he had his hand clenched into a fist. It was in his lap, so I doubt anyone else at the table noticed, but I did. I thought about going to him but stopped myself when I saw him smile up at his aunt. Whatever it was couldn't have been that bad, or he wouldn't have been smiling. I took a deep breath, stayed where I was, and helped Diane serve the slices of cake.

As everyone ate their dessert, I knew time was running out for me to ask Dr. Cooper my question. I knew what I wanted to ask. It was just a matter of opening my mouth and asking him.

His answer wasn't what I was expecting. Dr. Cooper struck me as a driven man, but I had no idea he chose his profession because of his father. In fact, his answer surprised me. His explanation made it sound like family was important to him, yet he'd believed that woman, a stranger, over his own flesh and blood. If he truly felt this way, I didn't understand how he could treat Stephan so badly.

The conversation stalled after that. Everyone finished eating their cake, and the men, including Stephan, gathered the dirty dishes and took them into the kitchen, leaving me alone with Diane and Samantha. I was okay with Diane. Samantha I wasn't sure about, so I tried to make myself seem small without disobeying Stephan's rule of not looking down.

It didn't work.

"I like your dress, Brianna. Is it new?" Samantha asked.

I knew I had to answer. Be polite.

"Yes."

"Where did you get it?" Her voice was pleasant enough, but I was suddenly nervous.

"Stephan. He gave it to me." My voice was shaking slightly. I couldn't help it. Something about the way she'd asked the question made me think she was fishing for information, not just asking about my dress. She didn't seem to like Stephan very much.

"Did Stephan give you that necklace?"

I glanced over at Diane, unsure if I should answer or not. Stephan was still in the other room with Jimmy and Dr. Cooper. I wished he were with me, but I knew he wanted me to try, so I would do my best.

"Yes."

"Maybe I should get us all some more coffee," Diane suggested, standing to walk over to the buffet table where a pot of coffee sat warming.

Unfortunately, Samantha didn't acknowledge Diane. She was completely focused on me, which made me even more nervous.

I closed my eyes briefly and thought about where I was. Stephan told me to let him know if I reached a five or higher. I wasn't there yet.

"Does he give you things often?" she probed.

"Samantha!" Diane snapped.

Finally Samantha turned her gaze away from me and looked at Diane as she walked back to the table with the coffee.

"Would you like some coffee, Brianna?"

I shook my head. "No, thank you."

She nodded and proceeded to top off Samantha's cup along with her own. "Samantha, dear, let's get one thing perfectly straight. I will not have you interrogating anyone in my home, especially a sweet girl like Brianna. If you continue to do so, then I will have to politely ask you to leave. It is your choice."

Samantha didn't answer immediately. Instead, she glanced back and forth from me to Diane as if searching for some answer.

"I meant no disrespect, Diane. I'm just concerned."

Diane picked up her coffee and took a sip. "While I'm sure Brianna appreciates your concern over where she acquires her clothing and jewelry, you and I both know that isn't the reason behind your inquiries. I don't know what my husband has told you, and I don't care. You are making Brianna uncomfortable, and I won't tolerate it. Are we clear?"

Samantha didn't comment.

"Are we clear?" Diane asked again. At that moment, I could see Stephan in the way she held herself, the tone of her voice. It made me miss him, even though he was only a few feet away. I glanced toward the opening that led to the kitchen, and willed him to walk through.

I was so focused on the doorway that I jerked when Jimmy appeared. Disappointment settled into the pit of my stomach when I realized it wasn't Stephan. Jimmy walked over to where his wife stood and whispered something in her ear. She nodded and stood.

"Thank you for the delicious meal, as always, Diane. I'm afraid the hospital called, though, and we need to go." He turned to me. "It was nice seeing you again, Brianna."

I nodded, not sure what to say back. He seemed like a nice man.

Movement drew my attention away from Jimmy and Samantha and back to the doorway. I smiled when I saw Stephan.

He strolled over to me and kissed my cheek before trailing his lips up to my ear. "Come. I want to show you something."

As we left the room, I saw Dr. Cooper reenter the dining room. He looked pensive but not angry. I was hoping that meant he and Stephan hadn't fought again. I wasn't crazy about Dr. Cooper, but he was Stephan's family. They should get along.

We entered the foyer as Jimmy and Samantha were walking out the door. Jimmy waved good-bye. Samantha managed a tight smile. I wasn't stupid. I knew what she'd been doing. For some reason, some people wanted to make Stephan look like he was hurting me. He wasn't. Ian had hurt me. All those men he'd given me to had hurt me.

Even my father.

Stephan was the most wonderful man I'd ever met. He cared for me, and he never forced me to do something I was uncomfortable doing. People might not understand, but that didn't make them right.

"Everything all right, Brianna?" Stephan asked as we stopped in front of a large picture. It was the same one I'd noticed when we'd arrived.

"Yes, Sir. I'm fine."

He hugged me close to his side before moving me to stand in front of him. Wrapping his arms around me, he pulled me back against him and laid his chin on top of my head. "This picture was taken two years before my parents died. I was twelve." He paused. "I remember not wanting to get dressed up, but my mom insisted. Now I'm glad."

"You miss them."

"Very much." He paused. "Their names were Katharine and Ronald."

We stood there for a long time looking at the picture of his family. He didn't say any more, and I didn't ask. There was something about just standing there together that was comforting. I didn't want to do anything to change that.

Chapter 12

Brianna

We ended up staying at Dr. Cooper and Diane's house until almost seven.
After we finished looking at the picture of his family, Stephan offered to
give me a tour of the rest of the house. The last two times I'd been there,
things had ended badly with Stephan and his uncle fighting. This time,
things seemed to be better between them, even if everything wasn't perfect.

My favorite room had to be his old bedroom. It was at the back of the
house, and outside one of the windows was a large oak tree. He explained
to me how he used to climb down the tree and sneak out to meet Logan. I
tried to imagine it, but all I kept seeing was a younger Stephan, all dressed
up in a suit and tie, trying to climb down the tree. The image caused me to
giggle, and Stephan made me tell him what was so funny.

We were standing at his bedroom window laughing when Diane found us.
She'd brought photo albums with her. "I thought you might like to see
these, Brianna."

I looked up at Stephan, making sure it was all right, before going to sit
beside her on the bed. Stephan sat down on the other side of me, placing a
hand on my back. Eventually, Dr. Cooper joined us.

I loved seeing pictures of Stephan as a little boy. The stories Diane told
helped me get to know Stephan better, too.

It was beginning to get dark by the time we said good-bye. His aunt and
uncle walked us to the door. Diane hugged us both and asked us to please
come back soon. For the first time, everyone seemed happy.

Stephan only drove about a mile down the road before he pulled off to the
side, unbuckling his seatbelt and mine. He took my face in his hands and
kissed me hard. "I've been wanting to do that for hours." He pressed his
fingers into the back of my scalp, holding my head firm in his hands. With
every exhale, I felt his breath brush against my cheek in heated waves. "I'm
so proud of you. You were amazing today."

I smiled at his praise. Pressure built in my chest to the point where it was almost painful, but somehow pleasant at the same time.

Headlights broke through the fog that seemed to have enveloped us, bringing us back to the present. Without the interruption, we might have remained there, frozen in time in our own perfect world until morning. Stephan sat back in his seat, sighing. "We should get home before someone stops, wondering if we're having car trouble or something."

I didn't say anything, only nodded.

"Put your seatbelt back on, sweetheart. Let's go home."

On Monday morning, before Stephan left for the office, he said he wanted me to think of three things about the weekend that stuck out to me and why. He didn't have to explain we'd be talking about them when he got home. I knew him well enough to know that.

I avoided coming up with my three things and instead cleaned every square inch of the condo, with the exception of the one room upstairs that was locked. Stephan had never said what was behind that door. I'd never asked. Some part of me was afraid of the answer, even though I knew eventually, if I continued to stay with him, I'd have to find out.

Cal called right after lunch. We talked for almost an hour, which had helped get my mind off the assignment I'd been given. Cal asked if I wanted to go see a concert with him and a couple of friends. "It'll be fun."

"I don't know."

"Consider it a birthday present." He paused. "Coleman can come, too, if you want."

I knew Cal wasn't Stephan's biggest fan, but I was glad he was trying. My mom had taken me to a concert right after she'd been diagnosed with terminal cancer, before she'd started getting really sick. It had been fun, but there'd also been crowds of people, and it was really loud.

"I'll think about it, okay?"

I knew he was disappointed that I hadn't immediately agreed, but I did need to think about it. While it was getting easier to talk to Cal, to be myself around him, I wasn't sure I could go to a concert with him and his friends by myself. I didn't know if I was ready for that.

It was three thirty. Stephan would be home in less than two hours, and I still had to make dinner. Pulling out the ingredients I needed from the refrigerator, I chopped the vegetables for tonight while I thought about the weekend. I couldn't put it off any longer.

The first thing that came to mind was my panic attack. He'd already said we would be revisiting the subject, so it seemed fitting to include it on the list. Even though I didn't want to think about it, I knew he wasn't going to let it go. That wasn't how he was.

What happened with Samantha and Diane stuck out as well. Her questions made me uncomfortable, but talking to people I didn't know usually did. What struck me more was why she wanted to know if Stephan had bought me things, and why she perceived that as a bad thing. Did she also think Stephan was hurting me? And if she did, why did she think that?

I was putting the casserole into the oven when I realized what the third thing was. Stephan hadn't qualified that the things had to be negative, only that they needed to be events that stuck out in my mind. Standing in front of his family's portrait certainly qualified. He had shared something with me, something special to him. That, in turn, had made me feel special. I was important to him, therefore he shared a part of himself with me. Warmth spread through me, and I smiled.

The table was set. Everything was ready but the food.

It was only a little after five, so I knew I had some time before Stephan arrived. I decided I should surprise him. Practically skipping across the living room to my bedroom, I walked quickly to my closet and retrieved one of my dresses. It was what Lily had called a wraparound dress, and it fell almost to my knees. I thought Stephan would like it, because it dipped low between my breasts and was loose enough to be pushed out of the way.

I left my feet bare as I walked back into the main room. Just as I was nearing the door, I saw the monitor turn on, and Stephan's image appeared on the screen. In a split second, I made a decision and dropped to my knees.

He opened the door. I heard him take two steps, then stop. There was a long pause, then the sound of the door being shut and locked.

I kept my head bowed and my hands resting in my lap as I waited. Still he didn't say anything. Didn't move from his spot near the door. My heart raced as I waited to see what he would do.

Finally, he took a step, then another, before stopping less than a foot in front of me.

He reached out with his right hand and tilted my chin up until I was looking at him. "You look stunning like this, sweetheart. What have I done to deserve such a beautiful gift?"

"I wanted to say thank you. For taking care of me. For sharing with me . . . about your mom and dad."

He took his other hand and threaded his fingers through my hair, lightly scratching my scalp. I closed my eyes automatically. A feeling of complete peace and relaxation flowed from my head down to the tips of my toes. I'd missed this.

The sound of the oven beeping startled me out of my trance. He chuckled. "Stay where you are, pet. I'll get the food."

Taking a deep breath, I tried not to miss the feeling of his hands in my hair. The way he'd rubbed his thumb along my cheek, my lips. I was beginning to think I could sit for hours while he ran his fingers through my hair.

I heard him moving around in the kitchen, but I didn't glance up to see what he was doing. Instead, I waited. Waited to see what would happen next. There was a voice inside me screaming, telling me that this was wrong, but it was overruled by how right it felt to be where I was. I was a little nervous, yes. I didn't know what he was going to do. However, my trust in Stephan kept that small voice from growing louder. I trusted him more than anything, anyone.

Stephan
Once the baking dish was removed and the oven turned off, I took a minute to catch my breath. To say Brianna had caught me off guard was an understatement. I'd missed coming home to find her kneeling, waiting for me, but seeing her that way brought images to my mind that couldn't come to pass. Not yet.

Thinking about the possibilities, though, had me growing harder. The moment I'd walked in the door and saw her there on the floor, my body had begun to react. There was no disguising my erection as it pressed against my slacks, begging to be let free.

I closed my eyes and took a deep breath. While I knew her seeing me aroused no longer caused her fear, I did need to remain in control of myself. I couldn't just do whatever I wanted without concern for her. We'd only started to discuss taking things further with the rope. It had to be a step at a time.

The thought of her tied up only made things worse, and I hoped I'd be able to survive the night, let alone the rest of the week. Sex with Brianna was amazing, but I longed to explore other things with her. Other kinky things.

Logan had been out of town for the last two weeks. We'd e-mailed back and forth a few times, but it was mostly mundane stuff. We didn't discuss details regarding our lifestyles. There were too many ways e-mails and texts could fall into the wrong hands. It wasn't something either of us needed. He was flying home tonight, and we were scheduled to have lunch on Thursday. Given some of my recent conversations with Brianna, added to what I'd come home to . . . I wanted to propose something to him that would require his and Lily's help.

Knowing I couldn't make her wait forever, I took a deep breath and walked as calmly as I could back to where Brianna remained kneeling on the floor. She was extremely patient, and I had no doubt it was a skill she'd been forced to acquire painfully at Ian's hands. I could, however, see the pulse in her neck beating out a steady but rapid rhythm. If I knew for sure she were ready for a good spanking, I would waste no time bending her over the back of the couch and giving her one. Then take her from behind as I enjoyed the view of her nice, red ass. Considering her reaction to the two single swats I'd given her, I knew that wasn't the case, though.

Plunging my fingers back into her hair, I drew her head to my groin and pressed, letting her feel what she was doing to me. The heat of her breath through my pants, knowing that her mouth was so close, made my resolve slowly disappear. I needed to feel her tongue, her lips, milking me.

"Undo my pants, Brianna."

She glanced up at me, unsure.

"If this isn't what you want, you need to tell me now."

Instead of answering verbally, she looked down at my crotch and then reached for the button on my slacks. My cock twitched in anticipation.

The last time she'd had her mouth on me, things hadn't ended well. She'd snuck into my bedroom while I was sleeping, still under the impression that she was my slave and thinking that waking me up, servicing me, would be a great way of thanking me for being nice to her. It had the opposite effect. I didn't want a mindless slave girl who did only what she was told and had no thoughts, feelings, or wants of her own.

She pulled my zipper down, the flaps falling to the side. All thoughts of the past slipped from my mind as I became intensely focused on the present.

"Take it out."

Brianna took a deep breath, reached back up to push my boxers down, and released my cock from its confines. It bobbed slightly and then pointed straight at her. She sat, waiting, watching, her hands in her lap.

I threaded my fingers through her hair, cupping the back of her head, holding it in place. Closing my eyes, I struggled for control. This was another first for us. I wanted to make this last.

Feeling slightly more centered, I looked down. Brianna stared up at me. There was no fear in her eyes, and it washed away any lingering doubts I had about continuing this.

With my left hand, I caressed the side of her face before brushing my thumb over her lips until she parted them. I slipped my thumb inside her mouth and pressed down on her tongue. Instinctively, she relaxed her jaw.

"If at any time you need to stop, to end this, I want you to tap my arm twice. Nod if you understand."

She nodded.

"Good girl. Now let's see if that mouth of yours is as good as I remember."

I stepped closer, the tip of my erection touching her lips. Just the feel of her breath was sending blood rushing from my brain down to my groin. If I waited any longer, I might explode before I ever got to relive the pleasure of her mouth enveloping my cock in its warmth. She wasn't giving me any indication that she didn't want this, so I was through holding back.

Allowing my thumb to slip from her mouth, I tangled my hand in her hair and waited to see what she would do. It didn't take long. Brianna opened her mouth wide, and nearly my entire length was surrounded by her warm, wet mouth.

She bobbed her head and ran her tongue up and down my length as she sucked. It was nothing short of heavenly. As I felt that tightening in my balls, I gathered her hair around my fist and guided her movements. There was something mesmerizing about watching a woman as she used her mouth. Something about watching my erection move in and out from between her beautiful pink lips. Every now and then, I got a glimpse of her tongue as it glided up, down, and around my entire length. The closer I got, the more I needed.

"Relax your throat." It was all the warning I gave her before tightening my hold on her hair and thrusting in her mouth.

Brianna didn't miss a beat. She closed her eyes, relaxed, and within seconds I was plunging down her throat and she was sucking with an intensity that sent the last of my self-control out the window. I pulled roughly on her hair as the evidence of my orgasm emptied down her throat. The surge of energy exploded until I was left breathless and certain that I'd just experienced the best blowjob of my life.

I opened my eyes and looked down as I pulled out of her mouth. She gazed up at me, her blue eyes darker than normal, and I knew she'd not been unaffected by what she'd just done. Untangling my hand from her hair, I trailed the backs of my fingers gently across the side of her face, down to the mouth that had just given me so much pleasure.

"Thank you."

She smiled, and it had to be one of the best things I'd ever seen.

"You're welcome, Sir."

I smiled back.

"Be a good girl and fix my pants, and then we'll go see what you made for dinner."

Brianna wasted no time doing as I'd instructed, all with a smug smile on her face. I'd been holding off pushing too much, for fear it might trigger a past memory for her. Maybe I'd been wrong to do so. She seemed ready for the next step, ready to explore. Brianna was the one who'd brought up the ropes. She was the one who'd been waiting at the door kneeling. My lunch with Logan couldn't come fast enough. I just hoped he and Lily agreed.

I helped her stand and then made my way to the table while she checked on the food. She was still smiling as she carried the baking dish over to the table and set it down. If nothing else, she seemed quite pleased with herself.

Once she sat down, and we each had food on our plates, I continued to watch her. She showed no signs of discomfort, regret, or anything other than happiness. It hadn't escaped my notice when I'd walked in, either, that she was wearing a dress. Brianna always chose to wear pants or shorts. I had to assume her wearing a dress held some significance.

"I like the dress."

"Thank you." The smile never slipped from her face, but she lowered her head and blushed. It was adorable.

I thought about beginning our normal, nightly conversation here at the table but reconsidered. Brianna was smiling and happy. Although I didn't want that to change, I knew there were some serious things we needed to discuss. I also had assignments for her to work on during the week. The topics were almost certain to wipe that smile from her face, at least temporarily, and I wasn't ready for that to happen yet.

"Did you read any more in your book today?" I asked later, once we were sitting in my chair.

"No. I cleaned."

I glanced around the room and frowned. The condo was clean when I left. There was no way it should have taken her an entire day. "You don't have to clean every day, you know. In fact, you don't have to clean at all if you won't want to. I used to have a maid who came in three days a week, and I can easily make that happen again."

"I like to clean. It . . . it helps me clear my head."

Her hair was still a bit messy from where I'd twisted and pulled it earlier, and I pushed it back out of the way. She was looking down, so I knew there was something on her mind she wasn't crazy about discussing. My guess was the assignment I'd given her, to come up with three things that had stuck out to her from the weekend. I didn't care if they were good things or bad things. I just wanted them to be important enough to stand out in her memory.

"Did you come up with three things from this weekend?"

She nodded.

I waited.

For the longest time she said nothing. I was almost ready to scold her when she answered. "Yes."

I rubbed her arm letting her know I was pleased. "Tell me the first one."

"I liked the picture of you and your family. I liked . . . I liked that you shared it with me," she whispered.

Hugging her closer, I kissed her forehead. "I enjoyed that, too. You are very special to me, Brianna. You make me want to share those things with you."

She snuggled closer, her lips grazing my neck as I held her. It brought back the memory of earlier, and my body reacted. I closed my eyes briefly, trying to concentrate on our current conversation.

"What was the second thing?" I asked, trying to refocus.

"Diane and . . . Samantha."

I halted the movement of my hand up and down her arm for a moment before resuming. "What about Diane and Samantha?"

"I don't think Samantha likes me either."

I heard the words, but I didn't like how detached they sounded. It was as if she expected to be disliked. "Why do you think Samantha doesn't like you?"

She didn't answer right away, but I gave her time to gather her thoughts. "She started asking me questions. I felt uncomfortable, like I was missing what she was really asking."

"Was this when I was in the kitchen?"

She nodded, her hair tickling my face as she moved.

"Did you tell her she was making you uncomfortable?"

She shook her head. "Diane did. She told her to stop or she'd have to ask her to leave." Brianna paused. "I don't like causing trouble."

"You didn't cause trouble, sweetheart. That was all Samantha's doing,

I'm sure. You have nothing to feel sorry about. Trust me. You were perfect yesterday."

I allowed a few minutes for both of us to sit and enjoy the time we had together. It upset me that I'd not been there for Samantha's little interrogation, but I supposed it had been inevitable. She'd been waiting for the time to pounce and had apparently felt that was her opportunity. I was eternally grateful to my aunt, however, that she'd jumped in and put Samantha in her place.

Although I wanted nothing more than to hold her all night, I knew there was more to discuss. "What was the third thing?"

"What happened before . . . before we left."

I could always tell how hard things were for Brianna emotionally by how many times she paused. Easy things that held little emotion for her were said without pause at all. The harder subjects, the ones that either held emotions or she was unsure of, she always hesitated. Either that or she said them with a robotic detachment.

"Your panic attack. Yes, we do need to discuss that further, don't we?"

She shivered.

"I know it's scary, Brianna, but it's not going to go away unless we deal with it."

"I know." Her voice was so soft I almost didn't hear her response.

"I'll be right there to catch you. I promise." It wasn't a vow I took lightly, and I meant every word.

Chapter 13

Brianna
Stephan's words comforted me, but they didn't take away the fear completely. I knew he was right. I knew I couldn't run away from what had happened to me. Even on my good days, which I had more often now, there was no way to forget. Every time I turned around, there were little things. It could be a word, a gesture, or even an object.

While brushing my hair out earlier that morning, I was hit by the memory of being beaten with the back of a hairbrush. The experience had left the back of my legs covered with welts for almost a week. I'd had to stop, close my eyes, and chant over and over again that it wasn't real. There was no rhyme or reason as to when a memory would hit me. Ones like the hairbrush weren't as bad as some of the others, and I was able to get them to go away on my own. I was afraid what had triggered my panic attack on Sunday morning would be a little harder to make disappear.

"Do you know what stands out the most for me from this past weekend?"

I shook my head. "No."

"It was when we were standing in my old bedroom and I was telling you about all those times I snuck out and climbed down the tree. That wasn't a good time for me in my life, but telling you about it made me realize how much things have changed. How much I've changed since then."

Hearing him talk about it again made me smile, which turned into giggles.

"Picturing me climbing trees in my suit again, Brianna?"

When I didn't answer, he moved his hand to my side and began tickling me. Before I knew it, I was hanging over the arm of his chair and laughing so hard I could barely breathe.

Eventually, he helped me to sit up, a huge smile on his face. I was panting, but it didn't seem to matter as he took hold of my face and kissed me.

It didn't take long for him to deepen the kiss. Soon I was straddling him and had my fingers tangled in his hair. When he broke the kiss, he rested his forehead against mine and chuckled. "It amazes me how easy it is to get sidetracked with you."

A thrill surged through me at his words. If kissing me was what he meant by getting sidetracked, I liked that.

He kissed me once again and then leaned back in his chair, leaving me sitting astride his lap. "As much as I'd love to forget about everything and take you to bed, there are things we still need to talk about, sweetheart."

He drew his hands down my side and gripped my hips. It probably took me longer than it should to realize he was holding me in place so I wouldn't bump the erection that was once again straining against the fabric of his slacks. I glanced down purely out of reflex.

Stephan dug his fingers into my hips and groaned. "That isn't helping. I need your eyes up here."

My face heated, and I knew I must have been blushing. Looking up, I met that dark look in his eyes that confirmed his desire to forget everything he wanted to talk about and skip straight to sex. It was strange how much my feelings on the subject had changed, but I didn't want to question it too much. Sex with Stephan was something I enjoyed and even looked forward to. I didn't want that to change.

He closed his eyes, and when he reopened them, they were more focused and the intense heat was gone. I couldn't help but be a little disappointed.

"Before we get into what I had planned for tonight, I want to talk about what happened earlier when I came home."

When he didn't continue, I felt I needed to respond in some way. "Okay."

"How do you feel about what happened?"

I was confused again.

"I don't understand."

He began rubbing his hands up and down my thighs absentmindedly. The fabric of my dress moved under his palms, scraping lightly against my skin. It was distracting.

"How did you feel about me pulling your hair and fucking your mouth?"

Time stopped.

"Brianna?"

I didn't answer. My mouth felt dry all of a sudden.

"Brianna, look at me."

I looked at him.

"What are you feeling right now?"

I thought about it for a moment before answering. It wasn't panic or fear exactly. There was some of that, but that wasn't it entirely. "I feel . . . numb? No. I don't know. Like . . ."

"Like, what?"

"Like I'm . . . waiting."

"Waiting for what?" he prompted when I didn't continue.

"I . . . I don't know."

He took my hands and placed them on his chest. "Can you feel me? Feel me under your hands?"

I nodded, and the strange suspended feeling began to fade.

"Better?"

"Yes."

He smiled.

"We need to talk about this, Brianna. I need to know how you feel, what you think about what happened tonight when I came home. Is that what you wanted? Is it what you expected to happen?"

I curled my fingers into the soft cotton of his shirt. "I . . . I didn't know . . . what would happen."

He lifted his right hand and began running his fingers along my scalp as he had when I was kneeling. "I know you've said you enjoy kneeling, and you like when I run my fingers through your hair like this."

I closed my eyes and reveled in the sensations his ministrations brought to the surface.

"What about the rest? You have to tell me, Brianna. I can't read your mind."

When I didn't say anything right away, he tugged on my hair. It wasn't as hard as he had before, but my body still responded.

He gave my hair another tug.

"I . . . I liked it."

Then as if to test the theory, he wrapped his hand around my hair as he had before and pulled hard enough to jerk my head back, exposing my neck. I automatically closed my eyes. "Eyes open, Brianna."

I opened my eyes, the long, straight beams of his ceiling in my direct line of sight. I couldn't see him, only feel.

He didn't release his hold on my hair as his other hand snaked up my dress. I gasped as his fingers came in contact with my damp panties.

"Does my pulling your hair make you wet, Brianna? Do you like that?"

It was impossible to nod given the tight hold he had on my hair. "Yes."

Stephan continued to rub up and down over my sensitive flesh. All too soon, the pressure began to build, and I knew my orgasm was approaching.

"You aren't to come until I say, Brianna."

I closed my eyes, trying to hold off what I knew was coming. My body felt overheated, like I was wearing a snow suit on a warm summer day. His lips brushed my skin along the edge of my dress above my breast moments before he moved the clingy fabric out of the way with his teeth. Ignoring my bra, he placed his mouth over my nipple and sucked. The sensation had me crying out.

Seconds later, two of his fingers dipped beneath my panties and plunged inside me. I held on for dear life. It was too much. Too much.

He blew on the wet fabric covering my nipple, and a shiver ran through me. This one had nothing to do with fear and everything to do with the wonderful things he was doing to my body.

He loosened his grip on my hair slightly, but I could still feel the controlling tug of his hand.

"Look at me," he demanded.

I opened my eyes and glanced toward him.

His eyes were dark with arousal. It was a look that used to scare me, but it didn't from him. Not anymore. Instead, the sight only increased the tension building between my legs to the point where it was almost unbearable. I was trying to obey, to not come before he said. But it was becoming difficult. I didn't know how much longer I would be able to hold on.

"Come," he whispered as he scraped his thumb against my clit and bit down on my nipple.

It was as if the world exploded into little shards of glass. I screamed, riding out my orgasm.

Stephan

I would never, ever get tired of seeing Brianna climax, feeling her body quake beneath my hands. She collapsed under her own weight, and I caught her before she lost her balance. I didn't want her falling to the floor and hurting herself.

Resting her head on my shoulder, I massaged her back and neck as her breathing returned to normal. The events of this evening gave me hope. Hope for our future. Whether Brianna realized it or not, she'd just proven that she could be what I needed in a submissive. Now it was up to her to decide if it was what she wanted for her life.

We sat there for almost half an hour, her arms wrapped around my neck, my hands rubbing her back. It was perfect. I couldn't have asked for a better way to spend my evening. Unfortunately, I would have to break the spell that had encompassed us.

"How do you feel?" I asked, sliding my hand up into her hair and grazing my fingers over her scalp.

She burrowed her head further into my shoulder.

"Good." Her response was muffled by my shirt, but I understood her.

"Does your head hurt at all?"

She shook her head. "No."

I realized she was blushing, and kissed the side of her head. "Does the fact that you like when I pull your hair embarrass you?"

Brianna didn't answer right away, and her fingers went to work on the buttons of my dress shirt. I held her and waited.

"I shouldn't like that," she whispered.

I couldn't stand not being able to see her face any longer, so I shifted us so I could look into her eyes as I spoke. "What makes you think you shouldn't like it?"

She glanced down. I tapped under her chin, and she looked back up at me. "I don't like . . . pain." The last word came out strangled.

I brushed my fingers from her temple to her chin and back, never taking my eyes off her. "What you went through, from what you've told me . . . from the evidence I've seen on your body . . ." I sighed, trying not to let the anger those thoughts evoked in me take over. "What was done to you was extreme. There are very few people who would actually enjoy the level of pain you endured."

I let that set in before I continued. "Remember the lesson with the cane?"

She nodded. "It's not the object, it's the person using it."

I smiled. "Good girl. And how do you think that applies here?"

Brianna looked down again, but I could still see her face clearly. She was thinking, trying to figure out the puzzle I'd given her. I had no doubts she would, however. It would just take her some time and thought to wrap her head around something she'd probably never considered.

Time ticked by, and the light coming through the window changed from sunlight to the artificial lights of the city. I reached over and turned on the lamp so we wouldn't be sitting in the dark.

"Pain is relative?"

"Meaning?"

"Everyone is different." She hesitated. "And . . . it depends on the person?"

"Very good." I kissed her forehead and smiled. "Pain isn't bad any more than a cane. It's the individual who is administering it, and the person who's receiving it, and the situation they're in. As long as they agree on the level, the use, then it can be pleasurable."

She nodded, then appeared to think very hard about something again.

"I'm scared."

I pushed her hair back behind her ears. "What has you scared?"

"I shouldn't . . . I shouldn't *like* it. I shouldn't—"

"Sweetheart, there is no right or wrong about what we like and what we don't like. It just is."

"And you . . . you like to pull my hair?"

I chuckled. "Yes. I like it a lot."

Now that the crisis appeared to be over, I changed positions again and tucked her head back into the crook of my neck.

"You should never feel ashamed or embarrassed about something you enjoy. Or something you don't enjoy, for that matter."

"What if . . ."

"Go on."

"What if I don't like something you do?"

I continued to caress her as we talked. Even though she was calm, I knew from experience that could change in an instant.

"First, we would talk about it like we're doing now. If it were something you truly didn't like, however, or were uncomfortable with doing, we wouldn't do it again. It's called a hard limit."

"A hard limit."

I wasn't sure if she was talking to me or herself, but I answered her anyway. "A hard limit is something you absolutely, under no circumstances, want to do or try."

She was thinking again.

"Do you have . . . hard limits, too?"

"Of course. Everyone has hard limits, even if they don't call them that."

She was quiet.

"Would you like to know what some of mine are?"

"Yes."

"You already know I don't do any type of toilet play. I also have blood play and needles on my list of hard limits. "

She shuddered in my arms when I mentioned needles. There were no marks on her skin from needles, but if it were done by someone with experience, there wouldn't be. It was a lot like acupuncture, although the needles weren't always as small. Considering the level of pain Ian preferred, my guess would be they were larger needles rather than smaller.

It took her several minutes to completely relax again in my arms. When she finally did, I glanced up at the clock and realized it was getting late. Her assignment was going to have to wait. It wasn't ideal, but I didn't want to get into anything major this late. The day had already been emotional for her, and we'd accomplished a lot.

I helped her up, and we walked hand in hand into my bathroom where I helped her strip. At my prompting, she did the same for me before we entered the large shower.

I kept everything chaste, more because I wanted to give her time to process everything than the lack of want. She glanced down a few times at my erection as if waiting for me to act upon my obvious desire. I pretended not to notice, concentrating on getting us both clean instead.

After drying off, we climbed into my bed together. I hadn't been lying to her when I said I might never let her sleep in her own bed again. Even though occasionally I'd wake up in the middle of the night and be startled by her presence in my bed, once my conscious mind kicked in I was filled with a sense of contentment seeing her lying there surrounded by my sheets and pillows, completely at peace and trusting.

It was usually those times when I couldn't resist pulling her into my arms and holding her. She'd woken up more than once, stiff and frightened. The second time it had happened, we'd ended up staying up for more than an hour talking through it. As with everything else that frightened her, she didn't want to shy away from it, and she'd been embarrassed to have reacted as she had.

Gathering her into my arms, I laid her head on my chest and kissed her forehead. I longed to tell her I loved her. My heart ached with the want to tell her.

Her fingers played absentmindedly with the brown hair below my navel. I sucked in a breath as she dipped a little too low, and grabbed her wrist.

She stilled.

"You didn't do anything wrong, Brianna, but I just want to hold you tonight."

When I let go of her, she retracted her hand and tucked it up under her chin.

"Sir?"

"Yes, Brianna?"

"I talked to Cal today."

I closed my eyes, hoping this wasn't bad news.

"And what did Ross have to say?"

"He . . . he invited me . . . us . . . to a concert."

"What kind of concert?"

"I . . . I don't know. I . . . I didn't ask. I should have . . ."

"Shh. It's fine." I soothed, running my fingers through her hair like she enjoyed. "Would you like to go?"

"I don't know if . . . what if I can't . . ."

Sitting up, I brought her with me. Once we were facing each other, I repeated the question. "Would you like to go?"

"I think . . . I'd like to try."

I nodded.

"I'll call Ross tomorrow and get the details."

Lying back down, I tucked her into my side and resumed petting her hair. We'd made great progress over the course of the evening. She was getting better at communicating her thoughts and feelings every day, even if sometimes she was unsure of them.

I had no idea what Cal was intending with this concert, although considering Brianna's birthday was only two weeks away, I hazarded a guess that was the underlying reason. Why he'd picked something so public was beyond me, but I doubted I'd ever understand Ross and his motivations or thinking. Hopefully, after talking to him, I'd have a better idea. If Brianna truly wanted to go, I wanted to attempt to make it a positive experience for her.

Brushing my lips against her hair, I realized she had already fallen asleep. Smiling, I lay back against my pillow and closed my eyes. Tomorrow was another day, but for now, Brianna was safe and happy. I couldn't ask for anything else.

Chapter 14

Stephan
Monday hadn't gone as planned, and Tuesday wasn't shaping up to be much better. It seemed every time I turned around something needed my attention. There was also the process of introducing the new CFO to his job and the other employees. After going through all the feedback from the board on Monday morning, I'd called and officially offered him the job with a bonus if he could start immediately. Lucky for me, he accepted.

Michael James spent the morning with Human Resources going through his contract and all the necessary paperwork, while Jamie and I tried to get his office in order. Jamie made sure everything was clean and that Michael had the office supplies he needed, while I organized spreadsheets and reports to make it a little easier for him. The other executives and I had been trying to keep up with the workload, but we'd only been able to deal with the most pressing issues. Michael would have plenty to keep him busy when he finally sat down in his office.

At lunch, I spent some time in the gym before calling Brianna to see how things were going. Hearing her voice always brightened my day, and this time wasn't any different. She was currently reading a book about a man who'd left his home on a ranch to go in search of a bride in the big city. I'd noticed that as we'd become more intimate, she'd begun to pick up more romance-driven books. Of course, Lily had also brought a stack with her the last time she'd come to visit—something I'd not realized until one night when I'd seen Brianna reading a book I hadn't recognized as being from my library.

We spoke until Jamie buzzed, letting me know I had a call. Regretfully, I said good-bye and let her get back to her book.

I picked up line one. "Stephan Coleman."

"Stephan, it's Oscar," my lawyer answered.

Taking a seat at my desk, I reached for a pen. "Tell me you have good news."

"I have good news. I was able to get a judge to approve a restraining order against Jonathan Reeves. They're planning to serve him with it today at the motel where he's been staying."

"Good. The sooner the better."

"I agree. If what you've told me is true, he needs to be kept as far away from his daughter as possible."

"Are you doubting me, Oscar?" I asked, joking. I knew he wasn't, but I couldn't resist commenting on his wording.

Oscar didn't answer immediately. "No. I'm not doubting you." He paused again. "I've known you for a long time, Stephan. Since you were in diapers. I don't ever think you've joked with me once in all those years. It's good to hear, and I can only guess it's because of Miss Reeves."

I leaned back in my leather chair and smiled. "I love her."

He sighed. "Stephan, I love hearing you so happy, but I wouldn't be doing my job if I didn't voice my concerns. Hearing you talk about Brianna Reeves, saying you love her . . . if it were anyone else, I'd be thrilled. But as your lawyer, I have to be upfront and honest with you. This is dangerous. Very dangerous. Especially with you going after Pierce."

"I know the risks, Oscar."

"I don't think you do," he said, interrupting me. "You are clearly involved with this girl. And considering you're a healthy twenty-four-year-old man, I'm not going to even pretend to assume it's platonic. Do you have any idea what a prosecuting attorney could do with that information? I'm a good lawyer, Stephan, but even I can't work miracles."

"I won't walk away from her, Oscar. That's not up for negotiation."

"I'm not telling you to. What I am saying is stop putting your sausage into her honeypot."

His voice was forceful and meant to drive home his point, but his choice of wording made it impossible to take him seriously. I understood what he was saying. I did. But that wouldn't change anything. As long as it was what Brianna wanted, I wouldn't change anything. Not even if it meant having to stare down the proverbial barrel of a gun.

"I appreciate the advice."

He sighed.

"I might as well be talking to a brick wall, right?"

I chuckled. "I didn't say that."

"You didn't have to." I heard some movement on his end. "Just be careful, all right? From what you've told me, this girl is vulnerable. The right attorney could work that in their favor. Who knows, Miss Reeves might even turn on you herself given the correct motivation."

"She wouldn't do that."

"I'm not saying she would," he said, defending himself. "I'm just saying I know some crafty lawyers out there who, with a little incentive—like, say, lots of media coverage—could spin this into a front-page story and launch a political career. All I'm saying is *be careful*. Don't do anything stupid."

"I'll keep that in mind, Oscar."

He sighed again, and I could almost see him shaking his head at my words.

"I'm sure you will. Now, I've sent you over Mr. Pierce's financials to look over via courier. You should be getting them sometime today."

"I'll let my assistant know to expect them."

"Call me if you need anything else, Stephan. I'm going to go help some clients who might actually take my advice."

"Thanks, Oscar."

He grunted. "You're welcome."

Since I already had my phone in my hand, I decided now was as good a time as any to call Ross. Looking up his office number, I dialed.

There were two rings before a woman answered. "Ross Builders. How may I help you?"

"Is Mr. Ross available?"

"I'm sorry, sir. Mr. Ross isn't in the office much anymore. His son has taken over running the business for the most part. Would you like to talk to Cal?"

I closed my eyes and begged for patience. "Yes, please."

"One moment."

At that point, I was forced to listen to some of the strangest music I'd ever heard. It wasn't jazz, although that was the closest genre I could fit it into. Instead, it had an abrupt start-and-stop feel to it every thirty to forty seconds. I had to wonder who had selected the hold music.

"Thank you for holding. This is Cal."

"Nice hold music you have there, Ross."

"Why thank you, Coleman. Our receptionist picked it out. She loves jazz. Thought it would soothe the customers."

"That's *not* jazz."

"Did you call to insult my receptionist or to talk about Anna?"

"She told me you invited her to a concert."

"I did. Are you going to tell her she can't go?"

Twisting in my chair so that I was facing the window, I looked out over the city toward the building that housed my condo . . . and Brianna. "No, but I'd like some more information. Where is it and who's playing?"

"It's at a club downtown. My girlfriend's brother is the manager of the club, and he can get us tickets. The band's local, but they're rumored to be in talks with a couple record labels, so they're good. I know what you're thinking, and I've already talked to Brian, the manager, about getting us a booth in the back so Brianna won't feel so crowded. There'll be a lot of people, but most of them should be up front, closer to the band."

"Seems you're starting to pay attention."

"I know you don't like me, Coleman, and quite frankly, I'm not a big fan of yours either, but I *do* care about Anna. I think she needs to get out and socialize, make friends."

"So it will be you, your girlfriend, me, and Brianna?"

"And three other friends."

"Who?"

"Calm down. They're friends. I wouldn't do anything to intentionally put Anna in danger."

I stood and walked to the window. Spending the evening with Ross and his friends wasn't my idea of fun, but I'd do it for Brianna. Plus, he was correct on one thing—Brianna needed to socialize.

"When, and what time?"

"Next Friday night at Crazy Lewie's. Seven o'clock."

I nodded, even though he couldn't see me. I'd never been to Crazy Lewie's, but I knew where it was. They prided themselves on live music and local talent. "Send our tickets to my office. We'll meet you there."

After a few more mumbled words, Ross hung up. How that man ran a business with such poor manners was beyond me. Given their ability to donate large sums to the foundation, however, they had to be doing well. Maybe it was just me he was rude with. He did seem to be getting better with Brianna.

I was impressed he'd thought to arrange for a table in the back to give her space. She would still be uncomfortable with so many people around, but Brianna did need to get out more. She couldn't stay shut up in my condo forever.

Brianna

I was really getting into my book when the phone rang. The hero, Jack, had just met Ronnie, a sassy waitress. He'd been checking her out, and she'd noticed. She'd just "accidentally" spilled his drink in his lap. I didn't want to stop reading. I wanted to see what happened next, but I knew I needed to answer the phone. It could be Stephan.

"Hello?"

I heard a sigh on the other end of the line and knew immediately it wasn't Stephan.

"Anna."

Cringing back into the couch, I almost threw the phone when my father spoke again. "Don't hang up. Please. Just hear me out."

I didn't know what to do. "What . . ." Closing my eyes, I reached up and held tight to the collar Stephan gave me. "What . . . do you want?"

"I'm sorry I scared you before. I didn't mean to. I just . . . I needed to get you out of there, away from that man."

All I could do was shake my head as I curled into a ball in the corner of the couch. A minute ago, I'd been lost in a world of promised romance. Now I was clinging to the only piece of Stephan I had at the moment and trying to not let my fear take over and send me into a spiral of panic.

"I'm asking for you to listen to my side of the story. That's all. Will you do that?"

I didn't answer, and he must have taken that for a yes.

"After I realized you'd been taken somewhere, I *did* look for you, Anna. I promise you I did. I called in favors with other law enforcement officers I knew across Minnesota. I didn't file an official missing person's report on you, but I checked the police wire every day. I looked for anything that might lead me to you, but until last month, there was nothing. Then I had a friend in Minneapolis call saying there was mention of a Brianna Reeves in one of the society pages. It was a long shot, and he didn't think it could be you, but I checked it out anyway. My heart almost stopped when I saw your picture staring back at me."

He paused.

"You looked so scared, Anna."

Somewhere along the way, I'd squeezed my eyes shut. I didn't want to hear him, but somehow I couldn't hang up on him either.

"I was served with a restraining order today. It says I can't come within five hundred feet of you."

That made me open my eyes, and I was able to take a deep breath for the first time since answering the phone.

"Don't do this, Anna. I'm your father. I love you. I wouldn't do anything to hurt you. Not intentionally. What happened with Dumas . . . it was a mistake. An accident. No matter what happened, I'm your only family. There's nothing that can change that."

The phone fell from my hand, and I rolled over onto my side.

A mistake.

An accident.

That's what he called the ten months I'd spent with Ian.

A sob ripped from my throat as I cried harder. I didn't bother to wipe away the tears. They didn't matter. It was all just . . . a mistake.

I reached in my pocket and retrieved my cell phone. My hands shook as I brought it up to eye level so I could dial Stephan. Just as I was about to push the buttons, however, the phone rang, startling me, and I dropped it.

The sound of the phone hitting the floor registered faintly as the blackness crept in. I knew I should fight it, and I tried, but it felt never-ending. The only thing I could hear was John's voice repeating over and over again that it was all just a mistake, an accident. None of it mattered. Not me. Not what Ian had done. Nothing.

Lying there, I heard the phone ringing, but I didn't move. The only thing keeping me from sinking into total darkness was Stephan. I wanted to be strong for him. It was just so hard.

There was a noise in the background, but I didn't know where it was coming from. I had no idea how long I'd been there. Minutes? Hours? Then a voice. *Stephan*. Was he here, or was I just imagining?

"Oh, Brianna," said the voice.

Arms lifted me up and cradled me.

Instinctively, I laid my head on his shoulder, breathing in the scent of him. Slowly, the blackness began to fade as I let his warmth sink into my bones. He was here. I had no idea how he knew I needed him, but I held on tight, clinging to the light in the sea of darkness that threatened to consume me.

He brushed his lips against my forehead repeatedly, until I was no longer holding on to his shirt as if I would fall off a ledge if I let go. "Can you tell me what happened, love?"

I shook my head. I couldn't talk about it. Not yet.

Instead of pressing, he wrapped his arms tighter around me. Closing my eyes, all the tension left, and peace took its place.

It was a long time before I was able to speak. I knew Stephan would want answers.

"Feeling better?" he asked.

"Yes."

"Who called you?"

I looked up at him. How did he know someone had called me?

"The phone was off the hook when I arrived." The question must have been clear on my face.

"John."

His chest vibrated beneath me, and an angry scowl formed on his face.

"I should have told you not to answer the phone today. I should've known he'd try to get around the restraining order in any way he could."

"He said . . ."

"Yes?"

"He said . . . he can't come within five hundred feet of me."

Stephan nodded.

"That's right. And if he does, Brianna, you need to let me know and I'll have him arrested. Even if you see him across the street or in a store, you need to say something. At five hundred feet, you shouldn't ever be able to see him. If you can, he's in violation of the restraining order."

"Okay."

"I have to ask you, sweetheart. What did he say that made you so upset? Ross called me saying he'd tried your cell several times and you wouldn't answer. After trying myself, and you still didn't pick up, I knew something was wrong. When I got home, you were curled up in a ball on your side, crying and rocking back and forth. I called your name, but you didn't answer."

"I thought you were a dream."

He smiled and kissed the tip of my nose. "Not a dream."

I smiled back, so glad he was here, and hugged him. "Thank you."

"Always," he whispered.

We were silent for a while, just holding each other.

"He said . . . he said it was a mistake. An . . . accident."

I felt Stephan's hands curl into fists at my back, and I cuddled closer.

"He's an idiot, Brianna. What happened was that he made a very bad decision, and you paid for it."

"I don't . . . I don't want to see him."

"And you don't have to. I'm also going to have the main phone routed to my office. Jamie can answer any calls. Lily and Ross have your cell. That way you don't have to worry about your father calling again like he did today."

I nodded, playing with the buttons on the front of his dress shirt. He hadn't bothered to take off his jacket, so I'd pushed the lapels out of my way. I wasn't sure what it was about buttoning and unbuttoning his shirt that was comforting to me, but it was and he didn't appear to mind.

"Tell me what else you did today," he prompted.

We sat and talked about what had transpired while he was at work up until the phone call from John, but eventually both of our stomachs began to growl. He kissed my forehead and told me to go change into a pair of my pajamas while he ordered pizza.

I did as he asked, but I was a little confused. Since we'd started having sex and I'd been sleeping in his bed, I hadn't worn pajamas at all. I hadn't worn anything. Did that mean I wouldn't be sleeping with him tonight?

When I walked back out into the main room, Stephan had moved the coffee table over to the side, and was laying a blanket out on the floor in front of the couch. "I'm going to go change. Can you get the plates and some drinks for us?"

"Yes, Sir."

He kissed me as he walked past toward his bedroom, leaving me even more perplexed than I'd been moments before. It didn't matter, though. I trusted him, so I went to the kitchen to do what he'd asked.

I'd just sat down when Stephan strolled back into the living room in a pair of sleep pants and a T-shirt. It was odd seeing him in pajamas. He normally slept naked, the same as me. Even before, when I'd slept on the floor in his room, he'd worn boxers. I'd never seen these before tonight.

He sat down beside me on the blanket. It was then I realized he had my journal in his hand.

When he noticed I'd caught sight of it, he handed it to me, along with a pen. "I want you to write about your day today. You can include as many details as you want, but I want you to concentrate on how those things made you feel. Start with this morning and work your way through. Don't skip anything."

I nodded as the phone rang. Our pizza was here, and he stood to go answer the phone and give the front desk permission to allow the deliveryman to come up to our floor.

The journal was heavy in my hands as I stared at it. It had been a few days since I'd written anything. Although Stephan had encouraged me to write in my journal, he'd not made it a rule.

Opening the front page, I read over some of the first words I'd written about Stephan. Back then, everything had seemed scary and confusing.

Now the things that frightened me were totally different.

Stephan returned to sit beside me, this time with a large pizza in his hands. I glanced over at him and then back to my journal.

"Eat first. Then you'll have time to write."

Laying down my journal beside me, I took the plate he offered and helped myself to some pizza.

Chapter 15

Brianna

We didn't talk much while we ate our pizza, but we rarely did during dinner. It was a little strange sitting on the floor, picnic fashion, in the middle of the living room, but I wasn't going to complain. The arrangement meant Stephan was almost constantly touching me in some way. At first, it was just our legs bumping each other as we moved. Then it was arms and hands and lips.

He offered me a slice of pizza but refused to give it to me. Instead, he insisted on breaking off a bite and feeding it to me. Once I'd taken the food from his fingers, he smiled and kissed the corner of my mouth. It was something silly, and it made me smile, too.

When we'd both had our fill, Stephan put the remaining pizza in the refrigerator and rejoined me on the blanket. To my surprise, he opened his legs and motioned for me to sit between them. The new position made me feel surrounded by him, even more so than I did when we were in his chair. It reminded me a little of when he held my wrists above my head and pressed against me. Knowing he was there, completely surrounding me, protecting me, made me feel safe. I knew he wouldn't let anything or anyone hurt me.

He picked up my journal from where I'd left it lying on the floor, and handed it to me. Brushing my hair out of the way, he placed a kiss on my shoulder. "Do you remember what I told you I want you to write in your journal?"

"Yes."

"Go ahead. I'm right here."

Taking a deep breath, I opened my journal.

Since he said not to skip anything, I started at the beginning.

I woke up this morning feeling warm. He . . .

I paused, feeling unsure.

"Don't worry about me being here, Brianna. Write how you normally do.

You can use my name."

Stephan had his arm wrapped around me, his hand on my breast. The sun was shining through the window, signaling the start of another day, but I didn't want to move. I wanted to stay there in bed with him.

He kissed me, and I felt even warmer. But after a couple of minutes, he left the bed to get ready for work. I could already feel the separation. I didn't want him to leave, even though I knew he had to. I never want him to leave me.

I glanced up at him. He was watching me, but I couldn't read the emotion in his face.

He smiled and then gave me a quick kiss. "No stopping now, sweetheart. Keep going."

I turned back to my journal.

We had breakfast, I made eggs and toast. Then he had to go. I stood just inside the door and watched him leave on the new monitor. When I saw him step into the elevator and disappear from the screen, I finally moved away, knowing I had almost ten hours before I would see him again.

I cleaned up the kitchen and loaded the dishes into the machine before going into the living room and picking up one of the books Lily had brought over for me. I like the book. Jake is funny. He is so out of his element in the city. The only women he's really been around were his mom, who was a rodeo rider, and a couple of local girls who'd also grown up on ranches. He's awkward and charming at the same time.

When he met Ronnie, she was everything all the other women he'd known weren't, and he liked that about her. It made me wonder about relationships in general.

"Go on," he said when I stopped writing.

I turned my head to the side and pressed my face against his chest. He smelled of soap and something else that was distinctly him. It comforted me and made me want to kiss him all at the same time.

He hugged me tighter to his chest. "Waiting isn't going to make it any easier. He isn't here. He can't hurt you. You don't have to write down everything that was said. I just want to know how it made you feel."

I nodded and turned back to my journal.

When the phone rang, I didn't want to put my book down, but I knew it could be Stephan so I answered it. As soon as I heard his voice, I knew it wasn't and I began to get nervous. All I wanted to do was hang up, not listen to him, but for some reason, I couldn't make myself do it.

Then he said . . .

The pen started shaking. Then I realized it wasn't the pen, it was me.

Stephan took hold of my free hand and squeezed. "Deep breaths, Brianna. You're doing great. Just a little more."

I felt like I couldn't breathe. Like walls were closing in on me and I couldn't get out. He dismissed what had happened to me like it didn't matter.

Like I didn't matter.

Stephan removed the journal from my hands, gathered me in his arms, and laid my head on his shoulder. "You matter, Brianna. You always matter. Don't ever think you don't."

I cried against his shoulder, soaking his shirt. He didn't say anything, only held me until the crying stopped.

"I got your shirt all wet."

He ignored my comment. "Are you feeling better?"

"Yes."

Stephan took my face in both his hands and kissed me. "I want you to do something for me."

I nodded. I'd do anything for him.

"I'm going to talk to Brad about teaching us some self-defense. We can add it to our workouts. I think it will help you with your confidence."

"You mean . . . learning to hit people?"

He chuckled.

"Kind of. But I was thinking more learning to get away from someone. I don't want you to ever feel helpless, Brianna."

"Okay."

"Good girl. Now, I think we've had enough for one day. Let's get our shower and crawl into bed. I have a feeling you might want to get back to that book you were reading, and I have some work to do."

After folding the blanket and putting it away, we took a quick shower before getting into bed. Neither of us wore any clothes, but it didn't feel strange. It felt natural. Normal.

Stephan leaned back against the headboard and placed his computer on his lap, while I opened my book to where I'd left off. I couldn't help but smile at how good it felt to be with him like this. Smiling, I began reading my book, getting lost once again in Jake and Ronnie's story, and really happy that Stephan was here beside me.

At eight thirty Wednesday morning, Stephan called on my cell phone to let me know that he'd talked to the phone company and the phones were now forwarded to his office during the day. He said I'd still be able to use the phone if I needed to, but no one would be able to call me. I released a sigh of relief knowing John wouldn't be able to call me again like he had the day before.

Lily called on her lunch break to ask if I wanted to go shopping with her the following week since Stephan had mentioned to her that we'd be going to a concert next Friday night. It took a little persuading on her part—I didn't like leaving the condo without Stephan—but she finally got me to agree.

I had to rush to make dinner. Before I knew it, it was almost four thirty, and I hadn't even begun to prep anything. I'd been too caught up in my book.

When the monitor flashed, letting me know someone was in the hall, I was still putting the finishing touches on dinner. Although I didn't think he'd get upset because things weren't ready yet, I wasn't sure, and I felt my anxiety level rise. The door opened. Stephan walked inside. I immediately stopped what I was doing and lowered my gaze to the floor.

The sound of his footsteps drawing closer brought with it both a sense of excitement and nervousness. I wanted to make him happy always. I never wanted to disappoint him.

He stood before me for only a moment before opening his arms. I stepped closer and hugged him.

Stephan tilted my head back and kissed me. "Dinner smells good."

"Thank you."

"How much longer till it's ready?" he asked, glancing at the pot on the stove.

I looked down, embarrassed.

"Fifteen minutes?"

He rubbed his thumbs over my cheekbones before tapping my chin to regain my attention. "Is something wrong, Brianna? Did something happen today while I was gone?"

I felt even worse. I'd let time get away from me, and now he thought something bad had happened.

"No. I just . . . I was reading and . . ." My face heated. "I lost track of time."

"Oh."

Stephan looked toward the couch where I liked to read and then back to me. To my surprise, he chuckled. "Must be a good book."

"You're not mad at me?" I knew my eyes must be wide with shock. Did he really not care his food wasn't ready when he arrived home?

"Of course not. I never told you dinner had to be done at a certain time. Why would I be upset that we have to wait fifteen minutes to start eating? It would be a longer wait if we went out."

"I don't know. I just thought . . ."

"Brianna, if you ever want to know how I feel, just ask. You know I won't lie to you. All right?"

"Okay."

"Good girl. Now, I'm going to go get out of this jacket and tie while you prepare dinner." He gave me one last kiss on the lips before going to his room. I turned back to the stove to finish cooking with a smile on my face.

Stephan

The new CFO was finally in his office, trying to wade through the mountain of paperwork that had built up over the last month. It was a blessing, especially since everyone who needed something from me seemed to be coming out of the woodwork. My office started to feel as if it had a revolving door.

Lily had stopped by twice needing my approval on items for the fall gala.

We'd both been extremely busy lately and hadn't spent much time together. The foundation's big fundraiser was only a little over three months away. Everything had to be finalized soon in order to make sure it would all arrive on time. With Logan having been away for the last week, I knew she was even more stressed as they'd not been able to play.

After Lily left my office for the second time, Gary, the marketing director, poked his head in to see if I had a minute to deal with some sort of mix-up in an ad campaign we'd launched six months ago. Thankfully it was an easy fix, but he was going to have to spend most of the afternoon on the phone with the ad agency we used to correct not only the ads currently running but also the ones that were scheduled to start next month. It wouldn't do us any good to run the ads if the website address was wrong.

The icing on the cake was a visit from Ross. He strolled in about two o'clock wanting to see me. Jamie, of course, told him I was very busy, but he insisted. In the end, it turned out to be a good thing.

I had Jamie hold all my calls while we talked. Ross was not my favorite person, but he was proving he would put Brianna's well-being first.

"John showed up at my place again last night."

"What did he want?"

"He said he was served with a restraining order. That was the start of it, anyway. Then he went on to say how he'd called and talked to Anna." Ross paused. "I guess I know why she didn't answer her phone when I called yesterday."

"I found her curled up in a ball on the couch, crying."

"But she's okay?"

"She is now. I've made arrangements to have the phone forwarded to my assistant during business hours, so if you want to reach Brianna, you're going to have to call her cell."

He nodded.

"Do you think he'll try to see her again?"

Ross didn't hesitate. "You can count on it. From what I saw last night, he was gearing up for an attack. I wouldn't put anything past him."

"If he comes near her, I'll have him arrested." I wanted to leave no doubt as to my intentions.

"I have an idea. I have no idea if it will work, but it might buy us a little time at least."

"I'm listening."

"Why don't I suggest to John that I talk to you . . . see if I can see Anna and talk to her? He trusts me. Maybe if I can assure him that she's really okay, he'll back off a little."

"It's worth a try."

"If we're going to make this look convincing, I'm going to need to come see her."

I nodded.

"Can you come for dinner Friday night?"

He frowned.

"Something wrong?"

"No. I'll just need to talk to Jade first. My girlfriend. We usually go out on Fridays."

I thought about it for a moment. "If she's willing, bring her along. Brianna needs to meet new people, and she's going to meet her at the concert anyway. This, at least, will be a safe environment for Brianna. If something goes wrong, it will be easier dealt with at home than out in public."

"Agreed." He looked around the room, spotting the picture of Brianna I had on my desk. "How is she doing?"

"You talk to her almost every day."

"I know that, but talking to her and seeing her are two different things."

Standing, I walked over to the window. It was crazy how much I missed her when she wasn't right there in front of me.

"She's doing better every day."

"I want to help her, you know."

I turned around, leaning on the window's ledge. "If I didn't believe that, you wouldn't be coming over to my home for dinner Friday."

He laughed.

"At least you're honest."

I walked back to the chair behind my desk and sat down again. Leaning forward to rest my elbows on the desk, I appraised Ross. Taking a chance, I filled him in on what was happening with Ian Pierce.

"I haven't had the opportunity to go through the files yet, but I'm hoping to find something—anything—that will put Peirce behind bars."

"What do you think the chances are of that happening?"

I shook my head. "I don't know, but there has to be something. Brianna didn't suffer through all that for ten months to have that bastard get away scot-free."

After Ross left, I finally had a few minutes to myself and took the time to open the envelope Oscar had sent over for me to look through. The stack was almost two inches thick. Going through everything would take a while, unfortunately. Oscar still had people sifting through everything, but an extra set of eyes wouldn't hurt, especially since we really didn't know what we were looking for.

I ended up spending the last hour of my day looking through the stack of spreadsheets detailing Pierce's bank account. There were large sums of money everywhere, both coming in and going out. By the time five o'clock rolled around, I was starting to see double.

After placing the seemingly endless amount of papers back into the manila envelope, I tucked them under some other paperwork on my desk and turned off my computer. I'd considered putting the papers in my safe or taking them home with me, but I wasn't worried about someone seeing them. All the account numbers had been blacked out. Plus, other than the cleaning lady, no one but Jamie came into my office while I wasn't there, and I wasn't overly concerned with either of them. Both had worked for me since I'd taken over the foundation.

I paused outside the door of my condo and wondered how and where I'd find Brianna. She always seemed to keep me on my toes one way or another. Would she be in the kitchen cooking? The living room, reading? Or would I find her kneeling, waiting for me?

Opening the door, I was hit with the scent of spices coming from the kitchen. Glancing over in that direction, I was disappointed when I didn't see her. She wasn't in the living room either.

"Brianna?"

I heard a noise coming from my bedroom, and then a handful of seconds later, Brianna appeared in the doorway. She looked . . . unsettled, guilty. It made no sense.

Taking a step toward her, I saw her tense. What in the world was going on?

Ignoring her discomfort for the moment since she didn't look hurt in any way, I removed my jacket as I walked across the room and threw it, along with my tie, over the back of the couch. By the time I stood in front of her, she was looking down, her shoulders hunched over, and she was wringing her hands. I had to admit, I was curious as to what had brought out such a reaction in her.

I pressed one finger under her chin and tilted it up so I could see her face. Her cheeks reddened under my scrutiny. I considered asking her to explain but thought of a better idea. Since she'd come from my bedroom, I was willing to bet that whatever was causing this was in there.

Releasing her chin, I reached for her hand and marched us both into my bedroom. She resisted for only a moment before reluctantly following. I had to stifle a laugh. I had no idea what she'd done, but I doubted it could be that bad. Brianna was such a good girl. She was always trying to please.

Once we were inside my bedroom, it didn't take me long to realize what had her feeling so guilty. The bottom drawer of my nightstand was lying on the floor, all its contents spilled out haphazardly on the carpet. From where I stood, I could see the ropes I'd used on Brianna's father along with several other toys I kept in there.

Glancing over at Brianna, she'd not moved much. She still looked as though she'd stolen a cookie from the cookie jar. I had to keep myself from laughing. She was too cute. Did she really think I'd be upset with her discovering my toys? Obviously she did.

"Do you mind telling me what happened here?" I asked, keeping the amusement out of my voice.

"I . . . I didn't mean to, Sir. I was cleaning, and . . . my shoestring got caught on the knob. The drawer opened and . . . before I knew it, the whole drawer had fallen out . . . and everything, and . . ." She paused for a long time. I wasn't sure she was going to finish her sentence at first. "I . . . was curious."

I released her hand and walked over to kneel beside the drawer and its contents. One by one, I picked them up and replaced them in the drawer with the exception of three items. With the drawer back in place, I went to the bed to sit down, patting the mattress beside me. Again, I had to suppress a chuckle as she literally dragged her feet.

"Give me your hand," I instructed once she'd sat down.

She held out her hand and closed her eyes. I wondered if she thought I would smack her hand or something. Instead, I ran the feather over her knuckles. She opened her eyes and glanced up at me. The look on her face was no longer that of apprehension, but of shock.

I saw her other hand twitch as I continued to move the feather back and forth lightly over her hand. "What does it feel like, Brianna?"

"It tickles, Sir."

I smiled and removed the feather.

I picked up the bamboo skewer and followed a similar path along her knuckles and the back of her hand.

"And this?"

"Sharp. Like a knife."

"Does it hurt?"

She shook her head. "No."

I removed the bamboo and reached for the last item. This time, I turned her hand over so I could reach the underside of her wrist. "Do you know what this is?"

"I think so."

Turning it on, I held it a couple of inches from her skin. "This is a bullet vibrator."

The gentle vibrations pulsed through my fingers as I placed it against her wrist. She held very still.

"This is the low setting."

I let her get used to it on low before I turned it up. When I finally had it on high, I ran it up the length of her arm to her elbow. "How does that feel?"

"Strange. But . . . good."

"Good," I said, smiling.

I turned the vibrator off and laid it on top of the nightstand along with the other two items before turning back to face her.

"First, is there anything in the kitchen that needs your attention?"

"No. The lasagna's done."

"Do you need to take it out of the oven?"

She shook her head.

"Good. Now tell me why you were looking so guilty when I came home. Did you really think I'd be upset you'd been in my toy drawer?"

"You didn't say I could get into your drawer, Sir."

"You're not answering the question, Brianna. Did you think I'd get upset with you?"

"Maybe? I wasn't sure."

"I see."

I thought I'd made myself perfectly clear weeks ago that Brianna was able to go anywhere in the house. The only exception to that had been the playroom, which I kept locked. I was hoping to show it to her one day, but as with many other things, I didn't think she was ready yet.

"Unless I tell you otherwise, Brianna, you are able to look at, touch, and use anything in this house. If you're curious about something, all you have to do is ask. Okay?"

"Okay."

There was a long pause.

"Have you used all those things?"

I knew she was asking not only about the three things I'd used on her but the other items in the drawer, which included nipple clamps, a flogger, several vibrators and dildos, and a paddle, along with the ropes I'd used on her father. "Yes."

She shivered, and I could see the fear in her eyes.

"What about the things you saw frightens you?"

"Will you put those things inside me?"

"Eventually."

Her body jerked.

"Do you trust me?"

Brianna looked up at me. "Yes."

I pulled her into my arms and held her.

"I do . . . trust you. I do."

"Just remember that, sweetheart. I would never do anything you didn't want me to do, but I can also show you things, make you feel things, you've never experienced before." I tilted her head up so I could kiss her lips. "Remember how you like kneeling before me? How you like it when I pull your hair? Did you like those things before?"

"No."

I kissed her again. "See? Everything is different now, which is why you have to trust me."

The guilty expression returned.

"Hey. None of that now. I know this is hard for you, Brianna. I don't expect it to be easy. Just remember you always have your numbers and your safewords. You can always stop anything we do together at any time."

She nodded.

"Now. I do believe you mentioned something about lasagna?"

Brianna giggled. "Yes."

"Wonderful," I said, patting her leg. "I'm starved."

Chapter 16

Stephan
Dinner was delicious as always. By the time we finished eating, I was stuffed. I seemed to do that all too often with her cooking.

After helping her clean up, I took a seat in my chair and pulled her down with me to sit on my lap. Sometimes I think this little ritual of ours had become as important to me as it had for her. It was a time for me to decompress and to reconnect with her after being gone all day. Being the president of The Coleman Foundation was a lot of work and even more pressure.

That first year out of college, I'd had to prove myself, show that it wasn't just my name on the letterhead but that I could contribute to the cause my parents had begun. I didn't date anyone seriously for that entire year. Only for the sake of needing to forget about work for a while had I gone to a few local private lifestyle parties. It was there I'd met Lily, so I couldn't regret the decision, although it made me realize the mountain I had ahead of me.

If recognition didn't occur the moment I introduced myself, it came quickly thereafter. The Coleman heir stepping into his role as president of The Coleman Foundation had been front-page news. One of the reasons I'd been attracted to Lily was that she didn't seem affected by who I was.

When women, and some men, at those parties had looked at me, I'd been able to tell they were seeing dollar signs. It had been more about what I could potentially give them financially if they were my submissive than what they were looking for in a relationship. That was why, after playing with Lily and deciding we were better off as friends, I'd decided to stay out of the dating scene for a while. I'd had enough on my plate at the time without having to worry about a woman looking to become a trophy wife.

In the end, I'd achieved my goal and earned the respect of my colleagues. I would do it again in a heartbeat.

Glancing down at Brianna where she lay with her head on my shoulder, I was reminded again of how different she was from the other women I'd met. It had nothing to do with what she'd been through and everything to do with who she was. I'd thought Tami had been different. When I'd first met her, she hadn't acted as if my wealth mattered to her. In the end, however, she began to show her true desires. She wanted to move in with me, have me put a ring on her finger, and a limitless credit card in her hand.

Brianna didn't care about any of those things. She wasn't fake. She didn't pretend. I could be myself with her, even if sometimes I had to keep in mind how fragile she was.

When we talked about my day, she was genuinely interested. If I told her about a family struggling, there were tears in her eyes—her heart went out to them. She cared about people, even though being around them scared her.

Closing my eyes, I relaxed and enjoyed the feel of her in my arms. She accepted me for me, not because of who I was. To me, that was invaluable.

"Sir?"

"Yes, Brianna?"

"Is everything . . . okay?"

I kissed the top of her head and rested my cheek against her hair. "Yes, sweetheart. Everything's fine. How about you? Tell me about your day."

"I finished my book." She reached for the buttons on my shirt and began playing with them.

"Did you like it?"

She nodded.

"Ronnie was funny. Jake kept trying to get her to go out with him, and she'd mouth off to him and put him in his place." She laughed. "She was mouthing off to him this one time and he backed her into a wall and kissed her."

I knew the book she was reading was a romance novel, so I had to assume the kiss was well received. "And what did she do when he kissed her?"

"She didn't like it at first. Well, she acted like she didn't. She kept trying to push him away."

"And then what?"

"She started kissing him back." She grew quiet. "They ended up having sex up against the wall."

Brianna whispered the last part as if she were telling some sort of naughty secret. I smiled.

"So do you think you'll read any more of the books Lily brought you?"

"Yes," she said, nodding her head enthusiastically.

I had to keep from laughing out loud. Sometimes, I had to wonder how she remained so seemingly innocent despite what she'd been through. My only guess was that it had to do with the detached state she zoned into sometimes. It was as if her body was there, but her mind wasn't. So, even though she was technically experiencing things, it wasn't the same as it would have been for someone else.

"Did you do anything else today besides read and explore my toy drawer?"

"I really didn't mean—"

"You can open that drawer whenever you want. I want to explore things with you . . . including toys. You need to be comfortable with them, and maybe holding them, feeling them in your hands, will help. I don't like the fact that inanimate objects frighten you."

"I don't want to be frightened," she whispered.

"It'll get better. We'll work on it together."

She cuddled closer.

"I spoke to Ross today." She tensed as I spoke. "I invited him and his girlfriend over for dinner Friday night."

Brianna sat up, her eyes wide with shock.

I laughed.

"Do you not want to see Ross?"

"Yes. I just thought . . . I thought you didn't like him."

Twining our fingers together, I brought our linked hands up to my mouth. "I can put up with him for your sake."

"Thank you, Sir." She smiled and leaned in to give me an awkward hug.

I released her hand and returned the gesture. "I'd do anything to make you happy, Brianna. Anything."

For the next hour, I held her. We talked here and there but about nothing particular.

When I couldn't put it off any longer, I told her to go get her journal. I went to the closet to get the blanket I'd had out the previous night for the floor, and tried to wipe any apprehension off my face. This wasn't something I was looking forward to, but it needed to be done. What had happened Sunday could have disastrous affects if it took place in a more public setting.

She walked back into the living room, clutching her journal and with her head bowed. I let her wait until I'd finished fixing the blanket. "Come."

We settled into our spots on the blanket with her sitting between my legs. I liked this position because it allowed me to both read over her shoulder and provide her comfort at the same time. Yes, I could have accomplished those two things in both my chair and in bed, but I didn't want either of those places tainted with any negatives. The chair and my bed were positive places for her. I wanted to keep them that way.

"Tonight I want us to start working on what happened Sunday morning." She stiffened, and I leaned down to brush my lips along her shoulder. "I want you to write in your journal the words you can remember the men using."

"Please . . ."

I turned her chin so that I could look at her. "They are only words, Brianna. Just words. They can't hurt you, just like those men can't hurt you anymore. You are safe here with me. Just. Words."

She pressed her lips together but didn't respond.

That fearful look in her eyes was back. I wished I could make it go away, but this was something we had to deal with.

Releasing her chin, I nodded toward her journal and waited for her to open it.

Slowly, she picked up her pen and opened to a fresh page. I could almost feel her giving herself a pep talk as she inched the writing utensil closer.

Then it was as if something clicked inside her, and she started to write. The words were written quickly, and I could barely make some of them out.

Whore.
Bitch.
Cunt.
Fuckhole.
Cumdump.
Slut.

The pen stopped moving and hovered over the paper before dropping from her hand, bouncing off my leg, and hitting the floor.

I reached out to touch her, and she flinched. It was subtle, but I noticed. Brianna hadn't pulled away from me since those first few weeks.

"Brianna."

Nothing.

"Brianna," I said with more force.

She jumped.

"Turn around and look at me."

When she did, I felt a sharp pain stab in my chest. The wonderful, strong woman I'd come to know these last two months wasn't there. Her face was devoid of emotion. Her eyes were distant and unfocused. The sight made me want to cry and hit something at the same time. Preferably Ian's face.

"Brianna, can you tell me what number?"

Still nothing.

Sighing, I removed the journal from her hands and stood. Picking her up, I situated us both back in my chair and wrapped my arms around her. She'd come out of it . . . eventually.

Brianna

I could feel movement under me, but it took me a while to realize it was someone breathing. Someone was holding me. It was as if I were underwater. I could hear things, but they all seemed muffled and far away. If someone was holding me, though, I couldn't be underwater, right?

Gradually the sounds became voices. A television.

There were arms around me, holding me against a chest. I breathed deep, and a familiar scent filled my nostrils. Stephan.

I opened my eyes to find him staring down at me.

"Welcome back."

His voice was calm, but I could see the worry in his eyes. I knew something must have happened to put it there.

"Hi."

"How are you feeling?"

I thought about it for a few moments. "A little tired, and . . ." Glancing down at my hand, I realized it didn't feel quite right. "My hand . . . aches?" He nodded.

"You were gripping your pen rather hard, and you've had your hand in a fist for the last forty-five minutes. I'm not surprised it's bothering you."

Stephan took my hand in both of his and massaged each finger until the ache began to subside. I relaxed into him, enjoying the sensation as the blood flow returned to my hand.

He kissed my palm before releasing it. "Better?"

"Yes. Thank you."

"Do you remember what happened?"

Thinking back, I told him what I could remember. "We were sitting on the floor. I was writing in my journal. And . . ."

"And?"

My memory returned. "I could hear the voices again."

"Brianna, look at me."

It took effort, but I pulled myself out of my thoughts to do as he told me.

"You are here with me, remember? Those voices? Those men? They're not here."

I nodded.

He sighed.

"Maybe we should get some rest and talk about this more tomorrow."

"No!"

I don't know why, but the thought of stopping whatever this was now frightened me. It was only after my initial reaction registered, however, that I realized I was not only holding Stephan's shirt in a death grip but that he was looking down at me, eyes wide, as if I'd grown two heads.

Thinking back on what I'd said, I started to feel the weight of what I'd just done. Not only had I said no, I'd also yelled at him. I'd yelled at Stephan.

Bowing my head, I placed my hands in my lap and waited.

Nothing happened for a very long time, and I began to get anxious. I'd never said no to him before, and I had no idea how he'd react. Stephan was completely different from Ian.

"Stand up." He didn't sound angry, but his voice wasn't soft and comforting as it had been earlier.

I scrambled to comply.

"Come with me."

Following as ordered, I trailed behind him into his bedroom. We didn't stop there, however. He kept walking until we were both standing in the large walk-in closet. I'd been in there a few times since I'd begun sleeping in his room, even though my clothes were still in my bedroom. It was about half the size of his bedroom, and one side was full of suits, ties, and shoes.

He bypassed everything, though, and went straight to the full-length mirror on the back wall. Not sure what he wanted me to do, I remained a couple of feet behind him.

He turned, a determined look on his face. "Stand here in front of me, facing the mirror." He pointed to a spot on the carpet.

I moved to where I was told. The last thing I wanted to do was upset him. I'd done wrong. I would have to face the consequences.

"Look in the mirror. Look at yourself. What do you see?"

"Me?"

"What about you?"

Unsure what he wanted, I listed the obvious. "Brown hair. Blue eyes. I'm wearing your collar. A dark green shirt. Jeans . . ." I stopped because I had no idea what else he wanted me to say. That was it. That was all I saw. There was nothing else.

"Remove your clothes."

I stared back at him in the mirror. The serious expression never faded.

Reaching for the hem of my shirt, I lifted it over my head, and let it drop to the floor. Quickly, I removed the rest of what I was wearing until I was completely naked.

Stephan picked up my discarded clothes and placed them on top of the large dresser in the center of the room. When he returned to stand behind me, he placed his hands on my shoulders and met my gaze in the mirror. "Now tell me what you see."

I looked. This time I saw all of my body's imperfections. The burn rings around my nipples. The marks on the inside of my thighs. I could even see the faint scar just above my knee where someone had taken a knife and cut me.

One by one, I relayed these things to him. With every word, I felt as if something were pressing down on my shoulders, although Stephan had removed his hands before I'd even started talking. I didn't like looking at myself in the mirror. My scars were permanent reminders of what had happened to me. Permanent reminders that I would never be normal.

"So you don't see a slut? A whore? A fuckhole? A bitch? A cumdump? A cunt?" I jerked as he said each word.

Closing my eyes, I began to cry.

"Open your eyes and look at yourself, Brianna."

I didn't want to. I didn't.

He took my chin in his hand, holding my head still. "Open your eyes. Now."

I did what he said, but I couldn't see anything through my tears.

Stephan didn't release my face as he lowered his mouth to whisper in my ear. "You are a beautiful woman, Brianna, on the inside and out. You are not any of those things. You are not a *thing* at all. You are a person. A person who deserves everything she wants out of life. Can you see that?"

I shook my head.

He sighed and took a step back. I could tell he was disappointed in me, but I didn't know how to fix it.

We took our shower and climbed into his bed. Unfortunately, he didn't try to have sex with me. He touched me like he always did, but I wanted to feel him surrounding me. I wanted him to make me stop thinking. The fact that he didn't made me wonder if I'd done something else wrong.

"What are you thinking, sweetheart?" He must have realized I wasn't actually reading the book I had in my hands.

"Did I do something wrong, Sir?"

Stephan brushed the hair away from my face and tilted my head up so I was looking at him. "No. Why would you think you have?"

"It's just . . . earlier . . . you seemed so disappointed in me. And then . . . you haven't . . . you haven't wanted to have sex . . . ."

"Brianna, I'm not disappointed in you exactly. I'm frustrated with the situation. More than anything, I want you to see how truly wonderful you are. It makes me angry to know not only what those men did to you physically but mentally as well. I want to help you fix it, but I'm just not sure I can—at least not quickly."

I didn't like the way he was talking, like he wasn't helping me. "You do help me. So much. I just . . ." Glancing down, I considered how best to word what I wanted to say. "I keep hearing them. In my head. It's not that I want to hear them. I can't help it," I cried.

"Shh." He pulled me into his arms and held me tight. "I know you're trying, Brianna. I do."

Finally, my tears dried, but I still wasn't willing to let him go. If I had my way, I would stay in his arms forever and never have to deal with the outside world again. I knew it wasn't ever going to happen, but I would take what I could get.

"Brianna?"

"Yes?"

"Why do you think I don't want to have sex with you? It couldn't be further from the truth."

"Then why haven't you?"

His chest vibrated beneath me with his laughter. "You've had a rough couple of nights emotionally, sweetheart. I was giving you time to adjust."

"Okay." I knew I didn't sound convincing, but it was the best I could do.

Then, before I knew what was happening, I was lying flat on my back and Stephan was hovering over me. He dragged my arms over my head and held them down with one hand as he reached between us with the other. The feeling of being surrounded by him permeated my bones, and all the stress and anxiety of the day faded away. For the first time in the last few hours, I could breathe.

Chapter 17

Stephan

I hadn't expected the night to turn out the way it had. I had thought I was protecting Brianna by not initiating sex the last two nights, but instead I'd made her feel insecure. That wasn't what I'd wanted at all. Quite the opposite, in fact.

Last night, I'd realized she was even stronger than what I'd understood her to be, yet she needed something from me. Brianna was submissive, at least to me. She trusted that I would take care of her, and there was nothing that said that more than the way her body became relaxed and pliant beneath me when I dominated her sexually.

She came twice—once with my fingers, once with my mouth—before I'd taken her. The instant connection I felt to her once we'd come together was hard to describe. It got better every time.

Her sleep had been interrupted only once during the night, which wasn't bad considering. She'd woken up screaming, not knowing where she was, just after two in the morning. Once I'd got her to calm down, I'd held her until she'd fallen back to sleep.

She was smiling as she served me breakfast, all signs of her distress gone. It was always difficult to leave her, but I also knew she would be waiting for me when I came home. The thought of her not being there one day was inconceivable to me, and I hoped it never happened. Until then, however, I would be there for her in whatever capacity she needed me to be, and at the moment, that included protecting her from her father.

To be safe, I stopped by the front desk to check in with Tom before going to my car. He was just getting in for the day.

"Hello, Mr. Coleman. How are you this morning?"

"I'm good, Tom. And you?"

"Can't complain. How is Miss Reeves?"

"She's doing well. I wanted to see if you'd heard or seen anything of Jonathan Reeves since the restraining order was issued."

"No. Nothing in the last three days."

"Good. I hope it stays that way."

"If I see him, sir, I'll call you."

"You're a good man, Tom. Thank you."

"No thanks needed, Mr. Coleman."

My morning at work went quickly. The pile on my desk didn't appear to be going away anytime soon, but at least I was making progress.

At eleven forty-five, I let Jamie know I was going out and headed to the local restaurant where Logan and I were meeting for lunch. It was almost exactly half the distance between my office and his, so it was perfect for these midday meetings. Plus, it was a little hole-in-the-wall place that was busier for dinner than lunch, which would mean more privacy for our conversation.

When I arrived, Logan was already seated at a small table in the back. I took a seat across from him. Before either of us was able to say anything, our server appeared to get my drink order.

"I think she may be new," Logan said, the minute our server left. "She was here within seconds of me sitting down as well."

"Nothing wrong with being prompt." He smiled, knowing how anal I could be sometimes about people being on time. I didn't have many pet peeves, but tardiness was one of them. "How was your trip?"

"New York is the same as always. It would have been nicer if Lily had been able to come with me."

"I'm sure. Unfortunately, she's up to her eyeballs in last-minute details for the fall fundraiser. October will be here before we know it."

"I know. I arrived home Saturday night to find our dining room table had disappeared. She'd covered it with fabric samples, different types and colors of paper, ribbons, sketches . . . I know there was a method to her madness, but I couldn't find it."

I laughed. "Sounds like her desk. I was down there last week and almost didn't find my way out."

He smiled. "You seem happy. Things must be going well with Brianna."

I didn't get to answer him before our server came back to the table with my water. We both placed our orders, and I waited until she'd disappeared again behind the partition.

"She's still having some issues, but I'm not sure those will ever completely go away. Our relationship, however, has improved, yes. That's what I wanted to talk to you about."

"Shoot."

"I'd like to have Brianna watch you and Lily in a scene." Logan nearly spit out his water, but I ignored him and continued. "Nothing overly complicated, of course. I was thinking some simple bondage. Spanking. That kind of thing."

"You don't think seeing us like that will freak her out?"

Feeling the need to be honest, I answered in the only way I could. "I truly don't know. She's asked about my ropes. She saw me use them on her father. I've also given her a swat on the ass here and there."

"There's a big difference between a swat and a spanking, Stephan, and you know it."

"Yes, I do, which is why I think it would be good for her to see a spanking involving a couple she knows, who are in a consensual, loving relationship. Brianna's seen and experienced so much negative. I'm only beginning to scratch the surface in getting her to realize that much of what she's experienced as negative can be positive when done the right way and with the right person."

"And you think her seeing Lily submit to me would do that?"

"I think it could help, yes."

Logan took several drinks of his soda before responding. "When did you want to do this?"

"Next weekend. I'd say this weekend, but we have some things to deal with that can't be put off."

"Okay."

"You'll do it?"

"I need to talk to Lily first, but I don't see a problem, no. We've played together at parties, so she's not opposed to people watching. My only concern is *her* concern for Brianna's mental well-being. If we're in a scene, I need to know she will be focused on me, not Brianna."

"I understand. I'd feel the same way."

We spent the next half hour catching up on our lives over lunch. Logan was rarely home anymore for longer than a week or two at a time. When he was home, he was catching up on things at the hospital and spending time with Lily. It didn't leave much room for anything else. Even now, he was planning to go on a quick trip to Chicago next week. Luckily, he'd only be gone until Thursday, and he wasn't leaving again for at least another week.

Stepping off the elevator back at the office, I noticed the new CFO waiting with the finance manager outside my office. Neither looked very happy, so I was hoping they didn't have bad news.

"Hello, Michael. Sheila."

"Sorry to catch you just coming back from lunch, but we needed to talk to you."

"Sure. Let's go in my office." I motioned for them to go ahead inside while I instructed Jamie to please hold my calls.

Sheila appeared rather nervous when I entered my office. Michael's expression was more confused. I took a seat behind my desk and waited for one of them to start.

"We were going over some of the numbers for the second quarter. Specifically the ones allocated to the fall fundraiser." Michael handed the papers to me. "The highlighted parts are what I'm most concerned about. We're going to go over the numbers again, but there's money that can't be accounted for."

I looked over the figures in front of me. It wouldn't be obvious unless one compared the pages carefully. "Have you double-checked the first quarter reports?"

He nodded. "So far we haven't found anything, but we're still looking."

"I'm sorry, Mr. Coleman. I should have caught this before. All the reports had to cross my desk before they came upstairs."

"I'm sure you didn't do it on purpose, Sheila. Do you think you'll be able to track down the source?"

"Given enough time, yes. I'll need to work with the IT department and see if we can figure out whose computer made the changes."

"Do what you need to do. If it was Karl Walker, then we'll pass the information along to legal and let them deal with him. But if not, we need to find out who and if they are still working here."

"Agreed."

"Do you mind if I keep this?" I asked. "I'd like to look over it a little more. I can bring it by your office before I leave."

"Of course."

I spent the rest of my day reading over the report. The more I went over the numbers, the more I was convinced it was Walker. All the withdrawals coincided with those Lily made but in roughly half the amounts. It's no wonder Sheila hadn't noticed them. Anyone would think they were payments for supplies. The only thing that signaled that wasn't the case was the account number the money was charged to. It was a single digit off the one Lily used.

A knock on my door caused me to look up. It was Jamie. "Sorry, Sir. I thought you'd like to know it's almost five."

Glancing over at my computer, I realized she was right. I thanked my assistant, laid the report aside for a moment, and checked my e-mail. Unfortunately, there were a handful that needed my attention before I could leave. Once they were taken care of, I shut everything down, slipped my jacket on, and grabbed the report from my desk.

By the time I made it to Michael's office, he was already gone. Laying the report directly in front of his chair, I left. After the day I'd had, I couldn't wait to get home to Brianna.

Brianna
While Stephan was at work, I spent some more time exploring his toy drawer. The rope was soft as I wound it around my hand. I remembered how Stephan secured it at my father's wrists and wondered if he'd do the same thing to me.

There was a man at a party Ian had taken me and Alex to who had tied intricate knots all over this woman's body, and then he'd used even more rope to hoist her up into the air. I hadn't gotten to see what happened after that. Ian hadn't been happy I was watching and forced me to spend the rest of the party with my head on the floor under his boot. I refused to think about what had happened later.

A chill ran though me as I pushed the memory aside and glanced up at the ceiling to see if there were any signs of hooks where ropes could be attached. There was nothing.

Moving on, I picked up what to me was the scariest thing in his drawer. It was shaped like a penis. I held it in my hand, trying to remember what Stephan told me. It was just a thing.

As I touched it, I realized it didn't feel all that much like a real penis. I knew male parts came in all shapes and sizes, but this was harder, stiffer. There was no give to it. When I touched Stephan, I could feel him pulse in my hand. This . . . thing . . . was lifeless.

After spending over an hour looking at his toys, I wasn't as scared as I had been. I still wasn't sure about his using them on me, but he was right—they were just things.

I was a little nervous what would happen after dinner. For the last two nights, Stephan had made me write in my journal about very unpleasant things. Last night, I'd had a nightmare about a time I'd been with two of the men Ian had loaned me out to. I'd been chained to a bench, unable to move. The two men took turns ramming their penises down my throat while spitting on me and calling me names. I was a thing to them. Just a thing.

When I'd woken up screaming, I'd thought I was there, tied to that bench. It was only Stephan's soothing words that brought me back to the present and calmed me. He always made everything better.

I was setting the table when Stephan walked through the door. He looked like he'd had a rough day, and as soon as he saw me across the room, he hurried toward me. Before I knew it, we were kissing, and I almost burnt dinner.

To my surprise, Brad showed up at seven. He usually came only on Monday, Wednesday, and Friday, so I was shocked to see him. He was there to show us some self-defense moves. Stephan had mentioned it, but I hadn't expected things to happen so soon.

Stephan and I changed into workout clothes and then headed upstairs to the gym.

"We'll start with something simple. Stand facing each other."

We did as instructed, and Brad came behind each of us and adjusted our positions slightly.

"Now, Stephan, grab hold of her wrist as if you are going to try and drag her away."

Even though I knew it was coming, I gasped when Stephan wrapped his hand around my wrist. There was a combination of uncertainty mixed with excitement. The memory from the night before of his hand holding my arms down as he'd thrust into me had me thinking of things that had nothing at all to do with self-defense.

"Anna?"

When I glanced over at Brad, he was looking at me with a knowing smirk on his face. I blushed.

He chuckled and shook his head.

"I want you to twist your wrist, like this." He demonstrated using his own hands.

I tried what he said, but nothing much happened.

"Good. Now put your whole body into it. Watch me."

Again, he showed me what he wanted, although the person holding his wrist was purely imaginary.

It went on like this for a good twenty minutes before he was satisfied I'd gotten it. Even then, I'd only been able to free my wrist twice.

"You'll get it, Anna. It just takes some time and practice. Plus, if you ever have to use it, your assailant won't have the advantage of knowing it's coming."

I nodded but didn't say anything. Stephan hadn't taken his eyes off me the entire time, and it was beginning to make me think I wasn't doing what I was supposed to do.

"One more thing, then we'll call it a night. Stephan, wrap your arms around her waist from behind."

Stephan pulled me tight against him. I could feel every inch of him. Closing my eyes, I relaxed. If I fell, he would catch me.

For the next half hour, Brad tried to show me how to run the side of my foot down the front of Stephan's leg and stomp on his foot. I couldn't do it, though. No matter how many assurances both of them gave me, I couldn't hurt Stephan. I couldn't.

Stephan finally called an end to it, and I breathed a sigh of relief. "Go wait for me in the bathroom. I'm going to see Brad out."

I hurried into his bathroom and removed my clothes.

Not sure what to do with myself while I waited, I sat down on the bench. I knew he must have wanted to talk to Brad alone, or he wouldn't have sent me in here.

The sound of running water made me look up. Stephan stood beside the large tub completely naked. He was leaning over, testing the temperature of the water. "I thought we'd try something a little different tonight."

"Okay."

"When was the last time you had a bath, Brianna?" he asked, walking to stand in front of me.

He offered his hand. I took it and stood.

"Not since I was with my mom."

"None when you were older? A teenager?"

"No."

Stephan glanced down, heat in his eyes. Warmth pooled between my thighs.

He ran his hand from my neck, down between my breasts, over my stomach, and then down between my legs. I jerked at the contact. Stephan smiled.

Lowering his mouth to mine, he rubbed his hand back and forth between my folds. He used his other hand to massage my breast. Every now and then, he'd take my nipple between his fingers and pull, causing almost an electric shock directly beneath where his other hand was rubbing. I held on to his arms, trying not to lose my balance. His hands felt so good. They always did. It was easy to forget everything else when he touched me like this.

"Mmm. I think our bath is ready," he whispered against my lips. I swayed from the loss of contact as he stepped back, but he steadied me.

The warm water engulfed us as we lowered ourselves into the bath. He sat behind me, much as he had on the floor the previous two nights. A shiver ran through me.

"Are you cold?"

"No."

He kissed my shoulder and then leaned back. "Place your hands behind my neck and lace your fingers together." I did what he asked. "Good girl. Keep them there."

I took a deep breath and nodded.

The position caused my breasts to jut out, and Stephan placed his hands on top of both of them. He began kneading and pulling on them. At first, it was gentle, but soon there wasn't anything soft about it. The strange thing was it felt good.

"Your tits are absolute perfection, Brianna."

He took hold of both of my nipples, pinching and pulling at the same time. I arched my back, not sure if I wanted more or if I wanted him to stop. Pressure built between my legs. How was this happening?

"That's it. You like that, don't you?" All I could concentrate on was the feel of his hands and fingers as they continued to tug and push and pinch. "Answer me."

Just the sound of his voice, firm and sure in my ear, sent a tingle down my spine and to the spot between my legs. "Yes."

"Such a good girl you are."

Suddenly his hands were gone. I opened my eyes. Where did his hands go?

His entire body vibrated beneath me as he chuckled at my reaction. He kissed my cheek. "No worries, sweetheart. I'm not nearly done with you. Lift your legs and put them on either side of mine."

Moving first one leg and then the other, I positioned them as he'd instructed, with a little help from him since I didn't have the use of my arms. My legs were spread wide, pinned to the sides of the large tub by his legs, and I could feel his erection pressed up against my backside.

"You are to stay in this position until I tell you otherwise."

I nodded.

He went back to playing with my breasts. I closed my eyes and leaned my head back against his shoulder.

Just when the buildup began again, he released my breasts. This time, however, his right hand snaked down my stomach and between my legs. He ran his fingers up and down several times before thrusting two fingers inside. "We are going to have to explore some more breast play, Brianna, if this is how wet you get when I play with them."

He continued to move his fingers in and out of me. My breasts ached, wanting to be touched again, but at the same time I didn't want him to stop what he was doing.

Then I felt something between my legs that wasn't him. I opened my eyes again and looked down.

"Keep your hands where they are, Brianna."

His voice startled me a little, but I tightened my grip around his neck and tried to breathe. What was he doing? What was that thing?

It began buzzing, and I realized it was a vibrator. I shook my head. No. I didn't want that. I didn't . . .

"Stop. It doesn't go inside you. It's only going to sit on either side of your clit and vibrate. It will feel good. I promise."

I didn't know. I just . . .

Closing my eyes, I answered. "Okay."

"Open your eyes and look at me."

I did, and he placed the vibrator back where it had been. It seemed to have two little arms.

The sensation was strange at first, but eventually, once I began to relax again, I realized just how good it felt. The vibrations increased the building pressure, as did his fingers as they continued to work their magic from the inside.

Somewhere along the line, I'd allowed my head to fall back against his shoulder again. The sensations were too much. Before long, I was climbing higher and higher toward climax. I was so close.

Stephan kissed my neck and added a third finger inside me. "That's it, Brianna. Let it go, pet. Come for me."

He licked and sucked where my neck met my shoulder. The vibrations increased their intensity, and then I couldn't take any more. My eyes rolled back in my head, and my back arched as a silent scream left my mouth. Every muscle in my body shook with my orgasm.

Stephan flattened his arm against my chest. He held me up because I no longer had the strength to hold the position without the use of my legs. Then again, I wasn't sure how much help they would have been.

The first thing I noticed as I came back to myself was Stephan touching and kissing me. He lowered both of our legs so I was no longer spread wide open and vulnerable. "We need to wash and get out, sweetheart. The water is getting cold."

I nodded but didn't move.

He laughed.

"How about you just lie there, and I'll take care of the cleaning."

Without waiting for my response, he picked up the shower gel, placed a soft kiss on my temple, and began washing both of us.

Chapter 18

Brianna

I couldn't believe Cal was coming over tonight to have dinner. He was bringing his girlfriend with him. He'd mentioned her a few times during our phone conversations, but I didn't know much about her other than they'd been going out for almost a year. I didn't know what she knew about me or Stephan either. I could only hope that she was nice, and that Stephan and Cal didn't get into one of their staring contests.

Stephan came home a little after four to help me get everything ready. He appeared to be in a good mood as we worked alongside each other in the kitchen, touching and kissing me every chance he got. At one point, I almost dropped the eggs I had in my hand. He'd come up behind me, wrapped his arms around my waist, and proceeded to kiss his way down my neck, over my shoulder, and then along the length of my arm.

It was always difficult to concentrate when his lips were on me like that. By the time he reached the tips of my fingers and kissed each one, my whole arm was tingling. He just smiled, released me, and smacked my behind, leaving a slight sting.

I stood motionless for a moment, not knowing what to do, but more importantly, I was still trying to recover from his kisses. It didn't make any sense to me. No matter where he touched me, whether with his mouth or his hands, my skin came alive from the contact, and I felt that stirring in the pit of my stomach.

"Those eggs aren't going to crack themselves, you know." He nodded to the eggs cradled protectively against my chest.

I blushed, lowered my head, and got back to work on dinner. Cal and his girlfriend would be there before I knew it. My anxiety was already building. Everything needed to be perfect.

A few minutes before six, the phone rang and Stephan went to answer it. I suddenly felt cold. What if she didn't like me? Dr. Cooper didn't. Samantha didn't. What would happen if Cal's girlfriend hated me? Would he stop talking to me? Stop coming around? My hands trembled, and the knife slipped from my fingers.

"Come here." Stephan's arms circled around me, pulling me against his chest. "I'll be right here with you, sweetheart. Everything will be fine."

I shook my head. "What if she doesn't like me? What if—"

"Shh. Deep breaths, Brianna."

Doing what he said, I let his scent permeate my senses. By the time a knock sounded on the door, I had myself mostly under control.

"Thank you, Sir."

He brushed his lips along my forehead before lowering his mouth to mine. "You're welcome. Are you ready to greet our guests?"

"Yes," I mumbled against his lips.

Stephan gave me a squeeze before opening the door.

Standing in the hallway was Cal and a beautiful woman with long blond hair. I assumed she was his girlfriend, Jade. She glanced at Stephan and then me. She seemed . . . curious.

"Ross." Stephan nodded and then turned his attention to Jade. "You must be Jade. I'm Stephan Coleman. It's nice to meet you." He held out his hand to her.

She hesitated for a moment before accepting. "Thank you."

"Please, come in. Dinner is almost ready." Stephan took a step back, moving me along with him, to allow Cal and Jade into the condo.

The door was closed, and Stephan paused. He appeared to be waiting for something. When nothing happened, my anxiety began to rise again. Sweat formed on my palms, and my stomach churned with unease. Why wasn't anyone saying anything?

Stephan sighed. "Jade, I don't believe you've met Brianna."

"Um. No. I haven't." She turned her attention to me. "It's good to finally meet you, Anna. I've heard so much about you from Cal." Jade paused. "Or do you prefer Brianna? Cal always calls you Anna, so . . ."

I didn't like being put on the spot, but I knew I had to answer. "Anna's fine."

She smiled.

"Why don't you both take a seat at the table while Brianna and I finish bringing over the food? There's a pitcher of water and iced tea already there, so help yourselves to something to drink," Stephan said as he guided me toward the kitchen.

"What? Keeping the good wine locked up tonight, Coleman?"

Stephan stopped and turned to look directly at Cal. "There is no good wine. Not in my home. I don't drink."

Ross's mouth fell open at Stephan's declaration. Stephan, however, seemed unfazed and resumed our progress to get the food. I stumbled slightly at the abrupt movement, but Stephan easily steadied me.

When we brought the food to the table, Cal and Jade were just taking their seats, and they glanced back and forth as if talking without words. It made me uncomfortable, so once I placed the platter I'd been carrying on the table, I took a step closer to Stephan. He trailed his fingers down my arm in a comforting gesture and held my chair out for me to sit down.

"Thank you—" I had to bite my tongue to keep myself from addressing him as *Sir*. What would Cal think if I did?

"Help yourselves. I don't want this to be a formal function."

Stephan reached for the meat. Cal and Jade followed suit. When Cal realized I wasn't doing the same, however, he scrunched up his eyebrows in confusion. "Aren't you eating?"

I glanced over at Stephan, and he nodded toward the food. "Um. Yes?" Cal frowned, but once I reached for the food, he did the same.

He continued to watch me, so I tried to keep putting food on my plate at a steady pace while keeping an eye on what Stephan was doing. He'd never said I couldn't start eating until after he'd started, but it was how I'd been taught when I was with Ian, and it seemed right. I didn't mind waiting. With Ian, it hadn't been an option. He'd made sure I understood how disrespectful it was to begin eating before my betters. It was different now, yet the same. To me, it was a sign of respect to allow Stephan to go first.

Once we all had food on our plates and began eating, the sound of forks and knives scraping plates was almost deafening. I knew I should probably say something, but I had no idea what. I gave an inward sigh of relief when Stephan broke the awkward silence.

"What do you do for a living, Jade?"

"I'm a student. My last year, thankfully."

"I remember that feeling. What are you studying?"

"Architecture." She smiled at Cal, and he smiled back. "It's how we met. Cal came to one of my classes to talk about construction and how important it is for architects to understand the process."

"She raised her hand to ask a question, and I knew right then I wanted to ask her out."

Cal obviously cared for her. I'd seen him touch her several times already, similar to the way Stephan was always touching me. I was comfortable with Stephan, just as they appeared to be with each other.

Jade laughed at something I missed and then focused her attention in our direction. "So how did the two of you meet?"

Everything stopped.

Stephan reached under the table and pried my fingers apart where I had them clasped in my lap. Something heavy settled on my chest, although I knew there wasn't anything there.

Stephan. Remember Stephan. His hand. He's holding my hand.

And the food. I can smell the food.

I'm . . . I'm sitting . . . on a soft chair . . . in Stephan's dining room.

Little by little, I felt as if I could breathe once more. The weight was lifting.

A warm hand caressed my face, and I leaned into it. "Open your eyes, sweetheart."

I opened them to find Stephan staring back at me with a mixture of worry and pride on his face. Glancing over my shoulder, I realized both Cal and Jade were watching, too. I lowered my gaze.

"Don't," Stephan whispered, lifting my chin. "You have nothing to be ashamed of."

"I'm sorry, Anna. I didn't realize. I hope you can forgive me."

"It's okay."

"No, it's not. I obviously upset you, and I didn't mean to."

Stephan pushed his chair back from the table and then moved it next to mine. "I know you didn't mean anything by your question. It's a sensitive subject, but one I'm sure will be asked in the future by others." He massaged my back as he spoke. "Brianna was in a bad situation, and I got her out of it. Our relationship developed from there."

Jade seemed to be at a loss for words. She picked up her fork again.

"I'm sorry. I didn't mean to—"

"No, it's my fault. I should have told Jade, but I wasn't sure how much you wanted her to know."

Jade looked confused again.

"I . . . I was with . . . a bad man. He . . . he hurt me."

Stephan

I was shocked when Brianna spoke up to explain. She hated talking about Ian or her time with him. Normally I had to pull every word out of her. I squeezed her hand in encouragement. She was doing so well. If she wanted to share with Jade, I wouldn't discourage it.

"He . . ." She took a deep breath. "I was his . . . slave."

Taking the opportunity to glance over at Jade, I saw first shock, then horror as she processed the information. Then she surprised me by abruptly standing, walking around the table, and kneeling next to Brianna. She reached out to touch her arm. Brianna was startled by the initial contact, but soon her muscles relaxed and she looked down at Jade.

"I'm so sorry that happened to you. I can understand why you're so shy now. I only hope that one day I can earn your trust. Did you cook all this?" Jade motioned toward the food on table.

Brianna didn't answer immediately. At first, I didn't think she was going to, but then I realized she was considering how to respond. I knew her well enough to know she wouldn't take all the credit since I'd helped her, even though what I did was minor in comparison.

"Sir helped me," she whispered.

Jade's gaze flickered to mine briefly, curiosity in her eyes, but she was quick to cover it. "Well, help or not, the food is delicious. I can't cook to save my life. Maybe one of these days you could teach me how to make something."

"You want me to . . . teach you how to cook?"

"It would have to be something basic, but yeah. I mean it would be nice if I could actually cook a meal for my boyfriend once in a while, right?"

Brianna looked over at Cal, and I followed.

"She's not exaggerating." Cal chuckled. "The last time she tried to make something, I had to get out the fire extinguisher. Since then, we pretty much stick to frozen dinners, boxed meals, and takeout."

"You'd really be helping me out, Anna. I don't want to burn down my boyfriend's house."

Brianna giggled. "Okay."

"You'll show me how to cook something?"

Jade was overexaggerating her enthusiasm, and Brianna began cracking up. I had to admit, her expressions were pretty funny.

"Yes. I'll . . . I'll show you." Brianna managed to respond between bursts of laughter.

All the sadness had disappeared and been replaced by smiles. I loved hearing Brianna laugh. It didn't happen often enough.

Jade stood. "Perfect. I'll see what my schedule looks like and we can plan something."

The second half of dinner went much smoother than the first half. Although I caught both Jade and Ross staring at me slightly longer than was normal every now and then, conversation flowed as Jade told Brianna about her studies. I was happy to hear Brianna opening up and asking a few questions of her own. Jade had made an impression, and it was a good one.

When it was time for dessert, I suggested we take it into the living room. Brianna was always more comfortable there in the less-formal setting, and I hoped she would continue talking.

Ross and Jade took seats on the couch while I sat down in my chair. There was still enough room on the couch for Brianna if she chose to sit there. She didn't, however. Without pause, Brianna walked up beside my chair and waited for permission to sit down. I opened my arms and gave her the okay. She hurriedly climbed into my lap, resting her head on my shoulder facing Ross and Jade.

That same look crossed both their faces. This time, however, there was something other than curiosity in Ross's. He was putting the pieces together between what he'd observed and what he'd heard about me from Karl Walker's drunken rants. The question was what he would do with his conclusions.

"Oh, my goodness!" Jade took a bite of the cake Brianna had made earlier in the day and closed her eyes. "This is magnificent."

Brianna blushed. "Thank you."

Jade took another bite, and I followed suit. After tasting it, I had to agree. "It really is spectacular, sweetheart." I gave her a soft kiss before feeding her a forkful from my plate.

She accepted it and then tucked her head into my neck. "Thank you, Sir."

"Are you still planning on school in the fall, Anna?"

"I don't know." Brianna glanced up at me before turning her attention to Ross. "I'm going to try. I don't know . . . if I can handle being around all those people."

Jade spoke up. "When are your classes? Maybe I could go with you the first few times or something. I might not be able to sit inside with you, but there are always benches out in the halls where I could wait."

"That's a great idea."

Cal seemed to love Jade's suggestion, and once I thought about it, I had to agree. The only other person I'd seen Brianna this comfortable with was Lily. If Jade was willing, I didn't see a problem in her going with Brianna to her class for a while. It would be good for her to have a female she knew and trusted on campus with her.

"Brianna's class doesn't start until the fall. It's an evening class. Would you still be on campus then?"

"I can be. There's always homework to do, and it would give me an excuse to go to the library and get it done."

Before we got too far off track, I wanted to get Brianna's opinion. "What do you think, Brianna? Would it help if Jade went to class with you for a while?"

"Yes," she said, picking nervously at her skirt. "I'm nervous about going on my own."

"It's settled, then. You just let me know when and where, and I'll be there." Jade smiled.

Everyone finished their cake, and Brianna stood up to take the empty dishes to the kitchen. I watched as she walked away, enjoying the view of her ass swaying slightly as she moved. Her legs were covered in thigh-high stockings. The lace around the top was hidden by her skirt, but I knew it was there. All that was missing was a pair of heels.

I shifted in my seat, trying to get comfortable without losing sight of her.

"What's going on?" Ross demanded in a furious whisper.

Reluctantly, I pulled my attention away from Brianna. "You're going to have to be more specific. What exactly are you referring to?"

He hesitated as Brianna rejoined the group.

"Do you have any moisturizer, Anna? I'm not sure why, but my hands are really dry."

Brianna turned toward me.

I nodded, letting her know it was all right.

"It's in my bedroom. I can go get it."

"Do you mind if I come with you?"

"Okay."

Once the women were out of the room, Ross leaned in, leveling an angry stare at me. "Those things Walker was saying about you were true, weren't they . . . *Sir*?"

"As I told you a minute ago, you're going to have to be more specific."

"Don't play dumb, Coleman. You're a lot of things, but dumb isn't one of them. You like to beat women. Tie them up and beat them. You like women who are able to be manipulated, bent to your will, so they won't fight you and what you want. What I want to know is how you hid the evidence? Do you only leave marks where they can't be seen?"

"I'd be very careful what you accuse me of, Ross."

"Then answer the question, damn it!"

"All right. I'm a Dominant."

"A what? Is that supposed to mean something to me?"

"You mean to tell me that you've never heard of BDSM? Domination and submission? Bondage and discipline?"

All the color drained from his face. "I'll kill you." He swiftly stood to his feet and moved toward me.

I stood, ready to go on the defensive should it be warranted.

Unfortunately he didn't get very far before Jade and Brianna strolled back into the room. They took one look at the two of us and reacted. Jade ran to Ross's side, and Brianna to mine. She surprised me, though. Instead of standing behind me or beside me, she stood in front of me, facing Ross.

"Get out of my way, Anna."

"No."

"Anna, I don't know what he's conned you into believing, but it isn't true. You don't have to let him touch you. You don't have to let him beat you, or whatever it is he likes to do. I promise you, you don't. You can stay with me if you want. I'll make sure your father stays away. He won't bother you."

"He doesn't hurt me."

"I know what he is."

She cocked her head to the side. I couldn't see her face, but I could imagine the confused look she was giving him.

"He's a Dominant, Anna. He admitted it to me himself. He likes to tie women up, beat them, and have his wicked way with them."

Ross's declaration was met with silence. The only sound that could be heard in the room was his ragged breathing. Everyone, including me, was waiting with bated breath for Brianna's response.

When she finally opened her mouth, she shocked all of us. "I know."

Chapter 19

Stephan

"You know? What do you mean you know?" Ross's chest moved up and down rapidly. I could tell he was trying to rein in his emotions so as not to upset Brianna, but I wasn't sure he was winning the battle.

"I know."

Ross ran a hand over his face and sighed. "Anna, I need you to explain this to me, please. If you *know*, as you say you do, then why . . . how could you possibly want to stay here with him? Haven't you been through enough? Or on some level did you enjoy having the shit beat out of you?"

Brianna jerked at his accusation. I took hold of her shoulders and pulled her protectively against me. She was stiff beneath my hands. "Watch it, Ross. I'm not above throwing you out of my house."

He glared at me.

"It's not the same," Brianna whispered, bringing everyone's attention back to her. She was nervous. She held her body in such a rigid position that her limbs began to tremble.

"Then explain it to me." Ross crossed his arms and stared, waiting for Brianna.

"He . . . he doesn't hurt me."

When she didn't continue, Ross began to get impatient. "You keep saying that, Anna, but BDSM is all about whips and chains and pain. If you really *know*, how can you say he doesn't hurt you?"

I was once again considering throwing him out and being done with it. Did the man not understand the meaning of boundaries? How was what Brianna and I did any of his concern as long as it was what she wanted?

"I don't know what you want me to say."

That robotic sound was creeping into her voice, but she appeared to fight it. The pride I had in her at that moment nearly knocked me off my feet. I realized it was Ross she was talking to, not some stranger, and that she was defending me rather than herself, but she was doing so without falling into a spiral of panic.

Ross glanced at me and then back to her, flexing his fingers. "Has he tied you up, Anna? Has he hit you?"

She shook her head. "No."

I saw his Adam's apple bob up and down as he took a deep swallow. Whatever he was going to ask next, I doubted I was going to like it.

"Has he made you have sex with him?"

Brianna cringed, leaning against me. Other than that, she didn't respond to his question.

"Answer the question, Anna." His voice was demanding and tainted with barely controlled anger. "Is he forcing you to have sex with him?"

"No."

"No?" Clearly Ross didn't believe her.

"No!" she cried. "He doesn't force me to do anything."

I wrapped my arms around her waist, resting my hands on her stomach. It was the best option at the moment. The other one was to toss him out as I'd threatened to do earlier. Unfortunately, that would only delay this conversation, and I wanted it over with.

Ross's eyes were wild, and he clenched his hands into fists. He was no longer focused on Brianna. "You're having sex with her? After knowing what she's been through?"

I rested my chin on the top of Brianna's head and spoke calmly. "I assume you and your girlfriend have sex. Why is the act so appalling to you when it comes to Brianna?"

"It's different."

"How? Brianna's an adult. She's been through more than most people can comprehend. She is perfectly capable of making decisions about her body." As I continued to hold her and speak in controlled tones, she gradually relaxed.

"You are a real piece of work, Coleman. Do you know that?"

He leaned forward, but Jade placed a hand on his arm. Her gesture seemed to snap him out of whatever action he was contemplating.

Refocusing on Brianna, there was a pleading in his eyes. "Why, Anna. Why?"

She laced our fingers together. "Stephan's good to me. He . . . he's helped me get better. To not be . . . afraid all the time. He doesn't hurt me." I could tell Ross was about to protest, and obviously so could Brianna. "He doesn't."

"Maybe we should sit back down and talk about this like adults?" Jade suggested, tugging on Ross's arm. He resisted for a moment and then followed her to the couch.

Once they were both seated, I situated Brianna back on my lap. She automatically went to her favorite position with her head on my shoulder. I was glad her tension from earlier had dissipated, and I wanted to keep it that way if possible. Running my hand over her hair, I did my best to comfort her.

"Why do you do that?" The abrupt question from Ross startled Brianna, and I mentally cursed him for his insensitivity.

I took a moment to make sure I was in control before I answered him. "Do what?"

Ross rolled his eyes as if what he was asking was obvious. "Why are you touching her like that? It's almost as if you're petting a dog or something."

"Brianna is *not* a dog. I touch her like this because it's something she enjoys." I continued to run my hand over her hair as I spoke.

He looked at her, disbelieving. "You really like that?"

She nodded but didn't leave the safety of my embrace.

"Why?"

"It feels nice."

"Cal, honey, she does seem happy with him." Jade turned to face Brianna. "You are happy, right?"

"Yes." Then Brianna looked in Ross's direction. "I don't want to leave. I like it here."

Ross sighed and leaned forward to rest his face in his hands.

"I worry about you, Anna. I really do. With everything you've been through, you're so vulnerable. I don't want him taking advantage of that. If he's into . . ." He took a deep breath and lifted his head. "I don't want to see you get hurt. Even if he hasn't tried any of that crazy stuff with you yet, that doesn't mean he won't. Is that truly what you want?"

"I want to stay with him."

He groaned and flopped back against the couch. If we weren't having such a serious conversation, his reaction might have been amusing.

While I disliked Ross, I was also under no illusion that he intended to be part of Brianna's life. He was her one link to her past that didn't cause her pain. Whether I liked it or not, he and I were going to have to come to some sort of common ground.

"I think you're under a misconception about my lifestyle."

"Oh really? And what misconception is that?"

"BDSM isn't about a Dominant forcing his will upon another. It's about fulfilling both individual's needs."

He snorted.

"And how exactly does tying a woman up and beating her meet *her* needs?" His tone was sarcastic, almost daring me to explain what he saw as impossible.

"Some women like pain." He started to interrupt, but I raised my hand to stop him. "I'm not saying that's Brianna's case. Honestly, what she likes and doesn't like sexually is none of your business. What I'm trying to explain, however, is that there are people who enjoy it, just as there are Doms who like inflicting it."

"And do you?"

"You do realize that if you were not Brianna's friend, I wouldn't be answering your rude questions at all, don't you?"

"And you realize I couldn't care less about your view of my rudeness, right?"

I shook my head. He was impossible.

"I prefer to use pain to create sensation rather than for pain itself."

"What's that supposed to mean?"

My frustration was mounting. He was deliberately being obtuse.

"Have you ever pinched a woman's nipples?"

"I don't think that's any of your business."

I laughed. "You can ask me questions about my sex life, but I can't ask about yours?"

"It's different."

"No. It's not."

I waited for him to answer the question. He continued to stare at me, however. It was almost as if he were measuring me up. Then again, maybe he was testing to see if I would break. He'd be sadly disappointed. My first submissive, Sarah, had been extremely bratty and stubborn when she'd wanted to be. I doubted he could match her in that department.

"Yes, he's pinched my nipples before."

"Jade!" Ross clearly couldn't believe she was sharing such private information, which I found rather amusing, considering.

I ignored him for the time being and directed my question to Jade. "Would you say his pinching your nipples hurts?"

"You don't have to answer that." Ross's expression was defiant.

I found it even funnier when she acted as if he hadn't spoken at all. "Yes, I guess it does. But . . . it feels good, too. It's hard to explain."

Ross flashed an angry glare back at me. "I don't understand what this has to do with Anna or you or anything else."

"It has everything to do with what we're discussing. You want to know about pain as it relates to sensation. As Jade just explained, pain is relative. In fact, I would be willing to bet that if you pinched her nipples right now, she wouldn't find it pleasurable at all. She's not aroused. In a sexual situation, though, the body reacts differently."

"I still don't understand what this has to do with your . . . 'lifestyle,' as you put it, and Anna. I don't want to see her get hurt. Period."

"Cal, honey. I think what he's trying to say is that you need to butt out."

I thought he was going to jump off the couch for a second, but he didn't. "What?"

"Cal, look at her. Stop trying to see something that isn't there. Anna is calm. She's happy. The only thing upsetting her is you and Stephan arguing. I know you're trying to protect her, but this isn't working. If Anna has truly been through what I think she has, then the last thing she needs is to have more of her choices taken away from her. If this is what she wants, if he's who she wants to be with, then you need to accept that."

Ross looked over at Brianna where she still sat in my arms. I wasn't wearing a dress shirt tonight, so she was playing with the collar on my T-shirt. My petting her hair, along with our more measured tones, had allowed her to relax. Finally.

"Fine." He looked me in the eyes as he spoke. "But if I ever find out you've done something, forced her into doing something she doesn't want, I will come after you, Coleman. I don't care how much money you have. I'll make sure you pay one way or another."

Brianna

It was all my fault. If I hadn't called Stephan *Sir*, Cal wouldn't have gotten upset. He and Stephan wouldn't have argued. Why had I done that?

I walked with Stephan to the door to see Cal and Jade out. Jade had stood up for Stephan, for us.

"I'll check my schedule and give you a call." She hugged me before stepping into the hall.

Cal watched me closely before taking a step toward me. "Am I allowed to hug you, too?"

Nodding, I took a deep breath and waited.

He wrapped his arms around me. "The offer stands. Always. If you ever need a place to go, you call me."

When he leaned back, I looked up at him. He seemed sad, but I didn't know how to fix it. He wanted me to leave Stephan, and I wouldn't do that.

Cal took several steps backward until he was also in the hallway. "I'll call you tomorrow."

He turned to go before I could respond, leaving me wondering if I'd done something else wrong.

"Brianna?"

"Yes?"

"What's going through that head of yours?"

I pressed my lips together, trying to decide how to put my feelings into words. "I don't know how to make it better."

"Oh, sweetheart," Stephan said, cradling me against his chest, surrounding me with his strength, his warmth. "It's not up to you to fix. Ross seems to be having a hard time with the fact that you're not a little girl anymore."

"Why can't he like you?" Holding on to the back of his shirt, I wanted . . . I *needed* to get closer to him.

He kissed the top of my head and then held my face in his hands, his face very serious. "There are a lot of people who won't understand our relationship, Brianna. I understand that what I like, what I need in a relationship isn't what many would consider normal, but I don't care about them or what they think. What I do care about is you and what you want. If at any time you want this, us, to stop, I want you to tell me, do you understand? I don't want you to ever think you don't have a choice."

"I want to stay with you." I was saying that a lot, but it was true. I didn't want to be anywhere he wasn't.

He smiled, and I smiled back.

"I was so proud of you tonight. You talked yourself through your panic, and then you stood up to Ross."

I dropped my gaze, heat staining my cheeks.

"No need to be embarrassed." He tilted my chin up until my mouth lined up with his. "I was thinking you did so well tonight that you should get a reward."

His lips hovered just an inch from mine. I could feel his hot breath, smell the coffee with a hint of chocolate from our dessert. I closed my eyes automatically, waiting for his kiss.

"Would you like a reward, Brianna?"

The waiting was almost intoxicating. I wanted him to kiss me. "Yes," I whispered.

"Mmm. And just what should I give you as your reward, hmm? A kiss perhaps?"

He closed the distance between us, brushing his mouth ever so gently against mine. Then, before I'd really gotten to savor them, they were gone again.

I opened my eyes to find him staring down at me with a smirk on his face. "Maybe more of that later. But for now, I want you to pick something you want to do for the rest of the evening. It can be anything you want."

It was a challenge to concentrate on anything other than the small taste of his lips I'd had just moments ago. He'd said maybe we could do more of that later, though, so that helped ease my disappointment. I had to focus.

At first, nothing came to my mind. Then . . . "Could we . . ."

"What is it, Brianna. What do you want to do?"

I glanced down, then over to the large windows and into the city lights. Disappointment dragged me down. It was too late. We wouldn't be able to go tonight. Maybe if I told him, though, we could go tomorrow? Or next week?

"Could we go to the library?"

He smiled, and it lit up his entire face. "Of course." He looked at his watch. "I'll need to make a call. Go get a sweater, just in case you get chilly. I'll be right back."

Before I could respond, he jogged across the room and up the stairs, leaving me staring after him. I didn't know what he was doing. It was after eight o'clock at night. Libraries didn't stay open that late, or at least they didn't in Two Harbors. They didn't even stay open that late in Dallas. Maybe it was different in Minneapolis.

Doing as I was told, I went to my bedroom to retrieve a sweater. It was June, so I didn't think I would need it, but I wouldn't question him.

When I returned to the living room, Stephan was back downstairs talking on his cell phone. "I appreciate it. We'll be there in about twenty minutes. Thanks." He hung up his phone and grinned. "Are you ready, sweetheart?"

I nodded.

He held out his hand, and I took it.

It was rare we went out at night. I wasn't sure if that was because of me or if it was what Stephan preferred. It was hard to imagine him sitting home alone at night in his condo. Did he used to go out with Logan and Lily? Were there parties, events, he was turning down because of me? I didn't want him to do that. It didn't seem fair.

As he drove, he kept glancing in my direction, smiling. I didn't understand what was going on, but I was glad he was happy.

We drove outside of the city and into an upscale residential area, and I became more confused. Where were we going? "We have to make a stop first. It won't take more than a few minutes." He answered my unspoken question.

I watched the houses as we passed by. They all looked the same except for small things. I couldn't tell in the dark, but I wondered if they were all the same color, too.

A few minutes later, he turned into a well-lit driveway. The porch light was on as if someone was expecting us. "Wait here. I'll be right back."

He left the car running and walked up to the front porch. Before he could ring the doorbell, an older woman appeared. She seemed amused as she talked to Stephan. Shaking her head, she handed him something before he hopped off the porch and strolled back to the car.

The lady stood outside her door, watching. She smiled at me and waved. I waved back. I had no idea who she was, but it would have been rude not to respond.

He slid behind the wheel and reached for his seatbelt. "Ready?"

"Yes."

Stephan backed out of the driveway and drove toward downtown once more. I wanted to ask him who that woman was, but I didn't. Stephan knew many people. She could have been anyone.

We came to a stop at the back of a large brick building. He exited the car and came around to open my door. Taking his hand, I stepped out of the vehicle.

Hand in hand, we walked up to a brown metal door on the far right-hand side of the structure. He pulled out a set of keys from his pocket and unlocked the door. It was then I noticed the sign to the left of the door. *Library staff only. All patrons please use the main entrance at the front of the building.*

He opened the door. It was pitch black until he turned on the lights. I nearly jumped for joy when I saw the piles of books stacked on the floor right inside the entrance. I glanced up at him, not sure what I was allowed to do. He chuckled. "Go on. The place is all ours for the evening."

Unable to contain myself, I ran to the nearest stack of books and began flipping through. There were so many. Stephan had a large collection of books, but it didn't compare to that of a community library.

I sat on the floor, leafing through the books around me until Stephan knelt down and rubbed the outside of my arms. "There's more, you know. We're only in the back room where they sort and process. The actual library is through there." He pointed to a long hallway on the other side of the room.

I looked first to the hall, then back to the books on the floor. I felt as if Christmas and my birthday had come all at once. I didn't know which to choose.

He laughed. "Why don't we take a look out there, and then if you want, you can come back here for a while."

That sounded reasonable. "Okay."

We stood. He took my hand again, and we walked past stack after stack of books on our way to the main part of the library. Some were on the floor. Some were on tables or carts. There were so many books!

Chapter 20

Stephan

I stood off to the side as Brianna walked down a third row of books. She held out her hand as she passed by, touching the bindings. Once she reached the end of the aisle, she switched to the other side to repeat the same action. I wasn't sure if she was reading the titles of the books or just enjoying the feel of them. It didn't matter to me either way. The only thing I cared about was the look of awe on her face.

There were times Brianna was childlike in her actions. From the time she'd laid eyes on that first stack of books, she'd been like a kid in a toy store who couldn't decide which toy to pull off the shelf and play with first. It was both amusing and slightly disturbing. Brianna was easy to please. She didn't require much, and she gave with her whole heart. I didn't know if that was because of who she was or if it had to do with what she'd been through. Maybe it was a little of both.

We gradually made it around the entire library in this fashion. I made sure to stay out of her way, but where I could see her and she could see me. Although we were the only ones there, it was a new place for her. Anything new was always an unknown with Brianna.

She stood in the main center aisle glancing back and forth at the bookshelves. I had no idea what was going through that mind of hers, but this was her reward. She could do anything she wanted. I was only along for the ride.

To my surprise, Brianna shifted her gaze to the long row of reference books along the wall. She went and sat down at one end of the encyclopedias and removed the first one from the shelf. As she flipped through the pages, I noticed she was mostly looking at the pictures rather than reading the pages. Only every now and then would she stop and read the caption or, even rarer, the article.

Once she was finished with the first book, she moved to the next. At first,

I didn't realize what she was doing, but then it dawned on me. Brianna had taken care of her mother while she'd been sick. It was doubtful she'd paid much attention to what was going on in the outside world when her immediate world was crumbling. Then she'd gone to live with her father in a small town where she'd had little freedom. It was hard to say how much access she'd had to information. I knew she went to school, but she'd also been grieving her mother at the time. I was well aware of how easy it was for people to get lost in their own world when going through something like that, and I'd been lucky enough to have Diane and Richard to help me. Brianna had been all alone.

Eventually, when I realized she was going to be there a while, I pulled out a chair at one of the tables and sat down. Taking out my phone, I checked my e-mail along with a few other sites I frequented. As I scrolled through, my gaze drifted back to Brianna. I'd tried to keep her sheltered from too much information because I hadn't wanted to overwhelm her given how easily she panicked. Seeing her tonight, however, devouring information, coupled with how she'd handled herself at dinner, I knew what I needed to do.

In just a few short months, Brianna would be going to school. She needed to be comfortable with technology and how to use it. It was then I knew the perfect birthday gift for her.

Using the time wisely, I pulled up the website for my favorite computer store and scanned their listing of laptops. After twenty minutes of searching, I found the one I wanted. It was perfect for anything she might want to do, and it was lightweight. She'd be able to carry it with her to her class if she wanted and take notes. I sent Jamie an e-mail with the laptop information and a note to have two of them delivered to my office the following week.

With that accomplished, I leaned back in my chair and watched Brianna as she continued down the bookshelf. The information she could access here was only a fraction of what would be available to her on the Internet. If I used her current reaction as a gauge, I would have to put some time restrictions on her, or she'd be glued to her computer all day.

It was almost midnight by the time she placed the last encyclopedia back on the shelf. She turned around to face me but didn't get off the floor. We stared at each other for several minutes before she began to crawl toward me. I remained still and waited to see what she would do.

She came to a stop beside my chair and laid her head in my lap. I didn't hesitate to reach down and begin stroking her hair. We remained that way until I felt drops of moisture seeping through the fabric of my pants. "Brianna?"

It was then I heard her choke out a sob, and I lifted her chin so that I could see her face. Tears streamed uncontrolled down her cheeks.

"Thank you."

"You're welcome." I brushed the moisture from her cheeks. "The reference books can't be checked out, but did you want to pick out any novels? You've been speeding through the ones Lily gave you."

Her eyes opened wide with both shock and excitement.

I chuckled. "Go on. Pick out some books and I'll make a list for Patty. She'll officially check them out for you tomorrow."

She scrambled to her feet and rushed off to the romance section. While she was looking, I went behind the circulation desk to get some paper and a pen. Patty had been one of my elementary school teachers. She'd heard about my parents' deaths and had come to the memorial service, along with several other teachers, to offer her condolences. After that, I hadn't seen her until I'd been invited to a "Friends of the Library" meeting to speak on the foundation's work and how we might be able to partner with the library to collect books and educational toys for children. She'd retired from teaching several years ago and was now the library director.

I returned to the table and waited for Brianna. One of the things that had changed with Brianna's arrival in my life was that I no longer attended many of the charity functions I once had. It was something I missed, but until I was sure Brianna would be able to accompany me or I felt comfortable with her being on her own, Jamie and the other executives would have to continue filling in for me. I left her home alone too much as it was already.

Brianna came around the corner, and I jumped up to help her. She had at least ten paperback novels in her arms, and she was about to lose at least two of them.

When I removed most of the books from her hands, she blushed and looked down. "I took too many."

Tucking the novels under one arm, I pulled her against my side. "Not at all. This will keep you busy for what? A week?"

I laid the books on the table and sat back down, pulling her with me. She quietly sat on my lap while I wrote down the titles and authors for Patty. She was doing me a favor tonight. I didn't want to mess up her inventory.

Once I had written down all twelve books Brianna had selected—some of which had rather racy covers, I might add—I led her over to the circulation desk and retrieved one of the plastic grocery bags I'd noticed earlier. Loading the books inside so they were easier to carry, I guided her back down the hall to the storage room where we'd entered. She looked sad to leave.

"Don't worry. We can come back."

"Okay." Her smile returned, and I couldn't resist giving her a kiss.

"Come on, sweetheart. It's late. Let's get home."

Brianna

"Good morning." Stephan smiled up at me from between my legs. He'd woken me up and then proceeded to trail kisses all the way down my body.

"Morning." I was still trying to catch my breath from the orgasm he'd just given me.

He smiled wider and crawled his way up to kiss me, plunging his tongue deep into my mouth. I could taste myself, smell myself, and I could feel his erection pressing against the inside of my thigh.

Sliding my fingers through his hair, I clung to him as he continued to kiss me. Heat was building again between my legs. I kissed him back with everything I had, waiting, hoping he'd move just a few inches and push inside me.

Just when I thought I would go crazy with the need to have him inside me, he shifted his hips just right and filled me. I would never get used to how good it felt being with him like this.

His movements were slow, measured. With every thrust and retreat, the pressure coiled tighter and tighter until I was once again ready to explode.

"Not yet," he warned. "I'm not quite done with you yet."

He propped himself up, causing me to lose my hold on his hair, and moved one of my legs, then the other, until my knees were resting on his shoulders. He leaned back down, stretching the muscles in my legs as he pushed them up flush with my chest. I was effectively pinned to the mattress, and for some reason, knowing he had me completely trapped and at his mercy didn't scare me. It had the opposite effect. Like when he held my arms down, I knew he would keep me safe, protected.

With this new position, he penetrated deeper, and his thrusts turned harder and faster. I climbed higher and higher. I was right there, on the verge of climax, and there was nothing I could do to stop it.

"That's it, sweetheart. Come for me."

He pounded into me three more times before I was screaming out my orgasm. My whole body shook, and I reached out, trying to hold on to something, anything. He grabbed hold of my hands and held tight, letting me ride out the ripples of sensation coursing through me.

When I finally became aware of my surroundings again, he'd released my legs and was placing featherlight kisses on my neck and collarbone. When he stopped kissing me and rolled off me completely, I frowned. I didn't want him to stop.

Stephan propped himself up on one elbow and laughed at my expression. "No need to be sad, sweetheart. The day is young." He ran a single finger from the tip of my nose, down over my lips, my throat . . . all the way down to the junction between my legs. "Trust me. I've in no way had my fill of you today."

A shiver of anticipation ran up my spine at his words even though I'd just climaxed twice in a matter of minutes.

"For now, though, we need to hit the gym. I want to work on the self-defense moves Brad showed us."

He got out of bed and padded over to his closet. Reluctantly, I went to my room to get my clothes, my legs feeling like there were no bones left in them. I had no idea how I was going to work out in the gym.

For the next hour, he encouraged me to try to get away from him. We started with him grabbing my wrist, just like the night Brad was there. I did better but was still only able to break his hold about fifty percent of the time.

When he saw I was getting frustrated with that, he'd moved onto the second technique. This one was a lot harder for me. I was supposed to run my foot along my attacker's—Stephan's—lower leg, and then stomp on his foot. I couldn't do it. I couldn't hurt Stephan. He kept telling me it was all right, to give it my all, but the one time I really tried I ended up in tears, so he stopped.

I hated that I couldn't do better. He'd explained to me why he wanted me to learn this, and I understood. It made sense. But logic didn't change how I felt.

After showering and eating breakfast, Stephan had me sit down at the dining room table. He stood by my chair, holding my journal out for me to see. It was as if a lead weight had settled into the pit of my stomach.

Instead of handing it to me or placing it down on the table in front of me, he flipped through some of the more recent pages. Then he took a paperclip I hadn't noticed before and clipped several pages together.

"I don't want you reading the pages I've placed between this paperclip unless I'm around, understood?"

I knew that tone. "Yes, Sir."

"Today, I want you to write down ten positive things about yourself in your journal. They can be anything as long as they are about you and they are positive. It can be something about yourself you like, not a thing but a personality trait. A physical feature. A talent. Anything."

I nodded in understanding although I had no idea how I was going to accomplish such a task.

"Let me be clear, Brianna. You will sit here until you finish, even if it takes all day. You may get up and go to the bathroom if you need to, and I will allow you periodic breaks to stretch your legs and eat. Other than that, I expect you to be writing or thinking about what to write."

"Okay," I whispered weakly.

"I'm sorry? I didn't hear you. What was that again?"

"Okay, Sir. I understand."

"Good. I have some work to do today. If you need me, I'll be upstairs." He handed me my journal, leaned down, and placed a kiss on the top of my head.

I watched him pick up his laptop and disappear up the stairs. With each step he took away from me, the feeling of dread increased. How was I going to come up with *ten* things?

For the first hour, I sat staring at the blank page in front of me. Not one thing had come to my mind that I could write down.

At eleven, he came downstairs. He walked into the kitchen, got two glasses out of the cabinet, and filled them both with water. Without saying a word, he strolled over to where I was sitting, set one of the glasses down in front of me, and then went back upstairs. I didn't know what to make of it. Why hadn't he said anything?

I took a drink of my water and then picked up my pen. One thing. I had to be able to come up with one thing. What did I like about myself?

As soon as I opened my mind, the flood of negative began to fill my head.

"You stupid cunt. This is all you're good for, isn't it?"

No. No!

I shook my head furiously, trying to block the voice from my head.

"What happened?" Stephan's voice beside me made me jump.

When I realized he was really there, I threw my arms around his neck.

"Shh. Tell me what's wrong?"

"I heard them again."

He didn't answer right away. "The voices?"

I nodded.

Stephan sighed. He glanced down at my empty page. "You haven't written anything."

"I know. I was trying. Honestly I was."

"Brianna, I want you to look at me." He waited until I was looking. "Tell me one thing you like about yourself."

I stared at him in disbelief.

"Right now. Tell me something."

"Um." He brushed a loose piece of hair out of my face, and I remembered how my mom used to tell me how pretty my hair was. It wasn't something I thought about, but . . . "My hair?"

"What about your hair?"

"I . . . like it?"

"What do you like about it?"

I scrunched up my nose and thought about it. "I like . . . I like how it's wavy. And . . . and I like the color."

He smiled. "Good girl. See? You can do this."

I wasn't so sure, but I nodded.

"I'll be upstairs," he announced, leaving me to my writing.

I picked my pen back up.

1. I like my wavy hair.

The next few came easier.

2. I'm a good cook.

3. I was good in school.

4. I like to read.

After that, I was stuck. I didn't know what else to add. It was so much easier to think of the bad things.

It was then I understood why Stephan was making me do this. It was easier to remember the bad things. Unfortunately, that revelation didn't make it any easier to come up with positives.

I was still pondering what else to write when Stephan came back down. This time, he walked directly behind me and read what I'd written. "Good girl. It looks like you've made some progress."

"Yes. A little."

He massaged my shoulders, easing tension I hadn't realized was there. "Getting hungry?" My stomach grumbled. "I guess that answers my question." He chuckled as he continued to work his magic on my upper back.

I closed my eyes, and for several minutes I forgot about the list I was making and relaxed into his touch. My skin warmed under his fingers. I tilted my head forward and groaned when he slid his hands up over my shoulders to rub the skin just above my collarbone. His touch was completely innocent, yet it already had me craving more.

Stephan kissed me softly just below my ear, and I sucked in a breath. "Take a break and go freshen up. I'm going to make us some sandwiches for lunch."

Before his words sunk in, he was already in the kitchen. I watched him for another minute, thinking about what he'd done to me earlier that morning, what he might do later. My heart sped up at the thought.

He glanced in my direction. "Are you not ready for a break?"

"No. I mean, yes. I would like a break."

He smirked as if he were well aware of what I'd been thinking. I forced myself to move.

When I came back, he already had two sandwiches ready. I sat down beside him at the island, and once he'd started eating, I did the same.

"Have you had any more trouble with the voices?" he asked.

"No." I didn't know why they were leaving me alone, but I wasn't going to dwell on it. They were gone, and I was hoping they stayed away.

He smiled but didn't comment. We finished the rest of our lunch in silence.

All too soon, it was time to return to my assignment. Even though I finally understood the why of it, it didn't help me get it done any faster.

I managed to add another four things to my list by the time he came back downstairs again.

5. *Like to write.*

6. *I have made two friends, Lily and Jade.*

7. *I'm a good listener.*

8. *I like that I can make Stephan smile.*

The last two had come back to back. They were sort of related. I loved listening to people but especially Stephan. He was always trying to get me to talk, but hearing him tell me about his day, his life, when he was growing up . . . I loved being able to just sit and listen.

"Have you taken a break recently, Brianna?"

I noticed it was almost five. "No."

He frowned. "You need to get up and walk around every once in a while, or you're going to put undue strain on your muscles."

"Yes, Sir. I'll do better."

When I didn't get up, he crossed his arms over his chest and cocked his head to the side. I jumped up out of my seat and walked quickly to my bedroom.

As I stood in front of the mirror washing my face, I took a moment to look at myself. *Really* look at myself. I was happy. That was something I liked about myself. I wasn't frightened all the time. I had long periods where I wasn't focused on what had happened to me and was just . . . happy. I smiled, pleased that I'd come up with yet another item for my list.

Turning off the water, I dried my hands and went back out into the main room. Stephan was still there. He stood at the island, reading what I'd written so far.

"I'm proud of you," he commented without raising his head. "You only have two more to go."

"I thought of another one in the bathroom."

He smiled at me and opened his arms. I went to him.

"What is it?"

"I like that I'm happy now. That I'm not always afraid."

"Mmm. Yes. That is a good one. I like that about you, too."

Stephan buried his face in my hair and took a deep breath. He did that sometimes, and when he exhaled, it always sent a chill through me.

"Only one more to go."

It took me another hour to come up with the last one. I'd reread over my list several times hoping it would help me come up with something, but it didn't. What did help was a memory of Stephan and me working out earlier that morning. He'd commented on how toned the muscles in my arms had become since I'd been working with Brad.

I tilted my arm back and forth. He was right. My skin was no longer pale and sickly. The muscles underneath were strong and healthy. I was strong and healthy.

10. I like that I'm strong and healthy.

Chapter 21

Stephan
After Brianna finished her list, I sent her to soak in the bathtub while I ordered us dinner. She was given instructions to relax. It also hadn't escaped my attention that she'd taken one of her library books in with her.

Our food arrived a little before seven, and I went to tell her it was time to get out. The sight that greeted me made my heart thud solidly in my chest. Her hair was pulled up into a high ponytail, exposing her neck and shoulders. She was almost completely surrounded by bubbles. To top everything off, she was leaning to the side, her right hand poking out from beneath the bubbles, to hold the book she was reading. She was completely engrossed. After five minutes of me standing there watching her, she was still unaware of my scrutiny.

"Enjoying your book?"

She jumped, nearly dropping her book in the water.

I laughed and walked toward her.

"I wasn't paying attention, Sir."

"Don't worry about it. I told you to relax. You should be able to do that without having to worry about your surroundings, but you didn't answer my question." She looked confused. "Are you enjoying your book?"

Brianna glanced at the now-closed novel. This was one of the ones with a racy cover. The man on the front was shirtless, and the woman in his arms was only half wearing her dress.

"Yes. I like it."

I took the book from her and pretended to skim some of the pages. "What's it about?"

Her face turned a brilliant shade of red.

Pretending not to notice, I waited for her to talk.

"Um. He's . . . a pirate."

"A pirate. Hmm." I turned a few more pages in the book, pretending to read. "What about the woman? Is she a pirate, too?"

She shook her head. The movement had her sinking a little farther down beneath the water. "She's running away from her family. They . . . they want her to marry this mean man."

"Ah. So this pirate saves her from having to marry." I laid the book on the edge of the bathtub. "Is he a nice pirate?" I asked, brushing the back of my fingers down the side of her face.

"Not at first, but . . ." Dipping my index finger down below the waterline, I traced the outline of her breast. "But now he's starting to like her . . . even though he says she's a spoiled brat."

"Ah. One of those."

She closed her eyes as I moved my attentions to her other breast. Brianna was extremely responsive to my hands.

"Dinner is here. Get out and dry off. Don't bother to get dressed. I'll meet you in the living room." Standing up, I reached for the towel, then dried my hand and left the room. I could only imagine what was going through her head at my instructions.

I cleared off the coffee table and laid out the food on top of it. There was a large variety of options, but it was mostly finger foods. I'd ordered everything from mini-pizzas to tapas and sushi. We were going to experiment a little with food and with Brianna's comfort level in regards to herself and nudity.

She hesitated in the doorway, glancing at the large windows showcasing downtown Minneapolis, before tentatively moving into the living room where I was waiting. I patted the floor beside me, letting her know I wanted her to sit. Her actions were rushed. She was clearly uncomfortable. I supposed I could tell her the windows had a mirrored shine on the outside preventing anyone from seeing in, but I wanted her a little on edge.

"I hope you're hungry." I pointed to the variety of food on the table.

Aside from a slight widening of her eyes, she didn't react to the spread.

Brianna bowed her head and crossed her arms over her chest. "Put your arms down, Brianna. You are not to hide yourself in any way from me tonight, understood?"

She nodded and lowered her arms.

I watched as she placed her hands in her lap, then placed them on her knees, and then dropped them to her side. She was unsure what do to with them. It was just as well. She wasn't quite in the exposed position I wanted her.

"Spread your legs apart and sit with your ass on the floor." I watched as she followed my instructions. "Spread your legs wider."

Reaching down, I cupped my hand possessively over her pussy. Brianna sucked in a breath and held it. I gently rocked my hand back and forth over her folds, bumping her clit, but not applying enough pressure to truly stimulate.

Her pubic hair tickled my hand in a reminder that she still needed to get waxed. Her shopping trip with Lily would be a perfect time to get that taken care of. Her birthday was in nine days, and I had plans for the two of us, especially if things went well with Logan and Lily next Saturday.

I'd talked to him earlier, and everything was set up as best as it could be for next weekend. We'd go over to their house at two on Saturday afternoon. It was agreed that Brianna would most likely react better if she could see things from beginning to end. Therefore, Lily would be clothed when we arrived, and she and Brianna were going to have some time to talk beforehand. Brianna needed to know with absolute certainty that Lily was doing this of her own free will, that it was what she wanted.

"Have Lily arrange a waxing appointment for you this week while you're shopping. I want you bare by the weekend."

I didn't wait for her to respond, and she apparently realized I didn't require an answer.

"Place your hands behind your back and keep them there."

Once her hands were out of the way, I picked up one of the tapas. I had the restaurant send over a sampling. This first one had tomato, basil, mushroom, and some rosemary. I placed it up against her lips. "Take a bite and tell me what you think."

She opened her mouth and bit down just shy of the middle. As she chewed and swallowed, I popped the remaining half into my mouth.

"It's good. I like it."

I smiled and reached for a deviled egg. Again, we shared it.

As our dinner of finger foods continued, I played with her a little, making her reach for the food or intentionally missing her mouth so bits of food would fall onto her chest and need to be removed. I started by using my fingers to retrieve the dropped food, then progressed to more creative means. When a bit of hummus dropped onto the top of her breast, I dipped my head and used my tongue to lick it off.

By the time we reached the dessert portion of the meal, I was more deliberate with strategically putting food on her body and removing it with my mouth. Gradually, I began to smell the scent of her arousal wafting up from between her legs. Her sex glistened, and the memory of feasting on her first thing that morning had my cock straining to get free.

I took a deep breath to steady myself. She was such a picture of beauty sitting like this, completely trusting . . . submitting. I debated my original plan, which was to finish dinner and then go over her journal with her. Sex was on the menu, yes, but not until later. I wanted to get her worked up, exposed, and go over her diary with her. She needed to see herself as a whole person, not just what those voices she kept hearing in her head told her she was.

After feeding her a chocolate-covered strawberry and watching the juice dribble down the corner of her mouth, my resolve went out the window. I lifted myself up off the floor and took a seat on the couch directly behind her. Completely forgetting about the food, I undid my jeans and pulled my cock out, holding it at the base. "Turn around, Brianna."

Like the obedient submissive she was, Brianna turned around, kneeling before me with her hands behind her back. Her only reaction to seeing my erection was to scoot herself closer to the edge of the couch and look up at me for permission. I placed my hand on the back of her head and gently guided her down. Leaning my head back on the couch, I allowed her to go at her own pace and enjoyed the feel of her mouth sucking on my cock.

Brianna

Stephan's fingers tightened on the back of my head, and it sent a thrill through me. I wasn't sure what it was about giving him a blowjob that I liked, but feeling him in my mouth, knowing I was giving him pleasure, only increased the heat between my legs.

I knew I was wet. With every lick and suck and slide of his fingers during dinner, I'd felt the moisture increasing. At first, I'd thought he had put a blanket on the floor to provide padding since we were both sitting. I wondered, however, if it had more to do with not wanting me to ruin his carpet. The area where I'd been sitting was now soaked. I had no doubt the new spot I was on soon would be, too.

The salty taste increased as I licked, removing the drops of moisture from the tip of his penis. I swirled my tongue around the head, just as I'd been taught, before sinking down and taking in as much of him as I could. He wrapped his hand around my hair, and I increased my movements, bobbing my head up and down faster. Sucking harder.

His breathing changed, and I knew he was close. The thought of him coming in my mouth again made me feel a mixture of pride and unease. I understood the first part. Stephan was allowing me to do this for him, to him. He was letting me give him pleasure. The latter confused me. I liked doing this for him.

His hips jerked forward, once, twice, before the taste of his cum hit the back of my tongue. "Swallow."

Working my throat muscles, I swallowed several times, and the thick liquid streamed down the back of my throat.

To my surprise, he didn't release his hold on my head. The pull sent sparks of arousal to my already-heated sex. He held me in place, his penis growing flaccid inside my mouth. He looked down at me, at my lips loosely surrounding him.

"I could quite literally sit here all night with you in this position." His admission did funny things to my insides.

Unwinding his hand from my hair, he indicated that he wanted me to sit up. He tucked himself back inside his jeans and reached behind me for the tray of desserts we'd been eating from before. Selecting what looked to be a chocolate ball, he picked it up and then placed it against my lips, indicating he wanted me to take a bite.

When I did, I realized the inside was filled with raspberries. He pulled the candy away, leaving a trail of red down my chin.

"Looks like you've made a mess again, Brianna."

The sensation of his tongue licking up the sugary treat only added to my excitement, and I wanted more. He fed me another candy, this one filled with peanut butter. Then yet another filled with caramel. By the time he set the tray back on the table, I was on fire.

That fire was banked significantly when I saw the next thing he held in his hand. My journal. Was he going to give me another assignment?

He didn't acknowledge me. Leaning back casually against the couch, he opened the pages and began reading out loud. He started at the beginning and continued to read. This wasn't the first time he'd read my journal, but he'd never spoken my words back to me in such a way, almost as if he were having a conversation with another person who wasn't contributing.

Memories of my early days with Stephan returned. In my first journal entries, I'd referred to him as 'Master', too afraid to call him Stephan, even if I'd been given permission to do so. In later passages, there was a shift. No fear, and confusion about my feelings for him rather than what was required of me.

Then there were more recent entries. Ones where I'd mentioned Lily, Logan, Cal, my father, and even my recent visit to Stephan's office. At times, I smiled. At others, I was close to tears. If not for the fact that I could remember every detail of my time with Ian and my first days with Stephan, it would be easy to think it had happened years ago rather than months.

I was so lost in my memories that I failed to realize the part the journal we'd come to until he read the words back to me.

" 'Whore. Bitch. Cunt. Fuckhole. Cumdump. Slut.' "

The words were like daggers to my heart, each and every one, even though he said them without feeling or emotion. His tone, his volume, stayed consistent from beginning to end.

The emptiness began to creep into the space the daggers created. It hurt too much. I didn't want to feel.

" 'Ten things I like about myself. One, I like my wavy hair. Two, I'm a good cook. Three, I was good in school. Four, I like to read. Five, I like to write. Six, I have made two friends, Lily and Jade. Seven, I'm a good listener. Eight, I like that I can make Stephan smile.' "

He paused for a moment there and smiled down at me. With each word he read, each of the good things that I'd written earlier, the emptiness and hurt faded.

Softly closing the journal, he laid it down beside him and held my face reverently in his hands. " 'Nine, I'm happy. Ten, I like that I'm strong and healthy.' " We sat there staring at each other for several minutes. It was easy to get lost in his eyes when he looked at me like that. "You are, you know. You are all of those things, love, and so much more."

The tears were back again, but this time they had nothing to do with sadness. Stephan always made everything better. He'd made my life better. Sex better. He took care of me in a way no one had done since my mom.

And he refused to let those men continue to have power over me. Every day he encouraged me and helped me fight my way back.

It was at that moment I realized why what I was feeling seemed so familiar. This was what I'd been reading about in all the books Lily had brought me. This connection. This longing. I wasn't just grateful to Stephan for all he'd given me. I loved him.

Chapter 22

Brianna

I was slightly disappointed when, as we lay in bed on Saturday night, Stephan announced that we'd be going to his aunt and uncle's for dinner the next day. It wasn't that I was averse to going. Diane had always been nice to me, and even Dr. Cooper hadn't been as distant the last time. He'd even laughed at some of the pictures Diane had showed me of Stephan.

I was disappointed because I had hoped Stephan and I would spend the day together. Most of Saturday had been spent working on my assignment. He'd been there, yes, but it wasn't the same. Plus, it seemed different. Or maybe it was me who was different. Knowing that I loved him had changed things for me. And when he'd entered me, all the things I usually felt were intensified. It was as if my heart and body were confirming what I already knew.

He caught me staring at him as he was dressing on Sunday morning after our shower. I stood in nothing but my bra and panties, clutching my dress. "You all right, sweetheart?"

He pulled a pair of dress pants up his legs and over his backside. The memory of him bending over in the gym earlier and watching his muscles contract . . . Stephan was absolutely gorgeous, and for now, he was mine.

"Yes." I hurried to get dressed before he stopped what he was doing and made me tell him what I was thinking. The women in my books always made it seem like it was a big thing, and they were scared to confess their feelings. It made me think I should be afraid, too. I'd always been honest with Stephan, however, and I knew I had to tell him. I just had to figure out how.

When we arrived at Dr. Cooper and Diane's house, Jimmy was there but Samantha wasn't. Jimmy mumbled something about his wife not feeling well. I didn't hear the entire conversation, because Diane asked for my help in the kitchen. Whatever the reason, I was glad Samantha wasn't there.

Dinner was good. I only caught Dr. Cooper giving Stephan a

disapproving look once, after he leaned over and placed an intimate kiss on my neck. I giggled, which probably drew the attention of everyone at the table, but I couldn't help it. Diane had a knowing smile on her face, a direct contrast to the look on Dr. Cooper's. Then there was Jimmy. He seemed lost in his own thoughts and didn't contribute all that much to the conversation.

Jimmy excused himself right after dinner, saying he wanted to get back home and check on Samantha. Once he left, Dr. Cooper and Stephan went to his study. I helped Diane clear off the table and put the food away.

"Have you thought about what you'd like to do for your birthday, Brianna?" While the subject of my birthday had come up over dinner, Diane's question caught me off guard.

"Cal is taking me to a concert." We were in the kitchen now, putting the leftovers into containers.

"Cal? Is he a friend of yours?"

I stopped what I was doing. She had paused as well, and was watching me closely. Had I said something wrong? "Yes."

"I see," she said, going back to rinsing off the plates before placing them in the dishwasher. "Does Stephan know you're going?"

"Yes. He's . . . we're all going together."

"So it's just going to be the three of you?"

I didn't understand. It felt like I was missing something. "No. Jade is coming, too. And I think some of his other friends as well. I don't know them, though." Then I realized there was something in the way she was standing that made me think she was upset. "Are you . . . did I do something wrong?"

She smiled at me, and I breathed a sigh of relief. "Not at all, dear."

A few minutes later, Stephan walked into the room. He didn't look overly happy until he saw me. Smiling, he walked behind me and pulled me back against him. "Almost done, sweetheart?"

"Um . . ."

"I can finish up here if you two need to go."

"We'll be back. I want to take her down by the creek." Stephan was already guiding me toward the back door.

"You two have fun," I heard her say through the open kitchen window.

We held hands as we walked down a winding path through several herb gardens. Being June, everything was in bloom. It was beautiful.

As we went farther, the path straightened out and we entered a canopy of trees. It was a warm day but overcast. The shading from the trees as we walked farther into the woods made it seem later in the day than what it actually was.

Soon I began to hear the sound of water. Mom and I had lived in the city, so it was rare for me to be near water unless it was a pool. In Two Harbors, however, there was water everywhere. Sometimes, when John had been at work, I had snuck down to the stream that ran not far from his house. It hadn't been much, but it got me out for a little while. There had been something about the water running freely that made me envious. I could have sat there watching it for hours had I not been afraid John would come home and realize I was gone.

"A penny for your thoughts?"

I'd been staring at the ground. When I looked up, we were standing on the banks of the creek he'd mentioned, although to me it appeared too wide for that title. There were at least twenty feet between where we stood and the other side.

He wrapped his arms around my waist, forcing me to face him.

"There was a small stream behind John's house."

"Did you used to go there?"

I nodded. "I liked the water."

"Come here. I want to show you something."

Very carefully, we walked along the rocky shore. He helped me jump over a few of the wetter areas, never releasing his hold on me for more than a second. Eventually we came to a small cliff-like structure made up of large rocks. It jutted out toward the water.

He helped me climb up, and we sat with our feet dangling over the edge. I could see the water flowing on both sides as well as beneath me.

"This is where I used to come when it got too much for me to handle." There was a note of melancholy in his voice, and I knew he was talking about missing his parents.

"How did they die?"

Stephan didn't look at me. Instead, he focused on the water. "Their plane crashed on the way back from New York." He paused. "I should have been with them."

"I'm sorry."

He turned to me and smiled, but there was no joy in it.

I reached out and touched his face. We stared into each other's eyes. I understood the loss, the emptiness that he still felt. I wanted to help him, but I didn't know how.

The air grew heavy around us, and he leaned forward. He brushed his lips against mine before cupping my face and deepening the kiss.

Although he'd kissed me many times, there was a raw emotion, a sadness that I understood. He was still mourning his parents just as I was my mom. It was something I doubted would ever go away for either of us.

"Brianna." He moaned against my mouth. There was something in his voice, almost a sound of desperation. I slid my arms around his neck and held on, letting him take whatever he needed from me.

He snaked his hand up under the hem of my dress, lifting my backside. Stephan had barely finished speaking before he raised me up, positioning me farther back on the rock. Moments later, he was on top of me, his weight pushing me against the hard surface. He found my mouth again with his, and he hitched my leg over his hip. His arousal was pressed firmly against me. Only our clothes separated us.

His hands were everywhere, roaming over my clothes and underneath the hem of my dress. I clung to his shoulders, his hair, anything I could get my hands on. I loved kissing Stephan, but our clothes were beginning to frustrate me. I wanted him closer. That we were outside didn't matter. He needed me, and I wanted him to take what he needed.

Our breathing became harsher as the intensity increased. My back scraped against the rock, and I briefly wondered if the dress would survive. He tilted my hips so I could feel more of him, and I forgot about anything else other than him.

Stephan kissed down the column of my neck, buried his head in my shoulder, and began mumbling. I couldn't understand what he was saying, but I was so far gone I didn't know if that was because he wasn't making sense or if I wasn't able to comprehend.

He shifted us again until his mouth hovered over mine. Our breath mingled, and I could taste him on my tongue even though our lips weren't touching. Stephan stared into my eyes. He ceased breathing for several seconds. Neither of us moved. It was as if time stopped.

Our breathing slowed as we continued to look into each other's eyes. The pained look that had furrowed his brow was gone. Pleasure filled me at the knowledge that I'd helped drive that haunted look from him. The love I had for him beat hard in my chest, and the need to tell him clawed its way to the surface. "I—"

"Stephan?"

We both turned at the sound of Dr. Cooper's voice. To my surprise, Stephan laughed. "Well, I guess this will confirm any lingering doubts Richard has about our relationship."

He pulled away from me, and I instantly felt the loss.

Stephan helped me to sit up. He checked the back of my dress and grimaced. "I should regret making out with you on a jagged rock like a horny teenager, but I don't. Are you hurt?"

"No. I'm fine."

He smiled and kissed my lips just as Dr. Cooper came into view. When I caught sight of Stephan's uncle's face, I knew he wasn't going to keep silent. I only hoped they didn't start fighting again. Not because of me.

Stephan

"Brianna." My uncle's voice was tight but pleasant enough as he greeted her. When he addressed me, however, there was a distinct edge. "Stephan."

I helped Brianna down from our rocky perch before turning us both toward my uncle. Brianna's hair was a mess. The back of her dress had tears from where it had scraped against the rock. Luckily, it seemed her dress got the worst of it. I didn't see any broken skin through the small rips, but I'd have to verify that once we got home.

Pulling Brianna to my side, I addressed my uncle. "You were looking for us?"

He pressed his lips together, and I could tell he was measuring his words carefully. Richard had promised he wouldn't say anything to upset Brianna. For her sake, I was glad he was trying to uphold that promise.

"I wanted to say good-bye. The hospital called. One of my patients was admitted, and I want to check on him before it gets too late."

I knew he wanted to say more. The small vein in his forehead was pulsing. It was a telltale sign of his agitation. I ignored it. "Thanks for letting us know. I hope your patient recovers."

My uncle dragged his attention away from Brianna's disheveled dress and back to me. "I'm sure he will. From what they tell me, it was minor, but I'll feel more comfortable overseeing things myself."

That was one thing my uncle and I had in common. I'd learned to delegate over the last two years, but it wasn't something that came naturally to me. Richard was the same. It was probably the reason we butted heads as often as we did.

"Stephan, may I speak privately with you for a moment?"

Smiling, I kissed Brianna's shoulder. "Do you think you can find your way back to the house on your own, sweetheart?"

Brianna glanced up at me, worry in her eyes. I'm sure she had some idea of what my uncle wanted to discuss with me. She didn't want to go. "Yes, I think so."

"Just follow that path there." I pointed to the opening in the trees Richard had emerged from a few minutes before. "As long as you stay on the path, it will take you directly to the gardens at the back of the house. I'll be there shortly."

She nodded and tentatively made her way over the rocky bank, past Richard, and up to the path. We both waited several minutes after we could no longer see her.

"Stephan." There was a mixture of anger, frustration, and exasperation in his voice. "What are you doing?"

"I think it's obvious."

He laughed, but there was no humor in it. "Yes. It is *quite* obvious."

We stood staring at each other for an extended period of time. His opinion of my relationship with Brianna didn't seem to have changed.

Running his hands over his face, he sighed. "I know there is nothing I can say to make you stop doing what you're doing, Stephan, but I'm still worried. I'm worried about her and how she's dealing with what happened to her. She seems to be getting better, but is she really, or is she just learning to rely on you?"

Before I could comment, he continued. "And what about you? What happens if this gets out? What you're doing. What you . . . are." He whispered the last word as if he were sharing some well-guarded secret. In a way, he was, but no one was around. Even if there were, they wouldn't have a clue what he was referring to. "You have a reputation, and people—

a foundation—that depend on you. What about them?"

"I understand the risks, Richard."

"Do you?"

"Yes."

He shook his head and looked down at the muddy ground before making eye contact again. "What would your parents think?"

It was like a blow to the gut. I couldn't believe he'd gone there.

"They'd want me to be happy."

"At the expense of others? No."

"It is not at the expense of others. I'm not hurting anyone."

"I think that's a matter of opinion."

"We're done here." I'd had enough. I wasn't going to continue to listen to his misguided condemnation.

I walked past him. He didn't try to stop me.

When I reached the tree line, however, his soft tone halted me in my tracks. "I don't want to fight anymore."

Tilting my head back, I looked up through the canopy of trees to the barely visible sky, and took a deep breath. "Neither do I."

"I know you're not my son, but I *do* love you like one, Stephan. I don't like what you're doing. I don't understand it. But . . . I won't say anything more."

I glanced over at him. He looked defeated. "Thank you."

He nodded.

I waited a few more seconds and then continued up the path to find Brianna.

Monday morning brought with it the usual headaches. Jamie knocked on my office door around nine with a stack of mail and all the paperwork I needed for my two afternoon meetings. I hurried to get through everything so I could take a break before being trapped in a conference room for the rest of the day.

I was just getting onto the elevator to go grab some lunch when I caught sight of Lily. "Hey."

"Hey." She looked happy. I could only imagine the reason for that since Logan had been home this past weekend. "You heading to lunch?"

"Yeah. I need a break before this afternoon."

"Mind if I join you?"

Lily and I ended up at a café two blocks from the office. We found a corner booth and sat down with our lunches.

"I spoke to Brianna this morning."

I nodded and took another bite of my sandwich.

"I'm leaving the office early on Wednesday so she and I can go shopping. She told me you want her to get waxed, too."

"Yes. I do."

Lily cocked her head to the side, considering. "Does this have to do with Saturday?"

I smirked. "Partly."

She huffed. "I hate when you and Logan do that, you know."

Laughing, I took another bite of my lunch. Dominants talked to each other, and it was rare they included their submissives unless it was to talk about limits or trying something new in a scene. My guess was that Logan hadn't told Lily much past asking her if she would be able to concentrate on the scene while Brianna and I watched. That, and perhaps that we wanted her to talk to Brianna both before and after so she'd know it was all completely consensual. Lily knew how it worked. But because we were friends outside the friendship Logan and I shared, she occasionally liked to push. Didn't mean she'd get anywhere, though.

"You know I'm not going to tell you anything, so I'm not sure why you ask."

"Because I want to know."

"Why? Do you not trust Logan?"

"Of course I do." She seemed offended by the suggestion.

"Then why are you asking something that is his concern, not yours?"

"Because he won't tell me anything. All I know is you and Brianna will be there."

"Then that's all he feels you need to know."

She threw her fork down on her plate, not happy that I wasn't giving up any information.

I laughed. "If you want to know something, ask Logan. Stop trying to go behind his back and ask me. You keep it up, and I'll have to share this information with him."

Her eyes got wide, and I suppressed a chuckle. Needless to say, after that she changed the subject.

At home that night, Brianna was quiet. I asked her if something was wrong, but she said no. Given her conversation with Lily, it was likely she was nervous about her waxing appointment on Wednesday. I decided to let it go for the time being. If it didn't get better, or got worse, I'd confront her about it.

As I was leaving the office on Tuesday, our new CFO caught me in the hall. "Do you have a minute?"

I glanced down at my watch. "Sure. I need to make a quick call, and then I'll meet you in your office."

Quickly dialing Brianna, I let her know I was going to be a little late. "Okay. I'll turn the oven down."

"No. You go ahead and eat. I don't know how long I'll be."

"Okay." She sounded disappointed.

"I'll be home as soon as I can." The urge to tell her I loved her sprang to the surface. It was getting harder and harder to keep inside. When we were making out on the rock by the creek Sunday afternoon, I'd let it slip. I didn't think she'd heard me, though.

Tucking the phone back into my pocket, I said goodnight to Jamie and went to find out what Michael needed.

When I knocked on the door to his office, he was looking down at a stack of papers and rubbing the back of his neck. "Mr. Coleman."

"Mr. James." I walked into the room and took a seat across from his desk.

"I'm . . ." He took a deep breath. "I was going through some paperwork this weekend, and I came across this." Michael handed me the papers he'd been looking at, and I recognized them immediately.

"Where did you get these?"

"They were on my desk, underneath the second quarter financial reports."

I tried to think back to last Friday when I'd returned the reports to his office. There was no one to blame here but myself.

"I have to ask, Mr. Coleman. Who is Ian Pierce, and what does he have to do with The Coleman Foundation? I can't find any record of him, and believe me, I've been trying after seeing that mess."

"He doesn't."

Michael blew out a breath he appeared to have been holding. "That's a relief."

His response had me intrigued. "Why do you say that?"

"Well, it's quite obvious there is some illegal activity going on there. I did my research on this organization before interviewing for this job, Mr. Coleman. Your parents were good people, and from what I can tell, so are you. It was bad enough finding out someone was skimming, but this . . ." He pointed to the documents in my hands. "That is something altogether different."

"Are you saying you can follow this? You can prove there is illegal activity here?"

He looked confused. "Of course."

"Mr. James, I need you to do something for me, and I need your assurance that you won't speak a word of this to anyone."

"I'll do my best."

"I need you to go through this with a fine-tooth comb, and tell me everything you can find that is questionable."

"All right," he said reluctantly. "But I don't understand. If this man has nothing to do with The Coleman Foundation, why am I looking into his bank statements? Shouldn't this be something for the FBI?"

"If you can prove illegal activity, then I'm sure they'll be involved at some point. Right now, I just need to know."

"Can I ask why?"

I handed the statements back to him and stood. "Because he hurt someone I love."

Chapter 23

Stephan

I was an emotional mess by the time I arrived home to Brianna.
Michael's news both thrilled and worried me. I was taking a gamble having
our new CFO go through Ian's bank statements. What he would do when he
discovered, if he hadn't already, that my name and bank account were on
there as well, I didn't know. Given what I knew about him, and that he'd
noticed something neither Oscar's experts nor I had, I doubted it had
escaped his attention.

Brianna was on the couch reading another one of her library books when
I walked through the door. She immediately laid it down on the coffee table
and came to me. As always, having her in my arms again calmed me. We'd
deal with whatever came, no matter what it was.

Leaning down, I brushed my lips against hers. "Did you eat?"

She nodded. "I made a plate for you."

Brianna sat beside me on the couch while I ate the dinner she made.
Maybe it was my conversation with Michael, but the dining room seemed
too far away from her. I needed her near me.

When I was finished, I laid my plate aside and pulled her onto my lap.
"Tell me about your day, sweetheart."

"Lily called. She's picking me up tomorrow at three." Brianna glanced up
at me, and I could see she was worried about something. "I won't be home
to make you dinner."

I smiled and tucked a strand of her hair behind her ear. "I think I'll be
able to fend for myself for one night." She still appeared unsure, so I
decided to move on. "What else did you do today?"

Over the next hour, Brianna told me about her new book and a phone call
she'd received from Jade. Cal's girlfriend wanted Brianna to go grocery
shopping with her. I wasn't sure how I felt about that, although Jade's
reaction to Brianna's meltdown the previous Friday was encouraging.
"When does she want to go?"

"Thursday. She says she doesn't have class that day."

"I want you to call me before you leave and the moment you return home." It was the only way I wouldn't drive myself crazy with worry. Knowing she was out with someone I barely knew was going to be bad enough.

"Yes, Sir."

Giving her a kiss to show her my pleasure, I let my lips linger against hers. It would be so easy to forget about everything else and take her to bed, but there were things we needed to discuss. I chose the easiest first. "Did Lily say anything to you about this weekend?"

She shook her head.

"You and I are going to be going over to Logan and Lily's Saturday afternoon."

I waited for that to sink in. "Okay."

Running my hands up and down her arms and back, I was hoping to detect any adverse reaction she might have to my next bit of information. "You know Logan and Lily have a Dominant and submissive relationship." She nodded. "I've asked them to perform a scene for us."

She was quiet. When she met my gaze, I could tell she was confused as to my meaning. "I don't understand."

"Brianna, you and I have talked about you being my submissive, correct?"

"Yes." The muscles under my hands tensed as her anxiety increased. I tried my best to comfort her without changing our position or breaking eye contact.

"I know the idea still scares you, sweetheart, and I want you to see a couple you know and trust engaging in a scene." Wanting to reassure her, I continued. "All we're going to do is observe. You'll be with me the entire time. I want you to watch, and if you have questions before or after, you may ask them to any of us, all right? I want you to be comfortable with this, Brianna. With us."

Her lower lip began to tremble before she pressed them both tightly together. Running my thumb over her lips, she gradually relaxed them.

"Talk to me."

"Is . . ."

"Go on, love. Tell me what's bothering you."

"Is he going to hurt Lily?"

"No. I promise you, he won't hurt Lily. It's what I've explained to you before. Everything they do together, everything he does to her, she has consented to. You remember your safewords?"

She nodded.

"Lily has safewords, too. If something is wrong, she can use them just as you can. And if something happens Saturday that bothers you, I'll be right there."

Brianna wasn't completely comfortable, so I waited for her to gather her thoughts. "Does Lily know?"

"Yes, Lily knows."

She considered this new information for several minutes before I felt her tension ease.

"You and Lily are going to talk both before and after the scene. I want you to ask anything you want to, Brianna. Anything, do you understand?"

"Yes, Sir. I understand."

"Good girl. Now why don't you tell me about this newest book you're reading? Is it as good as the last one?"

The rest of our evening was spent discussing her book and watching some television. There might have been some making out mixed in there, too . . . and some groping. I could try to pass it off as an attempt to get her mind off the serious things we'd talked about, but it would be a flat-out lie. Keeping my hands off Brianna was a near impossibility. Knowing she welcomed my attentions didn't help quell my impulses either.

On Wednesday morning, I woke her up before the alarm. There was nothing better than feasting on her pussy first thing, except maybe following that up with making love to her.

Morning sex was new to me. Before Brianna, I'd never had sex before breakfast. Prior to college, I'd never spent the whole night with a woman. It was usually a quick—or not so quick—fuck in the back of a car or up against a wall or, if we were lucky, in a bed. None of the women had been looking for anything long-term. They wanted a young stud to take care of their needs before going on their way. At the time, that had worked for me.

Sarah was perhaps the closest I'd come to what Brianna and I had. We had been together over a year. During the week, we would hang out, go to clubs or parties. It was college, so there had been plenty of opportunities to blow off some steam after classes. The sexual part of our relationship had typically been confined to the weekends and our arrangement. On the two occasions we'd fallen asleep studying, there'd been nothing remotely romantic about waking up the next morning.

Once we'd agreed to start playing together, I'd rented an apartment on the other side of town. College could be a lot like high school, and the last thing either of us had wanted was for someone to see us playing and spread it across campus. Since money hadn't been an issue, it had been easier to have a separate place to get away.

We would drive to the apartment on Friday nights and spend the evening eating pizza and doing homework. At the end of the night, she would go to her bedroom, and I to mine. From midnight until six o'clock on Sunday nights when we'd sit down to dinner, she would be my submissive.

I learned a lot about being a Dominant in that time. Sarah was a year older than me, and she'd been introduced to the lifestyle by her first boyfriend when she was sixteen. She knew what she wanted, what she liked, and she was a great teacher. In many ways, she'd taught me more than Daren had.

Brianna worked in the kitchen to make me breakfast while I sat at the table and watched her. No, none of my prior relationships came close to what I had with Brianna. I'd never loved any of my submissives before her. To be honest, I'd never wanted more. With Brianna, I wanted everything.

During breakfast, I couldn't stop touching her. It almost became a game as to how many times I could make her blush or giggle.

When I couldn't put it off any longer, I pulled her into my lap and gave her a long kiss good-bye. "Have fun with Lily today. Use the card I gave you to buy whatever you want, and I'll see you tonight when you get home."

Brianna
She would be here any minute.

The day had gone by too quickly. That might have been due to how nervous I was. I checked to make sure I had everything . . . again. My cell phone was in the pocket of my jeans, along with fifty dollars Stephan had insisted I take with me. He said you never knew when you'd need cash for something, and it was just safer that way.

For the first time, I was carrying one of the purses Lily bought me. There wasn't much in it other than the credit card Stephan had given me and the driver's license I hadn't gotten around to using yet. I knew I'd have to drive sooner or later. There was nothing keeping me from using the car parked down in the parking garage but me. I was worried something would happen, even if it was a memory, and I'd panic. I didn't want to cause an accident and risk hurting someone.

The panel by the door came alive, and I knew Lily had arrived. I stood, not sure what I should do. Normally Lily let herself inside on her own. Would she do that again?

My question was answered seconds later when she rang the doorbell. I rushed across the room to open the door.

"Hi." Lily smiled. She was wearing jeans, a fitted blouse, and heels. It was the most casual I'd ever seen her.

"Hi, Lily."

"Are you ready to go?"

I glanced behind me into the apartment. Everything was as it should be. There was no valid excuse for me not to leave with her. "Yes."

"Grab your keys and let's go. We have an appointment with Julie at four."

By the time Lily parked her car alongside a large stone building, I was concentrating on taking each breath. Julie was Lily's esthetician. We were going to get waxed before we went shopping. Lily said it would be easier that way, and Julie had blocked out her schedule for the rest of the day.

"Are you all right?"

I turned to see a worried Lily.

"I . . . I think so."

She took my hand and squeezed. "It'll be okay. I'll go first. You can watch everything she does, okay?"

I nodded, but I was still at a five. Stephan said Lily had safewords. Would she know what it meant if I said *yellow*? Or *red*?

Lily got out of the car. She stood a few feet in front of her vehicle and waited, hand on her hip. "You coming?"

Taking a deep breath, I reached for the handle and opened the door.

The inside of the building wasn't what I'd expected. I didn't know what I'd expected, really, but this wasn't it. There was a large desk in the center of the room. As we walked closer, I noticed there were two women sitting behind the high marble counters.

Lily stopped to talk to one of the women while I took in the rest of our surroundings. Music played overhead. It was soft and melodic. I realized it was meant to relax. Maybe that worked for most of their customers, but it wasn't helping me. I was just as nervous as when we'd walked into the place.

"Julie's ready for us."

I swallowed and clutched my purse to my stomach. With every step, my uneasiness grew, and so did the nausea building in the pit of my abdomen. *I'm doing this for Stephan. I'm doing this for Stephan.*

"Lily!" A petite woman with curly blond hair approached us.

"Hi, Julie. How've you been?"

Julie hugged Lily. "Oh, you know. Same old, same old. Although I did hear back from that guy I met at the gym. We're going out on Friday."

Hearing Julie talk to Lily settled my nerves a little. She didn't *seem* dangerous.

Just when I started to breathe a little easier, however, her attention refocused on me. "And this must be Brianna."

She held out her hand. I looked at it for longer than I should have before taking it. "Hi."

"Lily tells me this is your first time getting waxed."

I looked at Lily, eyes wide. What should I say?

When neither of us responded, Julie cocked her head to the side and wrinkled her brow. "Did I misunderstand?"

My anxiety began to rise again. This woman didn't know me. I didn't know her. There was no way I could tell her . . . tell her all of those things . . .

Lily took hold of my hand and pulled me closer to her. "Brianna's been waxed before, but it wasn't a good experience. I was hoping you could do me first so she can watch and see it's not so bad."

"Oh. I'm sorry. Yeah. There are some really bad estheticians out there. It was a man, right?"

I managed a small nod.

"They're the worst, especially when it comes to Brazilians. Like ripping a huge chunk of hair from our lady bits won't hurt. Please! I'd like to see how they'd react if someone did the same thing to their balls." She laughed and walked to the back of the room.

Once she was several feet away, Lily leaned in to whisper in my ear. "You going to be okay?"

"I have to be."

"You don't have to be anything, Brianna. If you don't want to do this, then you tell me. I know it's what Stephan wants, but he'll get over it. He won't want you to be traumatized over this either."

Julie glanced up from where she was now sitting on a rolling stool. It was similar to the one I'd seen in Dr. Cooper's office. That brought with it the memory of lying there, panicked, while Dr. Cooper examined me. Stephan had been there that time. He'd been there when I'd needed him. I remembered the look in his eyes, the sound of his voice. *Shh. No one is going to hurt you, Brianna.*

No one was going to hurt me. Stephan would never have asked this of me if he didn't know it was safe.

Lily hadn't moved from her spot even though Julie was waiting. She looked as if she were about to call the whole thing off.

"I'm okay."

"Are you sure?"

I nodded.

"We ready to get this show on the road?" Julie patted the end of the table.

Lily hugged me and then began removing her clothes.

I stood off to the side, still hugging my purse, while she climbed up on top of the table. Julie covered her discreetly with a large, white towel.

"You can pull that chair over if you'd like." Julie was turned away from me as she spoke.

Looking behind me, I noticed a chair pushed up against the wall. Without moving it, I sat down.

"The usual, Lily?"

"Yep. Make me hair-free." Lily made a sweeping motion with her hands down her body, and they both laughed. Neither of them appeared to be nervous about what was about to happen. Knowing that, I concentrated on my breathing and staying calm.

Julie dipped what looked to be a wooden tongue depressor into a ceramic pot. When she pulled it out, it was covered in hot wax. I cringed as she put the wax on Lily's leg.

"How are things with you and your man? He still traveling all the time?"

"Unfortunately." Lily didn't sound distressed at all. She sounded . . . relaxed. "He was home this past weekend, though, and he'll be here this coming weekend, too."

"Anything special planned?"

"No idea. He likes to surprise me."

"Nothing wrong with that. I love when a man shows up with some elaborate plan for us to spend an evening together."

"You'd love Logan, then. He always has something up his sleeve."

As Julie worked her way up Lily's leg, the sight and sound of her applying the wax and then ripping the cloth off didn't bother me as much as it had at the start. Every now and then Lily would wince, but after a second, it was gone and she was back to her conversation with Julie. Maybe this wouldn't be so bad.

Lily moved, and it caught my attention. She positioned herself farther down on the table, her legs bent and spread wide open. Julie pushed the towel up and reached for the wax.

It was strange. I didn't want to look, but I couldn't turn away.

"Brianna?"

I dragged my gaze up to Lily's face. "Yes?"

"Did you want to come closer so you can see what she's doing? I don't mind."

Did I?

She held out her hand, beckoning me.

When I reached her side, Lily took hold of my hand. "This part hurts more than the legs, but once it's done, it's done. The pain goes away after a few seconds, and I don't have to worry about hair for at least a month."

"Ready?"

Lily nodded to Julie, and I held my breath as Julie pulled the skin taut and ripped the cloth strip away.

Chapter 24

Brianna
Before I knew it, Lily was hopping off the table, and it was my turn. Julie looked concerned as I removed my clothes and lay down on the table, my hands holding tightly to the sides.

"Are you sure you want to do this?"

"Yes." I closed my eyes and tried to remember to breathe. It would be okay. I'd be fine.

The sound of a chair scraping across the floor, followed by the feeling of fingers prying my hand off the table, made me open my eyes. Lily sat next to me.

"I'm right here."

I nodded.

Lily glanced in Julie's direction, and there seemed to be some sort of unspoken communication that took place.

A hand touched my leg, and I jerked. "It's okay. I just want to see what direction your hair is growing. It will make removal easier and less painful."

"Okay."

She ran her hand up and down both my legs, turning each one to the side. "I'm going to get started now. If you need me to stop, just say so."

I didn't respond other than to hold tighter to Lily's hand.

Something warm coated a small section of my leg. To my surprise, it didn't hurt. It was the temperature of a relaxing bath, not that of a hot stove.

Something was placed over the warmth and pressed down. It reminded me of making a pie crust, and having to be sure you got all the air bubbles out of the dough.

"This may hurt some."

Julie's words barely registered before there was a flash of pain, like having an old Band-Aid ripped off. As quick as the pain had come, it was gone.

"How was that?"

For the first time since climbing on the table, I met Julie's gaze. "Not . . . not as bad as I thought it would be."

She smiled and patted my leg. "Good. The ankles are the worst part of the legs. Once those are done, the rest shouldn't be bad at all." Julie paused. "Are you getting a Brazilian as well?"

"Yes."

"That's going to hurt. I won't lie to you. But we'll take it slow, and if you need a minute to catch your breath, you just tell me. We're in no hurry."

Julie picked up her wooden stick again and slathered more wax on my leg. I relaxed this time and watched her. When it came time for her to remove the strip, I was prepared. While it wasn't pleasant, the pain was tolerable.

"So do you have a boyfriend, Brianna?"

"Um . . ."

"Yes, she does."

Julie smiled. "I thought maybe you might. Not many women come in here wanting the Full Monty if there isn't a guy going to see it." She winked at me before refocusing her attention on my leg. "What's his name?"

"Stephan."

"He sounds sophisticated. Is he older?"

I realized then that I had no idea how old Stephan was. He didn't look that much older than me, but that didn't mean he wasn't.

Lily noticed my struggling and jumped in with an answer. "He's twenty-four."

Twenty-four. That meant his parents had been gone ten years.

"Not too old, then."

Julie finished with my legs and asked me to scoot down farther on the table. A lump formed in my throat and I had difficulty swallowing.

"I'm right here," Lily assured me.

Once I was where Julie wanted me, she pushed the towel out of the way. She gasped. "What happened to you?"

I didn't need to look to know what she was referring to. The bruising had gone away over time, but the scars would always be there. They were high, mostly under my pubic hair, so she probably hadn't noticed them when she was waxing my legs. With my legs spread wide, and no towel to shade the area, there was no hiding.

"This wasn't done by wax, was it?" Julie's eyes were wide. Her face held a mixture of pity and outrage.

"I don't know."

That was honest. I really didn't know. So many things had been done to me, especially in that area of my body, that I didn't know what had left permanent marks and what hadn't.

Julie didn't move for a long time before she appeared to get a hold of herself. "We'll go really slow. I don't know how this scar tissue is going to react to the waxing. If something doesn't feel right, I need you to tell me right away, and we'll try something else." I could have been wrong, but I thought I saw a tear fall down her cheek as she turned away from me to reach for the wax.

She placed the wax on a small area of skin along the crease of my leg and pressed the cloth strip over top. For the first time since we'd started, Julie appeared more nervous than I was. I wasn't sure why, but knowing that gave me confidence.

"It's okay."

The look she gave me told me she understood more than she probably should, and it made me wonder if she'd ever been abused.

"Here we go."

I wasn't going to lie. The waxing hurt, especially between my legs. However, it wasn't nearly as painful as I remembered. I wasn't sure if that was because of Julie, or if it had to do with me.

Lily went to pay, but then I remembered Stephan had told me to use his card. I placed my hand on her arm, stopping her. "What is it?"

Pulling out the card, I held it up to her. "Stephan gave me this to pay."

She considered for a moment and then nodded. "Come on. I'll have them separate the charges."

The wind had picked up by the time we left the salon. It looked like it might rain, so we hurried to the car. "Good thing I always carry an umbrella."

Lily was always prepared. I wished I could be that way. It seemed like it was Stephan who always looked out for me and made sure things were taken care of.

Thinking of him made me smile.

"I know who's on *your* mind." Lily smirked as she pulled out into traffic.

I blushed.

"I'm going to assume by that blush things are going well between you two."

I nodded.

Lily glanced over at me. "I'll let you in on a little secret, Brianna. This is the part where you tell your friend all the things you can't talk about to anyone else. This is girl time."

"Oh. Um . . ."

"You can tell me anything." She paused. "Or if you have questions, I'll try to help. That's how it works."

"Okay." I was quiet for a few minutes as I tried to gather my thoughts. There was only one thing I really wanted to ask her. One thing I'd been dying to know the answer to. "Lily?"

"Yes?"

"How . . . how do I tell Stephan that . . . that I love him?"

Stephan

I was trying my very best to stay out of Michael's office. He would come find me once he was done analyzing Ian's statements. It wasn't as if he didn't have anything else to do.

At five o'clock, I forced myself to go home without making a detour to our new CFO's office. Being so close to having something that would put Ian Pierce behind bars was driving me crazy. I knew I needed to exercise patience. A distraction would have been good. Unfortunately, I was going home to an empty condo since Brianna was out shopping with Lily. I couldn't even call Logan to come keep me company since he was still out of town until the following day.

The first thing I noticed when I walked into my condo was the smell of food. Warm food. Going into the kitchen, I found a note on the counter in Brianna's handwriting.

I made dinner. Everything is in the crockpot. I hope you like it.

It was signed *Brianna*.

I smiled. She was taking care of me even when she wasn't there.

Lifting the lid of the crockpot, something in my kitchen I'd never used before, I saw a small roast, potatoes, and carrots simmering in brown gravy. If it tasted half as good as it smelled, I doubted there would be much, if any, left by the time she returned home.

Dinner was lonely. I was used to having her there with me. Even if we didn't typically talk much as we ate, her presence alone made a difference. I missed her.

I took my time cleaning up, even wiping down the already spotless counters. Once that was finished, I was at a loss. Sitting in my chair, reading a book, or watching television didn't hold any appeal without her, so I grabbed my laptop and went upstairs to my study. Maybe I could at least get some work done.

It was almost eight o'clock when I heard the door downstairs open. Without thinking, I was already on my feet and headed down the stairs.

"Sir?"

Brianna called out moments before she came into view. Her hair looked damp, and for the first time I realized it had started raining outside.

She smiled when she saw me. "Hi."

"Hi."

I walked toward her. She stood watching me, not moving, shopping bags in both hands.

"Did you have fun with Lily?" I asked, crowding closer to her.

"Yes." She looked up at me. Her chest rose and fell with ever-increasing speed as I backed her up against the door.

"Drop the bags, Brianna."

I still hadn't touched her, but that didn't matter. She did as I instructed.

Leaning in, I skimmed my nose along the skin of her neck, up to her ear. "I missed you."

She sighed. "I missed you, too."

"Did you eat?"

"Yes."

I towered over her, taking possession, control, while barely touching her.

"Good, because I don't plan on letting you out of my bed for the next couple of hours." Without waiting for her response, I swept her up in my arms and carried her to my bedroom.

True to my word, Brianna and I spent the next two hours in my bed. I'd even brought out the bullet vibrator and had some fun with her. She was now bare, and I loved it. The feel of her skin, sans hair, sliding against mine was something I couldn't quite put into words. The only thing that would have made it better was if I could have gone without a condom. I didn't want anything between us, but I knew I had to wait a little while longer. She'd gotten the all clear on her first blood test, but she would need another to be sure. The three-month mark couldn't come soon enough.

When I couldn't put it off any longer, we made our way into the shower to clean ourselves up. There hadn't been a lot of talking once I'd gotten her in bed, so I made the effort as we washed. "How did the waxing go?"

She reached up to run the loofah across my chest. It had become a ritual of sorts. Whenever we showered together, I washed her and she washed me.

"Julie noticed my scars."

I had to assume Julie was the esthetician. "Did you tell her how you got them?"

Brianna shook her head.

Taking the sponge from her, I had her turn around so I could wash her back. "Was the waxing what you expected?"

"No. It didn't hurt as much as I remember."

"That's good. I'm glad."

I kissed her shoulder before turning her and kneeling down between her legs. Opening her up, I cleaned away the remnants of the wax I'd noticed earlier.

When I stood back up, she had a look on her face I didn't understand. "What is it, Brianna?"

"I . . ."

Stepping closer, I aligned our bodies and held her face between my hands. "You can tell me, sweetheart."

"I love you."

My heart pounded at her words, as if it would beat out of my chest with the pure joy I felt. "You love me?"

She nodded.

Brianna pressed her lips together and lowered her gaze. I realized she was nervous about the confession she'd just made. Did she really think I didn't feel the same?

"Look at me."

I waited until her hesitant gaze met mine. "You have no idea how happy you've made me, sweetheart. I've been . . . I've been waiting . . . hoping . . . that one day you might feel for me as I do for you."

She still appeared confused, so I spelled it out for her.

"I love you, Brianna."

At first, there was no reaction. Then it was as if my words finally sunk in, and a beautiful smile spread across her face.

"Lily said I should tell you."

"Lily said?"

She nodded.

"How long ago did you realize how you felt?"

"Saturday."

"Saturday? This past Saturday?"

Brianna nodded again.

"When?"

"After you read my journal."

I pulled her against my chest and held her. "Is that what's had you worried this week, love?"

"Yes," she whispered against my chest.

"Here I thought it was the waxing appointment that had you all tied up in knots. Why didn't you tell me sooner?"

"I . . ."

I leaned back so I could see her face.

"The women in the books . . . they all were scared to tell the men how they felt. They were all worried that he wouldn't feel the same way and . . . and leave. I didn't . . . I didn't want you to leave me."

Hugging her back to me, I placed kisses all along her forehead, her face, wherever I could reach without releasing her. "I would never leave you. You are the strongest, most honest woman I've ever met. I want you in my life for as long as you'll have me."

We stood in the shower until the water began to cool. I had mixed feelings about leaving the cocoon the shower enclosure provided. The admission of our feelings had created a type of bubble, and I didn't want anything to break it.

Slipping back under the sheets, I held her as close as humanly possible. "Never be afraid to tell me something, love. It will never change my feelings for you. I love you, and I always will."

Chapter 25

Stephan

To my great disappointment, Michael still had not sought me out about Ian's bank statements. Other than passing him in the hallway, I hadn't seen him. By the end of the day on Friday I couldn't take it anymore and knocked on his office door.

"Come in." He glanced up from his computer. "Oh. Mr. Coleman."

"Sorry to bother you. Do you have a minute?"

"Of course." He gestured to the chair for me to sit down.

"I won't take up much of your time. I know you're swamped, but I was curious if you'd had the chance to look into the bank statements any further."

Michael removed his glasses and laid them down on the desk in front of him. "I have, although I'm not finished. I've mostly been going over them in the evenings at home."

I nodded in understanding. In a way, I felt guilty asking him to review bank documents that had nothing to do with his job. My need to make Ian pay quickly overrode any adverse feelings on the matter.

"I still have several pages to go through. I was planning to spend the weekend combing through the rest of them."

"I don't mean to rush you, it's just—"

He held up his hand to stop me. "If this man hurt someone you care about, I can understand your urgency. I have a daughter. She lives with her mother, so I don't get to see her as much as I'd like, but if someone hurt her . . ." Michael let the implication hang in the air for nearly a minute. "I should have something for you on Monday."

Monday. Brianna's birthday. For some reason, that seemed appropriate, considering she was the one who'd suffered most from his torturous ways.

"I'll let you get back to work."

Traffic on the way home was worse than normal for some reason, and I called Brianna to let her know I'd be a little late. Thankfully, since I didn't live that far from the office, I only had another fifteen minutes tacked on to my usual drive time.

Tonight we were going out with Ross, Jade, and their friends. The tickets had arrived at my office the previous day. According to the tickets, the band was called Black Diamond.

When I arrived home, Brianna was in the kitchen as usual. She smiled when she saw me, but I could see the apprehension in her eyes. We'd talked about the concert, and her biggest fear was that she would have a panic attack in the middle of the club. With so many people around, it was a valid concern.

I went to greet her, pulling her into my arms for a not-so-chaste kiss. "How was your day?"

It took her several seconds to get her breathing under control enough to answer me. "Good." She lowered her eyes.

"Did something happen, or are you just nervous about tonight?"

"Tonight."

I brushed my lips across her temple before burying my face in her hair and taking in her scent. "It'll be fine. I'll be right there with you." And as much as I didn't want to admit it, so would Cal and Jade.

As planned, Brianna and Jade had gone grocery shopping on Thursday. The whole time she was gone, I'd been worried. Everything had gone as well as it could have. Jade never left her side. The only hiccup they'd had was when a fellow student had recognized Jade and came over to say hello. It happened to be a male student. Brianna had reacted as she normally did around strange men and retreated into herself. Jade, luckily, had realized Brianna's distress and removed her from the situation as soon as she could.

I was glad Brianna was making friends. That didn't mean I didn't walk on eggshells every time she left our condo with someone else. Even with Lily, I waited with bated breath for Brianna to call me and let me know she'd arrived back home safely. As much as I hated to admit it, I wasn't sure that would ever change.

Brianna and I ate dinner, showered, and dressed for our night at the club. She'd asked what she should wear, so I'd picked out a simple black dress that clung to her body in all the right places. It was made out of some kind of stretch material that was clingy but not tight. I wanted her to be comfortable. As always, she looked beautiful.

Finding a place to park proved somewhat difficult. All the parking spots on the streets surrounding the club were full. If all of these people were going to the concert, the club was going to be at capacity. I reached into my pocket and palmed the collar and leash I'd brought with me. Hopefully I wouldn't have to use them, but it was better to be prepared.

After helping her from the vehicle, I linked our arms and walked toward the club. As we got closer, the number of people on the sidewalks increased. Brianna tightened her hold on my arm. In response, I placed my free hand where hers rested on my arm and squeezed, reminding her I was right there beside her.

When we turned the corner, the club entrance came into view. There was a line of people waiting to get inside. Brianna stopped walking, and I glanced down to find all color had left her face.

"Number?"

It took her more than a minute to answer me. "Five." She paused. "Six. Five."

I chuckled. "How about we go with five and a half?"

Kissing the top of her head, I moved us up against the building and wrapped both my arms around her. Brianna rested her cheek against my chest and fisted my shirt in both her hands.

"Do you want to go home?" Although I'd asked, I wasn't sure I would agree to it even if she said yes. She needed to be around people if she was ever going to get over her fear.

"No." Her voice was shaky, but I was pleased with her answer.

"Good girl."

She snuggled closer. We attracted some looks from passersby, but I don't think Brianna noticed. Her eyes were closed.

Checking my watch, I knew we needed to get in line. The concert would be starting in roughly half an hour, and we needed to find Ross and Jade.

As if on cue, Ross stepped outside. He looked down the line of people and then turned in our direction. When our gazes locked, I nodded, letting him know I saw him.

"Ross is waiting for us."

Brianna opened her eyes, looked up at me, and then glanced in the direction of the club. I knew the moment she saw him. She took a deep breath. "I'm ready."

Re-linking our arms, I guided her to where Ross was waiting. He ignored me and focused on Brianna.

"Everything all right?"

She nodded, but her entire body was rigid from her anxiety.

He looked to me for confirmation. "Perhaps getting inside and to our table will help."

Ross seemed to agree. After saying a few words to the bouncer, I handed him our tickets and we were through the door.

The club was dark, as most clubs were. People were everywhere, and I made sure to position Brianna in front of me as we started moving through the crowd. A woman bumped into us about halfway to our table, and Brianna froze. Without overthinking it, I halted our movement and reached into my pocket. Removing the collar, I used both hands to secure it to her wrist.

Her reaction was almost immediate. With the collar around her wrist, she calmed considerably. In this instance, the low light worked to our advantage. No one around us gave any indication that they'd noticed the addition to her wardrobe. No one but Ross. As we approached the table and he turned around, he zeroed in on the piece of leather around her wrist and followed the leash up to where I had it wrapped around my hand.

I was sure he was going to say something until Jade popped up from her seat and broke the growing tension. "I'm glad you came, Anna. This is going to be so much fun."

We all took our seats, and I positioned Brianna as close to me as possible. Ross frowned. Jade smiled knowingly.

"I guess we should introduce everyone." Ross was still giving me the evil eye, so Jade took over the introductions.

Brianna
There were people everywhere. I'd been close to saying *yellow* when that lady ran into us. Everyone was so close, pushing each other. Each breath had been an effort, and then when she'd touched me, everything stopped.

The feel of leather enclosing my wrist brought a sense of comfort and security. I knew Stephan had brought the collar. I'd seen him slip it into his pocket. Maybe I should have felt awkward or embarrassed because he had me on a leash, but I didn't. He knew what I needed, and I trusted him to do what was best.

Jade introduced us to the other people at the table while Cal sat grumpily by her side. I knew he still didn't care for Stephan, but his reaction seemed over the top given we'd only just arrived. I didn't understand it. Had something happened I wasn't aware of?

"Anna, Stephan, I'd like you to meet Justin, Mandy, and Phillip."

Stephan adjusted my hand so that it lay in his lap, just below his crotch. I knew without his saying anything that he wanted me to keep it there. "Nice to meet you."

A man approached the table, and I leaned into Stephan. He was about as tall as Stephan, maybe a little taller. The man smiled. He didn't seem threatening, but sometimes it was impossible to tell.

"I see your friends got here," the man said.

"Hey, Brian." Jade motioned to us. "This is Anna and Stephan."

"Nice to meet you."

"Likewise." Stephan held out his hand to greet Brian.

"Anyone been over to get your drink orders?"

The question was directed toward Stephan and me, but Jade answered. "No. Not yet. Everyone looks pretty busy."

"They are, but I'll send someone over. No matter how busy the bar gets, they still need to take care of the tables." He glanced at his watch. "I need to get backstage and check on the band. Make sure everything's ready to go." Then he turned his attention to us again. "If I don't make it back over later, it was nice meeting you." Brian's gaze lingered on me a little too long before he walked away from our table, and I shivered.

"I'm right here," Stephan whispered in my ear as he tugged on the leash.

I nodded and took a deep breath. Everything was fine.

Justin shifted in his chair and took a drink of the beer in front of him. Everyone at the table had a drink except Stephan and I. "Have you guys ever been to Crazy Lewie's before?"

"No. This is the first time."

"How about you?" This time his question was directed solely at me.

I shook my head.

"I didn't think I'd seen you around before. Cal here was telling us you and he grew up together."

Justin's continued scrutiny made me uneasy, but I tried to remember that this was a social get-together. We were all supposed to talk. "Yes."

He smiled and leaned in as if confiding some sort of secret. "Do you have any dirt on Cal we should know about? Any skeletons in his closet?"

Jade punched him in the arm.

"Ow!"

Everyone at the table laughed, except me.

"Stop bothering Anna with your silly questions. You're just mad about your birthday."

The entire group, minus Stephan and me, snickered.

"You would be, too!"

Cal rolled his eyes. "Oh, stop whining. It's not my fault your mom decided to drop by unannounced." At that, the snickers turned into full-blown laughter.

Philip noticed our confusion. "Justin's just a little sore because Cal threw him a big bash for his twenty-fifth birthday party last month that included some . . . female entertainment, and his mom showed up right as it was getting good."

"Yeah. And she didn't talk to me for a week after that. My own mother wouldn't even take my calls." Justin sank down in his chair.

Female entertainment?

My heart pounded in time with the words as they repeated over and over in my head. The palms of my hands began to sweat, and my breathing accelerated.

Suddenly there was a sharp tug on my arm, and a hand gripped the back of my neck. "Breathe, Brianna. Deep breath in. Now let it out. Again." I did as he said, taking one breath at a time.

When I opened my eyes, Cal was staring right at me.

"Good girl." Stephan's words pulled me out of my trance, and I turned to face him. He ran a finger down the side of my face, making me forget about everyone around us.

"Hey, you all right?" Mandy broke into our world with her question.

Stephan didn't take his eyes off me. "She's fine."

"I didn't mean to make you—"

"He said she's fine." There was finality in Cal's voice. Everyone at the table stopped talking.

"Well, it looks like we're going to have to go fetch our own drinks."

Mandy placed a hand on Philip's and Justin's shoulders. "Come help a girl out."

There was a brief exchange where Stephan told her we'd just take some water, and then they were gone.

"I'm so sorry, Anna. I wasn't even thinking when the subject of Justin's party came up." Jade's voice was full of regret.

By that point, I was resting my head on Stephan's shoulder, and he was playing with my fingers as they lay in his lap.

Cal leaned forward, resting his forearms on the table. "What can we do to make it better, Anna? I wanted you to have a good time tonight."

Stephan laid his cheek on my head, holding me close. "She'll be all right."

"Anna?" Cal didn't seem to be taking Stephan's word for it that I'd be okay. "Talk to me. Please."

Without lifting my head, I shifted so I could see Cal's face. "I'm fine. I didn't . . . I didn't mean to make you worry."

"Forget about me. I'm only concerned with you."

I smiled, trying to reassure him, but it was weak.

Activity on stage dragged our attention in that direction. The band was taking their places.

"You don't have to stay."

The thought of going was appealing. I could go back to the condo and hide with Stephan. It would be safe.

Without introduction, the band began to play, filling the room with sound and making talking difficult. Mandy, Phillip, and Justin rejoined our group a few minutes later and placed two waters down in front of us. Stephan picked up one of the glasses and handed it to me. I took it and drank. He did the same with the other glass.

As the band continued playing, I got caught up in the music. They were good. Some of the songs I recognized. Others were completely foreign to me.

Every now and then the lead singer would make a comment or tell a joke between songs, and I found myself laughing at some of them. I was having a good time. I didn't want to go home.

Chapter 26

Stephan
Brianna had finally calmed. As the music filled the club, and people's attention was redirected to the entertainment, her breathing mellowed. It was good to see her happy and content, especially given where we were and how many people were around us.

I'd shifted our position slightly. We were both facing the small stage, with her back against my chest. The leash was draped across my lap and loosely looped around my wrist. No one could see it unless they were looking, which Ross was. Every few minutes, he'd glance in our direction. Occasionally we'd make eye contact, but more often than not he'd look at Brianna then down to where the leather circled her wrist. He would frown, close his eyes, and then refocus on the band. It happened so often I was beginning to wonder how much attention he was paying to the concert.

When the band announced they were going to take a break, people began milling around again, and Brianna stiffened almost immediately. I was going to do my best not to let her mind get the better of her, though.

"Do you like the band?"

She nodded.

"Use your words, Brianna."

"Yes. I like them."

I kissed the side of her neck in a show of approval. "They're good. I can see why there's buzz about them."

All the guys, including Ross, left the table and headed toward the bar along with roughly half the club's patrons.

"Did you want anything to drink, Anna? The guys went up to get us something. I'm sure Stephan could get you something, too, if you wanted."

Jade was tilting her head to the side, and raising her eyebrows, making it obvious that she wanted some girl time with Brianna. I wasn't thrilled about leaving her alone in this crowd, and I shook my head, silently telling her what she wanted wasn't going to happen. She looked disappointed but didn't push it. I handed Brianna her water and nodded to Jade in thanks for not pressing the issue.

"So what do you think?" Mandy had a wistful look on her face as she gazed toward the stage.

"They're better than I expected them to be."

She shifted her attention back to us. "Yeah. Brian's really good at finding local talent. I don't know how he does it, but he always does."

I felt the need to keep the conversation going. The activity at our table was helping to keep Brianna from getting overwhelmed. "How long has your brother been the manager here?"

Jade finished off the last of whatever it was she was drinking. "It's been about two years now. He really loves it."

I'd caught sight of Jade's brother a few times throughout the night. He floated from one side of the club to the other, making sure everything was as it should be, but it was done in a way that wasn't intrusive. Jade was right. Brian did appear to be good at his job.

We talked some more about the band. Brianna listened for the most part. The one time she spoke up was when Mandy asked her if she'd had a favorite song. "*Forever*," Brianna mumbled, before blushing and hiding her face against my neck.

The song was one of the last the band had played before taking their break. It was a love song about unlikely lovers. Brianna was a romantic. I wasn't surprised with her choice.

Phillip and Justin returned to the table, followed by Ross, who set a glass filled with dark liquid in front of Brianna. "I considered getting you something stronger, but I figured he wouldn't let you have it anyway if I did."

I quirked one eyebrow up at him in question.

"Relax. It's only soda."

He acted as if I were a tyrant. Jade must have gotten the same vibe from his statement that I had, because I saw her elbow him in the side in response. I smiled.

I handed Brianna her new drink. She looked up at me, uncertain. I nodded, motioning toward the glass, letting her know it was all right.

The band retook the stage not long after Ross and his friends returned to the table, and our attention once again was on the performers. Brianna leaned back against me, her soda still in her hand, and listened to the music.

It was ten forty-five by the time the band called it quits for the night. For the second half of their act, they'd mixed it up with some cover songs and originals. To be honest, if I hadn't recognized the cover songs, I wouldn't have been able to tell the difference. They were that good.

Brianna finished off her soda, and we stood to leave. I turned to Phillip, Justin, and Mandy. "It was nice meeting you."

"Same."

"Yeah. We should get together again sometime."

I let the comment go without responding. Without speaking to Brianna first, I wouldn't make any type of commitments for the future. When it came to her, everything was one step at a time. She needed to socialize, yes, but not at the expense of her well-being. She also needed to get to the point where the leash wasn't necessary. It was one thing to have a submissive on a leash at a party. It was another to have to use it so Brianna felt safe enough to be in a crowd of people. I wasn't sure of the best way to accomplish that, but it was something we needed to work on.

Jade moved around the table toward us and hugged Brianna. "If I don't see you before Monday, happy birthday."

"Thanks." Brianna looked down, embarrassed.

Then it was Ross's turn. "I got you something for your birthday. I was hoping I could stop by on Monday and bring it to you."

She nodded.

Ross smiled. "Good."

Outside, the temperature had dropped, but it felt good after being inside the warm club for the last four hours. We found our car, and I opened the door for Brianna. Once we were both inside, I reached to remove the leather collar.

"You did well tonight. I'm proud of you."

She smiled.

I was grateful we didn't have to be up early the next morning, because I had no intention of allowing Brianna to sleep anytime soon. We needed to shower, talk, and the desire to be inside her after having her so close tonight and keeping my hands to myself was increasing with each passing moment. Maybe I could accomplish two things at one time.

Leading her into the bedroom, I sat down on the edge of the bed and pulled her into my lap. "How did you feel tonight being around all those people?"

"At first it was scary. When that lady . . ." A visible tremor flowed through her body.

"The leash and collar helped."

"Yes." She paused. "Thank you."

I lifted her hair and pushed it over onto one shoulder. "You're welcome, sweetheart. I knew tonight was going to be challenging, but you did so well."

Kissing a line up her shoulder and around to the back of her neck, I began unzipping her dress. The clingy fabric slowly pulled away from her skin, revealing the pale perfection beneath.

"Tell me what your favorite part of the evening was."

"The mu—sic." She gasped as my fingers slipped beneath her dress and around to palm her breasts. I pushed the cups of her bra out of the way and kneaded her flesh, paying extra attention to her nipples. I knew before long she'd be wiggling against me, looking for friction.

"Hmm. Yes. You did say you enjoyed that song. *Forever*, was it?" As I spoke, I tried to make it a sensual experience by keeping my voice low and even while nipping and sucking on her exposed skin.

"Yes," she hissed as I took both of her nipples between my thumbs and index fingers, twisted, and pulled. Her back arched away from me, and I couldn't help but smile. I knew her response was to my question, but her body also confirmed she was in complete agreement with the direction I was heading.

"What did you like about the song?"

Releasing one of her breasts, I inched my hand down her abdomen until I reached the edge of her silk panties. I'd watched her dress, so I knew they were a dark blue. I ran my finger along the top, teasing her, before slipping my hand underneath the material. The warmth and moisture that met my touch had my already-erect cock pressing eagerly against my pants.

She adjusted her position slightly. It was subtle but enough to confirm she was ready for more.

My fingers teased her entrance. "Answer the question, Brianna."

It took her almost a minute to answer me. "He . . . they . . ." I smiled watching her trying to concentrate on answering me while I continued to tease her. "No one . . . wanted them to be together. But . . . but they found a . . . a way." With her last words, I thrust two fingers inside her.

Brianna

I couldn't think. How was I supposed to think when he was touching me like that? His hands never seemed to stop.

Then they were gone.

"Stand."

It took me a moment to understand what he'd said, but when I did, I obeyed.

He followed me, helping to remove my dress. My bra and panties soon followed, until I was standing naked before him while he remained fully clothed.

Stephan circled me, as if inspecting. I felt his finger outline my shoulder blades, my spine, and the curve of my hip.

Returning to stand before me, he looked down upon me with eyes that left no question as to his desire. "You like the idea of forbidden love, do you, Brianna?"

"I like . . ." He stepped behind me again. "I like the idea of their love overcoming everything."

A shiver ran though me. I wasn't sure if it was because I was actually cold or if it had more to do with knowing I was standing in the middle of his bedroom, every item of my clothing removed.

He returned to stand behind me, wrapping his arms around my waist and pulling me up against him. His erection pressed against my backside. "We are going to try something new tonight, Brianna. Do you feel me like this? Do you feel my cock against your ass?"

I swallowed. *New?* We were going to try something new?

"Yes."

"Tonight, I'm going to take you from behind."

I felt panic rising until he slipped his fingers down between my legs and slid them inside me.

"That's right. Relax. It's still me. Nothing we haven't done before, except I'll be behind you and you won't be able to see me."

I nodded and tried not to let my imagination get away from me. It was Stephan. I'd be fine.

"Get on the bed."

He released me, and I walked to the bed.

"On your hands and knees. Face the headboard."

Taking a deep breath, I moved into the position he wanted. I could do this. It was just sex. With Stephan. I loved sex with Stephan. It wasn't any different. It wasn't.

The mattress dipped as Stephan climbed onto the bed. When he pressed against me, I realized he was no longer wearing any clothes. I gulped in a strangled breath and closed my eyes.

"Relax. Deep breaths." In addition to his erection, something cold touched the side of my hip. Then there were vibrations. "Do you remember this, Brianna?"

Opening my eyes, I looked back to where his hand was on my hip. The silver vibrator he called a bullet was encased in some sort of plastic or rubber and attached to his index finger.

Stephan didn't wait for me to respond to his question before he slowly dragged the bullet up my stomach to my breasts. He circled each one in turn. First the outsides and then my nipples, staying long enough to make sure they were hard and aching for more.

As he continued to use the vibrator on my breasts, he slid his other hand between my legs and moved his fingers up and down my folds. Every time the vibrations came close to my clit, he retreated. The teasing was beginning to drive me insane. I wanted him inside me.

"Patience. I'll take you when I'm good and ready, and not before."

He lowered the bullet down my torso, circling my belly button before gliding it between my legs. I tensed, preparing myself, but instead of going where I wanted it to go, he began outlining the creases of my legs. I closed my eyes again and fisted the sheets.

Just when I thought I couldn't take any more, the bullet found its target. I jumped as he pressed the vibrator directly against my clit.

"Is that what you were wanting, pet? Hmm. I like seeing you on edge, waiting for it."

The vibrations increased. My orgasm was building. It was right there. I just needed a little more, and his permission, and I could . . . I could . . .

Suddenly, the vibrations were gone, and I felt his length against my backside. I couldn't help the whimper that escaped me. I was nervous.

What if I didn't like this? What if . . . what if it was horrible, and I hated it, and then it made me hate sex like I did before?

He ran his hand along my back, soothing me. "Calm. It's only me, and I'm not going to hurt you. Shh."

His voice and his motions helped to release the tension in my muscles. I loved him. I trusted him. I could do this. I could give him this.

Without my saying a word, he seemed to know I was ready. He placed one hand on my hip, and then I felt his penis. He was right there . . .

As he eased inside, I realized it didn't feel that much different. It wasn't exactly the same, but it was still him. I still felt stretched and full and . . . right.

He began to move in and out. It was then I realized the difference. He was . . . deeper than he normally was. It wasn't bad, just more.

Then the vibrations started again. First at my hip and then between my legs. After that, thought left me as he circled my clit with the bullet and thrust harder. With every inward motion, I inched closer to my climax until it was right there. I just needed . . . I needed . . .

Stephan pressed the vibrator firmly against my clit and at the same time grabbed a fistful of my hair. "Come for me."

I was on the verge of my orgasm, and then I felt this . . . I didn't know what it was, exactly. It began just as all my other orgasms had, but then I saw white and my arms gave out.

When I became aware of my surroundings again, Stephan lay holding me, cradling me against his chest. "Feeling better?"

"I think so."

He chuckled.

"What happened?"

Stephan pulled the sheet I hadn't noticed tighter around us. "You had a really intense orgasm. You may also have gone slightly into subspace. If that's the case, we're going to have to be extra careful the first time we play with more intense toys."

I shivered.

"Are you cold?"

I shook my head.

He was quiet for a long time. "I scared you with the mention of intense toys, didn't I?"

Since I didn't want to lie, I nodded.

Stephan kissed the top of my head and caressed my arm with his free hand. The other was resting against my hip, holding me to him. "Don't be. We'll go slow and talk about everything like we always do."

I couldn't shake my nerves completely, but I also knew he was right. We always talked about things. On some level, I knew that if there was something I hated, he wouldn't force me to endure it. He wasn't like that.

We lay together for a long time before I remembered something else he'd said. "What's subspace?"

He rolled us so we were on our sides and looking at each other. "It's where you experience a type of high from sensation. It's described by some as an out-of-body experience. Some subs experience it often. For others, it's rarer. It depends on the person."

"Is . . . is it a bad thing?"

"No. Not at all." He ran his fingers along my face before tangling them in my hair. "It does create a shock to your system, however, which as your Dom I need to be aware of so that I know how best to take care of you after." I was still a little confused on what it was, but as long as he would be there to take care of me, I wasn't too worried.

Closing my eyes, I leaned into his hand.

"We need to go take our shower."

I groaned. The last thing I wanted to do was move. I was so comfortable.

He laughed and kissed me. His lips lingered for a moment too long, reminding me of other things.

When he pulled back, his face was serious. "I love you."

I smiled. "I love you, too."

Chapter 27

Brianna

I was starting to dread our workouts. After I'd followed the routine Brad had set up for me, Stephan had me stand on the weight-lifting mats and practice the self-defense stuff with him. I hated it. While I was getting better at the first move, the second—once again—left me near tears, because no matter how much he encouraged me, I couldn't cause him harm.

Just when I thought I'd reached my breaking point, Stephan called it quits. We took our shower and made breakfast. It wasn't fancy, just fruit and some muffins I'd made the other day. He praised me again for how good they were, and I blushed.

With breakfast out of the way, Stephan and I curled up on the couch to read for a while. Or I thought we were going to read for a while. I was on my side with my head in his lap, ready to read, when he reached for my book and closed it. Glancing up, I realized his book was closed, too.

I shut my eyes as he ran his hand through my hair. "We need to talk about last night and how you reacted to Justin's birthday party."

I stopped breathing for a second and opened my eyes. The conversation he was talking about came back to me as if I were sitting there again in the club.

Female entertainment.

"What if they were like me? What if they had no choice? What if—"

"Breathe, Brianna."

Pinching my eyes shut, I tried to push the images out of my head. I felt Stephan touching me, his hands calming. Rolling over, I buried my head in his waist and held tight to the fabric of his T-shirt.

"That's it. Good girl. I'm guessing I know where your mind went last night, and just now, which is why we need to talk about this. Phillip was talking about strippers."

I knew what strippers were. Although I'd never seen any in person, I'd watched movies and television shows. "They . . . they dance and . . . and take off their clothes?'"

Looking up, I saw him nod. "That's right. They get paid to dance and tease while removing their clothing."

"I don't understand. Why?"

Stephan chuckled, his chest vibrating beneath me. "Men are very visual creatures, and the female form, even if we can't touch, has a very stimulating effect."

I thought about what he said for a few minutes. It didn't make a lot of sense to me until I thought about how I liked looking at Stephan, watching him dress . . . or in the shower. Was it the same? "They only look?"

"Yes."

"Why?"

"Why what?"

"Why wouldn't they want to touch?"

He smiled. "Trust me, they want to touch. Strippers, at least most of them, aren't prostitutes. The men they're dancing for agree ahead of time that while the stripper can touch them, they can't touch her."

I knew what prostitutes were. "They don't have sex with them?"

"No."

Although I knew sex wasn't required to cause pain, knowing sex wasn't involved made me feel better. "So this . . . stripper . . . she danced and . . . took her clothes off while they watched?"

"Yes."

"It's what she wanted?"

"Yes, sweetheart. It's what she wanted. No one forced her to do anything."

The weight lifted from my chest, and I could breathe normally once more.

"Brianna people are going to say things, especially when you're outside these walls, that will sometimes upset you given what you've been through. I want you to try to do something for me, okay?"

I nodded.

"If that happens, I want you to try to remember this conversation. Things may not always be as they seem on the surface, and not everyone is going to know your history and watch what they say. But if something happens, if you hear something, remove yourself from the situation as quickly as possible and come find me. If something is truly wrong, I'll do something. I promise you that." He cradled my face in his hands. "And if not, we'll talk about it, like we're doing now."

"Okay."

He smiled and leaned down to brush his lips against mine. "Good girl."

Handing me my book, he encouraged me to get comfortable again and start reading. He picked up his own book and flipped to where the bookmark held his place. Settling in, he held the book in one hand while the other played with my hair. Sighing, I relaxed and picked up where I'd left off in my book.

The whole thing would have been perfect if not for my apprehension about what was going to happen that afternoon. As the day wore on, I began to get nervous, and my story could no longer hold my attention. I'd read the same page at least ten times. We were going to Logan and Lily's. To watch a scene. I had no idea what that meant exactly, but I knew it had to be significant, or Stephan wouldn't have told me ahead of time.

Stephan and I had just sat down to lunch when he must have decided I'd been quiet for too long. "What's on your mind, Brianna?"

Since I'd just taken a bite of the pasta we'd made together, I didn't answer right away. I knew I needed to be honest. "I'm nervous. About today."

He took my free hand in his and massaged my fingers. "There's nothing to be nervous about. We're observing. That's all."

I nodded. He'd said that before, but I couldn't help how I felt. I didn't want anything to happen. Not to me. Not to Lily. She was my friend.

"Do you recall our conversation about hard limits?"

We'd both stopped eating. "Yes."

"Lily has a list of them. I've seen them. Logan would never violate those limits. Any worthy Dominant wouldn't." He pulled me out of my chair and into his lap. "Brianna, Ian wasn't a worthy Dominant. He wasn't a Dominant at all, in my opinion. You've lived with me for almost three months now. I hope I've shown you there *is* a difference."

At the mention of Ian, he hugged me, and I welcomed it. "You're not like him."

He kissed the side of my face. "No. I'm not. And neither is Logan."

I nodded.

"Come on, love. You need to finish your lunch so we can leave. I told Logan two o'clock, and I don't want to be late."

On the drive over, he reminded me again of what would happen. Lily and I were going to talk. Then we would watch Lily and Logan in a scene. After the scene, I was going to talk to Lily again. Stephan said they were doing this because they didn't want there to be any doubt in my mind that Lily wasn't completely okay with what happened.

Stephan also gave me some rules I had to follow while I was there. I was to sit on his lap during the scene and watch the entire time. He also said I was not to talk to Logan or Lily during the scene, or in any other way try to interfere or interrupt it. And lastly, he told me that once we arrived home we would discuss what had happened throughout the scene and how I felt about it.

With less than a minute to spare, Stephan knocked on Logan and Lily's door. I was trying not to fidget. I didn't want to disappoint him or get into trouble.

The door opened, and Logan stood in the entryway wearing a pair of jeans. He had no shirt, and his feet were bare.

"Right on time." He smiled, and it made him less imposing.

Logan stepped back and let us into the apartment. Nothing much had changed since we'd been there last, except the furniture in the living room was arranged a little differently. It looked as if everything had been pushed back to make more space.

"Can I get you something to drink?"

"Water would be good."

Nodding, Logan went into the kitchen. He returned with two glasses of water that he handed to Stephan.

"Lily is in her room getting ready. I'll let her know you're here."

As soon as Logan disappeared down the hallway, Stephan guided me over to one of the chairs in the living room. He sat down first and indicated he wanted me to sit on his lap.

Once we were both seated, he handed me one of the glasses. "Drink. It didn't escape my notice that you picked at most of your lunch and barely drank anything. I don't want you to become dehydrated."

I sipped on my water, and tried to keep my anxiety under control.

Logan reappeared several minutes later and took a seat across from us on the couch. I didn't look at him. "I thought maybe it would be a good idea if Brianna spoke to Lily privately."

"I agree."

I gripped my glass tighter, hoping it wouldn't break as Stephan and Logan spoke.

"Lily's in the last room on the right."

Stephan lifted my chin so that I was looking at him. "Go talk to Lily. I'll wait here."

I swallowed. This was it. This was really happening.

Obediently, I stood, handed him my glass of water, and walked down the hallway. It was longer than I'd thought it would be. At Stephan's, the hallway was only about ten feet long. This had to be at least three times longer than that.

Following Logan's instructions, I walked until I came to the last door on the right. It had been left open a crack, but I couldn't see anything past the small opening, so I knocked.

"Come in."

When I stepped into the room, Lily was sitting on a bed, rolling a stocking up her left leg. She smiled when she saw me. "Hi."

"Hi." I looked over the rest of her outfit and quickly glanced away. She was wearing a corset, but the bra part was missing.

She giggled and patted the mattress next to her. "Come sit next to me while I finish getting ready. Logan said we could take our time, but I don't want to push my luck."

I went to sit next to her, but I still couldn't bring myself to look.

"Brianna, it's okay to look at me, you know. You're going to have to get used to it if you're watching us today."

Lily was right.

Preparing myself as best I could, I turned to face her. I tried not to stare, but it was hard when the black corset she was wearing pushed her breasts up and out. Add to that the contrast it had against her pale skin, and her breasts were hard to ignore.

"You've seen other women naked before, haven't you, Brianna?"

"Yes." I had seen other women naked. Alex, mostly, but she hadn't been the only one. This seemed different, though. I knew Lily. And even though I'd known Alex, she and I had never been friends.

"I figured you must have. Can I ask why seeing me bothers you, then?"

I shrugged. "You're my friend."

She smiled, but there was a sadness to it. "I don't want you to worry about me today, okay? Logan and I have been playing for over a year now, and he knows what I can take and what I can't. Do you remember what I told you about Stephan being a good man?"

I nodded.

"Logan's a good man, too."

Again, I nodded. What was I supposed to say? I didn't know what was going to happen, and I couldn't change that I was worried about her.

Lily finished with her stocking and took my hand in both of hers. "Logan and Stephan want us to talk before everything gets started. When we walk back out there, I won't be allowed to talk to you anymore, so if you have any questions . . ."

"You won't be allowed to talk?"

She shook her head. "It's one of my rules. When we're playing, I'm not allowed to speak unless Logan asks me a direct question."

I scrunched up my face in confusion. "Why?"

"During a scene, while we're playing, it's not my job to question him. I'm giving up control to him, and I have to trust that he knows what's best."

"But . . . but what if something's wrong? What if he . . . hurts you?"

"Then I have my safewords."

Pressing my lips together, I considered her words. Suddenly I realized what was bothering me. I didn't trust Logan. Lily did. She trusted Logan like I trusted Stephan. "You trust him."

She smiled. "Yes."

Lily released my hands and walked over to a large dressing table and mirror. She swept her hair up into a high ponytail and wrapped a black holder around it. "Logan likes my hair up when we play. He says it makes it easier for him to grab hold of."

She glanced at me through the mirror, and I realized she had a smirk on her face. I blushed and lowered my eyes to the floor.

"No need to be embarrassed, Brianna. I know Stephan likes hair pulling, too. And from the look on your face, you don't mind it either."

I shook my head but remained silent.

The next thing I knew, she was kneeling in front of me. "Don't ever be ashamed of what you enjoy. As long as it's something you both want, then who cares what other people think?"

"So it's not . . . weird?"

"That you like it when Stephan pulls your hair? No. Not at all. I happen to love when Logan pulls my hair. It reminds me that he's in complete control of me and my body, and that he can take what he wants from me."

"It doesn't . . . scare you?"

"Nope. Does it scare you when Stephan does it?"

"No. But sometimes . . . sometimes I think maybe it should?"

Lily smiled up at me. "Brianna, there are always going to be things in life other people don't understand about you. Last year, my sister found out about my lifestyle. Logan and I hadn't been dating all that long, and she still had a key to my apartment. She says she knocked, and when no one answered, she let herself in. When she walked into my bedroom, she found me tied to the bed, lying face up, with Logan's cock in my mouth."

My eyes went wide. "What . . ."

"What did she do?"

I nodded.

"She started screaming at Logan. Needless to say, it completely killed the mood, not that her walking in hadn't done that in and of itself, but . . . Logan immediately began untying me as I tried to calm her down, but she wouldn't listen. She pushed him out of the way and started loosening the ropes herself."

Lily seemed to be lost in a memory for a while, so I remained quiet and waited.

"After I was free, I put a robe on, sat her down, and explained what she walked in on." Lily paused. "She was furious."

"She was scared for you."

"Yes. I didn't understand it at the time, though." She seemed sad. "I found out later her husband had tried something like that with her once and she'd freaked out on him. She thought Logan was forcing me to do something I didn't want to do, and when I told her he wasn't, she couldn't wrap her mind around why or how I could want something like that."

"Stephan has ropes. He hasn't used them on me, but . . . but I told him he could." It felt strange admitting that, even to Lily.

She smiled. "I love ropes. They make you feel helpless, yet centered at the same time."

"I don't know if I'll like them."

Lily cocked her head to the side, studying me. "And you're afraid if you don't like them you'll upset Stephan?"

"Yes."

"Don't be. Stephan's a big boy. He'll get over it."

"But . . ."

"But?"

"I want to like it."

"Because he does?"

I nodded.

"I'll let you in on a little secret. When I first started playing, I was eighteen. During my first experience, my boyfriend at the time, Danny, put these nipple clamps on me. They were the adjustable kind, but he tightened them as far as they would go. After that, I swore I'd never let another set of nipple clamps near me again." She moved to sit back on the bed. "But do you know what? Now I love them. Danny had absolutely no idea what he was doing. He'd never used clamps before, and it showed."

"What changed your mind?"

"After we broke up, I realized a couple of things. First, I craved domination, especially in the bedroom. Sex was okay without it, but with it I'd experienced some of the most intense orgasms in my life." She shifted again, this time to face me. "So when I went looking for another relationship, I searched out the local BDSM community and started going to munches."

"What are . . . munches?"

"They're social events. Nothing fancy. Usually just dinner at a restaurant."

So people who liked ropes and nipple clamps and . . . well, I didn't know what else . . . all met for dinner and . . . what?

"A few months later, I started going to some of the play parties. That's where I met my first experienced Dom. He was older than I was and had been in the lifestyle for ten years. It took him about six months to get me to the point where I was willing to try clamps on my nipples again, but I will forever be grateful. It was amazing."

She told me a little more about this Dom and how he'd opened her eyes to many things. By the time he'd moved away for his job, her list of limits had become more defined. "It all came down to communication. He was willing to talk to me, explain things. Danny wasn't."

We talked a little more before she glanced up at the clock. "We should get out there. They're going to think something's wrong and come back to check on us soon."

Lily stood and slipped on a pair of heels.

I stood with her and walked toward the door.

She turned, reached for my hand, and squeezed. "I'll be okay, Brianna. I promise."

I nodded and hoped she was right.

Chapter 28

Stephan
"She seems nervous."
I watched until I could no longer see Brianna before answering Logan. "She is."

"Do you think she'll be all right with this?"

"I have no idea. Brianna has the tendency to surprise me. Sometimes that's good. Sometimes, bad. I never know until it happens. The only thing that I know is absolutely off limits is name calling. We've been working on it, but even the words themselves, without any context whatsoever, can set her off."

Logan nodded. "Lily was concerned about her this morning. We had a long conversation about it."

Brianna had handed me her glass before she'd gone to see Lily. I placed it on the floor beside my chair, and leaned back. "She was worried about Brianna?"

"Yep."

"Brianna's worried you'll hurt Lily."

"Hopefully the two of them talking beforehand helps calm her fears."

I took a drink of my water. "Hopefully."

"How was your trip?" I wanted to steer the conversation away from the purpose of our visit before my own anxiety increased. As much as I tried to downplay it for Brianna's sake, I was apprehensive about what might happen. Not with Logan and Lily, but with Brianna herself. As I'd mentioned to Logan, Brianna was unpredictable in new situations. I wanted this to be a positive experience for her, but that wasn't guaranteed.

"I have to fly back next week."

"I thought you were getting some time at home after this last trip."

"Yeah. So did I. Turns out some things that were supposed to be ready last week weren't."

"How'd Lily take the news?"

Logan pressed both index fingers against the bridge of his nose. I could tell he was agitated. Maybe work hadn't been the best topic of conversation. "She wasn't happy, that's for sure. I thought she was going to make me sleep out on the couch when I got home Thursday night."

I could see Lily doing exactly that. "You could have slept in her room, you know."

"No. That's her space. I wouldn't violate it like that. Plus, she'd probably come in the middle of the night and dump a bucket of ice water on me or something."

I laughed.

"It's different with you. You've never had a twenty-four-seven relationship with someone." He paused. "Well, until now."

"My relationship with Brianna isn't exactly what you'd call normal."

"No. It's not." He leaned forward, clasping his hands together. "She seems happier, though. Even with the stress today is obviously causing her, you can see a huge difference. Especially from the first time I met her."

"Yes. She has more good days than bad now."

As if hearing her name, Brianna appeared with Lily.

Lily stopped right inside the room, and Brianna looked back for several long seconds before walking the rest of the way to where I was sitting. I set my glass down and opened my arms. She hurried to climb into my lap.

"Did you have a nice chat with Lily?" I whispered in her ear.

She nodded.

"Good. Now I want you to turn and watch." She did as I instructed, maneuvering her body so that she was facing the center of the room. I wrapped my arms around her middle and rested my chin on her shoulder. "Just watch."

Lily stood with her head down, her hands behind her back, and her feet shoulder width apart. My guess was this was an instruction given to her by Logan earlier, since their normal starting position had her kneeling. It made sense, though, to have her enter the room and pause to get into her submissive mindset. It also gave her a little more freedom given the unknown Brianna added to the scenario.

Logan walked slowly over to her, observing. He circled her, not touching at first, and then glided his hands over her exposed skin. I could tell by the change in the rise and fall of Lily's chest that he was getting the reaction he wanted.

"Go stand in the middle of the rug and hold your position."

She moved to comply and was back in her pose within a matter of seconds. So far, Brianna was doing well, but then again, nothing had happened yet.

We watched as Logan picked up a brown leather bag and placed it beside the couch. Kneeling down, he unzipped it and removed a black leather collar with a D-ring. He walked behind her, unlocked the silver day collar she wore, and replaced it with the leather one.

Going back to his toy bag, Logan removed three lengths of rope. He returned to stand in front of Lily. "Lift your arms."

Lily stood with her arms out to her side at shoulder height. I'd told Logan I wanted there to be some simple bondage but hadn't clarified what type. He knew what Lily liked, so I'd thought it best to leave it up to him. It made me smile to see he'd chosen breast bondage. It was one of Lily's favorites, and something I'd love to try on Brianna one day. The ropes restricted blood flow to the breasts just enough to heighten sensation.

As I watched Logan bind Lily's breasts, I realized how much more proficient he'd become since the last time I'd seen him use any form of bondage. It made me wonder if he'd found a rope master to mentor him, or if he'd been studying up on his own and using Lily as a practice model. Either way, I was sure she didn't mind. Lily loved ropes.

Once the ropes were in place surrounding her breasts, he checked to make sure they weren't too tight before giving Lily permission to lower her arms. So far, so good. Brianna was watching. Her breathing was steady. All was good. Hopefully it would stay that way.

Logan threaded the second rope between the center of Lily's breasts, underneath her current bindings, and brought it up around her shoulders to create tension. The result was an increased tightening of the rope around each breast. Looking up at Lily's face, I could already see the euphoria building.

With the breast bondage in place, he took the third and final piece of rope and secured her wrists. When he was satisfied with that, Logan went back to his bag and pulled out a pair of nipple clamps. Brianna saw them as well, and jerked in my arms. I placed a soft kiss on her shoulder and gave her a gentle squeeze.

The clamps Logan had selected were connected by a silver chain. In Lily's current position, her back arched slightly causing her breasts to jut out.

Leaning down, Logan took her left breast into his mouth and sucked. Lily closed her eyes.

It took several minutes before he appeared to be satisfied and released her breast. He immediately took her nipple between his thumb and forefinger, pulled slightly, and then positioned the clamp. The whole process took less than three seconds. Lily sucked in a breath. Brianna cringed.

Logan moved on to Lily's other breast and did the same thing. With the clamps on both nipples, he released the chain and let it dangle between her breasts before giving it a light tug. I watched as her skin stretched in reaction to the pull. Lily remained unmoving except for another gulp of air.

"How does that feel?"

"Good, Sir."

He lowered his hand between Lily's legs and slipped two fingers beneath the small pair of panties she wore. "Hmm. I see you're already wet for me. Such a bad girl you are."

I glanced at Brianna. She was watching with wide eyes, but her breathing was still fairly normal and she wasn't clenching her fists. I kissed the side of her face and refocused on Logan and Lily.

Lily teetered a little on her heels as Logan thrust his fingers inside her. I couldn't see how many, but he wasn't being gentle about it. With every upward motion, she moved, even though I could tell she was attempting to remain still.

"What do you think I should do about your naughty behavior, Lily?"

The movement had been scarcely noticeable, but apparently it hadn't escaped Logan's attention. Lily wanted to be spanked, and she wasn't above being a brat to get it. Logan raised his hand and then slammed it down on her bare ass.

The sound of his hand connecting with her flesh had barely registered before Brianna was up and running. It took only a second for me to realize what had happened . . . and why.

I was up and out of my chair in a matter of moments, chasing after her. She hadn't headed toward the door, so there were only so many places she could go in the apartment.

After a few minutes, I found her. She was curled up in a ball in the back of one of Logan and Lily's closets. She rocked back and forth, mumbling to herself. I knelt down, reaching out to touch her arm, and she jerked away from me.

"Brianna? It's me, sweetheart."

No response.

"Brianna. Look at me."

Still nothing. This wasn't good.

I sat down crossed-legged in front of her, and waited. She'd come out of it. Eventually. I knew she would. I just had to be patient.

Brianna

Not real. Not real. Not real.

I squeezed my eyes shut, wrapped my arms around my body, and rocked. It would go away. It had to.

The voices. They were back. Screaming. Constantly screaming. And now there were sounds, too. Sounds of hitting and screaming and . . .

Grabbing fistfuls of my hair, I rocked harder.

Go away!

Please. Please! Go away.

"Brianna?"

I shook my head.

Eventually, the voices got quieter, and I could hear other things along with the sounds in my head. The first thing I heard was what I thought were pots and pans clanging against each other. It was far away, though.

As I calmed down further, I realized I was not alone. Someone was with me. I could hear their breathing.

Taking a deep breath, I caught a familiar scent. I opened my eyes cautiously.

My heart began to pound in my chest when I saw Stephan, and before I could question it, I launched myself from the floor and into his arms. He caught me and held me so tight it hurt, but I didn't care. *He's here. Right here.*

"Brianna." My name came out on a breath, barely loud enough for me to hear it. "You had me so worried, sweetheart."

I squeezed, holding him just as tight as he was holding me. "I'm sorry. I couldn't . . ." I began to sob.

"Shh. It's okay. You're safe. That's all that matters."

We sat holding each other for a long time. The clamoring in the other room had stopped, and silence replaced it.

Stephan straightened his legs and situated me in his lap as he leaned against the doorjamb. For the first time, I took in my surroundings. We were in . . . a closet.

As my memory of why we were there came back to me, I began to shiver. "Come here, love." He pressed my head down on his shoulder, resting his cheek on top of my hair.

Neither of us said anything as I did my best to remain calm. I wanted to leave this place.

"I want . . ."

He ran his hands through my hair, down my arm and back up again. "What do you want, Brianna?"

"I want . . . to go home."

Stephan sighed. "You weren't ready. I'm so sorry, sweetheart. I pushed you too much."

Sadness washed over me. The scene. He'd wanted me to watch, and I couldn't . . . I couldn't do it. I couldn't do it for him.

The tears returned. I clung to him as I cried. He just held me, brushing his lips over my hair every now and then.

There was movement behind me. The noise startled me.

"It's okay," Stephan said. "I'm right here."

"I wanted to see if you were hungry. I made dinner." At the sound of Lily's voice, I turned.

She stood against the far wall, looking fearful. I'd never seen her that way before, and I knew I needed to do something.

Scrambling out of Stephan's lap, I rushed to her side and hugged her. She lurched backward. "Lily. Are you okay?" I knew she was standing right there in front of me, but I didn't know why she was looking and acting the way she was.

It took her a few seconds to react, but then she threw her arms around me and hugged me back. "Shouldn't I be asking you that question?"

I didn't understand. "I'm . . . I'm fine. But . . . you . . ."

"I'm fine, Brianna. I promise."

"I thought . . ."

She didn't release me. "You thought what?"

"I thought he . . . I thought . . ."

"I think she thought Logan was going to hurt you," Stephan said from behind me.

"Oh." Lily stepped back and held both my hands. "No. Logan would never hurt me."

She looked okay. The corset was gone, and she was now wearing a T-shirt and skirt.

"But he . . . he hit you . . ."

Stephan reached up to cup my face with his hand, forcing me to focus on him. "Is that what upset you so much?"

Stephan didn't release me, so I couldn't turn to face Lily. "Y-yes."

"I'm sorry, Brianna. If I had known . . . it's not something I think about anymore. I like it, and so does he, so . . ."

Moisture pooled in my eyes. "But . . . why?"

"Why do I like it?"

I nodded, my focus never leaving Stephan even though Lily was the one talking.

"I'm his. I like it when he spanks me. It's something I get off on."

I didn't know how to respond, so I didn't. "Can . . . can we go home?"

Both Stephan and Lily immediately sobered at my question.

"Don't you want to eat something?" Lily asked, sounding disappointed.

Stephan searched my face. "Thank you, Lily, but I think we'll eat at home. I appreciate the effort, though."

Without pause, Stephan ushered me back into the living room. Logan was sitting on the couch and stood as we entered. I halted my movements upon seeing him, and stepped closer to Stephan.

Logan stopped and looked at Stephan before nodding. I watched Lily walk to stand at his side, and he wrapped his arm around her shoulders. She raised her hand and waved, a sad look on her face. I hated knowing that I'd put it there.

I couldn't stop fidgeting on the drive home. Disappointment, confusion, anger, and a variety of different emotions ebbed and flowed through me. It was as if my mind couldn't decide which feeling was the correct one.

Stephan didn't say anything until we were back inside his condo. "Do you want to go freshen up while I make us something to eat?"

I nodded and absentmindedly went to my room. Looking around, I realized how little time I'd spent in there lately. It didn't even feel like mine anymore. Then again, I wouldn't trade the nights I'd spent in Stephan's bed for anything.

As quickly as I could, I washed my face and hands, and then brushed out my hair. It didn't help how I was feeling inside at all, but it did make me look better on the outside. At the very least, I could try to look my best for Stephan.

Walking back out into the main room, I saw he had made us each a salad. "I wasn't sure how hungry you'd be, but you need to eat something."

"Thank you." I took my seat at the island, the same one I'd used since I'd been living with him.

I ate the salad he made, but I couldn't really taste it. When I was finished, I stood and took my plate to the sink like I always did. It was automatic.

"Come here, Brianna."

When I was close enough, Stephan reached for me and had me stand between his spread legs. "Talk to me, sweetheart. Please."

I couldn't stop the tears from falling, so I didn't even try. Stephan hugged me for several minutes before he stood and picked me up. He carried me into his room and over to his bed, where he laid me down with so much care it made me weep harder.

Taking off our shoes, he crawled onto the bed with me and pulled me into his arms. I embraced him, unable to help myself. Even if I would never be able to be a good submissive for him, I still loved him. Nothing would change that. I didn't ever want to let him go, but one day he was going to realize I was broken and I couldn't be fixed. One day, he was going to realize I wasn't the right one for him. I wasn't ever going to be enough. And when that day came, he was going to leave me.

Chapter 29

Stephan
How could I have been so stupid?

I spent the night comforting Brianna as best I could. She wouldn't talk to me, no matter how much I encouraged her to do so. That worried me more than anything did. I'd dealt with her fear, her nightmares, her panic . . . her silence was worse than all of those combined, and it was all my fault.

Brianna hadn't been ready—nowhere close to ready—to view a scene. Not even a simple one. I should never have arranged it. I'd let what I wanted from her get in the way of what was best for her.

Sunday was supposed to be a fun and relaxing day. The following day, June 18, was her nineteenth birthday. I had no idea how she'd spent her previous birthday. Her eighteenth, the one that should have been a time of celebrating her step into adulthood, had been more than likely shrouded in pain and horror. I'd wanted her nineteenth to be as different as possible, and now I was afraid I'd ruined any chance of that.

My aunt had invited us over for dinner, but I'd turned her down. I wanted to spend this day with Brianna, and only Brianna. Although Monday was her birthday, I wouldn't be able to spend the entire day with her, so Sunday was ours. I had plans to take her out to dinner on her birthday at a five-star restaurant. I'd rented the entire place and requested a female server to make sure she was comfortable. But that was tomorrow. Today I would let her choose.

"What would you like to do today, Brianna?" We were finishing our breakfast, and so far, she'd been as silent today as she had been the previous night.

She glanced up from her food and then quickly back down.

I sighed.

"Isn't there anything you want to do for your birthday? I have to work tomorrow, but today you can do anything you want." I paused and lifted her chin, making her look at me. "Anything."

Sadness filled her eyes. "Can I . . . can I see my mom?"

Her request brought me up short for a moment, until I realized what she was asking. From what I knew, Brianna had been taken by her father to live in Two Harbors when she was fifteen, after her mother had died. To my knowledge, she'd never been back to Dallas. "You want to go to your mom's grave?"

She nodded.

A sinking feeling settled in the pit of my stomach. "She's in Dallas, Texas?"

She nodded again.

I closed my eyes and took a deep breath. After what happened to my parents, I avoided planes at all costs. To fulfill her request, however, I would have little choice. The only way to travel from Minnesota to Texas and back in one day was to fly.

Anxiety bubbled up in my chest, causing my heart to beat faster. If anyone else had asked that of me, I would have said no. "Let me make a call." I released her and went to get my phone.

Jamie answered on the second ring. "Hello, Mr. Coleman."

"Morning, Jamie. I need you to do something for me."

"Of course. What can I do for you?"

"I'd like you to charter a plane to take Brianna and me to Dallas, Texas, and back today."

There was silence on the other end for a very long moment.

"Jamie?"

"I'm here, Mr. Coleman. Sorry. You . . . you want me to arrange a *plane* for you?"

I knew it was shocking. Since she'd been working for me, Jamie had only arranged two flights. She knew how I felt about flying. "Yes, and since we need to make this a round trip, the sooner the better."

"I'll make some calls."

"Thank you, Jamie. Let me know when we need to be at the airport."

As promised, Jamie called back twenty minutes later with instructions to be at the airport as soon as possible. The pilot needed about an hour to fuel up and go through a systems check, and then we could take off.

Bile rose in my throat as I thanked Jamie. It was only knowing I was doing this for Brianna that kept me moving one foot in front of the other. There wasn't anything I wouldn't do for her.

We didn't bother packing anything since this was only going to be a day trip. I did, however, take her collar and leash, just in case. Airports could be unpredictable places. I also had no idea what we might encounter once we arrived in Dallas.

Jamie had given me specific instructions on how to locate our plane and pilot, so it wasn't difficult. As promised, he was expecting us.

"You must be Mr. Coleman?"

He extended his hand, and I took it. "Yes. And this is Brianna."

"I'm Kevin. I'll be flying you to Dallas today." He glanced down toward our feet. "Did you have any luggage?"

"No. You're just taking us."

He nodded. "Feel free to get on board. I need to finish checking a few things, and then we'll get in the air."

I guided Brianna onto the plane. It was nice. Nicer than some boardrooms I'd been in. Too bad I wasn't going to be able to enjoy it. My palms were already sweating, and we hadn't even taken off yet.

Brianna seemed to sense something was wrong and leaned her head on my shoulder. I pulled her against me as best I could in the bucket-style seats. She wrapped her arms around my waist, and I felt better. Even if it didn't take my anxiety away completely, her being with me made more of a difference than she'd ever know.

The pilot boarded the plane about fifteen minutes later. He smiled at us before ducking into the cockpit. My stomach churned, and I closed my eyes, trying not to let my nerves get the best of me.

"Your heart is beating fast."

"Yes. I . . . I don't like . . . flying."

"Because of your parents?"

I kissed the top of her head and tightened my hold on her. "Yes. Because of my parents."

"I don't . . . we don't have to—"

"Yes. We do." Tilting her chin up, I rubbed my thumb over her beautiful lips before giving her a soft kiss. "Don't worry. I'll be fine. I've had to fly before—it's just not my preferred method of travel."

"What . . . happened? To the plane?"

I sighed. This wasn't something I wanted to talk about, especially not when we were minutes away from taking off, but she was talking—finally. "The pilot had a brain aneurism. It was sudden and completely unpredictable. The plane took a nosedive. My dad had his pilot's license, so he should have been able to take over, but he and my mom had been drinking. He could barely walk, let alone fly a plane."

"That's why you don't drink."

Tucking her head back underneath my chin, I took a deep breath and released it. "Yes. That's why I don't drink. I never want there to be a time when I'm not completely in control of myself. In college I tried it once, just to see what it was like. Even the buzz was too much. It left me feeling sort of disconnected from myself. I didn't like it."

She nodded but didn't comment. A few minutes later, the pilot's voice came over the intercom and announced we were ready to go. I made sure both of us were strapped securely in our seats as the plane taxied toward the runway.

Brianna

Maybe asking to see my mom's grave hadn't been the best idea. Stephan was tense the whole flight. I'd never seen him like that. It was strange. He was always so in control of everything, including himself.

When he told me about his parents, a lot of things I'd learned about him over the last few months began to make sense. His not drinking. His need to help others. His loyalty to his friends. It made me wish even more that I could give him what he desired from me. At one point, I'd thought I could, but now I knew that wasn't possible. What he wanted . . . truly wanted . . . I couldn't give.

The plane landed a little before one at the Dallas/Fort Worth International Airport. It had been years since I'd been there, but not much had changed. There were people everywhere, and I held tight to Stephan's hand as we weaved our way through the crowd to the rental cars.

Driving to the cemetery where my mom was buried took longer than I'd thought it would. I didn't remember traffic in Dallas being so bad.

The cemetery, though, was exactly as I remembered, minus the small tent that had been placed over my mom's grave the day she'd been buried. Stephan parked the car and helped me out, holding my hand the entire time. I knew he was concerned I'd have another panic attack. I didn't think that would happen, but I was grateful he was there none the less. He was the only one who knew . . . who understood.

There was no marker, just a round piece of metal with a number stamped on it. No one had cared enough to get her a gravestone, other than me, and back then that wasn't possible. As soon as the funeral had ended, John had driven us back to the house and had me pack my things. *"Our flight leaves in four hours."* I could hear his voice as clearly as if he were standing beside me.

Not caring what the dirt and grass would do to my jeans, I knelt down and touched the ground. She was gone, and I missed her. I missed her so much. She'd always been able to make things better. Even when she'd been sick, she'd always tried to make me laugh. Stephan's arms wrapped around me from behind as I sat there and cried, mourning my mother.

When I finally wiped the tears from my eyes and looked up, the sun was beginning to go down. "Thank you." I wasn't sure who I was saying it to, my mother or Stephan. Either way, neither of them answered me.

Turning, I circled my arms around Stephan's neck. "I love you." Whatever happened, I wanted him to know that.

"I love you, too, sweetheart. Are you ready to go?"

I nodded, and he helped me to stand. I didn't want to leave my mom, but I knew I had to. My life wasn't here anymore.

Stephan stopped at a drive-thru on the way back to the airport, insisting that I had to eat something. I was surprised to realize I was hungry, and I ate everything he'd ordered for me.

I fell asleep on the plane ride home. Stephan coaxed me awake once we'd landed back in Minneapolis. As always, the warmth of his lips on mine brought a feeling of comfort mixed with an electric charge. "We're home.

Did you have a nice nap?"

"I didn't mean to fall asleep."

He chuckled, all traces of the anxiety I'd seen from him earlier in the day gone. The flying part was over, and he was back to himself. "You had a trying day. You deserved some rest. Plus, you didn't sleep well last night."

I glanced down, not wanting to talk about my shortcomings. It was only a constant reminder of what I could never be.

"I need you to talk to me, love. Remember what I said about communication?"

As much as I wanted to forget about the previous day, I knew he wouldn't let me continue to avoid talking about it. The last thing I wanted to do, however, was point out what had become clear to me. I couldn't. I didn't want to give him up yet.

"I don't . . . I don't know what to say."

"Tell me how you're feeling."

The pilot emerged from the cockpit, breaking up our conversation, but I knew Stephan wouldn't let it go for long. He thanked the pilot, and we walked back to where we'd parked his car. The drive home was quiet, but I knew that would change once we were inside the condo.

"Come," he said as soon as the door was secure behind us.

He walked over to his chair, and I obediently followed.

Once I was seated on his lap in my favorite position, he took my hand and threaded our fingers together. "Now tell me how yesterday made you feel."

"I felt . . . I felt like I was back there."

"Logan spanking Lily is what triggered it?"

I nodded.

"Oh, Brianna. I wish I could take all those bad things away from you."

Not knowing what to say, I clung to him. I wished he could take them all away, too, but he couldn't. I was broken, and I knew it. There was nothing he could do to change that. There wasn't anything anyone could do.

"We won't do that again, all right? We'll just keep things between you and me, no one else."

I liked the thought of that. With Stephan, I felt safe. But for how long would he be content with that? How long until he wanted more again?

Since it was late, we went ahead and took our shower before getting into bed. He held me the same way he had the previous night, and I cherished every moment.

Chapter 30

Stephan

I woke up early. It was a rough night—for me anyway. Brianna had slept soundly even though she'd had a good two-hour nap on the flight back to Minneapolis. I just couldn't shake the feeling that she was keeping something from me. I had no idea what it was, however. Then again, I could have been imagining things. My guilt over what had happened on Saturday hadn't faded. Perhaps it was clouding my judgment.

Careful not to wake her, I tiptoed out of the bedroom to go get her gifts. I'd hidden the laptop in my briefcase and then secured it in one of the locked drawers upstairs. With it, I'd purchased a first edition of *Jane Eyre* for her. I'd been surfing online at the office for something else to get her, and an ad had come up for rare books. Once the idea had taken hold, I hadn't been able to shake it. *Jane Eyre* was one of her favorites, and I knew she would love it.

Brianna was still asleep when I returned. After carefully setting her presents on the floor on the other side of the nightstand, I slipped back in bed and began my efforts to wake her.

I started by barely touching her pale skin with my fingers. Soon after, I added my mouth, placing featherlight kisses along her neck and jaw. She stirred, and I increased my efforts. Before long, she opened her eyes. "Good morning, Brianna. Happy birthday."

She blinked. "Good morning."

I leaned down and gave her a gentle but thorough kiss, tangling my tongue with hers. When I pulled away, I didn't go far. "I'm taking you out to dinner tonight, but I wanted to go ahead and give you your presents."

"You got me presents?"

I looked at her, a bit dumbfounded. "Of course I got you something. It's your birthday."

Moisture welled in her eyes, and I quickly pulled her into my arms. "Shh. Why are you crying?"

She shook her head, but I wouldn't let her dismiss this. I needed to know the reason behind her tears.

"Tell me, sweetheart."

"You took me to see my mom."

"And you thought that was your present?"

She nodded.

"Brianna, I would give you the world if I could. I'd take you to see your mom every weekend if that's what you wanted. This is your birthday, though, and birthdays mean presents."

I smiled at her, hoping to lighten the mood, and it worked. She glanced up at me through wet lashes and smiled.

After a quick peck on the lips, I went to retrieve her presents. Both were wrapped, and I sat patiently as she tore the paper off her book. As soon as she saw it, her eyes lit up.

"It's a first edition. I know how much you love the story. Now you don't have to borrow my copy. You have one of your own."

She cradled the book to her chest. "Thank you."

"You're welcome."

Brianna removed the wrapping paper from the laptop. It was still in the box, but it didn't take her long to open that, too. "This is mine?" she asked reverently.

"It's yours. I figured you'd need a computer if you're going back to school. Besides, computers can be loads of fun. You can play games and look up all sorts of information. Talk to people halfway around the world . . ."

She was still looking at the computer in awe.

"I'm going to go make us breakfast. Come out when you're ready."

As I turned to leave, I heard movement behind me and knew she was already getting out of bed. She reached for the robe Lily had gotten her, and followed me out into the main room and then into the kitchen, where I began digging out the pots and pans I would need. "Can I help?"

I smiled and pointed to one of the stools. "Sit. It's your birthday. I'm cooking. You can keep me company."

"Okay." She looked disappointed, but she sat down.

As I worked to make our breakfast, we talked more about the books we were both reading. I also told her about the restaurant I was taking her to later that evening. It was a pleasant start to the day. Much better than the one previous. With any luck, that meant we could put what had happened on Saturday at Logan and Lily's behind us and move forward. That was what I was hoping anyway.

I gave her a long kiss good-bye before I left for work, promising to be home by four so we could head to the restaurant. Brianna appeared as reluctant to see me go as I was to leave. Leaving her was not something I wanted to do. If Michael hadn't promised to have something for me today, I would probably have taken the day off, or at the very least, worked from home. As it was, I needed to be there.

Jamie greeted me as I stepped off the elevator. "Good morning, Mr. Coleman."

"Morning, Jamie. How was your weekend?"

"Good. How was your flight?"

"It was fine. I'm glad to be back in Minneapolis."

I said hello to a few of the other executives as I grabbed something to drink before going to my office. The day was going to drag until Michael sought me out. The key was to keep busy, so that was exactly what I did. There was plenty of work on my desk. It was all about concentrating.

Thankfully he didn't make me wait all day. At ten, Jamie buzzed to let me know Michael wanted to see me in his office if I was available. There was no question of that. Although I was eager, I didn't want to appear too eager. Taking my time, I went into my bathroom, splashed some cold water on my face, and adjusted my already-straight tie.

Deciding I needed a little more encouragement, I sent Brianna a text. *Love you.*

In less than a minute, my phone dinged with a response. *Love you, too.*

Most people would have viewed Brianna as a burden, but I didn't. She was a phenomenal woman, and I was lucky to have her in my life.

At eight minutes, I couldn't hold off any longer and made my way down the hall to Michael's office. I knocked, even though he was expecting me, and he quickly waved me inside. Without prompting, I closed the door behind me and locked it. I didn't want anyone accidentally walking in on our conversation.

"First, let me say that this needs to be turned over to the FBI. After what I've seen, this Ian Pierce has his hand in more things than I could track. There's evidence of money laundering, as well as some extremely questionable transactions with a handful of men who are known fencers of stolen goods, especially rare artifacts and paintings."

I loved what I was hearing so far. "How did you find all this out?"

"I've been in the finance world for a long time, Mr. Coleman. It's been my job to go in and clean up companies whose books have been . . . less than honest. I know what I'm looking for, and I've made some contacts of my own in law enforcement."

Did that mean he'd already talked to the police? I wasn't sure how I felt about that. Yes, I wanted to get the law involved, but not yet. Not until I knew what I was dealing with.

"I noticed something extremely disturbing while I was digging."

He placed the stack of papers in front of me and flipped to the page he wanted. These weren't the same bank statements I'd given him. What I was looking at had details one would never find on a simple bank statement, including handwritten notes regarding individual transactions.

"There's a name here. Juliet Mullins. I searched every financial database I could to no avail. So then I tried the FBI's criminal database. Still nothing.

Given what I'd already found, that surprised me. I knew there had to be something out there somewhere, so I did a general search of the Internet and found this."

The paper he handed me next wasn't a bank statement or any other financial document. It was a missing person flyer. My heart felt like it had descended into my stomach. He'd taken someone else.

"Was she ever found?" The words sounded foreign to my own ears.

"Yes."

"Where?"

"She was found about fifty miles south of here. A construction crew was breaking ground on a new house and uncovered a body. It was her."

I stood, unable to sit any longer, and put my hand over my mouth. He'd killed her. I turned to look back down at the paper in my hands, at the picture of a young girl, aged eighteen, with long brown hair, and a face that spoke of innocence.

I had to know. "When . . . do they know when she was killed?"

"Her body was found about six months ago, and it was estimated she'd been dead about a year."

Tears clouded my vision as the reality of the situation sank in for the first time. If I'd not bought Brianna from Ian, she would have most likely suffered the same fate.

"Mr. Coleman?"

Looking up at the ceiling, I tried to get a grip on myself. I had to hear what else he had to say. "Go on. What else did you find?"

"Well, sir, I found your name, along with another woman's name. Brianna Reeves."

I nodded.

"I have to ask. Are you involved in something illegal? I know you said this man hurt someone you love, but . . . this looks bad from where I'm sitting."

Before I could answer him, my phone rang. It was Tom, so I knew I had to take it. "Excuse me for a moment. What is it, Tom?"

"Mr. Coleman, there is a delivery here for Miss Reeves that requires a signature."

That was strange. Although, Ross had said he was going to bring her birthday present over. Maybe he'd gotten busy or something. "What is it?"

"Flowers."

Ross was sending her flowers? I supposed it wasn't out of the realm of possibility. "Go ahead and sign for them, and I'll swing by the desk when I get home to pick them up."

"I was going to do that, sir, but the man says he was told that only Miss Reeves was allowed to sign for them."

I could turn the deliveryman away and tell him to come back later, or get his information and go to the shop and pick them up myself, but . . . "You're sure it's just flowers, Tom?"

"Yep. Just flowers."

"Is there a card? Does he know who they're from?"

I heard him talking to the other man before returning to the phone. "All he knows is that a guy came in early this morning and placed the order."

Looking over at Michael, I noticed he was watching me a lot closer than he had been. "Tell the man to wait there. I'll call Brianna. She can come down and sign for the flowers, but Tom . . ."

"I'll watch over her, Mr. Coleman. You have my word."

Quickly disconnecting from Tom, I called Brianna.

"Hi."

I could tell she was smiling. "Hello, sweetheart. I'm in a meeting, so I can't talk long, but I received a phone call from Tom downstairs. It seems you have a delivery that needs to be signed for."

"A delivery?"

"Yes. Flowers. The man won't let Tom sign for them, for some reason."

"Okay."

"You stay close to Tom, all right? And I want you to call me as soon as you get back upstairs, do you understand?"

"Yes, Sir."

"Good. Call me before then if you need to, Brianna."

Putting my cell phone back in my pocket, I turned to face Michael again. The look on his face had changed. "I guess I need to rephrase my last question. Did you buy Brianna Reeves from Ian Pierce, Mr. Coleman?"

I supposed there was no denying it. The evidence was right there, staring him in the face. "Yes. I did."

Chapter 31

Brianna
June 18

Today is my nineteenth birthday.

A year ago, I would never have imagined I would be here. I thought for sure I'd be dead. I had no hope.

So much has changed for me. I no longer live in fear, and I've fallen in love with a wonderful man. He has done more for me than I can ever repay him for.

This morning, he woke me up with kisses and gave me two lovely presents. I hadn't expected anything. He took me to see my mom yesterday, and that was more than I could have ever hoped for. To some people it may not have meant that much, but it did to me.

Since he left this morning, I can't stop running my hands over the copy of Jane Eyre *he bought me. It's perfect and something I will treasure forever. That is one of the reasons I love him. He doesn't just give because he can but because he wants to, and he takes the time to make it meaningful. With all the other books I've been reading lately, I hadn't even mentioned* Jane Eyre *for over a month, yet he remembered.*

The laptop was another special treat. I haven't opened it up, because I've been too busy with my new book, but I can't wait. Hopefully he will be able to show me how to use it. I've used a computer before, but only in high school. I'm sure it will come back to me, but I don't want to do something wrong and break it. I know he works with computers all the time, and I'm sure there are things he can show me.

He also made me breakfast this morning. I wanted to help, but he wouldn't let me. Instead, he had me talk to him while he was cooking. He told me he's taking me out to dinner tonight. I'm still nervous about it—I don't like being in strange places or around people I don't know—but Stephan said it would just be us and the server. I have no idea how he arranged something like that, but I was grateful.

My cell phone rang, dragging my attention away from my journal. I glanced down at the screen and eagerly answered it. He told me I had a delivery downstairs I needed to sign for.

After assuring him I would call him back once I returned to the condo, I grabbed my shoes and keys and then ventured out into the elevator. This was only the third time I'd gone out on my own like this. Both of the previous times, I'd been going to meet Cal.

As soon as I thought his name, I wondered if the delivery was from him. The only people I knew well enough for them to send me something were Cal and Lily. And maybe Jade.

The elevator doors opened, and I stepped inside. I knew some people found elevators to be stuffy and confining. They didn't feel that way to me, however, as long as I was alone or with Stephan. Elevators had four walls. An enclosed space. Once inside, the outside world had little effect. I liked that about them.

It didn't take long to reach the bottom floor, and when the doors opened I could see a man holding a large vase of flowers standing beside Tom. "Thank you for coming down, Miss Reeves. This man here has a delivery of flowers for you, and he insists you are the only one allowed to sign for them."

I looked at the man. He appeared to be in his early thirties and seemed to grow impatient when I didn't immediately approach him. "Are you Brianna Reeves?"

"Y-yes."

He seemed not to notice my anxiety. Or he was ignoring it.

"Look, I just need for you to sign this here, and I'll be on my way." The man took a step toward me, and I took a step back.

Thankfully, Tom stepped in front of the man, blocking his path. "Give me that."

"She needs to sign it."

"I'm well aware of that," Tom said, ripping the clipboard out of the man's hand. "But in case you didn't realize it, you're scaring her. Wait here, and I'll get you your signature. Then you can go."

The man didn't look happy, but he remained where he was while Tom brought the clipboard to me. "Sorry about that, Miss Reeves."

"Thank you."

Tom smiled. "Anytime."

I quickly signed my name and handed the clipboard back to Tom. He crossed the room and gave it to the man.

"Thanks for using Twin City Florist."

Once he was gone, I tentatively walked across the lobby to Tom's desk, where the flowers were sitting. I picked up the vase and sniffed. The flowers were beautiful. A mix of all different colors and sizes. It reminded me of a field of wild flowers.

Something caught my attention out of the corner of my eye, and I looked toward the front doors. There, striding toward me at a rapid pace, was my father. I dropped the vase and barely registered the sound of it shattering on the tile floor as I turned and ran in the opposite direction.

I heard Tom yelling, but I couldn't stop. An arm grabbed me from behind, and without thinking, I spun out of its grasp. Then I took off running again.

There was no way I could make it to the elevator and get inside before he caught up to me, so I headed toward the stairs. I reached out to open the door, but it opened on its own. A man appeared. A huge man. The one who'd come to the condo before with Tom to make sure John left.

I gasped, startled by his appearance. Before I could reverse direction, he wrapped his large hands around my upper arms and lifted, placing me behind him. Shocked, I stood immobile, not sure what had just happened or what I should do.

"What—" I heard John utter a second before I watched the fist of the man in front of me collide with John's face. He fell to the floor.

"That's for the Taser."

The big man stepped away from me, and I cringed back against the staircase.

I was about to take off up the stairs when I saw John trying to get up, but the big man pulled him up by his shirt and punched him again. "And that's for her."

This time, John didn't get up.

Tom appeared in the doorway looking flustered. "Are you all right, Miss Reeves?"

I nodded.

He watched me for a few moments and then held out his hand. "I've got to call the police. They'll come take him away since he violated the restraining order. Jesse will make sure he stays put until they get here."

I didn't move.

"Miss Reeves, I need you to come with me. We need to call the police, and Mr. Coleman."

At the mention of Stephan, I refocused on Tom. He held out his hand. I didn't take it, but I stood and followed him back to his desk.

He dialed and put the phone to his ear. "Mr. Coleman? Sir, you need to get here as soon as possible. Jonathan Reeves showed up. I'm calling the police now. I thought you should know."

Tom paused, and I knew Stephan must have been talking.

"Yes. She's right here."

There was another long silence.

"No. She's fine."

Tom handed the phone to me.

"Brianna?"

I sobbed. It was the only response I could manage.

"Sweetheart, I'm on my way. You stay with Tom until I get there."

"Okay."

Tom took the phone away from me again. "I won't let her out of my sight."

Everything else was a blur. I knew Tom called the police, but I didn't really remember it, or anything else that happened until I felt Stephan's hand on my face.

Stephan

I sat across from Michael, a man who didn't know me very well, and tried to figure out how to explain to him how I had come to purchase Brianna. There was no easy way to do it, so I stuck with the simplest version of events I could. "Someone brought to my attention that they thought Ian Pierce was holding a woman against her will. I went to check it out, and from everything I could see, I agreed with them. Brianna didn't want to be there."

Michael didn't comment or react in any way, other than to let me know he was still listening.

"If I'd gone to the police, they would have wanted proof. And if Ian had gotten wind of something before the police acted, I didn't want something to happen to her. So . . . yes, I bought her. I had to."

He was quiet for several minutes before breaking eye contact with me. "Mr. Coleman, you do realize human trafficking—which you've just admitted to—is a felony, right? You could go to prison for a very long time."

I leaned forward, resting my elbows on my knees. "I realize that."

Michael opened his mouth to speak, when my phone rang. I took it out of my pocket, thinking it would be Brianna, but it wasn't. It was the security desk at my building. Tom.

After speaking to Brianna and verifying that she was unharmed, I disconnected the call and stood. "I'm sorry. I need to go. We're going to have to continue this another time."

"Was that about the girl?"

I stopped.

"Her father, the one who's responsible for her being with Ian Pierce, showed up at my building and tried to kidnap her. Tom has called the police because we have a restraining order against him. I need to get to her."

"I'm coming with you."

I didn't have time to argue with him. The police were on their way to my building, and I knew they'd want to question Brianna. She would be scared, and I needed to be there for her. At the very least, if the police had to speak with her, I could make sure it was a female officer. She didn't need to be traumatized any more than she already had been.

Michael and I arrived on the scene just as the police car pulled up to the curb. Thankfully, we made it into the building before they could stop us. I would have ignored them in any event.

Rounding Tom's desk, I found Brianna curled up in his leather chair. She had her arms wrapped around her knees with her legs pulled up to her chest. In the closet, she'd done the same thing. I'd realized months ago she was trying to make herself as small as possible. She was trying to hide.

I touched her face, and this time she didn't cringe away from me. "Brianna. Look at me, love." She raised her head and met my gaze. "Good girl. Are you all right? Did he hurt you?"

Brianna hugged me, nearly knocking me off balance. I should have been used to her abrupt reactions by now, but I never seemed to be prepared enough.

"No. He didn't hurt me."

"Excuse me." A male police officer loomed over us, and Brianna ducked her head against my shoulder, shielding herself from the officer. "Are you Brianna Reeves, the one who has the restraining order?"

I shifted our positions slightly so that I could face the officer. "She is. I know you're going to need her statement, but we're going to need a female officer. Brianna is not comfortable around men she doesn't know."

He looked me over with curiosity. "And you are?"

"Stephan Coleman."

It took the officer a second before he recognized my name. "You run The Coleman Foundation?"

"That's right."

He nodded but continued to observe the way I was holding Brianna. I knew he was only doing his job, but I didn't like it.

The officer walked away, and Michael appeared. "I think you may want to call your lawyer."

I looked up at him in confusion. "Why is that?"

Michael motioned across the room where Jonathan Reeves was now handcuffed and talking to an officer. "He's telling the cops why he's here. And he's telling them about you, and what you have to do with his daughter."

He didn't need to say any more. I reached into my pocket, without losing my hold on Brianna, and retrieved my phone. Oscar was on speed dial, which was good since I could already see the officers looking our way. It wouldn't be long before they insisted on talking to me.

"Davis and Associates."

"This is Stephan Coleman. I need to speak to Oscar immediately."

"I'm sorry, Mr. Coleman. He's in a meeting."

"Get him out of it."

She hesitated only a moment before placing me on hold.

I looked at Michael. "If for some reason I can't finish this call, I need you to explain to Oscar what's going on and get him down here."

Michael nodded. I knew he was still weighing what I'd told him and whether to believe me or not, but I was glad he seemed to be giving me the benefit of the doubt.

"Stephan?"

One of the officers was headed my way. "Oscar, I need you to get down to my building. Now. The police are here, and I have a feeling they may try to arrest me."

His curse rang loud and clear through the phone. "Stall. I'll be there in ten minutes."

I'd barely disconnected the call when I heard the officer say, "Mr. Coleman, I need to speak with you. Privately."

Reluctantly, I separated myself from Brianna. "Stay here with Tom, Brianna. He'll make sure you're safe."

She nodded and curled back into her ball in the chair.

I looked to Tom, and he nodded.

The officer led me to the far corner of the room. I could no longer see Brianna, and that made me nervous, but I had to trust Tom would watch over her until I could get back to her.

"How do you know Brianna Reeves, Mr. Coleman?"

"She lives with me." To anyone else I would say she's my girlfriend, but I wasn't sure what Oscar would think best given the situation, so I decided to be as vague as possible.

"And you live here?"

"Yes. In the penthouse." I was not above throwing my money around if it gave the officer pause about questioning me. It wasn't something I did often, but under the circumstances, I didn't feel any guilt about it.

"And how long have you known Miss Reeves?"

"About three months."

"According to her father, she's been missing for over a year."

"Is there a missing person's report?" I knew there wasn't, and hopefully that alone would call into question whatever story Jonathan Reeves was telling.

He frowned and reached for his radio. "Dispatch?"

"This is dispatch."

"Can you run a check to see if there's a missing person's report for a Brianna Reeves?"

"Ten-four."

The officer and I stared at each other for several minutes, waiting for the dispatcher to return to the line.

"That's a negative."

"Thanks," he responded to the dispatcher as he readjusted his gaze to Jonathan Reeves.

"Do you know why Miss Reeves has a restraining order against her father?"

I nodded. "He broke into our apartment last month. To be safe, I had my lawyer file a restraining order on her behalf."

"Was a police report filed?"

"No. Security removed him from the building. You can confirm that with Tom and Jesse, if you'd like. They're the ones who escorted him out the last time."

"Why didn't you report it?"

"As I mentioned earlier, Brianna isn't comfortable around men she doesn't know. There would have been police in our home asking questions and looking for evidence. I didn't want to put her through that. I hoped being removed from the property and served with a restraining order would deter him. Apparently it didn't."

"And why is she so scared of men, Mr. Coleman?"

Luckily I didn't have to answer that as Oscar came storming into the building like he owned the place. He narrowed his gaze at me and the officer I'd been talking with, and strode over to our side. "Are you harassing my client, officer?"

Oscar handed him his card.

"No. Just asking a few questions."

"Well, the questions stop now."

"Sheriff Reeves has made some pretty hefty allegations against your client"—he glanced down at Oscar's business card—"Mr. Davis."

"Are you planning to arrest Mr. Coleman?"

The officer stood up straighter. "No. No one is under arrest but Mr. Reeves for violating his restraining order."

"Then I suggest you take care of Mr. Reeves and leave my client alone. He and Miss Reeves are the victims here."

Reluctantly, the officer strode away, back toward Jonathan Reeves.

Once he was out of earshot, Oscar turned to face me. "Now what in the hell were you doing talking to him in the first place?"

"You told me to stall."

Oscar shook his head, looked up at the sky, and mumbled something unintelligible.

Chapter 32

Stephan
The next hour about killed me. A female officer showed up ten minutes after Oscar and insisted on talking to Brianna alone. Thankfully, Oscar was allowed to be with her. That was both a blessing and a curse, since I knew he'd watch out for her best interests but also that she'd be scared to death because she didn't know him. I paced the entire time she was out of my sight.

Michael stayed with me. I had no idea what was going through his mind. Given everything he'd researched and what he'd both heard and seen, he knew more than most.

When the police had finally left the building, and Jonathan Reeves had been driven off in the back of a police cruiser, Oscar approached me with a face that warned me of the serious conversation that was coming. "We need to talk."

I nodded. "Let's go upstairs."

Brianna hesitated in the doorway to the small office off the lobby they'd used to question her about the incident. She looked from me to Oscar, then at the others in the room. To ease her concern, I motioned to her, and just like that, she was running across the room. She circled her arms around my waist, pressing her head against my chest. I cuddled her close and kissed the top of her head.

Once she was calm, I moved us toward the elevator. Oscar and Michael followed.

The doors opened, but as we stepped inside, my attention was once again drawn toward the front of the building as Ross walked through the doors. He spotted us, took in everyone's stiff posture, and frowned.

I sighed.

He strode straight to us, not bothering to acknowledge Tom or Jesse, who were still back behind the desk after the earlier incident.

"What happened?"

Michael looked at Ross with curiosity. Oscar, while never having met him before in person, knew who he was. I could tell by the expression on his face.

"Get in. We're going upstairs to talk." I tightened my hold on Brianna. "John paid Brianna a visit today."

An angry scowl took over Ross's face as he stepped inside the elevator.

No one said a word until we were all situated in various places around the living room. I held Brianna in my lap, threading my fingers through her hair, trying to comfort her as best I could with Oscar and Michael—people she didn't know—in the room with us. A charge of emotion hung in the air as we all stared at each other.

It was Ross who broke the silence. "Is someone going to tell me what happened, or I am supposed to guess?"

Before I could respond, Oscar leveled an even stare at Ross and answered. "From what we've been able to piece together so far, it appears Jonathan Reeves had a bouquet of flowers delivered to Brianna. When she came downstairs to sign for them, he rushed into the building and tried to grab her."

Ross's gaze fell on Brianna. "He didn't hurt her, did he?"

It was my turn to answer. "No. Thankfully, Tom and Jesse were there and took him out before he could."

Ross turned and paced toward the large bank of windows that ran the length of my living room. "I can't believe this. I thought . . . I mean . . . when I told him I'd seen Brianna and that she seemed fine, happy even . . . I thought he'd back off. Leave her alone. I didn't think he'd do this."

"He did."

"Yes, he did," Oscar said, bringing everyone's attention back to him. "Which brings us to our next problem."

I expected Oscar to elaborate, but he turned to Michael instead. "How much do you know?"

"If you're asking me if I know how Miss Reeves came to be with Mr. Coleman, then . . . I know enough."

"Actually, Oscar, you two need to talk. Michael looked over the bank statements you sent me, and—"

"What bank statements?" Ross rejoined the group as he took a seat on the couch next to Oscar.

Michael decided to answer him. "Mr. Coleman asked if I would look over some bank statements from a man named Ian Pierce."

Ross's gaze drifted to mine, and I nodded. "Please tell me you found something to nail that bastard."

"And then some."

Oscar leaned forward, clasping his hands together in front of him. "Good. Hopefully it will help."

"Help with what exactly?" I could tell Ross's patience was wearing thin.

Instead of answering Ross, however, Oscar focused on me. "You know, I've been doing this a long time, Stephan, and I hope that means you trust me."

"You know I do."

"That's good, because I don't think you're going to like what I have to say."

I braced myself as best I could.

"Jonathan Reeves strikes me as a person who has nothing to lose," Oscar said. "From the little I got from the officer questioning Miss Reeves, her father isn't holding back on what he knows."

"Which means what exactly?"

"It means that before long, they are going to link you to Ian Pierce. With the information Reeves has regarding his part of things, at the very least your life is going to become difficult. At most, you are looking at the inside of a federal prison."

I closed my eyes and breathed deep, taking in the scent and feel of the woman in my arms. My concern wasn't for me. It was for her. "What do we need to do?"

He looked at me, then down at Brianna. "She needs to leave."

I increased my hold on her. "No."

"Stephan, it's the only way. If this gets out, which I don't foresee a way of preventing, her living here is going to look very bad. She needs to have some distance from you so that it doesn't look like you've coerced her in any way. It needs to appear as if you bought her to help get her out of a horrid situation."

"I did."

He nodded and clasped his hands together in front of him. "I know that and you know that, but to an outside observer . . . to a federal prosecutor . . ."

"There has to be another way."

Oscar looked me in the eye, his expression sad but resolved. "There's not."

It was suddenly difficult to swallow.

"She can stay with me."

Everyone's attention shifted to Ross. "What?" I wasn't sure if I'd heard him right.

"She can move in with me. That would work, right?" he asked Oscar.

The thought of Brianna leaving me was abhorrent. Her moving in with Ross left me feeling as though my stomach had been ripped from my abdomen.

"You're an old family friend, so yes, it would look much better if she were living with you. Are you here in the city?"

He shook his head. "Not anymore. That's one of the reasons I was coming over today. Part of Brianna's birthday present . . . I wanted to take her to see my new place. I moved in this weekend. It was supposed to be a surprise."

I was about to open my mouth again when Brianna's timid voice rose above the others. "I'll go."

Brianna

As I clung to Stephan, listening to everyone talk, one thing had become clear. My being here was dangerous for Stephan. Even his lawyer, a man he'd told me time and time again he trusted, had said so. I had to do what was best for the man I loved even if it would nearly kill me to do it. I'd lived through Ian's torture—I could live with having my heart ripped out as well. At least he'd be safe.

Everyone was staring at me, which made me want to bury my head in Stephan's neck and hide, but I knew I couldn't. He'd given me so much. I could do this for him.

"Are you sure, Anna?"

Stephan turned me to look at him, holding my chin in his hand. "No."

"Yes," I whispered.

"It is the best way," Oscar insisted.

"No!"

I heard movement behind me, but I couldn't see. Stephan still held my face immobile. His hand flexed against my hip, and moisture began to pool in his eyes.

Cal stood. "I'll call Jade. She can skip out on her afternoon classes and come over to help you pack."

Several minutes passed as what I was doing started to sink in. My biggest fear had been his waking up one day and leaving me, and here I was, leaving him. Maybe that should have made it better . . . easier . . . but it didn't.

"Give us a minute." Stephan's voice was commanding, and no one questioned him as each walked past us and followed Oscar up the stairs.

Stephan took my face in both of his hands and kissed me until my head was spinning. "Don't go. We'll find another way."

"I have to."

"No." This time the word was soft, whispered, without any of the sting from before. He closed his eyes, and I saw a tear slip from beneath his lashes. "I love you."

As he'd done to me so many times before, I reached up and wiped the moisture from his cheek. "I love you, too."

We sat, unmoving, for what felt like forever. It was only the sound of the phone ringing that brought us back to reality.

Cal came down the stairs as the phone continued to ring. "Jade's here."

Stephan nodded but didn't move.

Cal sighed and answered the phone. "Hello? Yeah. She's expected. Mr. Coleman is busy at the moment. Fine. Hold on." He walked over to us and handed Stephan the phone. "He says he needs to speak to you."

Without taking his eyes off me, Stephan took the phone in one hand. "It's fine, Tom. Send her up." His voice sounded cold. Dead. So unlike the caring man I knew him to be.

He dropped the phone to the ground, not seeming to care what happened to it once it left his hand.

Minutes later, the monitor came alive, letting us know we had a visitor. Cal went to open the door since neither Stephan nor I had moved.

With Jade's arrival, I knew I had to go pack my belongings, even it was the last thing I wanted. For the first time, I willingly and knowingly pulled away from Stephan. He let his hands fall limply into his lap as I stood and stepped away, causing my heart to break even more.

An arm wrapped around my shoulders, and I looked up to see Jade standing beside me. "Come on. I'll help you get your things."

We didn't talk as we packed everything into the two duffle bags she'd brought with her. I doubted I would have any use for the fancier things, so I left them. The only person I wanted to dress up for was Stephan, so taking them would have been pointless.

When I had everything from my bedroom, I went into Stephan's to gather what little I had in there. I slowly looked around the room, allowing the memories to come, and then my gaze fell on the bed where we'd slept. The bed where he'd taught me sex could mean more than pain and suffering.

I quickly turned away and gathered my things as tears began to fill my vision. I needed to finish before I lost my nerve.

Jade met me at the door and helped me put the last of my stuff in the bags. She hugged me and then stepped back as Stephan approached.

He placed a hand on each side of my neck, and I felt his collar pressing down into my skin. Leaning down, he brushed his lips across mine so softly I wanted to weep. I knew what I needed to do.

Reaching up behind my neck, I went to unclasp the collar and remove it. Stephan's face fell. This was real, and there was nothing either of us could do to change it. He'd once told me that as long as I wore his collar, I was his and he would protect me. It was now my turn to protect him.

His hands wrapped around mine, stopping me.

I looked up, not understanding.

"No. Keep it."

"But—"

"Please."

When he was sure I wasn't going to continue trying to remove the collar, he ran his finger over the metal ring and then dropped his arms, the weight of them suddenly seeming too much for him. Cal and Jade stood behind me on either side, waiting.

Tears sprang to the surface again, and I knew I needed to leave. "Good-bye."

He raised his free hand and brushed his knuckles over my cheek. "Good-bye, Brianna. Be safe for me. Please."

I nodded, unable to speak.

"Come on. You can wait in the lobby with Jade while I bring around the car."

Cal picked up both the bags, and Jade guided me toward the door. I paused just outside and looked back. Stephan stood where I'd left him, his expression one of utter defeat. I wanted more than anything to make it better, but I knew I couldn't. Staying would only make it worse.

"You ready?" Jade asked when I remained motionless.

I pulled my gaze away from Stephan and closed my eyes. "Yes."

Look for the final installment in
Stephan and Brianna's story coming Spring 2014.

CPSIA information can be obtained at www.ICGtesting.com
Printed in the USA
LVOW01s0116300514

387864LV00010B/232/P